J.T. HOWELL

Devoted

BRAZEN LEAF

Contents

1	Vows	1
2	Oaths	17
3	Enlisted	30
4	Deployed	45
5	The Battle of Vilgast	60
6	Captain	74
7	Victory	86
8	Heptarch	98
9	The Devoted Company	112
10	Siege of Phalanaea	126
11	Changes	139
12	Recovery	153
13	Celebration	167
14	Flee	180
15	Exiles	193
16	Governor	204
17	Rebellion	217
18	Correspondence	230
19	Reunions	243
20	Convergence	257
21	Reclamation	270
22	Coronations	282
23	The Battle of Arachovia	295
24	Devoted	308

1

Vows

The afternoon sun spilled through the massive, arched window into the sensible but ornately furnished bedroom. Matthias Helianth stood pensively by the glass, looking out onto the city of Arachovia from the second story of his family's villa. The lavish gardens below him brimmed with fountains, topiaries, exotic flora, and even a cage of colorful birds his mother had spent half a fortune collecting. Beyond the villa walls, the upper city flourished, the broad cobblestone streets filled with chattering citizens going about their everyday lives. The sun gleamed off the sandstone buildings, many just as lavish as the Helianth villa, and quite a few were noticeably grander. The ancient city stretched almost a league in every direction until the buildings abruptly ended in the open air. The cliffs along the city's edge allowed for quite a dramatic scene.

Beyond those cliffs, Matthias could barely make out the dusty green plains beyond, spider-webbed with wide rivers. It was hard to believe that another half of the city sprawled at the cliff's base, hidden from view. He sighed, turned from the window, and began to pace the polished stone floor, wringing his hands nervously. The anxious noble often used this vantage point to calm his nerves and clear his mind during troubling times. However, his usual composing techniques proved futile against what he was about to face that day. He could feel his heart leaping from his chest; sweat dampened his hands. The act of rebellion he would commit today would alter the course of his life and his family forever.

Matthias was taller than most of the men in his family, with broad shoulders and the strong jaw of well-bred nobility, though he maintained the lankiness and awkward proportions of adolescent youth on the verge of manhood. He had always excelled in the physical aspects of his education like wrestling, swordplay, and fitness, resulting in a toned physique that attracted the attention of more than a few noblewomen. However, Lord Helianth was dismayed at Matthias' low aptitude in history, philosophy, and mathematics, which he considered more essential areas of study. The firstborn son of a noble house was expected to do more than swing a sword and run fast; he must take over the family estate and marry a woman of equal or greater nobility to carry on the bloodline. His father had made sure to remind Matthias of those duties constantly.

He examined his reflection in the bedside mirror and ran a hand through his messy, wavy hair. Matthias had a boyish face, full lips, and green eyes that his mother called lovely, while his father called them mischievous. A violent knock at the door jarred Matthias from his musings, immediately embarrassed by how much the unexpected sound caused him to jump.

"Yes?" he called as the door opened. Lord Helianth strode into the room with a regal posture, not bothering to close the door behind him. Matthias was the spitting image of his father, although he could not be more different than the pompous ass. The older man had grown thick around the middle and his hair had begun to thin. His otherwise handsome features were hard and sullen, and his mouth contorted in a resting sneer.

"Preening yourself, as usual, I see," Lord Helianth said dryly. Matthias opened his mouth to quip, but his father held his hand up and continued. "It is for the best, however. You must look your finest for our guests today."

"Surely you haven't arranged another betrothal for me—" Matthias began, but his father yet again silenced him with a raised hand. He hated how his father commanded him with such ease.

"Of course I have. After the last two that you ended with your ridiculous excuses, I was surprised there was another eligible lady of rank left in the city who would be interested in your childish antics." Lord Helianth spoke bitterly, and Matthias couldn't help but reciprocate his father's anger. "You have been considered an adult for a few months now, and it is high time you performed your duties to this house and choose a suitable wife."

Since Matthias had been a child, his father treated him as nothing more than his replacement, someone to marry off to a brainless twit and pump out babies to further the rotted family name of Helianth. He had hoped that his father wouldn't find another woman so soon, because what Matthias had planned for this evening would fix all of his problems.

Matthias decided not to press the matter further. The

sooner he could end this betrothal, the sooner he would make it to his scheduled rendezvous.

"Who is it this time?" Matthias asked.

"Follow me and find out." Lord Helianth smiled wolfishly, which did nothing to reassure Matthias. "I have a feeling that you will agree with this one."

The pair left the bedroom swiftly, and the lord arched an eyebrow at his son when he did not make any objection. Matthias could see his father puff his chest out in triumph as they quickly walked through the colonnaded halls of the villa. The arrogant lord of House Helianth thought that he had finally badgered Matthias into submission. He was sorely mistaken.

The lanky noble followed his father through the villa until they arrived at the top of the stairs that led downward into their home's lavish entry hall, trying to fabricate an acceptable excuse to not marry the poor girl waiting below. The grand hall, where the betrothal offers occurred, was immaculate and ornate. A large tapestry decorated the walls, detailing the family's illustrious genealogy to the mythic Ae'rach. Every noble villa in the city was adorned with a similar ornate hanging to boast their house's connection to the first known civilization to inhabit the known world. In Arachovia, the closer a noble's blood to the Ae'rach, the more dignified the family was regarded.

The Helianth genealogy was respectable but by no means the most impressive. Like many middling houses that vied for greater heights, the Helianth family tree had been slightly altered over the years to exaggerate their ties to the Ae'rach. Most historians could not tell the difference, but Matthias knew those fabrications were a sore spot for a man as proud as his father.

Matthias' mother and little brother, Markas, were waiting patiently at the bottom of the steps, facing the trio of visitors standing at the threshold. A lord and lady flanked a radiant woman with long, flowing hair. She awkwardly toyed with a small betrothal wreath in her hands and stared quietly at the floor. Matthias recognized the girl the moment he joined his mother and brother at the base of the steps and released a soft gasp. Kadri Lilias. His oldest and dearest friend in the entire world stood before him, proposing marriage.

He looked over to his father and shot him a nasty glare; only now did he understand the wolfish smile from earlier. It was a brilliant move; the Lilias family was a high-ranking house with impressive connections, not to mention how close Kadri and Matthias had become throughout their childhood. It was an excellent match. But he did not love her. His heart belonged to another, and he would not give it away so lightly, even for his father's pride and honor.

"I welcome you, Lord and Lady Lilias, to my hearth and home. I welcome you, as well, Kadri. You have mine and Lady Helianth's blessing to lay your betrothal wreath." Matthias' father spoke formally and calmly, yet his voice was the epitome of pride and smugness, causing Matthias' stomach to turn.

Reluctantly, Kadri stepped forward and paraded gracefully along the opulent hall. Lord Helianth gruffly pushed Matthias forward and toward the approaching woman. His mind raced as he met his friend in the middle of the hall. The second he reached her, Matthias understood by his friend's horrified expression that she was just as surprised by their current circumstance as he was.

"I'm sorry, Matthias, I would have warned you, but they didn't tell me until we were already on our way," Kadri whispered. She then raised her voice so the whole room could hear. "I present this wreath as a testament to our two families. Will you accept?"

The delicate ring of woven twine, vines, and flowers hung in front of him like a noose ready to strangle. He stood frozen until an idea finally popped into his head. He smiled, nodded, and took the wreath from Kadri. She gasped; brow furrowed in confusion. Kadri probably expected him to reject her outright. It was what they both wanted, but he knew better than to embarrass his father a third time. At least, not yet.

"I am gracious for your offer." Matthias held up the wreath for the whole room to see but did not put it around his wrist. "But before I can accept, I request to speak to the lady alone to discuss the terms of her proposal."

It was the best he could do; his parents would cast him out after a third refused proposal, and hopefully, his father would find it industrious of him to discuss terms of engagement before accepting. The corner of Kadri's mouth twisted subtly into a smirk as she realized what Matthias was doing. "Clever," she whispered under her breath.

"Very well," Lord Helianth called. His voice was neutral, not betraying a shred of emotion. "Please retire to the gardens. And make it quick."

Matthias and Kadri were halfway to the door when the lord had finished his statement. They glided silently through the villa, out the side door, and into the gardens. Matthias found a quiet alcove in the hedges with a bubbling fountain in its center, away from nosy family members and their spies. Once they were sure they were alone, they let out a collective breath, and Matthias chuckled slightly. Kadri punched him in the arm, which he reacted to melodramatically.

"Don't kill me," Matthias said, clutching his arm and doubling over in mock pain.

"Well, you nearly killed me with that stunt, Matthias, taking the wreath like that," Kadri said. "I thought you went mad and decided to go through with the whole thing and marry me."

"Could you imagine?" Matthias said, and the pair laughed at the prospect. "How would you become a priestess if you were married to a ruffian like me?"

"I was going to tell you," Kadri said, beaming, "I was accepted by the Temple of Sorilea this morning. Before this mess, I was going to break it to my parents tonight. But after this mess, I have a justifiable excuse to join the temple. A jilted woman, rejected by her best friend, who finds her place serving the great spirits of the city."

"You're very welcome for that cover story," Matthias said, "And congratulations, Kadri. I know how much you've wanted this. I am sure you will become a fury in no time."

For as long as Matthias could remember, his best friend wanted to join the army as an officer. Kadri was the most intelligent person he had ever met, a skilled tactician, she excelled in every aspect of their education. Although women were not forbidden to enlist, very few families allowed their daughters to do so. Prestige and power meant everything in the upper echelons of nobility and joining the Officer's Academy was social suicide for an ancient house, as such an act was reserved for lower families. His own father would drop dead if Matthias ever decided to join the army, though that was highly unlikely. Kadri, on the other hand, had devised a way to achieve her goal. Special priestesses, known as furies, specialized in the arts of war, and were allowed to join the army as a specialized unit. Kadri's acceptance into the Temple was just the first step on her journey to realizing her goals.

"Thank you, Matthias," Kadri smiled, "And speaking of long-awaited dreams becoming a reality, when is your appointment at the Shrine?"

"Sunset," Matthias answered, looking up at the afternoon sun falling beneath surrounding rooftops. He did not have much time. "And it cannot come soon enough. But we should hurry and break our parents' hearts sooner rather than later."

"You go on. I can handle the old fools," Kadri said.

"Are you certain?" Matthias asked hesitantly. He was eager to get to the Shrine of Isemelith, but asking her to carry the burden of delivering the news was too much.

"Of course, it will help my case with my parents," Kadri said. She bent over the nearby fountain, cupped her hands, and brought the water up to her face. The water dripped down her cheeks, and she rubbed her eyes vigorously as if she had been weeping. "But I cannot say my parents will ever forgive you."

Matthias beamed brightly, handed back the betrothal wreath, and kissed Kadri on the cheek, "You are simply the best friend a boy could ask for."

"And don't you dare forget it," Kadri replied. "Good luck, Matthias. I am happy for the two of you."

Matthias barely heard her as he raced down the garden path, toward the city beyond the villa's high wall. He couldn't escape fast enough.

* * *

Located on the other side of the upper city, the Shrine of Isemelith sat in the center of the extensive gardens near the Temple of Sorilea. The sun had almost set when Matthias arrived at the secluded shrine. His face flushed and chest heaved, nearly out of breath. He hadn't stopped running since leaving his family's villa, and though he was in reasonably good shape, he hadn't needed to run that far in quite some time. He hoped he did not draw too much attention during his run, grimacing when remembering how he had nearly barreled into a pair of soldiers. They were off duty, thankfully, but the Signata tattooed on each of their right forearms marked each of them as military.

The Shrine of Isemelith was an intimate, circular clearing in the center of high hedges. A shallow moat surrounded the cobblestone dais, filled with colorful fish. The giant statue in the shrine's center depicted two muscular men embracing one another. Words were carved into the plaque at the statue's base:

I Vow to respect your mind and consider you my partner in all things.

I Vow to protect your body, as it is more precious to me than mine.

I Vow to cherish your heart fully and share mine completely in return.

Until my own heart, mind, and body give way and until the end of my days.

Those were the Vows male lovers made to one another, to legally Devote themselves to one another and bond one to the other for the rest of their lives. It was not unlike marriage between a man and a woman, but it was much less common. Women who wanted to Devote themselves to another woman had a similar shrine with similar Vows, tucked somewhere in the gardens, though Matthias could not remember its name. The words etched on this shrine, however, were the very Vows he planned to share with the love of his life, Anton, that very night.

It wasn't the union his father had wanted for him, but Anton was from an equally respected noble family, and their Vows would bond the two families together just as a marriage would. His younger brother Markas could still marry, become Lord Helianth, and further the family name. It would take his father a while to accept the situation, especially after the debacle with Kadri, but he would eventually see reason and approve of his son's choices. His union with Anton would restore everything, and all would be right again. And he would finally stop having to keep Anton a secret from the world.

Matthias crossed the narrow moat on a wooden footbridge and sat on a stone bench in front of the plaque, reading the words and committing them to memory. He had met Anton Vandalia during his studies and quickly bonded over their love of the physical arts. No one was a better wrestler than Anton, and the pair soon fell in love. It was not unusual, but both were the eldest sons of noble families, and such an affair was not free of its complications, so they hid their love for years. Only Kadri knew of their relationship. But when they finished their studies and were seen as eligible bachelors in the eyes of society, the arranged proposals began for Matthias. Blessed with more amiable parents, Anton did not find himself subjugated to any unwanted proposals. Although the man was the most eligible bachelor in Arachovia, Anton's parents were waiting for their beloved son to choose a prospective wife before concocting any betrothals of their own.

However, even Lord and Lady Vandalia seemed to possess limits to their patience, and eventually, there was talk of potential unions as the months after graduation drew on. Anton and Matthias finally decided to end the charade and become Devoted to one another. It was the only solution to keep their family's honor intact and remain happy. All their dreams were about to come true.

Matthias tapped his foot to release his nervous energy, reciting the Vows repeatedly in his head. And then the sun fell beneath the horizon. He stared intently at the Shrine's entrance, expecting Anton to arrive at any moment, but the opening in the hedge remained empty. Twilight set in, and the pale moon became visible, but there was still no sign of Anton. Matthias stood up and began to pace, desperately wondering where his lover could be, for Matthias was usually the tardy one of the pair. Anton had always chided Matthias for making him wait; perhaps this was his way of getting revenge.

Twilight faded into the true darkness of night, the black jays sang their melancholy tune from the trees above, and Anton still had not arrived. Matthias was genuinely panicking. Maybe Lord Helianth had found out about the arrangement and went to Anton's home out of spite? That surely could not be it. He kept pacing around the Shrine, trying not to lose his composure as the minutes became hours.

"It's chilly tonight. We probably should have planned for that." Matthias whirled around, towards the speaker. Anton Vandalia was a handsome man with easy confidence and a robust, athletic frame. His beard had already fully grown in, and he was the most beautiful thing Matthias had ever seen.

"There you are, you big dolt. I nearly died, I was so worried," Matthias rushed to Anton and threw his arms around him. He was so big that Matthias' long wingspan had trouble encircling him. Anton returned the hug and kissed him softly. Matthias found himself lost in the warm, inviting embrace. He gazed lovingly at Anton and his face broke into a wide smile, his panic melting away. His lover pulled away, his lips pursed awkwardly, looking up at the dark sky solemnly.

"Now you finally know how I feel, Matt," Anton said, his voice oddly flat. "You've made me wait dozens of times. Not so fun, eh?"

"Sure," Matthias said slowly, confusion clouding his thoughts. Anton often teased him, but there was something off about his delivery, his voice was devoid of its usual jovial tone. Something about the man was off. "But I would never leave you waiting the evening we planned to say the Vows of Devotion to one another. Where have you—"

Matthias' words froze in his mouth, which simultaneously became dry. He noticed something around Anton's wrist. An accepted betrothal wreath of ornately woven vines, and golden flowers.

"Who is she?" Matthias breathed. Heat filled his body, his ears pounding, and the world began to spin.

"Matt, I—" Anton began.

"I SAID, WHO IS SHE?" Matthias screamed.

Anton gave a start. Matthias was shocked by the volume of his own voice, but he didn't care. He could only focus on the wreath around Anton's wrist.

"Evelin Rosalia," Anton said slowly.

"Evelin?" Matthias snorted in disbelief, "Evelin Rosalia? That prickly bully who used to make fun of me as a kid? How could you? After everything you told me about becoming Devoted."

"I had to!" Anton yelled, "You have a younger brother to carry your family's name. I do not. Your parents may have come around, but I surely would have been disowned. You must understand. I had no other choice, my love."

"Everything we discussed, everything we talked about, why didn't you speak of this before when we were planning?" Matthias asked. He could feel tears welling in his green eyes and solemnly asked, "You were always planning to accept a betrothal from Evelin. Weren't you?"

Anton stared sullenly at the ground, giving Matthias the answer he needed.

"You were," Matthias breathed, backing away from Anton, "This wasn't a surprise betrothal. You arranged this with your parents. If you never planned to say the Vows to me, then why did you ask me to come?"

Anton stepped forward and pulled Matthias back in. "This changes nothing, my love. It doesn't change the way I feel about you. I knew you wouldn't understand, so I couldn't tell you until now. I love you more than anything. I will marry Evelin and give her children, but you and I can still have what we've shared all these years. Why does anyone have to know about our love except for us?"

Anton leaned down for another kiss, tempting Matthias to accept it, but he pulled back and pushed the man off him. Anton looked stung, but it was nothing compared to Matthias' despair.

"It changes everything!" Matthias seethed, tears freely streaming down his face. "Do you think I enjoyed sneaking around with you all these years? I only did that because you promised we would be Devoted one day! Do I want to share you with that harpy, Evelin? If I am not Devoted to you, my father will force another poor girl on me, and we'll have two miserable wives to subject to adultery. I don't want to be your secret, Anton. I want to be your Devoted."

"Matthias…," Anton said, his eyes filling with tears, "I wish nothing more than to be Devoted to you and say the Vows here and now. But there is simply no other way."

"There was another course of action, Anton," Matthias said, deathly quiet, "And that involved you being truthful to me. While you were busy accepting Evelin's proposal and feasting with her family, I rejected a third of my father's arrangements. The only thing that would make him forgive me for such a slight was our Devotion to one another. Now there's no way to repair what I've broken. I'll be lucky if he doesn't cast me out!"

Anton pursed his lips and furrowed his brow. He had not taken Matthias' precarious position with his family into consideration. How could he have? "I am so sorry, Matthias. I never intended to harm you in any way. I love you."

"You didn't intend many things," Matthias said, "But I need you to know that I would have given up my entire future just to be with you. I risked everything tonight. And now I know you would never do that for me. Goodbye, Anton."

Glaring up at Anton, he mustered the last of his strength and pushed past him, running as fast as possible into the sleeping city.

"Matthias, wait. Please!" Anton called out after him.

Matthias ignored his lover's cries and sped into the night, tears streaming down his face. He desperately wanted to turn back, throw himself in Anton's arms, and forgive the handsome man. Every fiber of Matthias' being screamed at him to reconsider and find a way to make this arrangement work. Instead, the distraught noble forced himself to keep running down the quiet city streets. There was no turning back now; he could not possibly live the life Anton wanted for the two of them. Condemning Matthias to a life in the shadows, watching the man he loved start a family, raise children, and hide their true feelings from the rest of the world. It made him sick to his stomach.

The world began to spin, causing Matthias to stop in his tracks and double over in the street. His breath was short and raspy, his heartbeat erratic, and his vision blurred. Matthias breathed deeply, putting his hands on his knees to regain composure. The tactic proved to be fruitless. A storm of pain and anguish threatened to crush him and leave him destitute. He couldn't help but envision Anton kissing Evelin as two small children ran around them, laughing gleefully. Matthias wretched and emptied his stomach onto the cobblestones with a deep cough.

Matthias stumbled through the ancient streets, his eyes red, throat sore, and chest heaving violently.

One evening had irrecoverably ruined his life. Lord Helianth would never forgive his son for such a slight. He would never find another man who loved him the way Anton did; what they shared was unique. And in one night, the most amazing man Matthias had ever known threw all of that away. He began to question everything his lover had ever said and done since they began their relationship. Did Anton ever truly love him? Who would do this to the man they loved? Why would Anton speak of their future together when he had always planned to marry another?

Countless thoughts and questions came to Matthias utterly confused as he desperately searched for answers. None were to be found. The devastated noble stumbled through the empty streets of the sleeping city, heart completely shattered.

Matthias Helianth's life was over. The future he so desperately wanted was now forever out of reach.

2

Oaths

The proper night chill had set in when Matthias finally returned to his family's villa. The streets were almost empty, save for a few drunken youths and the occasional patrol of the civil guard. The city proved to be just as empty as his heart was. Tears still blurred his vision, and an aching in his chest threatened to tear his body apart. He breathed heavily between sobs as he stared up at the dark windows of the Helianth villa. After wandering the vacant streets of Arachovia for hours, Matthias' heart still told him to run back to the Shrine of Isemelith to find Anton and make things right. The confident and intelligent man was the reason Matthias woke up in the morning and was the reason he enjoyed every day.

But that was no longer an option, not anymore. Matthias would not live that life of secrecy and infidelity that Anton had offered him. Matthias shuddered when he imagined it. Anton had always been content with their clandestine rendezvous and stolen glances, but Matthias had desired more.

Matthias understood in a cruel turn of events that they had never wanted the same things.

As he gazed up at his childhood home, his mind wandered to what would happen once he entered. There would be shouting, disciplining, and scolding. His father would strip him of his inheritance and throw him into the street in the worst-case scenario. In the best-case scenario, he would find the first willing young noblewoman tomorrow and hurl Matthias into a loveless marriage. He couldn't live his father's life of duty and sorrow.

At that moment, Matthias realized he did not want the life either Anton or his father wanted for him, and in all truth, he did not want any life at all. Standing alone in the desolate, moonlit street, feeling empty and broken, he made a decision. He ground his teeth and turned away from the villa, back into the city. Making his way determinedly past the dark and sleeping houses, Matthias neared the southern cliffs at the upper city's edge.

The entirety of Arachovia's upper city was situated on a large mesa to protect it from being sacked by invading armies or bands of outlaws. It was a common practice for ancient cities in the region and only the most influential, like Arachovia, had expanded past their mesa. Within a few minutes, Matthias stood precariously at the top of mammoth-sized steps carved into the southern face of the mesa, snaking downwards to the plains below. The staircase was the only passage connecting the upper city with the lower city below, save for a few mechanized lifts scattered around the mesa's edge to transport goods to and from the outside. Arachovia had never been conquered by an army in its entire history, thanks to this strategic architectural design. One had only to defend the plaza at the top of the steps to keep enemies at bay.

He passed the soldiers guarding the entrance into the upper city as they eyed him suspiciously but did nothing to stop him as he descended the grand steps. A commoner would never interfere with a nobleman's business, even a soldier, unless they witnessed the noble committing a crime. Though practically unheard of, a noble entering the lower city late at night was not illegal.

A chest-high stone wall bordered the wide, zigzagging steps, but they still felt treacherous as Matthias made the long journey downward. He had never left the mesa of Arachovia or made the descent to the lower city before in his life. For a brief moment, Matthias considered hurling himself over the edge to rid himself of his grief but thought better of it. His plan this evening would lead to his death as surely as a fall from the cliffs.

The lights of the sprawling lower city soon came into view, followed by the rough stone roofs, and haphazardly built gravel streets. The lower city clung to the mesa cliffs and spilled out southward, contained by a high stone wall, lined with battlements to the south and east, with the wide River Palanthia to the east. The southern part of the city, nearest the high walls, was much neater and more organized than the rat's nest of hovels and alleys near the cliffs. They were the barracks of the sacred legions of Arachovia, one of the largest armies in the known world. The might of her soldiers was the second reason no army had ever conquered the city in its long and illustrious history.

After what seemed like an eternity, Matthias reached the bottom of the grand stairs after not meeting a single soul on his descent. He headed south on the dusty streets of the lower city, which were much more active and filled with drunken citizens. Matthias kept his head down and hoped that his fine clothes did not attract any attention, though the young noble still did not care if anything foul happened to him. He wanted to be free of this pain and hopelessness that seeped into his soul.

Matthias arrived at his destination after getting lost half a dozen times and asking for directions from a drunken degenerate. A low wall separated the army barracks from the rest of the lower city. The straight lines and clean streets were in stark contrast to the maze of dirty roads Matthias had just navigated. He ambled tiredly toward an opening in the wall, guarded by five soldiers. Unlike the guards in the upper city, the ones standing before Matthias had their Insignis weapons drawn. The steel of the swords shone, reflecting the moonlight like dark glass. Each soldier was clad in leather armor from head to toe, save for the officer who stood in the middle of the formation. Instead, the man's armor had been forged entirely of Insignis steel, and he practically glowed in the moonlight. It was uncommon for officers to summon their Insignis steel in the upper city, so Matthias stared at the man with his mouth agape.

"Please state your business," the officer said, in a lazy drawl, examining Matthias with particularly intense, brown eyes.

Matthias snapped his mouth shut and quickly stiffened his posture, embarrassed that he had forgotten his current situation. He raised his voice and tried his best to sound official. "I am Matthias Helianth and have come to take the Oaths of Service and enlist in the Sacred Legion of Arachovia."

One of the soldiers let out a stifled laugh, which elicited an icy stare from the officer. The soldier immediately fell silent and examined the ground in shame. The others merely looked at Matthias with confused curiosity.

"Are you sure you do not mean to enroll in the Officer's Academy or enlist yourself in the Cavalry?" the officer asked, examining Matthias' fine clothes. What Matthias had just announced was more than unusual. It was unprecedented. "You can come back tomorrow at midday and speak to the commander at arms. He will help you find a place for you that will be suitable for your family's name."

"No," Matthias said firmly. "I mean to enlist as a soldier and take the Oaths of Service. Tonight."

Most neighboring cities conscripted each of their citizens and required them to serve in their military, utilizing them as soldiers for most of their adult lives. It was the easiest way a city-state could amass an army large enough to defend itself from the constant chaos of the world. But Arachovia was prosperous, prominent, and filled with men and women who yearned to fight and protect their land, ensuring service was always voluntary. Many nobles from the lower houses took pride in their sons and daughters who served. In fact, the city's leaders, the seven Heptarchs, were directly in charge of Arachovia's defenses and martial forces. Most of them had a history of military service and were equivalent in rank to the generals of other nations. Only members from the most ancient and noble households could become a Heptarch without any ties to the military. Life as an officer or a cavalryman may have been acceptable and even highly regarded by noble families of lower regard. But not for the members of the houses who could trace their lineage back to the Ae'rach or even houses as middling as Lord Helianth's. A son who joined the Officer's Academy would greatly shame any such house. Matthias wanted more than shame brought upon his house. He desperately desired to humiliate any person he had ever met. Especially Anton.

"Very well," the officer sighed, "That explains the late hour of such a request. Follow me, and I will take you to the commander at arms."

The officer lazily gestured at the nearest soldier and walked into the encampment; Matthias ignored the dubious glances of the other guards left behind at the gate and followed the officer into the camp. The streets of the barracks were empty, and the efficiently constructed buildings were dark. The trio walked in silence through the buildings, across a few vast fields that must have been training grounds until they arrived at a large central structure capped with a shallow dome.

"Wait with the applicant while I alert the commander," the officer said to the surly soldier. Again, the man covered in Insignis armor seemed almost bored with the situation. The soldier saluted, and the officer called back, "Please don't do anything foolish while I'm gone, Matthias Helianth. Bruno hasn't seen a battle in a few months and is always eager to use his sword."

Matthias swallowed hard and regarded the soldier who stayed behind to guard him. Bruno was a hulking man with arms thicker than Matthias' legs. The giant man's face was blunt and covered by a thick beard; Matthias did his best to avoid staring at the intricate Signata on Bruno's forearm. The dark swirls of ink marked the man as a soldier, and Matthias did his best to not gape at the tattoo, for it was the closest he had ever been to one. Matthias smiled awkwardly at the man, who returned it with a stern nod and a sullen stare. He would keep his distance from the dangerous-looking soldier, planting his feet and barely breathing to not give the soldier a reason to use force.

After a few minutes, the officer returned with another man who may have been the most imposing person Matthias had ever seen. The man was handsome, bearded, extremely muscular, and carried himself with more confidence and grace than any nobleman Matthias had met before. He did not wear any armor but was covered neck down in the tattoos of his Signata. Matthias knew him to be the commander at arms in a heartbeat.

"Matthias Helianth?" he bellowed in a deep voice, "I am Commander Hendrick. Are you sure you are not mistaken with your request and instead wish to join the Cavalry or the Academy?"

"No, sir," Matthias said adamantly. "I wish to take the Oaths and become a soldier."

"I told you, commander," the armor-clad officer said dryly.

To Matthias' surprise, the muscular commander chuckled at the sly comment and flashed the shorter officer a warm smile. The grin faded as quickly as it appeared as Hendrick directed his attention back to Matthias, assessing the uneasy noble from head to toe in a similar way the officer had.

"Very well," Hendrick said, sighing. "Let's not waste any more time. I'd like to get some sleep tonight. Follow me, Matthias."

The tattooed commander led Matthias into the domed building, dimly lit by half a dozen torches hanging along the perimeter of the vast interior. Matthias could barely see a few paces before him, but Hendrick confidently strode through the darkness and another doorway on the far wall.

"Do you know much about the Oaths?" Hendrick asked

over his shoulder as he led Matthias down a narrow hall lined with dozens of doors.

"No, sir. I only know that they are taken when a citizen enlists. That is all," Matthias answered, trying not to sound too ignorant, for he knew next to nothing about the Oaths.

"Typically, the ceremony of the Oaths is officiated by the commander at arms each day for whoever wishes to lend their services to the legions. Every commoner knows that," Hendrick said. The exact words would have sounded condescending from another man, but the commander spoke matter-of-factly. "But as you are not a commoner, I don't hold that ignorance against you. However, I am curious as to why you are making this odd request. Though your reasons are yours to keep, as everyone is entitled, I can't say anything against it."

The hallway ended in a dimly lit chamber with a stone plinth in the center. Lining the room were dozens of swords hanging on wooden shelves. Hendrick strode over to the nearest one, regarded it for a moment, and carried it to the plinth, setting it gingerly on the stone surface. The dark steel glinted in the firelight. It was an Insignis blade.

"Tonight, you will receive your Signata, which will forever mark you as a member of this sacred military," Hendrick said, "I am sure your education covered the Signata and Insignis steel?"

Matthias nodded, looking at the sword like a poisonous viper. He hadn't imagined events would move this quickly. He expected to receive his blade after some training, but tonight Matthias would receive his sword and crest and forever be tied to the military. A part of him wished he had simply thrown himself off the city's cliffs instead of going through with this ridiculous scheme, but it was too late now.

"Great, then you are prepared for what is about to happen," Hendrick said, approvingly, "Now rest your hand on the sword's hilt with your dominant hand."

Matthias obeyed and grasped the metal hilt with his right hand. It was cold to the touch but seemed oddly pliable. The blade was double-edged, razor-sharp, and about three paces long. It appeared to Matthias that the hilt and blade were forged from the same dark gray metal piece.

"Repeat after me," Hendrick said. "I Pledge to serve the legion with my entire being, body, mind, and soul, laying down my desires and passions."

Matthias repeated the words and felt a slight tingle in his right hand while his eyes deceived him. It seemed as if the blade's surface rippled like a pool of water.

"I Pledge to protect my shield-brothers, commanding officers, and the people of Arachovia above my own life." Hendrick paused for Matthias to repeat, continuing when it was completed, "I Pledge to obey my Heptarch and the noble officers of the legion and to strive for courage, honor, and victory. Until my veins run dry, and my life ends."

As Matthias finished the last oath, the blade seemed to come alive. The metal pulsed and rippled, losing its shape and appearing to melt into some sort of oily, dark liquid. The hilt seemed to dissolve in Matthias' hand, but instead of cascading to the ground, the liquid crept up and latched onto his hand. The sentient gray oil laced around his hand in intricate and random patterns and crept up his wrist. He gasped and began to panic, pulling his hand back, but the liquid held him tightly in place. The frigid substance did not hurt him but gave him a strange itching sensation wherever it touched.

"Easy, boy," Hendrick said gently, putting a firm hand on his shoulder, keeping him in place, "Don't be frightened. The bonding is simply part of the process. Just breathe."

The writhing metal pool on the stone plinth was now only two paces long as the tentacles of gray liquid made their way slowly up his right forearm. Matthias could only watch in horror and wonder as the rest of the metal wrapped around him until the inky substance covered his arm up to his elbow. It writhed and pulsed until it finally lay dormant. What was left was an intricate, dark tattoo. He held up his arm and examined it in awe.

"I take it you did not pay much attention to your studies, boy," Hendrick said, chuckling heartily. "The Insignis blade and the Signata are one and the same. The Signata is just the blade in its dormant state. Let me demonstrate."

The tall commander closed his eyes, and his tattoos began to move and come alive. The same inky liquid that had just covered Matthias now covered Hendrick's entire body. The commander was enveloped in the strange substance for a few seconds until it settled and formed into a complete set of armor: helmet, chest plate, bracers, gauntlets, boots, shield, and sword. The steel shifted, boiled again, and within seconds had reverted to intricate tattoos. Hendrick grinned, and Matthias could only guess how ridiculous the expression on his face was.

"That is enough for now, soldier," Hendrick said, "It is late, and you have plenty of drilling in store for you tomorrow. You don't have the luxury of training like the legion's officers do; you must drill with your squad and learn by action, as all new soldiers do."

The commander led Matthias back the way they came, and

the young noble spent the entire short journey ogling his newly marked arm. It did not feel any different to the touch and did not seem to be anything other than an ordinary tattoo, though until an hour ago he had never known a soldier well enough to see one up close before.

The officer Matthias had first met at the entryway was still waiting alone, standing casually in his gleaming metal armor. He nodded as the pair approached the man.

"You will be assigned to the fourth battalion, which is under my leadership," Hendrick explained and then turned to the officer, "Captain Rain, I believe you have a position open in your squad; you will take the recruit to your barracks. Hopefully, the boy will learn quickly with the Sand Ferret Squad."

Captain Rain nodded, "Very well, commander. Is there anything else you need from me, sir?"

"Not tonight, Rain," Hendrick said, turning to leave, "See that the boy isn't torn apart tomorrow. I'm not sure if your squad will take kindly to a nobleman fighting alongside them as a shield-brother."

"Very well," Captain Rain said, and Matthias could almost hear a sense of disappointment in his voice for the first time as the commander left them alone.

"This way, Matthias," Captain Rain said, any emotion that may have been in his voice now absent. "Let me show you to your new quarters."

The pair walked through the simple buildings, and the captain spoke casually, explaining the basic regulations and laws of the army as if he were merely chatting about the weather. His blade was never to be summoned unless on duty or asked by a superior officer during training sessions.

Consorting with soldiers from other squads was not allowed. Being outside one's quarters was not allowed unless on duty or expressly directed by an officer. Matthias barely paid attention while the man continued; he was never one who learned well during lectures.

Finally, they reached a door halfway down an empty avenue, and the captain opened it, revealing a long, narrow room lined with tiny beds on either end. Matthias counted about twenty. The one next to the door seemed to be the only vacant bed in the room; the rest held massive, snoring shapes.

"The empty bed at the end is yours, soldier. You will find a uniform and armor in the trunk at its foot," Captain Rain said quietly. "When the sun is up, the squad will begin its drills, and please make sure to make a good impression on the others. You heard what Hendrick said. I suggest you change into your uniform before the others wake up."

The odd officer nodded awkwardly and stalked back the way he came. Matthias looked after his new commanding officer, furrowing his brow, unsure what to make of the strange, aloof man.

Closing the door behind him, Matthias laid down on the lumpy and stiff bed, with a pillow to match, accompanied by a thin and scratchy blanket. The dark room smelled stale, and the grating sounds of snoring filled the dark space. Absentmindedly clutching his right forearm, his mind went straight to Anton, imagining what he would say at this moment. He tried to shake the thought out of his head as fresh tears trickled down his cheeks. Never again would he experience his lover's embrace, feel Anton's kiss, or hear the man profess his love. Quietly sobbing, Matthias curled into a ball on the hard mattress, wishing the love of his life had chosen him instead of Evelin fucking Rosalia. That sniveling shrew obtained the life Matthias had always wanted and she had done nothing but be a woman. Anton did not even love her. The sorrow and anguish of the night caused Matthias' thoughts to spiral until the sudden realization of his decision to enlist gripped him. What had he done?

He wanted to enlist to spite his bullying and scheming father. He wanted to enlist to spite Anton, for his betrayal and for breaking his heart. He wanted to enlist to show that neither of them controlled his life and to ensure that he would never end up living the life that either of them wanted.

He was enlisted and tied to the army from now on until the end of his life. He closed his eyes and allowed sleep to take him. Matthias solemnly hoped that his new life would be short.

3

Enlisted

The following day was not particularly easy for Matthias, partially due to the emotionally draining events of the night prior, partially due to the lack of sleep, but mostly because he had never experienced a more physically grueling activity than drilling with his new unit.

Matthias considered himself an above-average athlete and enjoyed various physical activities. Still, nothing he had ever done in his youth prepared him for the archaic torture known as drilling. After being rudely awakened by a horn and the thundering laughter of those in his squad, he followed the group to the sprawling central training ground. Off to one side of the dusty field lay a pile of large boulders, and one by one, his new compatriots each took a stone and began to run along the perimeter of the camp. After completing a loop around the entire encampment, the soldiers dropped their rocks and spent a few minutes repeating strenuous exercises. They picked up their boulders and ran around the encampment again. One circuit, two circuits, three circuits,

Matthias lost count until the sun was high in the sky and he was following his unit back to the training field.

At first, the boulder seemed manageable, but after hours of keeping it lofted while he ran, his arms screamed for sweet release. He prided himself on only dropping it a mere ten times, but the nasty grins and chuckles from the other soldiers said otherwise.

After a grueling session of morning drilling, the Sand Ferrets marched to an open pavilion near the training grounds to partake in a quick meal of cold porridge with a few dozen other squads. Matthias ate silently at the end of his squad's table, not a soul acknowledging his existence. He had been too tired and distracted to heed Captain Rain's advice and had awoken in his fine silk clothes instead of the leather uniform of a soldier. To his horror, all the soldiers he had encountered at the entry gate were, unfortunately, part of the Sand Ferret Squad, including the massive Bruno. By the midday meal, Matthias was already referred to as "your highness" or "the prince" and received nothing but chortles behind his back and gruff shoulders during the grueling drilling exercises.

Captain Rain accompanied the squad throughout the day. Without his Insignis armor, Matthias could see the handsome man was lean and fit, with short-cropped, dark curly hair. The man was present throughout the day, but Matthias did not hear him give a single order or even say more than two words. He sat off to the side at lunch, lazily played the flute, and stared off into the distance. If it were not for the Signata tattooed across his body, Matthias would have never known he was the unit's commanding officer. It seemed as if most of the soldiers had been members of the Sand Ferret Squad for years, and each was a seasoned warrior. They moved as a single unit and did not need direction from any superior officer.

After the meal, the squad returned to the training yard and paired up to practice grappling. Matthias was excited about the prospect, as he had been an excellent wrestler during his studies. But his hopes of excelling were quickly snuffed out by the massive Bruno. After hours of being tossed around like a child, Matthias' pride was as bruised as his aching body.

Once grappling was finished and Matthias was sufficiently exhausted by Bruno's onslaught, the Sand Ferret Squad practiced with swords. Instead of being asked to draw their Insignis blades, something Matthias still had not been taught to do; the squad used wooden swords. Again, Matthias thought he would have an advantage with his prior training, and again, he was sorely mistaken. His partner for the sparring was one of the guards he saw at the front gate, the one who laughed at him mockingly. Ferron was his name, and the older soldier enjoyed trouncing Matthias with the practice sword.

After combat training and a dozen newly formed bruises, the squad returned to drilling. To Matthias' utter dismay, he dropped his boulder even more times than the morning session and struggled to keep up. Drilling was followed by another meal in which he sat in silence, trying to ignore his squad mates' crude jokes and laughter. After dinner, Matthias was surprised by another round of drilling. When the squad returned to their barracks after evening drilling, every inch of his body screamed for sweet release. He had made a grave mistake not throwing himself off those damned cliffs.

Instead of falling asleep, Matthias ruminated over Anton for hours. His idle mind was no longer distracted by his new surroundings. Instead, Matthias focused his thoughts solely on the man who had ruined his life. He silently sobbed until tears no longer came out, and his chest hurt from heaving. He did not know what was most excruciating: sore muscles, hunger, thirst, or his broken heart. After drifting to sleep, the blasted morning horns woke Matthias after what felt like mere seconds of rest.

After the horn, the second day progressed just like the first, only more arduous, with the effects of the first day taking a toll on his body: drilling, lunch, grappling, combat training, drilling, dinner, drilling, and sleep. With Bruno always his grappling partner and Ferron always his sparring partner, he soon realized the two men were the most formidable warriors in the entire squad.

The grueling monotony repeated for the third day, save for a stark difference in the morning. After just an hour of drilling, three other squads joined the Sand Ferrets in the large practice field. Matthias followed the others to a tiny building on the edge of the area where equipment hung neatly on pegs along the exterior wall. Each soldier grabbed a long wooden pole with a blunted tip and a heavy, circular shield made of iron and wood. Matthias struggled to carry his equipment back to the center of the field since the buckler weighed more than the rock he held during drilling, and the javelin-like piece of wood was over six paces in length.

To Matthias' dismay, the sour-faced Ferron grabbed him roughly by the shoulder and pulled him in line where the rest of the squad was slowly forming.

"Follow my lead, boy," Ferron said, "Do not make a fool out of yourself."

Matthias found himself in a line between Ferron and the grizzled veteran Tomal. Captain Rain stood aloofly on the other side of the old soldier. Ten Sand Ferrets formed a row, with the other half situated directly behind. One of the other squads joined the back of the formation in two rows of ten while the remaining squads faced Matthias, mirroring the Sand Ferrets.

"What are we doing?" Matthias asked the older veteran quietly.

"Practicing our battle formations," Ferron said, "You'll get a real taste of what war will look like. Now hoist your buckler up like this."

With a grunt, the older man heaved his shield high and locked it in place to the woman on his right. All of the Sand Ferrets around did the same. Matthias' arms screamed as he lifted the disk of wood and iron up and wobbled, trying to fit it in between Tomal's and Ferron's.

"Careful, boy," Ferron hissed as Matthias' shield nearly hit the man square in the jaw, "If that shield strikes me, you will regret the day you were born."

As Matthias struggled to keep his shield simultaneously aloft and wedged between the two bucklers on either side, he saw the soldiers around him lift their javelins high. Grunting, he struggled to hoist his heavy wooden shaft above the shield wall and keep it parallel to the ground like Ferron's. The practice spear stuck out five paces from his shield, and Matthias feared that he would lose control.

The other formation faced Matthias, menacingly. Their first two lines held their spears out like the Sand Ferrets. However, the two lines behind them kept their wooden poles up at an angle toward the sky. The line behind Matthias pressed in, and he felt a buckler pressed roughly between his shoulder blades. The whole affair was grueling and uncomfortable and caused Matthias' pulse to race in anticipation.

"Ready yourselves!" Rain yelled, uncharacteristically commanding and forceful. The men and women around Matthias tensed, and the shield behind him pressed harder, almost shoving him to the ground. "Push!"

The captain at the head of the opposing formation yelled in unison, and in seconds, Matthias was thrown into the heavy shields of the soldiers in front of him. His teeth chattered at the collision, and his knees quaked. Ferron screamed something at him, but he was too shocked by the clashing formations to notice. Then, a wooden stave appeared between the crack of his and Tomal's shields and smashed into Matthias' jaw. He screamed in pain, and the world spun. His legs turned to jelly, and he dropped his spear. The man in front of him rammed his shield again, and Matthias panicked, falling into Ferron. The pair crashed to the dirt with a grunt. A few other Ferrets screamed and fell as the entire formation broke.

Matthias lay on his back, dazed and terrified, as the others clambered to their feet.

"You idiot," Ferron screamed. "If this were a real battle, you would've gotten the whole squad killed. I should slit your throat before we're deployed."

"That is enough, Ferron," Captain Rain said coolly, extending a hand to Matthias. The captain pulled Matthias up with surprising ease. "No need to scare recruits."

"Thank you, captain," Matthias said. It was the first time anyone had shown him an ounce of kindness since he enlisted.

"Heed Ferron's words, Helianth," Rain whispered coldly, "This may be your first formation drill, but it is nothing compared to battle. Now form up!"

Matthias groaned in dismay as the Sand Ferrets began the exercise again. And again.

Training continued for a fourth and a fifth day. Formation drilling was now a morning staple, to Matthias' sheer horror. No one, including Captain Rain, spoke more than a few words to Matthias during the drilling, and any interaction he had with the other soldiers consisted of mocking or scolding him for his performance. His pain and their cruel words fueled Matthias' anger, which seemed to give him strength. Matthias had always excelled at the physical aspects of his studies, and these rough fighters would not make him a fool. After the fifth day, his body seemed to adjust to the torment, and he could finally ignore the pain to hone his performance.

Matthias slept more soundly, ignoring the grunting and loud snoring that persisted throughout the night. He dropped his boulder less, fell behind less, and was defeated less by Bruno and Ferron. The former seemed to take pride in Matthias' improvements, while the latter seemed infuriated by his development.

By the ninth day, both of his training partners were replaced by other members of the Sand Ferret Squad. Matthias' new grappling partner, Darius, was just as large and powerful as Bruno but much less brutal in his tactics. He even had an encouraging word to say during their bouts. The giant, bearded behemoth shared a few notes and tips to help Matthias with his form and stamina.

His new sword sparring partner was an energetic man named Veiko. He was thinner and smaller than most, but his slender frame was wiry and extremely well-toned. He was just as difficult an opponent as Ferron but a much more enjoyable one. Matthias found himself laughing a few times during his session with Veiko, as his tongue was as fast as his sword arm.

That evening, at dinner, Matthias was surprised when his two new training partners joined him at his lonely end of the dining table. The pair smiled as if they were his old friends as they began to tear into their only hot meal of the day.

"You have quite the sword arm there, princeling," Veiko grinned between mouthfuls. His voice had no vehemence; the cheerful soldier spoke with a surprising fondness. "You almost got the better of me a few times."

"Maybe it says less of our new squad mate and more about you, my dear," Darius said, slapping Veiko on the back cheerfully. "Though I am impressed by how well you've handled eight days of Bruno and Ferron's torture; they tend to spend only two or three days hazing the recruits. They must see some potential in you, or at least Bruno does. Ferron seems to simply enjoy inflicting pain. Or he feels threatened by you, the spineless weasel."

Matthias looked at the burly man incredulously, unsure how to respond. He hadn't had a real conversation since the night he enlisted and had almost forgotten how to carry a conversation.

Matthias had thousands of questions and was desperate for answers, but instead, he replied sarcastically, "I think you're right, Darius. Ferron would delight in slapping his own mother if he knew who she was."

Darius erupted in hearty laughter; his dark eyes sparkled. "You were right, Veiko. This one has some spirit in him."

"I am always right, you big ape. How many years will it take for you to realize that?" Veiko replied, smiling as the bigger man scowled back in mock disgust. "But I do want to commend you, princeling. I've seen harder people crack and renounce their Oaths after the first few days of hazing."

"So, this happens to everyone?" Matthias asked.

"Oh yes," Veiko said reassuringly, "The first few days are hard on everyone, it takes a while for even the most athletic body to adjust to a soldier's life, and it is tradition to ignore, mock and rough up recruits to help harden them. Our life is not an easy one. But it usually lasts a day or two, not more, until we start treating a squad mate as one of our own. You had the unlucky pleasure of enduring eight full days. And it may take even longer for some of the others to come around."

"Ah, I see," Matthias said, "Is that because…?"

"Because you are nobly born and the first nobleman to enlist as a soldier in living memory?" Veiko said, chuckling. "Yes, I think that has something to do with it. Or perhaps Ferron is giving you a harder time because you have been assigned as his shield-brother."

"What is that?" Matthias asked. "And why does it make Ferron so angry?"

"A shield-brother is your partner in battle, son," Darius said. "The squad is split into ten pairs to make sure there is someone to protect you if the formation is broken. Veiko is my shield-brother, Leonas and Bruno are paired, and crusty Tomal is the captain's shield-brother—a soldier's high honor. Ferron's shield-brother died during the last campaign. Which leaves you as his new shield-brother by default."

"So that is why he has been so hard on me," Matthias said, "and why he has been next to me for formation drills. Though I don't think I'll feel very safe with him next to me in battle. He'll sooner stab me before an enemy does."

"I wouldn't worry much about that now," Veiko said. "You

two have plenty of time to bond and become our newest pair. Your Signata will attune to one another in time. Our swords speak to each other. The longer you fight alongside a shield-brother, the stronger the friendship, the stronger the bond becomes. But I wouldn't expect Ferron to be warming up anytime soon."

Matthias found himself laughing along with the young soldier; it was good to finally be able to speak to someone who wasn't trying to impale him with a practice sword.

"But I'm curious, how is a sword long enough to penetrate an enemy shield line effectively?" Matthias asked. "We have swords but practice with spears during our formation drills."

"I shouldn't be surprised at your curiosity, princeling. It seems you missed your calling as an officer. Let me show you." Veiko's eyes gleamed in response, and he sat up from his shield-brother's side. Veiko called across the table, holding up his sword arm expectantly. "Permission to summon my steel, captain. I would like to demonstrate Insignis art to Helianth."

"Permission granted," Captain Rain replied lazily.

"Thank you, captain," Veiko said, grinning devilishly. The wiry soldier turned to Matthias and motioned him to follow. "Let us get clear of the pavilion. It is forbidden to summon your blade within a camp, but you should have a little experience with summoning before you are thrown into battle."

Veiko took Matthias out of the pavilion and into the vast space beyond. Darius followed closely behind until the three were a dozen paces away from the nearest table. Veiko smiled and summoned his sword. In seconds, the gray-black blade was in his hand, pointing towards the sky. The sun's reflection danced along its face.

"This is the standard size of an Insignis blade," Veiko explained. "You can summon your sword a thousand times, and it will be shaped exactly like this. However, it doesn't always have to be."

The blade pulsed and turned into thick liquid once more, but instead of retreating onto the toned soldier's forearm, the mysterious weapon reshaped itself. The hilt remained the same, but the blade elongated and narrowed until the weapon was over eight paces long. It almost resembled a cavalryman's spear. Matthias' mouth hung agape in wonder.

"And that is how you penetrate an enemy shield wall. And the reason we practice with those fake javelins," Veiko said, brandishing his newly formed weapon. "Just imagine any shape, and your blade will change its form to match your desires."

The metal pulsed again, and the blade writhed until it formed into a scythe. It pulsed again and was a short dagger, a broadsword, and a thin, serrated blade. The sword flowed into different angles, and positions, forming a dozen times until Veiko called it back into its dormant Signata state.

"Permission to summon my blade, captain?" Matthias blurted out, desperate to try the trick.

From his place under the pavilion, Captain Rain watched the display with a critical eye. The brooding officer thought for a moment and slowly nodded. Matthias' heart leaped with excitement, and he held up his arm, but nothing happened.

"Just imagine the sword in your hand, lad," Darius said reassuringly.

Matthias concentrated, followed the burly man's instructions and envisioned a blade in his hand. Suddenly the tattoo on his arm came to life, and in seconds, his hand was holding the cold steel of the sword's hilt.

"Now lengthen the sword," Veiko said. "Just visualize it growing, and it will obey."

Matthias stared at his sword and envisioned a longer blade, similar to Veiko's. His hand itched slightly, and the blade flowed into the spear-like image in Matthias' mind. Laughing, Matthias willed his sword into shape after shape.

Men and women began leaving the pavilion, signaling that mealtime was over. Matthias called his blade back into his arm.

"Good work, lad," Darius said, "The sword is an extension of your spirit and will obey your will. Trust it, and you will survive the weeks to come."

Matthias smiled at the brawny soldier, feeling confident for the first time since enlisting.

The post-dinner drill became significantly more bearable now that Matthias could join his newfound friends. The following days progressively became more tolerable, and soon Matthias was just as comfortable with his daily training as any other soldier in the Sand Ferrets. One by one, the other soldiers saw Matthias' grit and natural talent with the sword and gradually warmed up to him, even Bruno. The only people who continued to treat Matthias as scenery were Ferron, who clearly resented him, and Captain Rain, who paid attention to no one.

Once his mind wasn't preoccupied with adapting to the physical demands of the daily life of a soldier, Matthias had the liberty of learning more about the army and his role from Darius, Veiko, and other squad members. The Sand Ferret Squad had twenty men and women in its ranks, including himself and Captain Rain. Darius explained that twenty was the standard number for squads unless it changed due to death or injury. Twenty squads formed a battalion and a commander, like Hendrick, led each battalion. Ten battalions and a contingent of cavalry formed a legion, each led by a Heptarch, the highest-ranking officer in the city. The Heptarch who commanded their legion was none other than Aleksandra Passiflor, the most famous and decorated living human in Arachovia.

More than just structural knowledge, Matthias learned of battle formations, signals, how to prepare for marching, and even how to summon his Insignis blade. The last piece was simple, for all he needed was to focus on the forearm that held his Signata and imagine the sword in his hand, and within seconds, the magic metal did its duty and formed the blade. It all became fascinating, and Matthias began to enjoy the rhythm of his daily life and the odd security that accompanied it.

Four weeks after his enlistment, that rhythm was interrupted for the first time when a captain, previously unknown to Matthias, interrupted his lunchtime. Veiko was in the middle of a particularly embarrassing story about his first battle with Darius when the woman, clad in Insignis armor, approached the table.

"Enlisted Helianth?" The officer called for the entire table to hear.

Veiko shot the woman with a look of sheer annoyance; the gregarious man appreciated nothing less than being interrupted mid-story. Matthias stood clumsily and saluted the officer, which he was not accustomed to since Captain Rain did not seem to require any formality from his squad.

"You have a visitor from the upper city, Helianth," the officer roared. A murmur rose across the table, and Matthias winced. He wouldn't hear the end of this. The others had only just begun to call him by his real name not two days ago.

Matthias nodded and followed the armored woman out of the dining pavilion and across the encampment. He knew who this visitor was. There was only one person who it could be—his father.

Lord Helianth was a passionate yet methodical man; he took long to forgive and even longer to forget. Four weeks was not enough time for him to settle his rage sufficiently for a proper dress down for his son. The failed betrothal with Kadri coupled with the scandal of his eldest son enlisting as a lowly soldier would take years for the bombastic man to forgive. Still, a month was enough time to let his son stew in his "poor" decisions before forcing him back into noble society. That was the true nature of his father's visit, to attempt to salvage Matthias' scandal, force him to renounce his Oaths and return home to marry some poor woman from the lowest of noble families. But the man would be sorely mistaken if he thought his son would bend to his will now. Matthias had indeed hardened by the short weeks in the army. He would not be as malleable as he had been in the past.

An entire speech began to form in his mind, and he followed the officer toward the northern gate of the encampment. The argument was simple, and Matthias was almost excited to see his father for the first time in his life, to finally stand up to the man.

"Here you are, Helianth," the officer said as they rounded the gate, "You have ten minutes. Then return directly to your squad."

Matthias stopped in his tracks; the person waiting on the other side of the gate was not his father.

4

Deployed

Kadri stood before Matthias outside the barracks, dressed in a flowing silk gown embroidered in gold and wearing brilliant jewels around her neck that reflected the noonday sun. Becoming a priestess was something Kadri had always been transparent about but seeing her dressed as one was another thing entirely. Matthias would have laughed at the comically elegant outfit worn by his best friend if he hadn't been so shocked.

"Are you out of your mind?" Kadri chided the moment the officer was out of earshot. "What could possibly possess you to do such a stupid thing?"

"So, we are starting with anger, are we?" Matthias said dryly, and a small smile bloomed on his best friend's otherwise angry face. She could never stay mad at him for long, not even now.

"Yes, you dolt," Kadri said, trying her best to resist smiling, "You have no idea what a storm you caused back in the upper city. It is still the only subject anyone wants to discuss. Why on earth did you enlist?"

"Anton," Matthias answered, and suddenly a new emotion blossomed on Kadri's face. Pity. "You must have heard about his gorgeous, blushing bride Evelin fucking Rosalia."

"I did," Kadri said quietly, "I am truly sorry, but a broken heart is not a legitimate reason to throw your life away."

"How could I do that if Anton already took it from me?" Matthias said exasperatedly. "Or at least the life I wanted. In the course of one night, he denied that to me, which presented two options to me in its place—one by Anton and the other by my father. I decided there was a third option. At first, I wanted to die on some far-off battlefield to make them both suffer, but now I'm beginning to think I was born to do this."

"Oh, Matthias," Kadri exclaimed, throwing her arms around him and pulling him in tight.

It felt wonderful to be with someone he cared for again.

"My stupid, bull-headed Matthias. This stunt you just pulled is by far the dumbest thing anyone has done in the history of Arachovia. However, I agree with you; you seem exactly where you need to be, as strange as it sounds. Just as I am."

"I am tired of being the topic of conversation," Matthias said, "How is the Temple of Sorilea, anyways?"

"Dark and stuffy," Kadri said, "Filled with old women with slow wits and no sense of humor, but I am learning so much. You have no idea what things the spirits can do if we simply ask them, Matthias. I wish you could see it all."

Very little was known about what occurred inside the Temple of Sorilea. Most Arachovians avoided the place out of fear, respect, or a healthy mixture of both. The spirits of Arachovia, otherwise known as the rach, were said to have built the city from the foundations and protected the city. A few Arachovians claimed to have seen them as shimmering lights floating above the rooftops, but that was all hearsay. Only priestesses accepted into the temple were able to commune with them and understand their true nature. Matthias agreed it was best to leave such spiritual matters to them.

"Maybe one day I can," he said, nonchalantly, eager to change the topic. "Kadri, I'm so glad you're here, but I did fully expect to see my father when I heard I had a visitor."

The smile immediately fell off Kadri's face, and she studied his feet. "Oh…Matthias, there is something you should know about your father. I don't think he will be coming here anytime soon."

"Why is that?" Matthias said, "What do you mean? What happened?"

"Matthias," she said, choosing her words carefully, "After the night you refused my betrothal and enlisted, your father publicly disowned you outright. He named your younger brother, Markas, as his new heir and legally stripped you of title, inheritance, and all social standing. I'm so sorry."

Matthias looked at his friend, stunned. Of course, his father disowned him. Why wouldn't he, after threatening it so many times? He meant to insult his father and disgrace his reputation, and he had done exactly that. There was no other course of action.

After sharing the revelation about Matthias' father, Kadri's visit to the barracks did not last much longer. The circumstances of their conversation and his military duties forced brevity on the reunion, for which he was rather grateful. As much as he enjoyed seeing his dear friend, he was not ready to fully process the news she had delivered. The distraction had proven an excellent tactic to deal with his excessive emotions of late, and he was eager to return to his training, which allowed for an ample diversion from his deepest thoughts.

Three more weeks passed after Kadri's visit, and Matthias quickly developed calloused hands, sun-kissed skin, and denser muscles than he had ever been graced with. He was starting to understand why giant men like Bruno and Darius were ordinary in the army, though he wondered how Veiko had been enlisted for so long and remained so wiry. The young man packed away more food in his slender frame at mealtimes than his massive lover.

Seven weeks had passed since Matthias' spontaneous enlistment, and he had felt as if he had finally earned the full respect of the entire squad, except for Ferron, of course. The older soldier would continue to hate him until the day one of them died and probably continue his hatred after.

The squad's approval could not have come at a more opportune time, as one morning during his eighth week, he was awoken by not one but dozens of brass horns. The soldiers around him shot out of bed and furiously ran around the narrow sleeping hall, grabbing their belongings from various trunks and stuffing them into small packs. Matthias wearily stood up and gave Darius, who was helping his lover find his bracers under their bed, a questioning look.

"Those are the horns of battle, lad," Darius said, pointing towards the open doorway, "We are being deployed."

Within an hour after the horns, Matthias found himself standing at attention outside the southern city gates, staring at the vast plains that stretched southward. The Sand Ferret Squad formed two neat rows of ten soldiers; Matthias was wedged uncomfortably between Darius and Ferron, to his dismay. The other nineteen squads of his battalion were positioned in identical formations around them so that the force of four hundred was forty wide and ten deep. The gleaming armor of Commander Hendrick could be seen beyond the front line of soldiers, awaiting orders from further up the column. Three battalions formed before them, and six behind in a long line of metal, leather, and sweat.

He could see the cavalry for the first time since his enlistment, men and women in full Insignis armor riding armored mountain elk. Instead of swords, the mounted soldiers carried bows, quivers, and long deadly spears. The tall steeds they sat upon trotted gracefully on slender, toned legs. Long, curved horns twisted up out of steel helmets, looking just as deadly as the spears their masters brandished. Hundreds of mounted warriors passed the column of soldiers to form at the front where Heptarch Aleksandra and the other senior officers awaited them.

A second peculiar group formed behind the cavalry; many women in flowing gowns picked their way past the contingent, followed by their pack animals. The women were almost an entire battalion in number.

"Those are the furies," Darius whispered as the procession of women passed. "Priestesses trained in either the art of healing or destruction. They say Heptarch Aleksandra was the first to use them in battle. Now, almost every legion in the city uses at least a few. I've never seen anything more ferocious in battle than those women."

Matthias anxiously waited in his leather armor, the leather pack hoisted around his shoulder, weighed down by a water skin, ration kit, and other items he needed to make the journey. A heavy round shield made of wood and iron was strapped to his left forearm; it felt as if he had a boulder tied to his arm. A horn sounded, and the earth shook as thousands of soldiers began to trot forward, leather sandals, steel boots, and cloven hoofs beating against the dusty plains southward. The purpose of the daily drills had finally become clear to Matthias as he slowly jogged with his heavy equipment alongside Darius, Veiko, Ferron, and his other shield-brothers. Marching was like drilling, only much more strenuous.

Hours passed, the mesa of Arachovia faded away into the horizon, and Matthias felt a pang of sadness when he could not see his home anymore. He had never excelled in his geography lessons, but he knew enough to maintain his bearings. The massive mountain range that split the earth in two was to his right, known as the Dragon's Teeth. No one living had ever seen the other side, but historians said that the first humans, the Ae'rach, had traveled from the mystical lands on the other side. In the far distance, on his left, was the hazy outline of the forested mountains named the Sytharen Range. The two ranges formed the perimeter of the vast valley Arachovia sat in, protecting it from the outside world. A world in which Matthias would soon find himself.

Matthias knew that two great city-states controlled the lands to the south, but he could not remember either of their names. The legion made their way southward along the great River Palanthia, crossing smaller rivers and offshoots on wide stone bridges. The road they marched upon was well-worn from years of heavy use.

As the blood-red sun set under the peaks of the Dragon's Teeth, the legion halted and made camp on the bank of the Palanthia. Before the darkness of the evening set in, thousands of tents were constructed, and hundreds of campfires lit the camp. The Sand Ferret Squad lounged on the dusty earth in a circle around their fire, situated at the mouth of their long tent.

"Now you see why we constantly drill," Darius said, noticing Matthias massaging his sore feet. "But you're doing well. Prepare yourself. It's about another week until the Gap of Tanaegra and probably another week until we reach our final destination. Make sure you sleep well tonight."

"Have you heard what the purpose of our deployment is?" Matthias asked. "I hoped you had some idea what we were marching toward."

"I hear the Kyriaki and Raephinans are at war again; it happens at least once a year these days," Veiko said, laying his head on Darius' lap, looking up at the night sky.

Kyriak and Raephina. Matthias could not recall anything about either city.

"Word is that this time we are to side with Kyriaki during this campaign, though we side against them just as often. We don't hold a grudge against either, but we choose to oppose whoever poses the greater threat," Darius said. "As long as neither finds their way north into our valley."

Matthias nodded and gazed into the fire; the camp was eerily quiet that evening. Half of their squad had already retired to the tent after dinner. Most stared somberly into the distance, and very little laughter came from the other fires.

"What is a battle like?" Matthias asked in a low whisper.

Darius sighed and took a moment before speaking, as if deciding how to approach the topic. "Not as glorious as the histories would like you to believe, lad. I don't want to scare you, but you should know what awaits us in the south. A battle is a bloody and terrible business. You must rely on your brothers as much as your sword or shield if you want to survive. Good thing you have me and this sorry excuse for a soldier to keep you safe on the field."

"But what should I expect?" Matthias said, unsatisfied with the answer. "No one has spoken of what actually takes place during a battle. What happens?"

"Do you mean the specifics of our formations and such?" Veiko said, "We line up very much as we do during marching, forty soldiers wide and ten deep, each paired with a shield-brother to protect as fiercely as your own life. Shoulder to shoulder, we hold up our shields like a wall, push into the enemy, and try to break their line before breaking ours. The Insignis swords we are given come in handy. You don't need to know the specifics. Just listen for Captain Rain's voice if anything goes south. He'll make sure we're taken care of."

Matthias stared across the campfire at Captain Rain; the dark-haired man sat casually on the ground, toned limbs sprawled lazily to the sides as he regarded the stars with a blank expression, his curly hair obscuring half his face. Matthias turned to Veiko and dramatically raised an eyebrow.

"Don't be fooled by his carefree attitude on the training field. He's the sharpest captain I've ever had and fights like a tiger on the battlefield." Veiko said. "The Sand Ferrets lose fewer lives in battle than any other squad in the entire legion, thanks to him."

Matthias glanced back at the man. He did not have the same severe and pompous air as the other officers in the legion and wore tattered clothes, unlike his counterparts. The man was most likely from one of the lowest-born noble families that could barely trace their line back to the Ae'rach. That sort of man was the most common to serve in the army, and the captain reminded Matthias of the lower-born nobles he had grown up with, unassuming and undisciplined.

"I am curious about one thing, lad," Darius said. "What was the reason you joined up in the first place? The entire squad has been buzzing. No, the entire army is, probably the whole city."

Matthias' stomach churned violently as his mind wandered back to Anton and his betrayal for the umpteenth time that day. The physically excruciating training and mentally taxing hazing he had endured in the last week had done little to preoccupy his broken heart. The wound was still fresh, and the second he thought of Anton, all the despair and pain came flooding back.

"It was a matter of love, wasn't it?" Veiko had seen the visible torment on Matthias' face, "That has always been my theory. The heart is always the culprit when it comes to extreme decisions."

"Well, Darius, it does seem like Veiko is always right," Matthias said, chuckling dryly, ignoring the younger man's triumphant smile.

"Aye," Darius said empathetically, "It must have been a rough go for you to end up here, wasn't it, lad?"

Nodding absentmindedly, Matthias began to explain. Before he knew what he was doing, the lanky noble found himself telling the pair his entire story, from the day he met Anton, to the bevy of proposals, to the betrayal at the Shrine of Isemelith. Matthias wasn't sure if he trusted the two men or if he was just eager to get everything off his chest. He decided it was the mixture of the two.

Once he finished telling his short and bitter tale, tears began to well up in his eyes, and to his surprise, the same was true of both Veiko and Darius.

"I am so sorry, lad," Darius said, placing his hand on Matthias' shoulder comfortingly. "'Twas worse than I could have imagined, you poor thing."

"That bastard, Anton," Veiko said, wiping a tear from his eye. "Darius, I would've flayed you alive if you did anything like that to me at the Shrine."

Matthias smiled broadly. "How long have the two of you been Devoted to one another?" he asked, kicking himself for not realizing the apparent sooner. The love the two had for one another was more than palpable.

"A little over two years," Darius said, smiling fondly. "It was after Veiko's first campaign when we were randomly assigned as shield-brothers, and I just knew he couldn't survive another battle without me."

Veiko scoffed and punched the giant man playfully. "I believe I was the one who kept a Raephinan soldier from impaling you with his sword, you big lummox. I've been saving that giant ass of yours ever since."

Darius pulled Veiko in with a thick arm and kissed him sweetly on the top of his head. "And I wouldn't have it any other way."

Matthias smiled at the display of affection while simultaneously racked with jealousy. Darius and Veiko had what he lost a couple of months prior, but it was undeniably heartwarming to see. He glanced over and realized Captain Rain had already retired for the evening. Only Darius, Veiko, and Matthias remained around the fire.

"Seems as if our dear captain has made his way to his lover's bed," Darius said. "No worries, lad, you will have plenty of time to practice during our march south."

"Lover?" Matthias said slowly. "Are you saying that Captain Rain is…?"

"Like us?" Darius completed the unfinished question. "Oh yes. You will find that many men in the military are much more like you than you would realize, and a few women, too. Often, there is no other place for a man who loves another man or a woman who loves another woman in our world. Nearly half of the Sand Ferret Squad are Devoted; Bruno and Leonas have been Devoted to one another for just shy of ten years. It makes it easier in a battle to know the man next to you would do anything to keep you safe, isn't that right, my love?"

Veiko smiled and responded by planting a kiss sweetly on his lover's cheek. Once again, a wave of mixed feelings of happiness and jealousy for the pair crashed over Matthias.

"What of Captain Rain?" Matthias asked incredulously, his curiosity piqued, "Is he Devoted to someone in the squad?"

"Oh no, relations between officers and enlisted are strictly forbidden. No, our dear captain has found love outside of our little band of degenerates," Veiko said. "Haven't you noticed that the captain has never slept in our barracks since you enlisted? The night he brought you to the barracks, where did you think he went after?"

"Who is his lover?" Matthias leaned forward, surprised by his fascination with the aloof officer's personal life.

"Rumor has it that it is none other than Commander Hendrick himself," Veiko said with great satisfaction. It was no secret to anyone in the squad that the man loved a good piece of gossip.

Matthias nodded and thought back to his first night when he met both officers. He had noticed how familiar they were with one another and how casual the junior had been to the senior. Matthias had simply chalked it up to his odd personality. But it wasn't the case; Rain and Hendrick were lovers.

"I had heard that Hendrick was the captain's mentor before either of them joined the army. The man taught Captain Rain everything he knows if you know what I mean." Veiko giggled, and Darius' face flushed.

"Speaking of lover's beds," Darius said, "I think it is high time the three of us get some rest. The pair of you could gossip the entire night away, and I'll have to carry both of you to Tanaegra myself."

Veiko let out a scoff but went to work dousing the fire and cleaning up the camp, making quick work of it. Matthias found an empty patch of hard earth in the tent to set up his blankets next to Darius and Veiko, who combined their two woolen sheets together into a veritable cloth fortress. He soon fell asleep on the cold ground, ignoring the soft moans under the blankets next to him.

The following days progressed painstakingly as the legion moved slowly southward across the plains, past a few tiny villages and over dozens of winding rivers. In a week, the soldiers had made it to the valley's southern entrance, a treacherous pass between the rolling foothills of the Sytharen Range and the cliffs and slopes of the Dragon's Teeth. A few leagues north of the Gap was a short mesa, jutting out from the plains.

Matthias could distinguish buildings on top of the plateau and realized he was looking at a small city. As they approached the mesa, he could make out a walled encampment at the rock formation's base. Tanaegra, the city named after the mountain pass, was an industrious settlement under the protection of

Arachovia. It served as a southern outpost for the legions with strategic proximity to the Gap. A fully functioning encampment roughly half the size of the Arachovia's hosted the legion for the night, and Matthias was grateful to sleep on a bed.

The following day, the legion embarked southward, and through the pass, the narrow canyon allowed only ten people to walk abreast, forcing the entire column to enter the canyon one squad at a time. Matthias gazed around in wonder; he had never seen cliffs so tall before. The Dragon's Teeth made both the mesas at Arachovia and Tanaegra seem like anthills in comparison.

After an arduous march through the Gap, the legion arrived in the sprawling plains beyond. The terrain was almost the same as the valley, vast plains covered in short shrubs, hundreds of winding rivers, and the occasional butte or mesa. The plains, however, were not contained by anything save for the Dragon's Teeth. The massive mountain range continued its way south and west, dividing the world as it went. Looking south and east, Matthias could only see the blue horizon; it was a thrilling and unsettling sight, the boundless plains spilling into nothingness.

Kyriak, as Darius explained, was a powerful and formidable city-state that had conquered all of the lands south and west of the valley along the length of the Dragon's Teeth. They were brutal warriors and conscripted all their citizens to fight, starting at age ten. The legion continued south and west.

Rumor was that one of the Kyriaki fortresses was threatened by a Raephinan legion. Raephina, according to Darius, lay to the south and east and was very much like Arachovia in many ways. It had flourishing arts and culture and was renowned across the world for training the most talented artisans and craftsmen. Raephinan pottery and metalworking were priceless.

Veiko believed that the Raephinans were much more enjoyable to support, having fought beside both armies throughout the fierce war between the two superpowers. But the Raephinans had gained too much power in the past year. Their vast troops were stationed so dangerously close to the Gap of Tanaegra that the Arachovian Heptarchs had no choice but to align themselves with Kyriak. Matthias was surprised that the pair knew much about politics as soldiers in the legion. Still, Veiko explained that rumor was more powerful than any sword in the legion.

Ten days of marching followed the Gap of Tanaegra, and Matthias thought that the army would soon march over the world's edge, but every day the horizon continued, and so did the endless plains.

That was until the tenth day. A mesa, relatively the same size as Arachovia's, came into view an hour after midday. As the army approached, Matthias' jaw dropped. Buildings were not only built on top of the elevated land but carved into the sides as well. There was no lower city like Tanaegra or Arachovia, and the fortress' architects dug a large trench at the base of the cliffs. Tall stone cylinders coughed out black smoke, the product from the fire of a thousand forges. A single drawbridge connected the mesa from the surrounding plains. It was a veritable fortress in every right.

When the legion had arrived at the fortress, Veiko had discovered its name from the surrounding soldiers. Vilgast was an odd name for a strange city, but Matthias reminded himself he was in another realm entirely. The drawbridge lowered, and hundreds of soldiers marched out, brandishing red banners with what seemed to be a coiled snake. A single man with glinting armor rode out to meet the head of the contingent, and within minutes, Veiko learned the man's name was General Zsolt.

A horn sounded, and the army began the quick work of setting up camp, wearily unpacking their belongings and setting up neat rows of thousands of tents. A few minutes later, a messenger tore through the encampment, found Captain Rain, whispered in his ear, and ran towards the next officer he could find.

"I hope that means the Heptarch finished her council with General Zsolt, and we are allowed to make an early dinner," Veiko said brightly, "My stomach is growling."

"There will be no time for dinner, unfortunately," Captain Rain announced, so the whole squad could hear. "The Raephinan forces will reach the fortress within the hour. It is time to prepare for battle."

5

The Battle of Vilgast

Before the hour was over, the Arachovian Legion had assembled its defense of the great fortress of Vilgast. After a long day of marching and little rest, the soldiers were worse for wear; Matthias was certainly drained and wished he could rest. However, the warriors around him gritted their teeth and emanated a steadfast resolve that encouraged him to ignore his fatigue and focus on the eastern horizon.

Heptarch Aleksandra had positioned her ten battalions in a neat row, north to south, just a quarter mile east of Vilgast. The soldiers held tight formations, standing shoulder to shoulder, in a line four hundred souls long and ten deep. The Sand Ferret Squad was positioned on the right side of the fourth battalion near the front, placing them near the center of the grander formation. Matthias' squad formed the third and fourth rows of the configuration; there was only one other squad between them and the open plains ahead. Standing in the third row, Matthias found himself between Ferron and Tomal. Though he had hoped to be near Darius and Veiko, they were on the opposite side of the squad in the fourth row. Matthias realized that the Sand Ferrets were in the exact order as they did during training.

The long column of infantry was flanked on either end by a large contingent of cavalrymen; Matthias could see the horns of their steeds jostling above soldiers' heads like a chaotic forest of bones. It seemed as if the beasts were just as nervous about the impending violence as Matthias was.

The battalion of furies was positioned directly behind the tight formation of soldiers, spread out in seemingly random clusters. Matthias could hear their chants from his place along the front lines, spoken in ancient languages that made the hair on the back of his head rise. Behind the Arachovians were the Kyriaki defenders led by General Zsolt. They outnumbered the Arachovians by almost two to one but safely situated themselves hundreds of paces behind, acting as a reserve force. Matthias thought it unsuitable that the larger and better-rested army would allow their allies to fight their battles for them. It was an embarrassing display of cowardice.

A horn sounded and shields rose; Matthias hefted his heavy wooden disc with a grunt and locked it against Ferron and Tomal's buckler on either side. At the same time, thousands of Insignis blades pierced the heavens, and Matthias summoned his sword frantically. The first two rows shaped their blades like Veiko had demonstrated the first night of marching, nine paces long and narrow like spears. They held them parallel to the ground, and the blades protruded from the shield wall like a field of giant, deadly needles. Matthias glanced at Ferron's sword, which was just as long as those on the front lines but angled upward into the sky. He willed his sword to mimic the others in his row and smiled broadly when the metal obeyed.

Another horn sounded, but it did not sound like the brass instrument he had heard in the Arachovian barracks. The new sound that pierced through the air was high and reedy, carrying across the plains from the east. Then he heard them, thousands of feet beating against the ground. For a brief moment, he thought that the earth had begun to shake. Then he saw their opponents and nearly wet himself.

The Raephinans marched beneath hundreds of green banners, a veritable ocean of metal helms that stretched out to the north and south as far as the eye could see. There must have been at least ten thousand souls advancing towards them, though Matthias had never been great with numbers. Each warrior was heavily armored in metal, unlike the leather of the Arachovians. Thousands of spears pierced the sky, and battle cries echoed across the plains. Even from that distance, Matthias could see that none of the enemy's equipment was forged of Insignis steel, simply because the armor failed to catch the sunlight. The strange horn sounded again, and the Raephinan forces surged forward. A tide of metal, flesh, and wood threatened to completely swallow the inferior forces of the Arachovians.

"Spearmen, swordsmen, archers!" Captain Rain cried out to his squad, "Spearmen swordsmen, archers!"

After looking over at his commanding officer quizzically, Matthias suddenly realized he was describing the formation of the enemy troops. The Raephinans would try to batter open their shield walls with their wooden spears, allowing the swordsmen to rush while simultaneously protecting the archers once they were in range to shower death from above.

Matthias was not leaving these strange lands alive.

Then the sky exploded. A deafening peal of thunder rocked

the battlefield, then a violent bolt of lightning struck the center of the charging Raephinans, sending pieces of earth and soldiers flying. A second lightning strike fell upon the enemy forces, followed by another, then yet another. The destructive power of the Arachovian priestesses wreaked havoc upon the poor soldiers. Soon, dust, the sounds of the dying, and the rotten smell of burnt flesh filled his nostrils.

But still, the enemy charge continued.

The lightning was not all the Arachovian furies had in store for their enemies. Massive fireballs the size of cattle arched high above Matthias' head, leaving a simmering, black column of smoke in their wake. The flames crashed into the Raephinans, shrieks of terror erupted within their rank as the short grass beneath them was set ablaze.

But still, the enemy charge continued.

As the head of the attacking horde drew nearer, they passed out of the barrage of fire and lightning into safety, too close to the front lines to be attacked by the priestesses without collateral damage. A brass Arachovian horn sounded, and the cavalry lurched forward, hooves beating against the dusty plains. Instead of charging ahead, the mounted forces spread out like great wings until the farthest mountain elk had passed the flanks of the now haphazard Raephinan formation. Only then did the cavalry attack, barreling into the far sides of the enemy infantry in a torrent of fur, flesh, and blood. It was the most grotesque display Matthias had seen in his entire life.

But still, the enemy charge continued.

Forty paces.

Despite the onslaught of the defenders, the wave of Raephinan soldiers still outnumbered the Arachovian forces.

Thirty paces.

The cavalry funneled the vanguard survivors in a tight fist, and they hurtled towards the defenders with a bloody cry.

Twenty paces.

"Brace!" Captain Rain cried, and a shield rammed against his back forcefully.

Ten paces.

After a nasty look from Ferron, Matthias leaned against the soldier directly in front of him, placing his heavy buckler against their shoulder blades.

The Raephinan's force was enough to knock Matthias off his feet, which it would have done if the warrior behind hadn't pressed a shield roughly against his back. He cried out as the weight of thousands of soldiers pushed against him, threatening to crush him. The young soldier struggled to keep his sword held aloft as the ranks of the Sand Ferrets pressed in tightly.

The warriors in front of him stabbed brutally with their long swords, often finding their targets resulting in a sickening scream and shower of blood. Once or twice, the tip of a spear found its way through the first two rows and almost impaled Matthias through the skull. Arrows began to rain from above; one glanced off his helmet. He heard guttural howls all around him. Matthias cried out in fear, feeling trapped and helpless. Eventually, one of those metal blades would find him, which would mean his end.

"Push!" Captain Rain shouted. The other captains in the battalion echoed his shout. Only a few moments had transpired since the initial collision, though it had felt like a lifetime.

The fighters around him grunted, and the shield behind Matthias slammed into him so hard he thought he felt a bone break. He screamed and leaned forward, shoving his buckler forward with all his might.

"Push!" Captain Rain roared, and the Sand Ferrets lurched forward again.

The rows in front of him stabbed ferociously at the enemy, the wooden spears no match for the unbreakable Insignis steel. The battalion lurched forward a third, a fourth, a fifth time, and Matthias' foot landed on something soft. He glanced down briefly and almost vomited. The lifeless eyes of a Raephinan soldier stared up at him, skull crushed, and body broken.

"Push! Almost there!" Captain Rain yelled. "Push! Once more!"

With one final thrust, the last of the enemy spearmen broke, falling back to allow the swordsmen to lurch forward. They held their swords low, attempting to slash the Arachovian's legs and feet.

"Break!" The squad captain on the front lines bellowed, and the fighters in the first two rows suddenly lurched forward, swords reshaping to their standard sizes. They met the enemy in pairs, slashing and hacking, pushing the invaders back a few steps.

"Hold!" Rain yelled, and the Sand Ferret Squad lowered their swords as the squad in front had done. Matthias watched as ferocious warriors slaughtered each other in front of him. His stomach was in his throat, and the rank of death filled his nose.

"In a few moments, we will break," Ferron sneered at Matthias. "Stay near, you piece of filth, and don't let the—" His words ended abruptly in a gurgle as an arrow protruded from the man's neck.

The old soldier let out a bloody gasp and clutched his throat. After an excruciating moment, Ferron's eyes rolled in his head, and he crumpled to the ground, lifeless.

"Break!" Rain screamed as an arrow sprouted from Tomal's head. The veteran fell soundlessly, dead before he hit the ground.

The others lurched forward in pairs, Bruno and Leonas on the left, Veiko and Darius on the right. The squad behind stepped forward, pushing Matthias out of the way, and lowered their swords, becoming the front of the shield wall. Matthias scanned his surroundings, stunned by the bodies beneath his feet, feeling exposed. The world began to spin.

"Helianth, with me!" Captain Rain shouted. The armored man drew close, waving a hand in front of Matthias' face. "Do you hear me, Helianth?"

Matthias nodded.

"Good." Captain Rain smiled. "Stay close and keep your shield up and we will get out of this. Keep an eye out for their officers!"

With that, the armored captain brandished his weapon and stalked into the fray; Matthias jogged after him, hoisting his heavy shield and readjusting the length of his blade for the melee.

Years of combat training could never prepare Matthias for the chaotic storm that was an actual battle. As Captain Rain pressed into the mass of bodies, the swords of friend and foe alike cut through the melee like a violent storm. There was barely a patch of ground uncovered by blood or corpses, and its smell was enough to make Matthias gag every few seconds. Nevertheless, he kept close to the captain, who expertly fought his way through the enemy soldiers, slicing through them with shocking ease. The way he battled was almost like a dance, all fluid movements and athletic grace. Matthias simply walked in the man's wake, aimlessly slashing and pushing attacks away with his massive shield. He couldn't land any blows, but the least he could do was make sure no one attacked the captain from behind. Most of the Raephinan swordsmen held simple iron swords and wore iron armor, save for a few in full Insignis regalia. Matthias would bet his life that those formidable fighters were the enemy's officers.

Captain Rain seemed to ignore most of the soldiers and focused his attacks primarily on the enemy officers. Three Insignis bearers had already fallen to his sword before Matthias and Rain managed to fight their way through the dense front lines. Beyond, there was a small open space where the pair took refuge; the fighting here was spread out and gave Matthias a moment to assess their surroundings.

The fourth battalion was the first to break the enemy line, and already half its forces had joined the melee. A group had veered right, led by Leonas and Bruno, attacking the Raephinan spearmen from the side. They cut through the battlefield like a pair of bulls, tossing their opponents aside and scattering their ranks, allowing the soldiers of the fifth battalion to push forward and engage the Raephinan swordsmen. Veiko and Darius had already crossed the melee with a few other pairs of Sand Ferrets and reached the archers' line. Darius fought like a bear and Veiko like a panther, one powerful and brutal and the other fast and ferocious. Their foe fell like wheat to a scythe in close combat. The rest scattered, dropping their bows.

A heavy sword flew out of nowhere as Matthias was preoccupied with watching his friends. Hoisting the shield with all his might, he blocked the blow milliseconds before the dark gray blade found his neck. The decisive strike knocked the wind out of him, and it sent him falling onto his back. His attacker was a broad man covered in Insignis metal; the intricate helmet marked him as a high officer, most likely a Raephinan equivalent to a commander.

Lifting his sword above his head, the enemy commander prepared to bring it down on Matthias while stepping on his shield with a heavily armed foot to prevent him from escaping. Captain Rain wildly slashed at the commander from behind like a bolt of gray lightning.

Whirling around with surprising grace, the enemy commander expertly parried Rain's attack and, in the same motion, kicked Matthias in the face with his armored boot. Pain laced through his body, and his vision blurred; Matthias lay on the ground for a few moments. Gathering himself, he sat up and raised his blade defensively, but Rain and the Raephinan commander were no longer above him. He looked around frantically and found the pair dueling ten paces to his left. Rain may have been one of the most skilled swordsmen Matthias had ever seen, but the enemy commander was severely testing him. Every jab was parried with ease and was swiftly followed by a blow that knocked Rain off his balance; the captain gritted his teeth in desperation. An expert parry by the commander sent Rain's Insignis sword flying, disarming the curly-haired man. Matthias gasped. The ferocious enemy officer lifted his sword in triumph.

There was nothing Matthias could do; he would never get to him in time, not with the massive shield strapped to his arm. Spontaneously, he frantically unlatched the leather straps of his shield, scrambled to his feet, and lunged toward his opponent. Matthias was still out of range and would never reach the commander in time.

A wild notion flitted through his mind. It couldn't possibly work, but he had to try.

He raised his sword and pointed it at the commander, aiming it towards the unprotected gap in armor at the man's neck. He willed his sword to change, and the blade complied, stretching and thinning into the spear-like weapon he had formed at the beginning of the battle.

The blade's tip shot out with lightning speed, right into the commander's neck. The sword dropped from the man's hand as blood squirted out of the hole Matthias had just made. He retracted the blade quickly as the man fell to the ground in a crash.

"Thank you, Helianth," Rain said, breathing heavily. "That was quick thinking."

Matthias did not hear a word the captain spoke; he was too focused on the glazed eyes and the gaping hole in the neck of the man he had just killed, the life he had just stolen. He wondered if the man had a wife or children, and then his stomach decided to empty itself finally. His green eyes watered, and his throat strained as he wretched.

A man's life had just ended because of him.

He was jarred out of contemplation by the screams of three soldiers charging at them from the side. He held up his sword, wishing he hadn't discarded his shield. Rain reached out his hand, groping thin air. Matthias thought that the man had lost his mind. A sword sailed through the air and landed neatly in Rain's hand, just in time for him to decapitate the nearest soldier with it. Matthias blocked the blow of the second man and whirled around, and slashed the man in the shoulder, dropping him. Fighting seemed much easier without a cumbersome shield to get in his way. Rain's blade ran through the third. Matthias stared at the three fresh corpses below and felt like puking yet again, but nothing was left in his stomach.

An armored hand patted his shoulder, causing him to jump. "You will never get used to it, but it does get easier, however sick that sounds," Rain said quietly, staring at the bodies.

A few more enemy soldiers rushed Matthias and Rain, and the pair dispatched them with considerably less ease than the last group. They were drenched in sweat and blood, both their own and others'; Matthias felt like he was about to drop dead from exhaustion. Rain sported a few nasty wounds on his elbows and knees where he was unprotected, and Matthias realized he also had been cut in a few places. The adrenaline of battle had spared him of the initial pain.

More and more Raephinan soldiers were leaving the front lines, it seemed as if the fourth battalion had turned the tide against all odds, but Matthias and Rain still had to deal with the retreating swordsmen.

"Sand Ferrets to me!" Rain yelled; his voice echoed across the battlefield, and eight pairs of soldiers joined their side within mere moments.

By some sort of miracle, not a single soldier of Rain's squad had perished after the sudden deaths of Tomal and Ferron. Many were bruised and bloodied, but Matthias was relieved that the rest had survived. The remaining squad mates surrounded their captain in a semicircle, swords extended and shields raised, pointing at the retreating enemy. The archers had long since dispersed, so there was no point in guarding their rear. The squad fought their way back to join the rest of the battalion, who had begun to regroup.

Drums began to beat, and the Kyriaki army finally decided to join the battle. They poured around the Arachovian ranks and swarmed the dispersed Raephinan troops, forcing the survivors back to the east from whence they came. Matthias looked at the ally forces with disgust as they quickly tore through the fleeing Raephinan soldiers. The Kyriaki suffered almost no casualties that day due solely to the bravery of the Arachovians at their expense. Hundreds of brass horns sounded the victory, and the jubilant warriors beat their swords against their shields in triumph.

Captain Rain led the Sand Ferrets westward, past the carnage of the battlefield and towards their encampment. Ravens and other scavengers had already descended upon the fields. Priestesses picked their way through the fallen bodies, healing who they could with a chant and a glimmer of brilliant light. The squad met up with the rest of the fourth battalion and Commander Hendrick. Although they had seen the most fighting, the battalion had lost very few lives in the battle, which seemed to enhance the celebration of the fourth battalion. The captain did not join the revelry; his brown eyes focused and jaw set. Matthias could not blame the man. His own body was too busy shaking to celebrate the victory.

The sun had set by the time Matthias had returned to his tent; the world seemed to pass by silently as he stared at the ground. He overlooked the priestess who visited their camp to heal his wounds, did not enjoy the hot stew Leonas made for dinner, and hardly heard any of the conversations around the fire. The young soldier could not shake the grotesque image of the gaping wound that his sword had made in the commander's neck. He didn't even notice his friends when they sat down beside him.

"You did well out there, lad," Darius said, slapping Matthias on the back, "You fight like a true Sand Ferret!"

"Everyone is talking about how you saved the captain," Veiko said. "Shifting your weapon mid-stroke. I should use that trick more in battle. I usually just throw my sword."

Matthias looked at both men and opened his mouth to thank them but began to bawl. His shoulders shook, and tears streamed down his face. He was disgusted by what he saw that day, disgusted by what he had done to allow the Kyriaki to keep a fort in their possession. It all seemed so pointless. So hopeless.

"Oh, my sweet boy," Darius said. He wrapped his arms around Matthias and pulled him in tight, allowing him to cry into his shoulder. "Let it all out. You are safe now."

"Does it get any easier?" Matthias asked, between sobs.

"No," Darius admitted, "But you learn how to cope with the pain in time. You should not be alone tonight, not after what you experienced. Join us in our blankets. I have always said a good cuddle does the heart good. What do you say, Veiko, my love?"

Veiko nodded enthusiastically, his hand stroking Matthias' shoulder. "I think it will do you good to be warm tonight."

Matthias was in no position to disagree or make any decisions. He had longed for Anton's touch for weeks now, and with Darius' arms around him, he understood how much he simply needed someone to hold him. Matthias followed his friends into the tent, and the trio combined their blankets and settled into them, Darius and Veiko on either end, holding him gingerly, arms wrapped around him, making him feel safe and secure. He took solace in their embrace, and soon his sobbing stopped, oddly comforted by Darius' loud snoring. At last, sleep took him, and he fell into a dreamless slumber.

6

Captain

Captain Rain stood on the edge of the camp as the red sun rose over the plains the morning after the battle. Thousands of ravens descended upon the fresh battlefield, eager to find a feast. Dozens of soldiers picked through the bodies, carrying their fallen brothers to the funeral pyres built by the camp overnight. The unfortunate Raephinan casualties remained on the battlefield, left for the scavengers of the plains.

Rain had snuck out of Hendrick's tent before the sun had risen, careful not to wake the commander, and watched the scene with unblinking eyes. Attending the ceremony was a habit of his, the morning after a battle, so he would never forget the price of victory. Or the greater one of defeat. Crumpled and broken soldiers lay on the field, left to rot. The enemy's front line consisted of primarily conscripted soldiers, the poor men and women forced into battle against their will. The vast majority were not even citizens of the great city-state but peasants and farmers from outlying lands. The cruelty and brutality that influenced the tactics of the southern lands disgusted Rain to no end.

Shortly after sunrise, the pyres burned brightly, lit by the priestesses who began to chant a funeral dirge, soon joined by the few soldiers who had decided to attend. It was a crucial ceremony to Arachovian culture but a poorly attended one. Rain believed there was no single way to handle the pain of loss and respected each squad member for their decision. He looked up into the flames and spoke a few words to Tomal and Ferron, apologizing that he could not protect them.

Attending the ceremony was part of Rain's ritual, for if he held the guilt of each soldier who perished under his command, he would never survive it. Ferron had been a vile man with a quick temper and poor attitude, but he had been one of Rain's best swordsmen. Tomal had spent decades with the Sand Ferret Squad and had held the privilege of the previous captain's shield-brother long before Rain joined as its captain. They would be missed.

The sun had risen, and the ceremonial flames had ceased as Rain made his way through the waking encampment. Most officers allowed their subordinates to sleep in after a battle unless the skirmish had ended in a retreat or if the legion built the encampment in hostile territory. The hulking fortress of Vilgast would offer enough protection for at least a few days of respite and the Raephinans had suffered too many casualties to attempt another assault. The Sand Ferret Squad had taken advantage of the lazy morning and lounged around the fire, breaking their fast when Rain arrived at their camp. Some had minor scrapes and bruises, deemed too frivolous to be healed by a priestess when so many more dire situations required their attention.

Few of the Sand Ferrets acknowledged his arrival, and none

of them saluted, just the way Rain preferred; he did not like to feel above anyone, no matter the circumstances. Morale seemed high, given the circumstances. Despite seeing the most action in battle, the fourth suffered significantly fewer losses than other battalions. The seventh and ninth battalions had lost half of their forces, while the third lost its commander and most of its captains.

Despite losing Tomal and Ferron, the Sand Ferret Squad survived the battle relatively unscathed; Rain accounted for this fact by the unique connections half of his squad had cultivated over the years. Two couples were already Devoted to one another, while two more would almost certainly say the Vows within the following year. Rain suspected the first to the Shrine would be the younger pair of soldiers, Jonas and Taimo, who had been inseparable since they enlisted a few years ago. A man's undying love for another was more excellent armor than any helmet or shield. Rain had relied on Tomal's grizzled experience and unrivaled skill to keep him safe in battle, but a pang of guilt reminded him that arrangement was firmly in the past.

Rain examined his newest recruit, Matthias Helianth, who stared blankly into the fire with tired, red eyes. When the lanky noble unceremoniously joined the Sand Ferret Squad in the dead of night, Rain had simply dismissed him as a petulant and pampered brat who had enlisted merely to garner sympathy and attention from the other Arachovian nobles. After each day of training, he had expected Matthias to renounce his Oaths and sulk back to the upper city where he belonged. However, Rain was surprised by Matthias' resolve; he had endured more hazing than any soldier in the squad's history. Despite the battle the day before being the new recruit's first foray into war, Rain was surprised by the man's performance. Yes, he was traumatized and more terrified than a field mouse, but what man wasn't after his first taste of actual fighting? Matthias had excellent reflexes, an instinct in battle, and had bested a Raephinan veteran who had Rain himself cornered.

Moreover, Rain saw the recruit scan the battlefield moments before the skirmish began. He analyzed the situation with keen efficiency. The man had clearly missed his calling as an officer in the legion, but Rain would not allow his potential to go to waste.

"Helianth, do you have a moment?" Rain called, and Matthias slowly raised his head, looking confused, but nodded.

Rain took Matthias aside, out of earshot of the others but not out of sight. A freshly grown beard had begun to hide the new soldier's boyish features, but neither the facial hair nor the shock of battle did anything to hide the mischievous glint in his green eyes. The man was probably trouble, but nothing Rain could not handle.

"Yes, sir, what is it?" Matthias asked pensively.

There it was again, just like before the battle. Matthias clenched his jaw resolutely, taking in the situation. The handsome noble was much more intelligent than he would like people to believe.

"I wanted to thank you for what happened on the battlefield yesterday," Rain said. "If it were not for your actions, I would most likely be dead. You exhibited exemplary skills on the battlefield, which is commendable for someone so fresh to the army. We are lucky to have you in the Sand Ferret Squad."

"Thank you, captain," Matthias said warmly, but he continued to intently analyze Rain as he spoke.

"It also seems," Rain continued, "that you and I have both lost our shield-brothers. The entire squad will miss Ferron and Tomal. Furthermore, the likelihood of receiving reinforcements from Tanaegra before our next battle is severely low, especially since the other battalions will no doubt receive priority over us. In that case, I would like to ask you to become my shield-brother for the remainder of the campaign. If yesterday was any measurement of your skills, I have no doubt you will be a fine replacement for Tomal. May his soul rest in peace in the afterlife."

"M-me?" Matthias asked, uncertainly, "Is there anyone else in the Sand Ferrets who would be more suited or experienced?"

"Would you like me to ask Veiko or Darius?" Rain said, dripping with sarcasm, "Or would you prefer me to split up Bruno and Leonas?"

"I did not survive a battle just to get myself killed today, captain," Matthias flashed a devilish smile; thankfully, the man possessed a fine sense of humor.

Rain chuckled, "In that case, it looks like you are my best option, albeit my only one. But do not be mistaken. If your performance yesterday is any indication, you will bring great honor to your name in the battles to come."

"Very well, though I'm not sure honor has anything to do with what acts I committed yesterday," Matthias said bitterly, gazing up at the fortress that towered above them. "All those lives, just for a piece of land and a few dozen forges."

"I do not revel in it either," Rain said, surprised that the man so freely shared an opinion he wholeheartedly sympathized with. Most nobles were obsessed with glory and fame. He should not have been surprised, considering Matthias was the first noble in history to renounce his right by birth to become an officer and enlist as a lowly soldier instead. "The greed and pride of powerful men result in unimaginable pain and chaos. Our duty as soldiers of the realm is to do our best to mitigate that disaster where we can. As captain, all I can do is protect the lives of my squad and the other soldiers of the battalion, in that order."

"I think that very wise, captain," Matthias regarded Rain with a peculiar look and then nodded for a few silent moments. "Is there anything else you need from me this morning?"

"No, Helianth, you are dismissed," Rain said absentmindedly, looking up at the great forges of Vilgast and regarding the soldier's statement. He was right. There was no point in bloodshed other than the aspirations of a few greedy nobles.

After a few moments of quiet contemplation, Rain joined the squad, sitting off to the side, and took out his flute to play a soulful melody. Since childhood, music had been his passion, inherited from his mother. She had always excelled at the harp, but he found the instrument too ethereal for his liking. He much preferred to express his creativity and emotions through the flute. In his opinion, it was a more versatile instrument than people gave it credit.

The day passed slowly, and the warriors lounged, sang, and laughed with one another, desperately trying to suppress the memories of the day before. The senior officers were undoubtedly busy with General Zsolt and the rest of the Kyriaki command, so there would be no orders today. Rain sat with his squad until nightfall and made his way back to Hendrick's tent in the center of camp.

The commander's tent was spacious and warmly lit by a few

lanterns. A sturdy, wide cot was built on the far side, covered in thick fur blankets to protect from the harsh nights of the great southern plains. Across from the bed was a tiny, wooden table with charts, maps, and diagrams scattered across its face. Hendrick hunched over it, examining various drawings and battle strategies. He was naked above his waist; his sculpted and freshly bathed body seemed to glow in the lamplight, his Signata a dark tapestry on his smooth skin.

Hearing Rain enter, the large man turned around and smiled warmly. "Was wondering when you would finally return. How is your squad?"

"Better than most," Rain replied as his lover walked over, pulled him close, and delivered a sweet kiss on his lips. His face flushed as he returned the kiss eagerly. "We only lost two men, though one was my shield-brother. I decided to replace him with my newest recruit."

"The noble boy who bested the Raephinan veteran?" Hendrick asked. "Suitable choice. You will make an excellent commander one day soon."

Rain blushed. Hendrick's approval always gave him a warmth that would carry him through the coldest nights. He'd had that effect on him since becoming his private tutor all those years ago. Making Hendrick proud was reward enough for the horrors he endured in battle, almost as good a reward as sharing his bed every night. Almost.

"How was your summit with high command?" Rain asked.

Hendrick's handsomely bearded face split into a wide grin. "Fantastic, Rain. It was beyond fantastic. Look here." He gently took Rain by his hand and led him to the rickety wooden table, rustling through the paper. "Heptarch Aleksandra singled me out for a commendation in front of the other commanders; you should have seen Tyrial's face, the witless brute. General Zsolt even mentioned that our battalion's actions won the battle. Aleksandra has requested me to be her chief strategy officer for the remainder of the campaign. All of this work is finally paying off, Rain. I will finally get the honor of the entire legion."

"That is wonderful news, my love," Rain said, kissing the joyful man's cheek gingerly. "I am certain your tactics will secure us more victories in the battles to come. What is the Kyriaki general like?"

"Oh, he is an agreeable man, soft-spoken. Surprisingly kind and cordial for a Kyriaki. I quite like him," Hendrick said. "Why do you ask?"

"Just wondering about the man's character after his tactics yesterday," Rain replied.

"You do not agree with methods." Hendrick's brow furrowed. "Why is that?"

"It unsettles me when the larger forces sacrifice their allies when they have the strength to beat their foes themselves. There is no honor in it," Rain said bitterly.

"As the greater force, he has every right to use any advantage he sees fit. It was wise of him to use our forces as a pawn. Regrettably, the seventh and the ninth battalions were devastated as a result, but such is war. You must always take any opportunity in your path to achieve victory," Hendrick said.

"I just do not have the stomach for such decisions," Rain glanced down. He could not understand how certain men could be so calculatingly cruel, especially the love of his life.

"Hush, my sweet, come here." Hendrick placed a hand on Rain's cheek and brought his eyes to meet his. "Let us not dwell anymore on these matters. Not tonight."

Rain opened his mouth to respond, but Hendrick leaned down, covering his lips with his own, kissing him deeply and passionately. He wrapped his powerful arms around Rain in a tight embrace, then suddenly pulled back from the long kiss and locked eyes with his lover. Hendrick gazed down at Rain, breathing heavily and almost feral. The bearded man had always exuded primal lust after a battle, filled with desire after the adrenaline of the fray and the excitement of victory wore off. Their nighttime activities were Rain's favorite post-battle tradition.

Hendrick smiled and began to unbutton Rain's uniform, taking his time with each button and ensuring his strong yet deft fingers caressed his skin gently. Hendrick enjoyed nothing more than teasing Rain, which made his heart race and his face burn with passionate intensity. After an agonizing minute, Rain's shirt was stripped off his body and discarded to the ground. Hendrick tenderly ran his hands down Rain's torso, grinning in delight at the soft moans his mere touch had created. His gentle caress stopped at the hips, where his large hands grasped tightly and pulled Rain closer forcefully. Their bare skin touched as Rain draped his arms around his lover's chest, running his hands across the broad, tattooed back. Rain ran his tongue along his neck and kissed it voraciously, spurred on by Hendrick's deep moans.

Hendrick wrapped one large arm around Rain's shoulders, locking him in place; the other hand wandered southwards and underneath his trousers, massaging the smooth skin below. Following suit, his trembling hands worked furiously to unbuckle Hendrick's belt. Once released, he eased the pants downward, exposing Hendrick's naked flesh to the warm firelight.

With an eager grunt, Hendrick aggressively ripped Rain's pants off, baring his sensitive skin to the chill of the night. Rain began to shake due to the pleasure of his lover's naked body and the frigid temperature. Their lips locked again as their passions and desires grew, exploring each other's bodies and kicking off their trousers and sandals until both were completely nude.

Hendrick hoisted Rain off the ground with a grunt and held him suspended in the air. Rain clung to his lover, feeling safe in the man's powerful arms. Without ending their kiss, Hendrick walked over to the cot, laid the trembling man gently on his back, and fell on top of him.

Rain loved feeling the total weight of Hendrick's massive frame on top of him and let out more moans as they continued to kiss. Then the larger pushed his body off of him and diligently worked his mouth down to his neck, then his chest, running his tongue down Rain's stomach. He tasted and savored every inch of Rain's body, taking extra time at the most sensitive regions. Rain's eyes rolled back in his head in pleasure, and a few soft moans escaped his lips.

After his tongue had done its solemn duty of relaxing and loosening Rain, Hendrick smiled wickedly. He grabbed Rain's hips again, flipping him over on his stomach and climbing on top, teasing the younger man with his body. He gyrated erotically, kissing Rain's neck and slowly entering him. Rain let out a cry of pleasure.

Gently yet firmly, Hendrick began to make love to him; the brawny giant filled every inch of Rain's body with delight as he built up speed and force. The bliss was almost too much for Rain to take. He savored every moment, every thrust, and moan from his lover. The man was insatiable and continued for some time, only stopping to flip Rain on his back to kiss him while continuing to make love.

Again, he gently and steadily increased his speed as Rain wrapped his legs around his torso, begging for more. Harder and faster, Hendrick picked up his rhythm, letting out guttural growls. The pleasure was too much to bear. It built up like ocean waves crashing on the sand until the climax overtook them both. They cried out in unison as their love washed over one another, filling them with a warmth they could never escape.

Hendrick collapsed onto his back, physically spent and breathing heavily. Rain curled up next to him and laid his head on Hendrick's sweaty chest, wrapping himself around his muscular body. He looked up at his lover and smiled sincerely, filled with contentment and love.

Rain had been in love with Hendrick since childhood, a secret crush he had no idea was reciprocated until he joined the Officer's Academy. By then, Hendrick was already a captain, but the man grew to love Rain after a few months of late-night walks and stolen kisses. The two had shared a bed ever since. But a bed was not enough for Rain; he coveted what Veiko and Darius, Bruno and Leonas shared. He wanted to fight by Hendrick's side and wanted the world to know about their love for one another.

"Hendrick," Rain said slowly. Caught up in the moment, he found betrothing words pouring out of his mouth. "I have been thinking, when this campaign is over, will you say the Vows with me? I want to be yours forever, my love. Finally, will you be Devoted to me after all these years?"

Hendrick sighed and rotated his thick torso to look him

in the eyes. "My sweet Rain, I love you with all my heart. Isn't this enough for you? Isn't what we have together special enough? Why do we need a set of silly vows to bind us when we know how we feel about each other?"

"But—" Rain began to speak, but Hendrick kissed him before any words could form.

"Mere words and an ancient statue can't fully express what I feel for you, Rain," Hendrick smiled and quickly switched the subject. "Besides, you and I will be too busy to worry about such matters in the coming days. I can finally show Heptarch Aleksandra all of my ideas and your ideas, too. She will finally see my potential, and there's a chance future generations will write about my tactics in the histories, maybe even taught in the academies; we just have to keep up our victories and get through this campaign. Isn't that wonderful? I wanted to run a few ideas by you tonight. Is that alright?"

Rain nodded, defeated.

Hendrick suddenly jumped up and hurried over to the nearby table, rustling through the papers. Trying not to betray his disappointment, Rain pretended to listen to Hendrick's intricate strategies and grand campaign plans.

Tonight was not the first time Rain had asked Hendrick this question. At this point, he had lost track. Hendrick responded the same each time, minimizing the Vows' power and quickly changing the subject. The most common topic was his absolute favorite, his career.

Rain gazed up at the canvas above and wondered what Hendrick truly loved more, his lover or his own ambitions.

7

Victory

An arrow shot past Matthias' head, grazing his cheek, as he charged across the wide, wooden bridge shoulder to shoulder with Rain. He had already lost his shield in the frantic climb up the muddy riverbank, so he kept close behind the captain to avoid the Raephinan rear guard's arrows. Matthias needed to stop losing his shield in battle so often. Feet caked in mud and body drenched from the river, he and the other Sand Ferrets sprinted toward the enemy along with the rest of the fourth battalion. Commander Hendrick held his heavy Insignis blade in the air, leading the attack with a great bellow. The Arachovians crashed into the unprepared forces with a flash of metal and blood; Matthias followed Rain into the fray, their blades reserved for senior enemy officers.

On the bridge's western end, the bulk of the Raephinan forces engaged Heptarch Aleksandra and General Zsolt's unified forces. The two allied armies had surprised the enemy with a pincer attack on the western banks. The battle had been raging for quite some time, but the fourth battalion had just joined moments ago. Hours before the Raephinans marched across the bridge, Hendrick snuck his battalion underneath the west bank, waiting until the enemy had spanned the crossing to swim to the east bank. A dozen furies joined them to make the river's waters shallow and moderately calm, but despite their efforts, the battalion still lost a few lives to the current during the crossing.

Once safely across, under the protection of the bridge, they lay in wait until the signal. Zsolt and Aleksandra had managed to drive the Raephinan forces back towards the river, using Hendrick's pushing technique from the battle of Vilgast. The plan was to wait until the Raephinan senior command retreated to the bridge's safety, a very defensible position in most circumstances. However, what the enemy did not expect was an attack from behind. The Raephinan high command had nowhere to go. Their vanguard was locked in battle with Aleksandra, and Zsolt had trapped them on the bridge.

With ease, Matthias and Rain sliced into enemy ranks; the Raephinan elite were not exceptionally skilled fighters and relied on the brute strength of their conscripted in battle. Matthias focused on the enemy officers; killing a soldier who was forced into combat did not seem honorable, so the young soldier saved his blade for those in elaborate Insignis armor. He danced through the battle without a shield, dodging clumsy blows and adapting his sword to find his targets. Every time the steel hit home, his stomach lurched. Regardless of how many enemy soldiers he slew, he would never grow accustomed to killing. Each pair of glassy eyes would haunt him until the end of his days.

A Raephinan officer pushed his way past an archer and stabbed at Rain from behind; Matthias lunged forward to block the blow and kicked the man away. A loud clang of metal against metal rang out behind, and he found Rain holding off an enemy blade with his own. Whirling around, Matthias sunk his sword into the second officer's neck, and the man fell back. Rain used the opportunity to slay the first Raephinan, who had recovered from Matthias' kick.

The pair had quickly become an effective team over the last four battles since Vilgast; they had reached the point where they could predict the other's movements and communicate with one another with no more than a glance. Matthias was shocked by how easily their partnership had been as shield-brothers and was confident he would have been slain a dozen times over if it were not for the captain's skill.

The fourth battalion made quick work of the Raephinans on the bridge, and suddenly Hendrick cried out, holding his sword aloft, covered in blood and gristle. The commander had killed the Raephinan general.

Within seconds, the survivors of the enemy high command retracted their swords and armor and threw themselves upon the wooden bridge in surrender. A reedy horn sounded in three short blasts, and Matthias could see the remaining enemy forces throw their weapons down at the mercy of Aleksandra and Zsolt. A triumphant bellow erupted from the fourth battalion. Within minutes of their unit joining, the battle was over.

The following day, Matthias sat alone on the edge of the river between his squad's tent and the rushing water, looking into its murky depths. A few days before the battle, the Arachovian forces had set up camp a few leagues south of the ambush point, enough distance to avoid detection from enemy scouts.

His ears perked up at the sound of boots crunching the dry grass behind him, and in a cloud of dust, Captain Rain sat down on the riverbank next to him. Matthias barely acknowledged his superior officer, as it had become commonplace for the pair to sit together the morning after a battle. Neither could entirely relate to the bold and aggressive behavior the rest of the squad exhibited the day after a victory. Instead, they took refuge together isolated from their brothers and spoke of small things. It was a refreshing break.

"How are you faring this morning?" Rain asked casually after the pair sat in contented silence for a few minutes.

"As fine as could be expected," Matthias replied, massaging his sore muscles. "Any word from the high command? I am sure Commander Hendrick is pleased by yet another victory delivered by the fourth."

"Yes, he is," Rain said, "especially since he slew the Raephinan equivalent of a Heptarch yesterday. It turns out the man was the leader of the entire enemy forces in this region."

"Truly?" Matthias asked, and the captain nodded. "What happens now?"

"We have marching orders to return to Arachovia. We will rest a day here, break camp tomorrow and march north," Rain said. "After this battle, the Raephinans will not have the strength to launch another attack for quite some time. The campaign is officially complete. The elections are only a month from now so the law would have required us to return. But now we go home with the city's honor intact."

Matthias couldn't help but smile; elated by the wonderful news his shield-brother had just delivered. The bloodshed was over, for now at least, and he could finally sleep under a roof and fall asleep knowing he was safe. He was surprised that he was longing for the dank barracks; that was the effect of the horrors of the campaign.

But something still bothered him. "And what of the Raephinans who surrendered today? What do you think will happen to them?"

"Oh, the Kyriaki have already seen to that," Rain said, spitting venom when saying their ally's names. "The Raephinan officers have already been executed. General Zsolt will take the rest back to Kyriak. If a conscripted soldier can fight for one city-state, they can fight for another just as easily."

"It will never make sense to me how such cruelty can exist. And this is the outcome we fought for. Killed for." Ever since Vilgast, Matthias felt comfortable speaking candidly to the captain; sometimes, he forgot that Rain was his superior.

"I'm glad to see that this campaign has not diminished your altruism, Matthias," Rain said. It was always odd when the man was sincere. It almost seemed unnatural.

"Can I ask you a personal question?" Matthias asked, waiting for Rain to nod before continuing. "You clearly have the same distaste for battle as I do, so I am curious, why did you become an officer in the first place?"

"I will tell you under one condition," Rain said, after a moment of contemplation. "You reveal to me the true reason why you enlisted instead of joining the cavalry or the Academy like any other nobleman. I have heard too many rumors throughout the camp and have always been curious to know the truth."

Matthias briefly considered Rain's proposition, he thought his story was common knowledge by now. Veiko's mouth was more prolific than any messenger in the legion. There was no way Rain had not heard it, though rumor did have a way of twisting itself until the truth became unrecognizable. Matthias' curiosity was too strong to deny it.

"Very well. My father surprised me with an unexpected betrothal to my dearest friend the day I enlisted. I refused him because I had plans to meet my lover, Anton, at the Shrine of Isemelith that night. When Anton arrived, I discovered that he never intended to become Devoted to me and instead had accepted a betrothal. From a woman. I am still unsure what possessed me to do such a stupid thing as enlisting. Part of it was out of spite for both of them, part of it was because of a broken heart, and part was a hope to end my life. But I think all I truly wanted was to be free of their influence over my life and make decisions for myself for the first time. Not for my father, not for my lover, for me." Matthias was pleasantly surprised that he wasn't as affected by the story as when he told Darius and Veiko. It still pained him to think of his lover's betrayal, but it was like a muffled scream compared to what used to be a raging storm.

If the story affected Rain, he did not show it. The man was impossible to read. It took a while until he eventually spoke.

"Your reason is much more honorable than mine," Rain said.

"And what was your reason?" Matthias asked expectantly. "I held up my end of the bargain. Why did you decide to join the Academy?"

"I became an officer to follow the man I love," Rain said simply.

Matthias waited for him to continue, but no further explanation came. He knew the lover Rain referred to was Hendrick; their love affair was a poorly kept secret. "And how is love not honorable? I would do anything for the one I love. How is something so selfless better than my selfish actions?"

"Because you acted out of defiance and dared to choose your fate," Rain said. "I allowed another to choose."

Not knowing how to respond, Matthias continued the silence, staring into the rushing river and pondering Rain's melancholy words. After a while, Rain sat up and left the riverbank without a word.

Hoping his words had not struck a chord, Matthias followed Rain back into camp. Leonas was busy preparing breakfast while Darius and Veiko wrestled playfully near the fire. After a few minutes, Rain disappeared, most likely returning to his lover's bed for their last day of the campaign. He did not return to the Sand Ferret's fire for the rest of the day, which Matthias spent relaxing with his friends and trying his best to suppress the memories of battle.

As Rain had said, the legion packed up and marched northward the next day. The pace of the return journey was noticeably laxer than the initial march southward; after a campaign that lasted a month and a half, the Heptarch obviously did not want to strain her troops any further. The days passed slowly; as the adrenaline of battle wore off and the fatigue of marching set in, the Sand Ferret Squad was noticeably quieter. They only had two injured men besides the death of Ferron and Tomal, like some miracle. The first took a spear to the gut, while the other lost his hand. Both were sent home with the caravan of the injured. The squad's survival was a testament to Rain's leadership and the soldiers' love for one another.

Matthias and Rain continued to chat during the long days of marching; Rain taught Matthias about his favorite composers and his love of music, while Matthias shared his favorite sports. Rain politely yet apathetically followed along.

Matthias realized they could bond over their general disdain for other nobles, the abundant wealth both of them had grown up in, and how shocked they both had been when they saw the poverty in the lower city. Matthias admired his captain's sense of justice and equality, most likely due to him coming from a lowly noble house. The middle and upper classes of nobles could care nothing for the suffering of the commoners. Their privilege too far removed them from the harsh realities of the world. Matthias and Rain shared ideas on what they would do to change their city and the world to make it a better place.

Rain would leave the squad at night to join Hendrick in his tent, and Matthias would pass the dark hours telling stories with his friends. It mainly was Veiko telling elaborate stories and Darius occasionally interjecting to change a detail or give context. The duo bickered more often than not, resulting in a loud fit of laughter from Bruno. The beast of a man had a strange sense of humor.

Eleven straight days of marching until the column reached the Gap of Tanaegra and another seven until they reached the great city of Arachovia. The closer they were to their home city, the faster Heptarch Aleksandra pushed them. Elections were a few weeks away, and a Heptarch could not be as foolish as to be absent during them; the consequences of such an act were more than severe.

On the third day of marching in the valley, the legion passed a small village nestled between the River Palanthia and the main road. Unlike Tanaegra or Arachovia, the settlement had no walls, no natural cliffs, or any form of defense around it. Children ran between the humble buildings, laughing and playing with glee. Villagers gathered under trees to avoid the harsh midday sun and chatted jovially together. Matthias smiled at the display.

"Rain," Matthias said quietly as they marched forward. "Have you ever wondered what it would be like if the Ae'rach never built Arachovia on a mesa? But instead, they decided to settle on the plains? What if there was no upper city or lower city at all?"

"Well," Rain said. "I assume there would be no city at all. The mesa offers unequal protection from raiders and enemy cities. You have seen the battles in the south; just imagine that carnage here if Arachovia did not have its cliffs to defend it."

"But when was the last time there were any enemies in our valley?" Matthias asked sincerely, gesturing to the ancient structures of the nearby village. "Nearly centuries since an enemy boot has stepped foot here, the villager's ancestors probably built their homes since the last incursion."

"What has passed does not always dictate what will be," Rain said. "The peace our valley has seen is no reason to lower our guard. That is exactly when the enemy would strike."

"I am not saying we should not protect ourselves," Matthias said. "We deem our walls sufficient to protect our lower city, so why would we need cliffs? Why do we protect our rich more than our poor? All the mesa does is separate our nobles from the ones they exploit."

"You make a good point," Rain said. "If the city walls fell, there would be no stopping an army from reaching the upper city, even with the stairs providing some deterrence. But what are you suggesting, relocating the entire city and rebuilding it brick by brick? It would not be a popular decision, especially with the nobility."

"Or we could just eliminate the mesa altogether," Matthias

laughed, "Maybe the furies could ask the spirits for some help. You've seen them in action."

Rain let out a choked laugh, "Bring the upper city down using magic? Oh yes, that is much less drastic. You would be a fine statesman with ideas like that."

"I will ignore your sarcastic tone and take that as a compliment," Matthias said.

The two men laughed and continued marching, discussing other drastic or fantastical changes to improve their city.

The legion continued their march northward through the plains of the massive valley, resting each night under the stars. On the seventh day, the rough outline of the mesa became visible along the horizon. Matthias felt a tear run down his cheek. He was finally home.

The Sand Ferrets settled in quickly to the barracks, and Matthias was relieved that the stench of body odor had aired out during their long absence. Hopefully, it would not return to its former acrid smell.

He was sorely mistaken. After two days of total relaxation, the barracks smelled worse than the farms the army had passed on their marches through the valley. After their short break, the squad resumed their regular hard training, just as they had before the campaign. However, the exercise and training were much more manageable for Matthias to handle. The general morale of the squad was high, without the scowling Ferron dragging the mood down. However, it was primarily due to the effervescent joy that radiated from the fresh-faced couple Jonas and Taimo, who visited the Shrine of Isemelith the day the squad returned and pledged the Vows to one another. Matthias shared their happiness, but jealousy always crept into his heart whenever he looked at the pair of soldiers cuddling in the barracks or kissing around corners.

Trying his best to shove the upcoming election out of his mind, Matthias concentrated on folding his uniform neatly in his trunk beside his bed. His was nestled between Rain's ever-vacant bed by the door and the two beds Veiko and Darius had pushed together. Participating in the annual elections was a dream for every noble new to adulthood, every esteemed man and woman of age could participate in selecting the seven Heptarchs. He had heard stories, but he always wanted to see the Solarch's Palace on the inside for himself.

Unfortunately, his claim to the ancient blood had been stripped away by his father months ago. No longer a noble, he had no right to participate in the elections, just like the other commoners with whom he shared a room. Restricting elections solely to the noble class was yet another peculiar societal rule Matthias did not understand, for the Heptarchs acted as the generals of the armies. If anyone had the power to choose the leaders, why not those whose lives were directly impacted?

There was a sharp knock at the door; before anyone could react, it was flung open, and a tall officer, armor summoned, walked into the barracks and sneered at the enlisted. Most officers in the army were not as cordial as Rain and often treated the enlisted worse than dogs. For that, Matthias considered himself lucky.

"Captain Rain Cassian!" the officer called. "Attention to Captain Rain Cassian!"

"Excuse me, sir," Darius said respectfully, "The captain is not currently here; you could check Commander Hendrick's quarters. The commander called on him earlier this evening to go over some strategies for the next campaign."

The officer nodded curtly and exited the barracks without another word. Veiko threw a crude hand gesture at the closed door, and Darius shoved him playfully onto their bed.

"Nice cover story, my love," Veiko said sweetly, though he smirked dryly when the bear of a soldier turned his back. Unless the officer had lived under a rock for the past century, he knew the relationship between Hendrick and Rain.

"What did that man say, Darius?" Matthias asked softly.

"Oh, you didn't hear? He asked for the captain, probably summoning him to the upper city for the elections tomorrow like the rest of the…nobles…I mean the officers. I hear there are feasts the night before elections in front of the Solarch's Palace…but you knew that…sorry." Darius shifted his gaze awkwardly, obviously forgetting that Matthias was a noble himself, or used to be. He was now a commoner, just as Darius and Veiko were.

"No, not that," Matthias was surprised by how sharp his tone was, "What did the man call Captain Rain? What surname did he use?"

"Cassian," Darius said, and Matthias drew a quick breath. Darius furrowed his brow in curiosity. "Why do you ask? Do you recognize it from your life…from your time before enlisting?"

"No," Matthias lied. Of course, he knew the name Cassian. It was one of the most ancient and noble houses in Arachovia, undisputedly direct descendants of the Ae'rach. Matthias had been mistaken when he assumed Rain's noble position, for he was one of the most powerful nobles in the city by birth.

Looking out of the window at the sheer cliffs of Arachovia, Matthias wondered who the man he had been fighting alongside truly was.

8

Heptarch

Thousands of ornate lanterns hung from a golden string, illuminating the grand plaza in front of the Solarch's Palace. Dozens of dining pavilions with intricately embroidered canvas encircled the square, hundreds of revelers sat beneath them, indulging themselves with expensive wines and delicacies from the palace kitchens. Flutists, harpists, cellists, and many other musicians were stationed around the festival, playing a rich tapestry of chords and songs that echoed through the night. Nobles from every house in Arachovia danced to the upbeat tunes, laughing, kissing, and enjoying the illustrious evening. The feast night that occurred before the annual elections was the most anticipated event in the entire city.

Rain despised it.

Wishing he could have stayed in the barracks, he sulked behind Hendrick as the confident commander eagerly pushed through the crowds. Rain kept his head downcast to avoid eye contact with the wrong people. Hendrick had practically carried Rain from the lower city to get him this far, and it was the last place he wanted to be. Tugging at the silk sleeves of his horrendous dress uniform, wishing he could burn it or give it away to someone in need, he scowled at the nobles in their ridiculous costumes.

The festival was overly indulgent and an unnecessary waste of money. It celebrated the unadulterated and unearned power the nobility possessed over those less fortunate. Rain knew that half of the genealogy tapestries in the upper city had been forged and had always taken issue with the idea that one's blood was what made someone better than another. The garish display was sickening.

"Isn't it wonderful, my love," Hendrick said, grabbing Rain by the hand and swinging him around as they entered one of the many dance floors. "My favorite night of the year!"

Mumbling a half-hearted agreement, Rain danced with Hendrick and tried his best to enjoy being in his arms. It wasn't very often that the pair could dance or even be together outside of the barracks, and the music was quite lovely. Looking up into his lover's dark eyes, he couldn't resist a small smile. Hendrick suddenly tugged him away from the dance floor and into a nearby pavilion, quickly snuffing out Rain's momentary bliss. Rain could sense the judgmental glares of a few nobles who recognized him and tried his best to ignore the whispers as Hendrick pulled him past dozens of elegantly clad men and women.

"Will you grab us some wine, my dear?" Hendrick pointed towards the nearest elegant table surrounded by finely dressed nobles. "I need to speak with Heptarch Paulius for a few moments; he wants to hear about my...our victories in the south. I won't be long, I promise."

Without waiting for a reply, Hendrick kissed Rain gently on the cheek and ran off to the nearby table, eager to share his exploits with Paulius. Feeling exposed and not keen to attract the attention of old acquaintances or—the spirits forbid—his family, Rain trudged over to the serving table. If he had to endure a night like this alone, he could at least be inebriated for it. However, before reaching the wine, he felt a hand on his shoulder, stopping him in his tracks. His heart sank. Preparing himself for some mind-numbing small talk with a close-minded noble he had forgotten the name of, he turned around to face his assailant.

"Who are you?" he found himself asking rather bluntly.

He did not recognize the woman in front of him; he had never seen her before in his life. She was of average height and sported flowing hair that cascaded in thick locks below her shoulders. Intricately crafted jewelry hung from her neck and wrists, almost covered by her oversized silk robes. A priestess, but not any of the furies of whom he had fought alongside. Why was a woman of the temple interested in his company?

"Kadri Lilias, my lord." The woman spoke politely but rather tersely. She clearly had not appreciated Rain's tone. "Are you, in fact, Captain Rain Cassian of Heptarch Aleksandra's legion? Captain of the Sand Ferret Squad of the fourth battalion?"

"I suppose that is me," Rain said formally. His fury acquaintances had warned him about the temperamental nature of priestesses who chose to stay in the upper city, and he did not want to get on her bad side. "How may I assist you this evening, Priestess Lilias?"

"Oh, perfect." Kadri relaxed her shoulders, apparently satisfied by his answer. "You have no idea how difficult it is to contact anyone in the military. I have been turned away from the barracks three times now. Three! I am looking for someone, captain. A dear friend of mine is assigned to your squad. Broad shoulder, mischievous grin, and bullheaded, his name Matthias Helianth. Do you know him? Did he survive the campaign?"

"He is in my squad," Rain said. "He is still alive, and I am too because of him. You should be proud of your friend."

"So that idiot is still in one piece." Kadri breathed a sigh of relief. "The rach answered my prayers. Though I probably have you to thank for his safe return, captain. You have quite the reputation up here. I would love to hear all about my friend right now, but I don't have much time. Can you relay a message to Matthias for me?"

"Of course," Rain said. He was beginning to like this woman.

"Tell him that I will see him soon," Kadri announced, "I have decided to join the furies in Heptarch Aleksandra's legion. I will be transferred before the month is over."

"I have many friends within the furies," Rain said. "From our short conversation, I do not doubt that you will make an excellent addition to their numbers."

"Thank you, captain, I appreciate it," Kadri said, "but I should go before the mistress of the Temple realizes I have snuck out. Enjoy the rest of the festival."

Bowing politely to the priestess as she left, Rain reached the serving table, grabbed the closest wine glass, and drained its contents. Discarding it roughly on the table, he took two of the fullest glasses and carried them cautiously towards Paulius' table. The older, kindly-looking Heptarch was in the middle of telling a story to a captivated audience of high nobles, but Rain couldn't seem to find Hendrick anywhere. Frowning, Rain scoured the pavilion with keen eyes, but his lover was nowhere to be found. He guzzled both his wine glasses and stormed out of the pavilion in a sour mood.

Over the next few hours, he searched pavilion after pavilion while numbing himself with wine but could not find Hendrick anywhere. The man was hard to miss, standing a head taller than the average Arachovian and almost twice as wide. The crowds thinned as the night wore on, and Rain still failed to spot Hendrick, finding it hard to dodge old acquaintances in the quickly diminishing group.

Abandoning his search, he left the plaza and sauntered past other drunken party-goers through the dimly lit city. The only place left to look was Hendrick's villa, which the pair had agreed to share that night. The modest yet beautiful home sat near the city's eastern edge and was rarely used by the busy commander. Rain was always conflicted when the pair stayed there, although it was nice to have romantic holidays away from the army. But it sat vacant most of the year, which seemed like a waste.

Finally arriving, he squinted through the murky night at the dark villa. Though his vision was slightly blurred, he could see well enough to know that the estate was dark; even if Hendrick had retired for the evening, he had not waited for Rain to return. Not wanting to break in or cause the city guard, Rain turned and trudged back the way he came. The night air grew colder, and Rain felt the fatigue of the wine set in. He needed to sleep somewhere soon, but he would freeze if he slept in one of the gardens. The elections would take place early the next morning and he would most likely miss them if he spent the night in the barracks. There was only one option left, and that was to go home.

The Cassian estate was built near the city's center, beside

the Solarch's Palace. One of the city's most ancient and massive villas, owned by one of the oldest and most respected Arachovian families. Reaching the intricately designed iron front gate, he nodded wearily to his father's guards, who furiously bowed and unlocked the gate when they recognized his face. They had every right to be surprised, for it had been years since Rain Cassian had visited the family estate, not since he left to join the army. Being the Cassian's third child, he was under no obligation to marry to carry on the bloodline. But Lord Cassian had not been happy with the decision, seeing the army as beneath even his youngest child, and the two hadn't spoken since.

Stalking carefully through the gardens, Rain found his way to his old bedroom chamber, careful not to wake the dormant house. Even if he alerted his father, mother, sister, or brother, he doubted they would pay him any mind. The great family wanted nothing to do with their oddly quiet, disrespectful son, who enjoyed wearing rags and playing the flute like a commoner. He arrived at his old patio door, quietly slid it open, and snuck inside.

The dark room, dimly lit by the moonlight, was just as he remembered. Rain collapsed on the large bed, hating himself for coming home. Hundreds of children slept on pallets in the lower city; some slept in the streets, and here was this luxurious bed that no one had used since the day he left. It was disgusting. He wished he could smuggle the room's furniture to the lower city, each gilded piece was worth a small fortune. But the guards would never allow it, and even the lavish contents of the room would not be enough to correct the significant imbalance in the city. Pushing the idea out of his mind, he let the fatigue and the wine overcome him and fell asleep.

The bright rays of the morning sun woke Rain from his slumber; his head felt as if it would split in two. He would never drink wine again. To his surprise, a tray had been placed on the bedside table, filled with fresh fruit, biscuits, and a pitcher of water. Regretfully he ate a few grapes and drank the water ravenously. He did not want to accept the generosity of his family, but his hangover said otherwise. His body needed sustenance. Hopefully, the gallon of water would soon ease his headache. Then he noticed the height of the morning sun through the window. He was late.

Rain dashed out of the room, through the gardens, and into the empty city street. Turning the corner, he saw the aftermath of the feast. Servants picked through the trash and the discarded wine chalices, carefully deconstructing the pavilions systematically and efficiently. Not a single noble was in sight, for they were all in the palace. He was going to miss the elections. Racing through the plaza, dodging around the servants, Rain climbed the marble steps and rushed through the grand archway of the palace. The chamber beyond was massive and circular, topped with a soaring marble dome. Rain stood at the top of a magnificent amphitheater. Dozens of tiered semicircular platforms descended downward, form-ing around an ornate dais, the room's focal point.

Thousands of nobles from the city and the surrounding countryside filled the massive arena. An older man in illustrious robes was speaking on the dais, his feeble voice projected across the hall, bouncing off the marble. Rain sighed and found the nearest open spot on a bench in the highest row. Thanks to the long-winded man on the dais, he hadn't missed anything.

The frail noble delivering the speech in the gilded robes was Solarch Eirenan himself, who had served in the position for almost four decades. The term of the Solarch was lifelong and chosen from one of the current Heptarchs upon the last Solarch's death, but the title itself was mostly a figurehead. The only true power the Solarch possessed was the one the older man wielded today, and that was to be the officiant and judge of the elections.

"Now let us begin," Solarch Eirenan said after droning on about the history and splendor of Arachovia for what seemed like ages. "We shall start with the First District. If the incumbent Heptarch would like to maintain their position, please step forward."

A uniformed woman from the front row strode proudly onto the stage, covered in Insignis tattoos and wearing a golden crown nestled that gleamed brightly. She looked like a bird of prey with cunning eyes and a hook-like nose, and her dark hair was cut shoulder length. She stood proudly before the assembly, towering above the decrepit Solarch. The Heptarch removed her crown, handed it to the older man, and waited expectantly.

"I, Heptarch Aleksandra Passiflor, hereby declare my intent on retaining my seat," the powerful woman proclaimed in a deep voice.

"Does anyone elect themselves to challenge Heptarch Aleksandra's claim?" Solarch Eirenan asked. He waited a moment for someone to speak, but no one did. Aleksandra was the most decorated and renowned general in the city. Only a fool would run against her. "Very well, who in this assembly accepts Aleksandra Passiflor as the Heptarch of the First

District?"

Most of the hands in the room shot up, including Rain's.

The Solarch nodded and cried, "So the people proclaim! Heptarch Aleksandra Passiflor!"

The proud woman bowed slightly as the older man placed the golden crown back on her head. With a smattering of applause, she returned to her seat.

"Now, the Second District." The Solarch said, "If the incumbent Heptarch would like to maintain their position, please step forward."

The silver-haired Paulius Serriphine climbed onto the dais; the man had kept his seat longer than Aleksandra, though he had never seen a single battle. The regal man instead commanded the city defenses and civil guard. Rain didn't understand how a man without an ounce of military experience could hold onto his seat for so many years. However, he had no doubt it had something to do with the bottomless coffers of the Serriphine family fortune.

"I, Heptarch Paulius Serriphine, hereby declare my intent on retaining my seat," the pompous noble said nonchalantly.

"Does anyone elect themselves to challenge Heptarch Serriphine's claim?" Solarch Eirenan asked.

"I do." A spirited officer sprang up to the stage, followed by a few gasps. It was not unheard of for ambitious youth to challenge the more powerful Heptarchs, but it was not very common. Rain could not hear the man's name when he declared it, for his voice was shaking more than his legs. He was a military man through and through and probably a great strategist, but he lacked the charisma or nerve to be in public. He stood on the other side of the Solarch, who had already taken Paulius' crown.

"Very well, who in this assembly accepts Paulius Serriphine as the Heptarch of the Second District?" Solarch asked. Most of the hands shot up into the air, but not Rain's. "And who accepts his challenger?" Very few hands joined Rain's. The Solarch did not wait for the hands to fall before shouting, "So the people proclaim! Heptarch Paulius Serriphine!"

Paulius man took his crown, unsurprised at the outcome, and the dejected officer sulked off the stage. As uncommon an event as a challenger was, it was even rarer for the incumbent to lose to one. Rain watched the man fade back into the crowd. According to their laws, he would never be able to challenge again.

"Now, the Third District," the Solarch said. "If the incumbent Heptarch would like to maintain their position, please step forward."

Another older gentleman with a permanent scowl plastered on his face joined the stage. The man spoke in a nasally rasp. "I, Heptarch Ventin Vallin, hereby declare my intent on retaining my seat." The old noble had been one of the more formidable Heptarchs in his prime, but that was long past. Vallin had suffered considerable losses in his most recent campaigns due to his fading mind and quickly lost favor from his battalion.

"Does anyone elect themselves to challenge Heptarch Vallin's claim?" Solarch Eirenan asked.

"I do," A deep voice bellowed from the middle rows; Rain's heart jumped when he recognized the man stalking onto the stage. "I, Commander Hendrick Ixora, challenge the claim to the Third District."

Rain froze, staring at his beloved, standing proudly on the dais, and gasped along with the rest of the assembly. Hendrick had not spoken once of this to Rain. He knew the man had grand ambitions and had garnered attention for his recent victories in the south, but he had no idea he would try something as bold as this.

The powerful man calmly faced the audience with a confident smile. His challenge to the older Heptarch was not a spontaneous decision made at the time; this was a carefully curated plan. Hendrick's absence after he met with Paulius suddenly started to make sense. He was busy securing the votes he needed to unseat the unpopular Heptarch.

"Very well, who in this assembly accepts Ventin Vallin as the Heptarch of the Third District?" Solarch asked, followed by about a third of the hands. Rain breathed heavily, his stomach in his throat. That was a dismal number of votes for such a tenured Heptarch. Maybe now Hendrick would have a chance at victory. "And who accepts his challenger?" Rain shot his hand in the air with another third of the assembly. Surveying the crowd around him, he couldn't tell if it was enough. The Solarch did not wait for the hands to fall before shouting, "So the people proclaim! Heptarch Hendrick Ixora!"

The building erupted, the majority who voted for Hendrick cheered and applauded victoriously, while the rest voiced their dissent. Hendrick graciously bowed as he accepted the golden crown from the Solarch, ignoring the screams and the profanity spewed by Ventin Vallin.

"I accept this crown with humility and promise to honor this title and great city," Hendrick's voice roared above the din. "The courage and bravery of my warriors are the reason I am here today. Many of them have shown me the raw passion and courage that Devoted men have for one another. Because of this, I hereby pledge to this assembly and to the rach that I, Heptarch Hendrick Ixora, will forge a new elite fighting force built upon this love and devotion. Not a legion, but a company of Devoted men who will prove the strength of their love to the world!"

The theater exploded once more as Hendrick left the dais, leaving Rain in utter shock. The rest of the ceremony passed by in a blur. Rain did not even know the outcomes of the remaining four elections. He was too busy rejoicing for Hendrick's victory and wondering why the man hadn't confided in him about his plans. It was the first he had heard of this company of Devoted, and it was an unprecedented and thrilling concept.

When the ceremony concluded, he rushed down to the dais to find Hendrick, but he could not locate the large man, even with a golden crown. He pushed through the crowds and returned to the city's eastern edge. The only place he could think to wait for him was his villa, hoping that he would not first return to the barracks. He found a spot under a tree in Hendrick's garden and waited.

The sun was already descending when Hendrick returned to his small villa; his golden crown glinted brightly. The man smiled fondly when he saw Rain, who immediately jumped up and threw his arms around his love.

"Oh, Hendrick," Rain whispered. "Today is such a happy day, my love. Congratulations."

"Hello, my dear Rain," Hendrick kissed him sweetly, glancing at Rain's bloodshot eyes. "I see you enjoyed yourself at the feast. It isn't every day that you overindulge. I am ashamed I missed the spectacle."

"You were busy making deals, which seemed to have paid off tenfold. I'll forgive you this time." Rain smiled and playfully punched the man in his muscular shoulder. "But

I will not forgive you for hiding your plans for this company you announced today. I assume we should start selecting candidates. I think there are about four couples in my squad alone. What size of force do you have in mind?"

"One hundred and fifty pairs of Devoted," Hendrick said. "Led by their Heptarch."

"So, the company will be three hundred and two strong?" Rain asked, sensing there was something the man was hesitant to say. "When will our selection begin? Do you know how you will test the candidates?"

"Rain," Hendrick said, his eyes studying the dirt below. "You will not be joining me."

"What?" That was all Rain could manage to say.

"You will stay in the fourth battalion under Aleksandra and continue your career as a captain." With a cold air of finality, Hendrick said. "You will flourish in her legion, just as I have. Maybe one day you will become a Heptarch just like me. But from now on, you will have to do so without my guidance."

"But shouldn't the leader of such an elite squad of lovers be Devoted himself?" Rain said, pulling away from Hendrick. His heart felt heavy as the new Heptarch's words sunk in.

"How can I be focused on my troops when I am worried about you in battle? I could not focus, knowing you were in danger. I need to focus on my soldiers, on my company. Not on you," Hendrick said firmly. "What you and I have shared has meant the world to me, but it must end as I fulfill my destiny. Alone."

"That doesn't make sense, Hendrick," Rain said, "You are missing the true meaning of what being Devoted—"

"Enough!" Hendrick shouted, cutting him off, "You will just be a distraction, and I cannot allow that! Not when my every move will be over-analyzed and ridiculed in the coming months, half of the city expects me to fail. I cannot fail, Rain. I will not!"

Rain looked back at him, stung. "A distraction? That is what our love has been to you all of these years? I feel pity for your future company, bonded together by a sacred love but led by a man who doesn't even understand the true power of Devotion. Blinded by his own selfish ambition."

Hendrick opened his mouth to speak but stopped himself; he leaned down and kissed Rain on the forehead, whispering, "I am sorry, my dear."

Hendrick turned and entered his villa with one final glance, leaving his ex-lover alone in the garden. Rain watched Hendrick walk away, leaving everything they shared behind.

He sank to his knees and wept.

9

The Devoted Company

The morning horn blared directly outside the Sand Ferret's sleeping quarters, violently pulling Matthias from his slumber. Mumbling various profanities at the horn bearer outside, he clumsily rolled out of his cot. He was having a lovely dream involving his bed in his parent's villa, but in the dream, it was the size of the practice field, and the blankets were weaved entirely from gold. One day he would sleep in a bed that did not leave his back feeling trampled on in the morning.

Wearily, he prepared himself for the morning drilling as Rain lounged patiently on the bed next to him, waiting lazily for the rest of the squad. The man always managed to be awake and dressed when the morning horn sounded; he was a true monster. Matthias was still not used to sharing quarters with Rain, but it proved to be the least intrusive change to the squad in the last few weeks.

Within minutes, the column of soldiers jogged briskly towards the practice field in the dim morning light, and Matthias thought he heard a few of the recruits crying. It had been two months since the elections, and the fourth battalion was almost unrecognizable.

By the time Rain had returned to the barracks the night after the annual ceremony to crown new Heptarchs, the word of Hendrick's surprise victory in the elections had swept through the camp like wildfire. Even more shocking was the new company that Devoted couples would exclusively fill. Veiko could not stop chattering about it, the thin man almost shaking with excitement. No one could have imagined that something like this new company was attainable in their lifetime. Devoted men were not ridiculed in society but were never celebrated, merely tolerated. Matthias thought the idea was lovely but was shocked by Hendrick's abrupt rise to Heptarch; he was sure Rain would have said something to suggest such an occurrence. When he finally returned to the barracks and slept in the quarters with the troops, Matthias understood what had happened between the two lovers. Rain did not speak much or show emotion during the days proceeding, even when his former love reformed the world around them.

Hendrick wasted no time recruiting for his elite force. Every squad was given a pamphlet within days of his election. Within a week, he was already holding trials to select his one hundred and fifty couples. Veiko and Darius, as well as Bruno and Leonas, were among the first to be tested, and to no one's surprise, Hendrick's company accepted both pairs of Devoted. All four left the next day; Matthias could not help but cry as they packed their belongings. Veiko shed tears and Darius pulled Matthias in for a bear hug, promising him that Rain would keep him safe. Even Bruno hugged him tearfully as he and Leonas departed to their new quarters;

Matthias had always secretly known the man was soft-hearted. Rain seemed unbothered by the departure of four of his most skilled soldiers. Only a few days later, the new couple, Jonas and Taimo, were the next to leave. The next day, Arvo and Gvidas, a pair of grizzled veterans Matthias did not know very well, went straight to the Shrine of Isemelith, pledged the sacred Vows to one another, and promptly passed Hendrick's trials. Two short weeks passed, and Hendrick had filled his company with three hundred of the most trained, ferocious, and capable Devoted soldiers in Arachovia.

The Sand Ferrets lost four Devoted couples to Hendrick's Devoted Company; after losing four people in the previous campaign, the squad had dwindled to six soldiers besides Matthias and Rain. The same was true of most squads in the fourth battalion, since Devoted couples were more common under Hendrick's tolerant command. Almost half of his new company had been selected from the fourth, leaving the battalion leaderless and a hollow shell of its former self. The slow re-population of both the squad and the battalion was underway when Hendrick marched his new troops south to Tanaegra for training. The finality of their departure might have been the only time Captain Rain allowed his mask of apathy to crack, although he merely frowned at the grand procession.

The reinforcements that joined the Sand Ferrets shortly after the Devoted Company's departure were less than exemplary, consisting of two types of soldiers. The first were bright-eyed recruits who did not last for more than a few days, breaking under the pressures of training and having to be replaced by freshly enlisted recruits. The second group may have been more trained and experienced but were transferred from other legions or battalions due to disciplinary or behavioral issues. The new recruits were lazy, antagonistic, and temperamental, forcing Rain to become more rigid and punitive, which annoyed the usually calm man to no end. Matthias' heart ached for his dear friends who had become like brothers and wondered what a battle would be like fighting side by side with these undisciplined ruffians.

According to Rain, the new officers of the battalion were no better. Ten new officers replaced those lost in combat or recruited to the Devoted Company. They were either fresh out of the Academy or transferred from other legions due to poor performance, like the soldiers.

The new commander of the fourth was no better. Commander Ventin Vallin, recently demoted from his position of Heptarch, was a decorated officer and a strategist with decades of experience. However, the petulant man was past his prime, irritable and spiteful. Instead of retiring from service after losing the election, Vallin refused and demanded a place among the legions. Being the only sympathetic Heptarch, Aleksandra offered the man a position commanding her fourth battalion, which he quickly accepted. Matthias could hear Commander Ventin's screams of indignation when he discovered that he was replacing the same man who stole his crown from him.

The only silver lining in the past two months of restructuring was Kadri. Rain had informed Matthias the day after the elections that he had spoken to the priestess, and she intended to join the battle furies. Matthias was less than surprised; Kadri was fearless, loyal, and determined and would make an excellent addition to the battle priestesses. She enlisted days later and frequently joined the Sand Ferrets in the dining pavilion during their mealtimes, along with a few of her sisters.

Matthias was grateful to have Kadri as a companion during the long days, since Rain was his only remaining friend in his squad. The other Sand Ferrets were either crying throughout the day or preoccupied with traumatizing and jeering at the sobbing recruits. Two other priestesses would often join Kadri during mealtimes, twin sisters Vilja and Silja, though the two were anything but identical. Vilja was sweet, carefree, and hilarious. She often made Matthias choke on his food with laughter. Her sister Silja was quiet, reserved, and serious. She barely talked, and if she did, the comment would always be melancholy and off-putting.

Matthias learned more about his friends' mysterious battalion of priestesses during his daily interactions with the trio. However, they avoided discussing many of the order's secrets. They inhabited a small temple on the far end of the encampment with training grounds and walled gardens. The priestesses would train and strengthen their bonds to the many spirits associated with war within those protective walls. Many were noblewomen, but the mysterious rach did not view humans as society did, so any woman from any social caste was welcome. There were no actual ranks among the priestesses, just respect for seniority and longevity; the eldest priestess was called Mother. She ranked like a commander, and all other priestesses were regarded as rough equivalents to captains and had free range of the encampment. A fact that Kadri relished in lording over Matthias; she often shouted orders to him to no effect.

Most furies focused on one of two paths, restoration or destruction. Furies like Vilja prayed to the rach of war, chaos, storms, fire, and lightning to master the terrible power Matthias had witnessed firsthand in battle. Despite her sunny disposition, Matthias kept a distance from Vilja when he discovered her specialty. Other furies, like Silja, focused their energies on rach of nature, protection, and healing to cast barriers of protection and harness natural forces like wind and water to help turn the tide of battle. Then there were furies like Kadri, who walked a path between the two and could communicate with all spirits. A priestess like her was well regarded among the furies, so both Vilja and Silja treated Kadri with deference, even though she was their junior.

A few weeks after the Devoted Company's departure, rumors rushed through the camp about a new war between Kyriak and Raephina. Heptarch Hendrick had immediately marched south with his newly formed company, eager to prove their might and strategic worth, and aligned himself with their former Kyriaki allies and General Zsolt. Reports reached northward of fantastic tales of victory and battles won by the company against forces ten times their size. Almost every day, Matthias heard of yet another couple making the journey to the Shrine of Isemelith, desperate to join the now famous and celebrated company when Hendrick would eventually need reinforcements. Their efforts, though heart-warming, may not have been practical, for rumor reported that in over three battles, Hendrick had only lost six warriors despite placing the Devoted Company on the front lines each time. Matthias desperately wished those rumors were true and that his friends were not one of the three unfortunate couples who perished in battle. He could simply not endure the loss of Veiko, Darius, or even Bruno and Leonas. They were like his brothers; even though he would probably never again fight by their side.

As the weeks progressed, Rain gradually began to soften his silently stony exterior and began to speak more and act like his usual self, though the man was not very sociable to begin with. Since the other veterans had left, he often asked Matthias to join him during guard duties or various assignments that required them to be separated from the squad. Matthias always accepted eagerly, delighted to be free from the now-toxic group of fighters and with someone he now considered a friend. He avoided any conversation that had to do with Hendrick, the war in the south, or the Devoted Company.

At first, it presented a challenge since almost everything they experienced during the day directly resulted from the mass exodus from the fourth battalion. But that meant the pair could talk of lighter things, topics that had nothing to do with the army or the strife of their daily lives. It was a refreshing escape from the stress of the military, and Matthias soon looked forward to their late-night patrols. Rain would talk about his favorite musicians and composers, and Matthias would share stories about various sports he used to play as a child, similar to conversations they had on the previous campaign. The topics also extended into deeper passions the pair shared, philosophy, history, and various mythic tales.

But the one topic they always reverted to was a typical conversation they'd had on their march home from the campaign: how Matthias and Rain could make the city a better place for all its inhabitants. Matthias was surprised by how interested Rain was in politics and general equality in the city. He frequently complained about the various injustices and the imbalance of power, which was always a shock coming from a man from the wealthiest family in the entire city.

One night, in particular, Rain changed the topic to one they hadn't discussed before.

"Did you hear about the Devoted Company's recent victory?" As the pair guarded the eastern gate, he asked casually, "I hear that it is their sixth successful skirmish since deploying southward."

"I-I think so," Matthias stammered, not quite sure how to approach the sensitive topic. "Though I have only heard vague bits and pieces from an old codger from the third battalion, and you can never be sure if he's telling the truth." It was a lie, but Matthias wanted to spare his friend's feelings.

"Don't be foolish; the entire city is talking about it." Rain scoffed, "Even the most absent-minded noble could write an entire play about the battle, down to every last detail. Have you heard about what tactics they used?"

Matthias took a moment, studying Rain's face. His upper lip quivered slightly, and he clenched his jaw tightly. He had rarely seen such an expression on Rain's face before, and it had always been in battle. The man was angry. More than that, he was filled with sadness. Conflicted with how to respond, Matthias considered his options carefully. He did not want to add fuel to his friend's outrage, but he also knew not to mess with the captain when he was in this state.

"I believe I did," Matthias said, choosing his words with the utmost care. "They charged the enemy in a tight semicircle, two fighters deep. Shields up and swords extended, just like our defensive formations. The soldiers behind the formation closed the flanks, forming a circle as the company punched through the enemy. I heard it was only minutes until they reached the Raephinan high command."

"Correct," Rain said, his voice now uncharacteristically

wavering with emotion. "Does that formation remind you of anything in particular? Anything specific from our last campaign together? Think hard."

Matthias furrowed his brow and raised it once the answer dawned on him. "Vilgast," he breathed. "We used a similar formation when we returned to the main forces."

"Correct," Rain seethed. "That formation was my creation. My idea. One of many that Hend—the Heptarch of the Devoted Company has used during his numerous victories in the south. I hear that he is now regarded by many in the city as Arachovia's most brilliant military strategist even greater than Aleksandra herself! All with the strategies I helped him create!"

Matthias' heart went out to his friend, who was now shaking. The man had never raised his voice outside of battle like this before. It was odd to see the man overcome by emotion. He put a hand on his shoulder and waited in silence before speaking. "I am sorry, Rain. For what the bastard has done to you. Taking your ideas and the honor that should be yours as well. What a reprehensible thing to do."

"I do not care about glory or honor or victory in battle! I never did! I only cared about him so much, and that blinded me. Instead of loving me in return, he was using me." A single tear ran down Rain's cheek. "At first, I thought he did not bring me along with him because he was a fool who thought he was protecting me and protecting his legacy. But now I know him for the shrewd manipulator that he is. He didn't want me with him because he didn't want to share the glory. He wanted me to share his bed so I could share my ideas with him. That was all it ever was."

"Rain," Matthias said gently, "I understand what betrayal

feels like better than most. Especially from the one you love most in this world. Now I know what Hendrick and Anton did are not truly comparable, but their betrayal resulted in heartbreak the same. I do not know the commander...the Heptarch...personally, but I know his love for you was real despite what he did to you. It was not the love you deserved, and it was not stronger than his love for himself, just like Anton. He never spoke the Vows to you because how could he? The Vows of Devotion speak of partnership, of equals sharing one life. Men like Anton and Hendrick are not built for a bond like that, forcing them to think of others as much as themselves. It's not that they do not understand the Vows. It is that they understand they will never be able to fulfill them. You and I are better without them."

"Thank you," Rain said. "I never thought about it in that context. I have known for quite some time that the man would always put his ambitions before me, but I thought that the harder I tried and the more fiercely I loved him, that maybe he would eventually come around. I was so preoccupied with my feelings for him that I never considered once that he was incapable of the Vows in the first place."

"It is not your fault whatsoever," Matthias said kindly. "We do not choose who we love, nor can we change them or force them to love us in return. A love that comes with stipulations, limitations, or requirements is not love."

"You're a good man, Matthias," Rain said, "and wiser than you look."

Matthias smiled brightly and the pair continued their patrol in silence, contented by the fact that someone understood a pain he had held for almost a year. A pain so specific and agonizing that it was refreshing to finally speak to someone who did not respond with pity or confusion. Matthias no longer felt the excruciating pain like he used to, just the mild sorrow of lost love. He may have been soothing Rain's tortured soul, but he was aiding in his own healing in return.

Rain's mood slightly improved as the days passed, and their patrols became a nightly ritual. Matthias knew all too well that the monotony of training and the slow passage of time did wonders for a broken heart. That and friends to help ease the pain. Matthias once had Veiko and Darius, and now he could do the same thing for Rain.

Training with Rain in the practice fields rapidly became the best part of Matthias' day. After struggling with formations with the recruits, the captain would disperse the squad to practice the sword with their shield-brothers. Instead of using the practice swords, Matthias and Rain summoned their blades and sparred with one another. The pair would dance around the field in a flurry of Insignis steel, honing their skills and pushing one another to their limits.

Matthias was impulsive and wild, forcing the captain back with random blows, combinations and formations of his sword; he tended to rely entirely on his instincts. Rain, however, was cunning and meticulous in his fighting style, always thinking two steps ahead, and each strike and counter-strike had a purpose. The pair could not be any different in their approaches, which forced both to grow and change as fighters. Matthias learned to reason and plan, while Rain became more adaptable. The more the pair fought together, the more they understood the other's movements and intentions. Matthias could read Rain's minute gestures and facial expressions to predict his next action.

The Sand Ferrets would soon gather to watch the daily

spectacle of their captain and his shield-brother dancing with their swords. Word spread through the camp, and their audience steadily grew. Matthias did not particularly mind; he quite enjoyed showing off his newly refined skills. However, one day after their hour-long bout, they realized their training had garnered the attention of more than just the soldiers. After the crowd dispersed, they were shocked to find Heptarch Aleksandra herself standing before them, peering down with her hawk-like eyes. Matthias mimicked Rain's salute as the intimidating woman sauntered over to them. He had never seen the famous woman up close, but within seconds in her presence, Matthias knew that she was every bit of the leader as the stories suggested.

"A fine display, Captain Rain," Aleksandra said, "What is the name of your shield-brother?"

"Matthias Helianth," the captain promptly said.

Her piercing gaze descended on Matthias, and his face felt red under her scrutiny; he stared at the ground sheepishly, waiting an eternity for her to speak. His Insignis blade felt heavy in his hand, fully aware that it was not customary to have his sword summoned during training. Practicing with a blade was considered highly dangerous under most circumstances. Matthias prepared for a severe reprimanding from the legion's highest officer.

"Helianth," she said, tasting the word in her mouth. "Interesting. Well, you are to be commended, young man. I have seen few people with better instincts than you; your captain is lucky to have you as his right hand. Skills like yours can be the difference between victory and defeat on the battlefield."

He tried his best to be respectful to Aleksandra, but it wasn't in his nature; the moment he realized he wasn't in any trouble, he relaxed his shoulders and looked her directly in the eye. "Thank you, Aleksandra," Matthias said. "I appreciate it."

After speaking so casually to his superior officer, Matthias could feel Rain tense next to him.

"You are welcome, Helianth," she said with a wry smile. Her sharp eyes glistened with a peculiar light. Aleksandra turned her attention back to Rain. "I needed an excuse to watch the two of you, but I'm afraid there are pressing matters I need to discuss with you, captain. Will you follow me?"

Rain nodded curtly and shot Matthias a confused look as he accompanied the Heptarch across the training field and out of sight. He stood awkwardly as Aleksandra left without a farewell, wondering what she wanted with his friend on such short notice.

Matthias continued the morning with the Sand Ferrets, assuming leadership in Rain's absence. It was arduous work without his friend for company.

After training, the Sand Ferrets sat eating lunch with the rest of the fourth battalion. Rain had still not returned from his meeting with Aleksandra. After a few minutes, Matthias realized that none of the captains were in the pavilion. For that matter, Kadri, Vilja, and Silja were also absent, which was unusual for them as of late.

Towards the end of the meal, Matthias saw Rain at the head of a small group of officers, marching through the pavilion with gusto. The Sand Ferret Captain's face was dark, and his brown eyes filled with fierce determination.

"I just received orders from Heptarch Aleksandra," Rain announced to the entire table, loud enough for the whole dining pavilion to hear, "We are to march at first light tomorrow. Southward. We are to join the current campaign and act as reinforcements to Heptarch Hendrick and the Devoted Company."

Captain Rain canceled afternoon training and drilling as the legion prepared for their journey. It was the first campaign of many in the fourth, and a silent air of dread covered their section of the camp. Inexperienced soldiers stared blankly into space as they packed their bags and received their battle shields for the first time. As they fell asleep, Matthias could hear many of them crying. He did not blame them in the slightest.

The chorus of horns that echoed through the barracks had ended their precious few hours of sleep. Sullenly, the Sand Ferrets rose and marched out of their quarters. Matthias would miss his bed, even if it was harder than stone. Soon, they were marching southward along the plains in the long procession; Matthias briefly saw Kadri and the twins as the priestesses glided past them. Once again, Aleksandra's legion marched away from Arachovia and toward the vast southern plains, towards the battle, glory, and death.

10

Siege of Phalanaea

The air was hot and muggy, and the overcast sky hid the midday sun, casting dark shadows across the southern plains. Sweat was already dripping down from Matthias' helmet, threatening to blind him. He ignored the metallic taste in his mouth and the quickening heart rate that he experienced directly before a battle.

The unified forces of Kyriak and Arachovia marched southward from their camps in tight formation. Hendrick strode proudly at the head of the army, his Devoted Company marching directly behind. Aleksandra's legion marched on the company's right flank while General Zsolt led his Kyriaki troops on the left side; both forces vastly outnumbered the Devoted at the front. Still, the new Heptarch was eager to impress his former superior officer, who had yet to experience his prowess in battle. Hendrick shouted encouragement to his troops, who chanted back in unison.

Matthias was relieved that his old friends from the Sand Ferret Squad had survived the campaign thus far, having rushed to their camp when Aleksandra's forces arrived the day before. They all had dozens of stories and exploits to tell; though Veiko did most of the talking, rumors had confirmed that not one man from the Devoted Company had perished thus far. A lover would do anything to ensure his man would leave a battle alive, a fact the whole world was now discovering.

The legion's formation was an odd one, in Matthias' opinion. The cavalry trotted slowly at the front of the troops, bows drawn and mountain elk baying in anticipation. The Kyriaki archers were also at the forefront of their contingent, a strategy that puzzled Matthias. The priestesses from Arachovia walked in clusters between the archers, cavalry and the great host of soldiers at the rear. Flanked by Vilja and Silja, Kadri marched only a few dozen paces in front of the fourth battalion, robes flowing violently in the wind. Matthias and Rain and the rest of the Sand Ferrets marched in the dead center of the fourth, led by a scowling Commander Vallin. Like the other high commanding officers, he was unaccustomed to marching in front of his troops; Matthias could hear the man's bitter curses from across the battalion.

"What do you think he is planning?" Matthias asked his captain over the din of the moving army.

"We will soon find out, won't we?" Rain gestured at the mesa that loomed before them.

The city of Phalanaea was the northernmost stronghold for the Raephinan forces and functioned as a garrison during its recent campaigns against Kyriak. The large town was built upon a mesa at least twice the size of Arachovia's, and tall domes and spires reached the heavens above. A grand staircase carved into its northern cliffs led up to the city above, similar to Matthias' home city. But instead of the rambling lower city built beneath the cliffs of Arachovia, the only structure at the base of Phalanaea's mesa was a great fortress with high walls, a heavy wooden gate, and ramparts filled with archers.

A small but sizable force of Raephinans stood before the great gate in a tight defensive position. They must have outnumbered the Devoted Company three to one but were nothing compared to the great host of the attacking forces. The rest of the enemy forces were undoubtedly assembled beyond the fortress gate, protecting the precious staircase that led into the city above.

The priestesses chanted loudly, filling the air with a chorus of varying songs, each more haunting than the last. The wind started to howl, picking up and changing directions southward towards the Raephinan city. Hendrick shouted, and the Devoted Company immediately shifted in shape to match the width of the defender's formation. Heptarch Hendrick's elite squad was now seventy-five wide and four soldiers deep. The fortress was only a few hundred paces away, and the Devoted on the front lines were out of range from the enemy arrows. Suddenly, a horn sounded the signal to halt. Matthias stopped along with the rest of his legion and the Kyriaki forces, but the Devoted Company continued marching determinedly forward, the sky shimmering above them.

A reedy Raephinan horn blew behind the high walls, and hundreds of arrows arched toward the Arachovian forces, raining down on Hendrick and his Company in a deadly downpour. Matthias' heart stopped as they fell, but so did the arrows. As if caught by some invisible hand, each arrow hung in the shimmering cloud above the soldiers. The projectiles kept coming, but not one found its way past the shining cloud. The chant of the priestesses grew louder, and the arrows began to glow in a blinding display. Hundreds of deadly arrows rotated slowly until the invisible hand pointed them in the opposite direction toward the fortress. In a flash of light, half of the arrows shot back towards the fortress-like lightning and slammed into the ramparts, resulting in scores of screams of falling and dying archers. The remaining projectiles hovered in place for a moment until they shot violently into the soldiers who were guarding the gate. Tearing through shields, armor, and flesh, the deadly bullets of light killed dozens of defenders instantly. The Raephinan soldiers scrambled to keep the front line steady. Still, the right side of the formation had been particularly devastated by the blast.

Hendrick bellowed, and the Devoted Company charged forward, Insignis blades extended like spears. The elite troop's formation transformed once more. The soldiers on the left flank rushed and fell in behind the right in a long column, leaving the entire left wing only two warriors deep. The two forces clashed in a deafening din of metal clanging against metal and the dying screams of men and women. The Devoted troops on the left flank kept the defenders occupied, but the right column hammered into the Raephinans with unbelievable power, propelled by the strength of twenty soldiers deep. The overwhelmed defenders stood no chance, and soon the charge had reached the fortress wall, completely flanking the Raephinans on the right side. Archers desperately fired at the Devoted, but their arrows were stopped by the shimmering barrier directly above the company and reflected back like tiny bolts of lightning. A brass horn sounded, and the

Arachovian cavalry and the Kyriaki archers released a volley at the enemy, felling dozens of archers along the ramparts and soldiers closest to the fortress wall, careful to avoid hitting any of the Devoted.

The column that flanked the Raephinans on the right had now pivoted and attacked the defenders from the side. They pushed the enemy soldiers back, attacking from two sides and leaving a sea of blood and broken bodies in their wake. Hendrick stood at the rear now, directing a few Devoted to the left flank to avoid any Raephinan escape. Still, the Devoted continued to push the surviving enemy forces against the fortress wall. Matthias suddenly realized that Hendrick was trying to drive the enemy away from the wooden gate to expose it for an attack. It was a brilliant and horrifying display that left a rotting feeling in Matthias' stomach.

Within a few bloody minutes, only a third of the Raephinan forces were left standing, and those that survived had been pushed entirely past the giant wooden gate. The moment the Devoted Company exposed the heavy set of doors, the priestesses all began to chant in unison. The sky above the entire army began to glimmer and shine, writhing and roiling like ocean waves. Then flames burst to life, a few people screamed, and a few fell to their knees in terror.

The fire folded into itself and began to take shape. A great serpent made entirely of fire danced above the troops with sinuous grace, coiling itself into hundreds of graceful loops. Matthias could feel the heat of the flaming behemoth and thought the serpent singed his eyebrows. Suddenly, the snake lashed out, striking the gate in a chaotic, fiery explosion and splintered wood. The impact crushed the gate easily, and the serpent passed through the jagged opening into the fortress courtyard. Pained screams of the dying cut through the battlefield, and Matthias heard a few new recruits around him empty their stomachs in disgust. The serpent glided out of the fortress and spiraled upwards triumphantly, then dissipated into nothing, taking the flames and eating the remnants of the gate along with it.

The moment the priestesses extinguished the flames, the cavalry rushed forward, splitting into two columns. The first galloped through the broken gate and ran into the chaos of the courtyard beyond. The second curved around and rammed into the remaining defenders, cutting through them like rag dolls. A few brutal minutes passed, and the Devoted rushed into the fortress along with the remaining cavalry. Not a single defender had been left alive.

"Odd," Rain said as the remaining Devoted disappeared behind the wreckage of the gate. "It does not seem like many forces were defending the gate. The Raephinan forces stationed here must have been much smaller than our intel suggested."

"Maybe they are positioned in the city above?" Matthias suggested. "The plaza at the top of the stairs would make an excellent defensive point. We can only send a few soldiers at a time."

"The Raephinans are not cruel enough to risk the lives of their citizens for a mere strategy." Rain said, his intense and dark eyes searching the cliffs above. "There will be some resistance in the city, but they would never plan a full-scale attack in the city proper."

The pair were interrupted by a series of horn blasts announcing the legion's deployment. The first three battalions marched into the fortress with a small force of Kyriaki.

The remaining seven battalions marched close to the high walls, whose battlements were now free of enemy archers. They surrounded the fortress in a quarter circle, the tenth battalion stationed outside the broken gate, arching around to the cliffs where the fourth found themselves. The Kyriaki formed a mirroring configuration to complete the massive semicircle of troops. By the time the fourth had reached the rocky outcropping, the sounds of battles echoed from above. Matthias scanned the battlements above and saw the Devoted Company rapidly ascending the long stairs, killing guards at each landing efficiently and rapidly. Soon they would reach the city of Phalanaea, overtake its central bastion, and the siege would be over. Rain scowled at the charging troops high above; his feelings were being vocally reciprocated by Commander Ventin, sulking at the front of the battalion and yelling at an unfortunate junior officer.

"No doubt he feels slighted, being on the flanks like this," Matthias said, chuckling, "I do not begrudge him for it, but I am happy to be out of the fighting. Though it does seem illogical to reverse the order of battalions and make us march over here."

"It is a message from Hendrick, so Ventin understands his new place and can watch his successor achieve victory where he couldn't," Rain said. "And a message to me, I suppose. To also remind me of my new place."

Matthias studied the man's pensive features, trying to decide how to console him. Before any words came to mind, an arrow flew between their heads and struck the soldier before them, who fell to the ground with a grunt. Dozens of arrows streaked through the air, cutting soldiers down from behind. Rain and Matthias whirled around and raised their shields, the captain screaming at the rest of the squad to do the same. Raephinan archers stood in a deadly line on the other side of a rocky outcrop, raining death onto the fourth. A great roar followed the arrows, and Matthias watched in horror as thousands of soldiers poured out behind the nearest corner of the mesa.

Rain had wondered where the main Raephinan forces had been this entire time, and now he had his answer. Massive warriors in metal armor charged at the unsuspecting Arachovians with a blood-curdling battle cry. The fourth battalion was in disarray, dozens already dead in the first few volleys, and the Sand Ferrets were the only squad to have fully reformed, though they had lost over a third of their number. A few Arachovians near the fortress had abandoned the line and fled, including Commander Vallin. The older man ran with his arms over his head, racing towards the safety of the cliffs. The ambush had taken out half of the captains, and the soldiers, half of them fresh recruits, were left leaderless and horrified.

"Hold the line! Keep your shields raised!" Rain shouted. He turned to Matthias and spoke quietly, "I have to reach Commander Vallin. The battalion needs the commander to regroup. Otherwise, we will all die in minutes. Can you hold the line until I return?"

Matthias nodded and looked back as Rain pushed his way through the screaming troops, ordering soldiers to stand and reform as he went. He was halfway to the cliffs when the Raephinan forces hit. They tore through the disorganized flanks with a frenzy of steel and blood, only taking seconds to reach Matthias and the Sand Ferrets.

He dug his heels into the dirt below and leaned against the

shield behind him as the enemy barreled into him. He willed his sword into a spear-like shape and stabbed wildly over his buckler. The blade struck home once, twice, and three times. The remaining Sand Ferrets held the formation, following Matthias' lead, but very few found their targets since most had their eyes closed and their hands shook with terror. If only Veiko and Darius were with him, they might have stood a chance. But with the slovenly and poorly trained recruits around him now, he wasn't sure if they could hold before Rain returned. If the captain hadn't died already.

He heard a gurgling sound as an enemy sword stabbed through the soldier's throat to his right. The poor soul dropped to the ground, dead, while the enemy soldier slashed at Matthias. He dodged the attack and willed his blade to shift and curve, slicing into the enemy's face. She grunted in pain and collapsed in a pool of blood. Matthias yelled in defiance at the next soldier on his right to fill in the gap, but an arrow sunk into his forehead before he could, killing him instantly.

The Raephinan charge continued, and three more enemy soldiers replaced the woman Matthias had slain. He bellowed in defiance and rewound his sword arm to strike. But then he lost his footing and stumbled backward as the soldier behind him fled. The rest of the Sand Ferrets followed the first coward or found a blade in their chest. Matthias lay on the ground among fresh corpses, utterly defenseless and surrounded by jeering Raephinan soldiers. The enemy had decimated the Sand Ferret line.

He lengthened his blade and jabbed at the closest enemy, impaling her in the head. He reformed the sword into a scythe and slashed the next one at the ankles, who hit the ground hard with a stomach-turning scream. Trying to stand, he unbuckled his shield from his left hand but was kicked back down by a third soldier. Falling hard on his stomach, Matthias landed on the corpse of one of the new Sand Ferrets. Blank eyes stared at the sky, and a limp hand held a dormant Insignis sword. Without thinking, Matthias grabbed the fallen soldier's blade, twisted it around in one motion, and stabbed the Raephinan soldier in his heart. He pulled the new weapon from the dead Sand Ferret and tried to reshape it, but to no avail. The sword was not his. It was not bound to him. He stood, holding two swords in his hands, surrounded by enemy soldiers, who watched him with wary eyes after seeing him dispatch the last enemy so effortlessly. He had no chance of defeating all of them with one and a half swords. If only he had complete control over both, there was a chance to survive this melee.

Maybe there was a way to control the new sword.

"I Pledge to serve the legion with my entire being, body, mind, and soul, laying down my desires and passions." He decapitated the nearest soldier with his scythe-shaped sword on the right. "I Pledge to protect my shield-brothers, commanding officers, and the people of Arachovia above my own life." Matthias ducked a wild blow with his right and disemboweled the enemy with his left. "I Pledge to obey my Heptarch and the noble officers of the legion and to strive for valor, honor, and victory." Spinning around with both arms extended, he cut into the survivors, sending them back. "Until my veins run dry and my life ends."

The sword on his left suddenly boiled and came alive, quickly forming into a Signata on his left forearm. Before it had even settled, he called the blade out and formed it into a long scythe, like his right-hand sword. Gracefully, he danced and twirled through the enemy, cutting down Raephinan warriors on all sides, angling the blades to cut at ankles, necks, and chests in an almost random pattern of carnage.

After a few moments, he crouched in a small clearing of the battle, breathing heavily and dripping in blood. Matthias took a moment to assess his surroundings, alone in the eye of broiling melee. Arachovians desperately fought off the ambushing Raephinans, but they were losing. To his right, the fifth and sixth battalions had managed to form a defensive line after taking heavy casualties and were trying their hardest to repel the ferocious assault. Up against the cliffs, to his left, was a strong force of Arachovian survivors about one hundred strong. They had formed a tight defensive formation with their backs against the cliffs but were slowly swinging out, driving the forces back. Matthias could not see Commander Vallin anywhere. At the end of the human-formed lever was Rain. The captain deftly cut down enemy officers and soldiers alike, directing stray Arachovians into his swinging formation. A few more seconds and Rain's formation would be perpendicular to the cliffs. He was only a few dozen paces away but that was leagues on a battlefield.

He smiled and took a deep breath to begin his bloody path toward his friend; they needed to close the gap between the fifth battalion and the cliffs. An enemy officer charged him from behind, and Matthias swung his blades furiously to cut the man down, but they clashed against Insignis steel and bounced off.

Before Matthias could regroup, the officer's sword came from below in a blur of dark gray steel. Matthias grunted as the blade ran him through. His mind turned numb as the steel tore through his stomach and sprouted out of his back. The world began to spin as the enemy pulled the blade out from his wound, and he fell to his knees, dropping both swords.

He thought that he could hear someone yelling in the distance as darkness took him, and he knew no more.

* * *

Rain saw the blade impale Matthias and his blood ran cold; he heard an ear-splitting scream and realized it was coming from him. He absentmindedly ordered a stray trio of Arachovians into his defensive formation and commanded a few more to defend the flanks. The words had barely left his mouth as he sliced his way across the melee, eyes focused on the officer standing above his friend's freshly fallen body. He willed his sword to lengthen and sharpen and savagely cut through soldier after soldier, throwing his allies back and ordering them to the line as he went.

In seconds he had torn through a dozen enemy soldiers and made his way to his fallen friend and the man who impaled him. The enemy officer held his sword in defense, but Rain's blade had already sunk deep into his skull. He knelt to his friend as the officer fell. Matthias' green, sightless eyes were open and staring up into the sky.

He was already dead.

Rain pushed back his tears and stood over his friend as three more Raephinans charged, blades drawn. Slashing the air and extending his sword to its limit, Rain decapitated all three at once. More of the enemy came, and more corpses fell. He would not allow a single soul near his friend. No one would be able to touch him. Rain slashed through countless enemies, pushing them back, not leaving his friend's corpse. Dozens of enemy swords glanced off his Insignis armor; none could find his flesh.

Nothing else mattered in the world. It was just Rain, Matthias' body, and the enemy before him. He would not allow anyone past; not one soul would get close. After what seemed like a lifetime, a flurry of motion was behind him. He looked back and saw the cavalry racing around the fortress, cutting down a few Raephinans who had broken through. Rain realized he was standing alone in the center of the gap between the surviving fourth battalion and the fifth, now only a dozen paces wide. The cavalry column was headed right for the opening, right at him.

Quickly, he threw himself over Matthias' body as the mounted reinforcements tore through the melee and into the mass beyond. A few hooves glanced off his armor, but most of the spry mountain elk could leap over and avoid him.

As the mounted troops finally passed, Rain lifted his head, picked up his friend's body from the bloody dirt, and carried it through the closing gap. The formation would hold, and reinforcements would arrive soon. But none of that mattered now.

He stumbled past the front lines, Matthias' lifeless body hanging from his arms, screaming for the aid of a priestess.

11

Changes

The soldier drifted aimlessly through the inky black void surrounding him like a soundless, numbing blanket. Suspended in oblivion, the man could not see, hear, or feel a thing. No sound, no emotion, no sensation of any kind, just blackness remained. Not long ago, he existed, but how did he even know that? Was he a soldier? He seemed to recall that he was a noble. Or was he both? Soldier. Noble. Both words seemed foreign to him, the meanings remained elusive, just out of reach.

Matthias. That was his name. Was. Past tense. Did he not exist anymore? If so, where was he? But more importantly, who was he?

Images began to flash across his mind—a great battle. Soldiers were dying around him; their screams pierced the void. A storm of metal, dirt, and broken flesh. Men and women dying by his hands. Two swords sliced through air, leather, and flesh. Then the pain blossomed from his abdomen and lanced outwards, consuming him. He had been stabbed, run through by a blade. The pain tore through him, opening up his memories all at once. He was scraping his knee in the markets as a boy, running through his parents' garden at night with Anton, stealing his father's wine with Kadri, joining the military, and fighting alongside Rain.

The void began to fade away gradually, and his senses slowly returned. At first, he heard a quiet mumbling in the distance. As the voice grew louder, Matthias thought it sounded like chanting of some sort. His lungs filled with the acrid smell of disinfectant mixed with an odd fragrance that reminded him of incense. His eyes fluttered, and a blurry image of a canvas roof began to fill his vision. The one constant thing was the pain. His abdomen throbbed with excruciating pain, and his muscles felt as if he had just run straight in full armor for a week.

A hand gently cupped the back of his head and lifted him so he was angled upright while a cup touched his lips, and cool water poured into his mouth. He swallowed the refreshing liquid eagerly, feeling a cold sensation spread down his throat and throughout his body, pulling him back into reality.

The world finally came into view; he could see that he was in a small, dimly lit tent and lying on a hard cot. Two women, priestesses, sat next to the bed, looking down at him intently. Silja, running a hand impatiently through her short hair, scowled at the foot of the bed. Kadri was holding Matthias's head and holding the cup to his lips.

"Kadri—" Matthias said hoarsely. The word felt like fire in his throat, and he began to cough violently, his abdomen laced with pain at every wheezing breath, threatening to tear open.

"Do not speak yet," Silja said, sharply. "Keep drinking and

allow the healing to take full effect. You are fortunate the spirits decided to spare you; do not mock them now by dying."

"You are a lucky idiot. I hope you know that," Kadri said dryly, but tears rolled down her face. She gingerly set the cup against his lips, and he gratefully took another long swig.

"Where...what?" Matthias croaked, ignoring Silja's stern glare and the pain of speaking. He did not have the energy to form sentences, but that did not change the fact that he had millions of questions.

"You are in the healing tent of the priestesses in Heptarch Aleksandra's camp, just a few leagues north of Phalanaea," Kadri explained softly.

"The battle..." Matthias rasped. He was able to hold the glass in his hand and took another gulp, allowing the water to soothe his aching throat.

"Ended in our victory," Kadri said, "The Raephinan forces surrendered after the Devoted breached their upper city and rebuffed their final assault. I hear that you and Captain Rain were instrumental in the final moments of the battle. But that was three days ago. You...you were badly injured during the ambush and have been here ever since. Silja has prayed over you every night. Tonight, the spirits finally answered."

"The rach decided to bring you back from the brink. Their reasons are beyond my reckoning," Silja said matter-of-factly. "They have decided, however, not to restore you fully. You will have to recover on your own, but the only thing that will be lasting from the wound is the scar. They must have great plans for you."

"Th-thank you," Matthias said weakly. He ran his hand down to his bandaged stomach. It felt tender and still ached, but he trusted Silja's diagnosis.

"Do not thank me, thank the spirits. And him," Silja said sternly, gesturing to the corner. Matthias turned to see Rain lying in the corner, asleep. "He's the one who carried you from the battlefield on his shoulders, ignoring his own wounds. The fool had thought you were already dead, though you would have been if he hadn't reached us in the fortress when he did."

"He hasn't left this tent in three days," Kadri said, "I am not sure what his commanding officers think about his absence from his duties, but who am I to judge?"

As if on cue, the captain stirred from his slumber, lazily rubbed his eyes, and sat up wearily. Rain Cassian rarely ever smiled—emotion was relatively rare on his normally detached face—but the man beamed so brightly as he stood that Matthias could not help but grin.

"So, it seems that the spirits aren't a cabal of self-serving narcissists," Rain swiftly walked across the small tent and knelt by Matthias' side, opposite Kadri.

"I should be on my way," Silja announced loudly, looking at Rain pointedly. "There are more casualties in this camp that require the divine mercy of the spirits."

Kadri smiled fondly and waved at her friend as she departed, but did not leave Matthias' side for an instant.

"Matthias," Rain spoke softly, hand on Matthias' shoulder. He looked at Kadri awkwardly, as if she was intruding on a confidential strategy meeting, but he continued when she showed no sign of leaving. "I wanted to apologize to you for failing you as a shield-brother and captain. I should never have left you during the ambush. The Sand Ferrets may have survived if I had stayed and you wouldn't be here."

"Apologize?" Matthias said, incredulously. The man was

always too critical of himself. "You are the only reason I am still alive today, Rain. And the reason why the battle did not end in defeat. I saw the formation you orchestrated along the cliffs. How did that pompous blowhard Vallin let you take over his command so easily?"

"Commander Vallin did not survive the initial assault," Rain explained, "An arrow struck the man before I could reach him."

"Ah," Matthias said, regretting speaking ill of the dead, however true it might have been. Deciding to change the subject, Matthias was curious about how the Arachovians could have turned the battle around so swiftly. The last he remembered, Raephinan forces had entirely overrun the Arachovians. "What happened after I…after you carried me to safety?"

"Aleksandra sent the cavalry through the gap between my formation and the remnants of the fifth, pushing the Raephinan forces back," Rain explained. "By the time the other battalions reinforced our lines, the Devoted Company had reached the top of the stairs and claimed the defenseless city, forcing the enemy below to surrender. The Raephinans did not expect us to break through their defenses with such ease; they meant to ambush and defeat us before we breached the fortress gate."

"How did the rest of the fourth fare? You said the Sand Ferrets were…destroyed." Matthias asked.

"Only four of the squad survived, including you and I," Rain said bitterly, "About a quarter of the fourth battalion survived the ambush, taking the brunt of the casualties. Most of the captains are now dead."

"It is not your fault," Matthias said, seeing the pain on his friend's face. "Vallin was in no shape to lead the defenses. You and I both saw the coward running away from the battle. If you hadn't stepped in, there is no telling what could have happened."

Suddenly the flap opened and a heavily armored figure walked in, chin held high and peering down at Matthias' cot over a hook-like nose. With Insignis armor drawn and a golden crown gleaming in the candlelight, Heptarch Aleksandra Passiflor was the most intimidating person Matthias had ever seen.

"How fortunate for me that so many people I want to speak to are all in one place," Aleksandra said, studying the three with an unsettling intensity.

Matthias swallowed nervously; a personal visit from the Heptarch was never a good omen. Rain sprang from the cot and saluted his superior dutifully, though his face was uncertain. Much slower than Rain, Kadri stood and gave Aleksandra a slight curtsy. The furies may have been an integral part of the Heptarch's legion, but they were not bound by the same formal rules and command structures as officers and soldiers were.

"Are you Kadri Lilias?" Aleksandra's question sounded more like a command.

"Yes," Kadri replied apprehensively.

"I have been told that this is your first campaign, is that correct?" Her angular face was unreadable; Matthias wondered whether Aleksandra was angry or pleased to see them.

"That is correct, Heptarch," Kadri said cordially. She gave the older woman a modicum of reverence.

"The Mother of the furies informed me that you were the one responsible for summoning the great fire serpent that destroyed the enemy gate," Aleksandra said. Matthias shot Kadri a quick look. He had no idea how the priestesses harnessed their powers, but he was equally impressed and terrified that his friend could do something so powerful. "I wanted to give you my thanks, Kadri. What you accomplished was something I had never witnessed before and was one of the keys to our victory."

"Thank you, Heptarch. I had help from my sisters, especially sister Vilja," Kadri said. "Without their help and guidance, I would not have had the strength for such a feat on my own.

"Your humility and loyalty to your peers are quite commendable, but you would do well to accept a compliment. I am not known to hand them out very lightly," Aleksandra said, her eyes lit with a peculiar fire. It seemed as if she had some semblance of a sense of humor. "I will have to keep my eye on you in the future. I expect you to join the Mother for my strategy meetings with the fury battalion."

"Thank you," Kadri said, smiling slightly. "I will make sure to keep your advice in mind."

"Very good," Aleksandra nodded briskly and turned her attention to Rain. "Which brings me to one of the few surviving captains of the fourth battalion. I saw your tactics with the cliffs firsthand and wanted to say how they impressed me personally. If you had not held that line, the enemy forces would have surely overwhelmed the rest of the legion. We may all have perished if it were not for your skill and courage. I also wanted to apologize for the cowardly actions of Commander Vallin that forced you to act. His appointment was a personal decision that was regrettable, in retrospect. The officers under my command must be of sterner stuff and the man was much past his prime. I apologize."

"Thank you, your eminence," Rain said, bowing, studying the ground. "I was just upholding my Oaths and you have nothing to apologize for."

"I must have spent too much time around old and stodgy veterans. Are the youth these days so formal? You may call me Heptarch or simply Aleksandra. I have never enjoyed the nonsensical etiquette that comes with my position." She smiled. "Rumor has it that you trained under Heptarch Hendrick himself, and some say that he collaborated with you on many of his strategies. After seeing you in action, I can only assume that these rumors are true. If that is the case, I would be a fool to not promote you to the commander of the fourth. How does that sound?"

"I accept your promotion with honor," Rain said curtly, saluting his superior.

His calm demeanor betrayed no strong emotion, but Matthias knew that his friend was not elated by the surprise promotion. The last thing his friend wanted was glory or to be responsible for more lives or more deaths.

There was a long silence as Aleksandra regarded Rain for a few moments. With a calculating expression, she considered the new commander's reaction to his position. Aleksandra must not have been used to a noble as uninterested in power as Rain. Matthias took the opportunity to ask something that had been troubling him.

"Aleksandra, I am curious," Matthias ignored the sharp breaths his two friends took when he spoke. "How did our scouts not detect the ambushing forces?

"Ah, Matthias Helianth, the man with two blades." She carefully inspected the second Signata on his left forearm. "Excellent question. The Raephinans waited until we had begun our assault and then transferred their forces using their lifts on the far side of the mesa. I suspect the attack was supposed to catch us before we breached the fortress, but Kadri here foiled that part of the plan, and they did not arrive soon enough."

"Clever," Rain said under his breath. Matthias could imagine his friend currently conceiving hundreds of possible scenarios. He couldn't help himself.

"Which brings me to my third and final reason for visiting the healing tents this evening," Aleksandra continued. "I was also able to witness your exploits on the battlefield, it has been years since I saw someone fight so ferociously and I would never have thought to take a fallen sword as my own. After this siege, I would consider you and your commander two of the best fighters in my legion."

Matthias nodded and tried to smile but only managed a grimace, and he could see a similar expression on Rain's face. Neither man had ever delighted in the killing and being congratulated for it was rather sickening.

"That is why I would like to promote you to captain," Aleksandra said, noticeably taking satisfaction from the stunned look on Matthias' face.

"But I am no noble, Aleksandra," Matthias said, breathless. "I have no claim to be an officer."

"You were a noble once, and frankly that has always been a foolish rule," Aleksandra said dismissively.

"So, you have heard about how I joined the army?" Matthias asked.

"Of course, I heard of your peculiar enlistment. The entire city was gossiping about it for months, and I know all that goes on in my legion." Aleksandra chuckled. "Though I wouldn't mind if you told me the real truth behind that story one day."

"I could arrange that, Aleksandra," Matthias said with a devilish smile. He quite liked this woman. "Though it still does not change that I am not a noble, and by law, only nobles can become officers."

"I suppose the old senile crows in the palace would take issue with such a promotion," Aleksandra said thoughtfully, then she smiled suddenly. "I have an easy way to remedy that. With the powers granted to me as Heptarch, I hereby proclaim you as my ward and adopt you into the house of Passiflor. You will henceforth be known as Captain Matthias Passiflor."

The tent sat in stunned silence. Kadri, Matthias, and Rain gaped at Aleksandra as she stood with a satisfied grin. Not even a Heptarch had the power to grant nobility as it was a matter of genealogy and blood. But in Matthias' case, there was no genuine issue in the adoption. She simply adopted a disowned noble with pre-existing ties to the mythic Ae'rach. Some of the older and more conservative members of the nobility would take issue, but she was well within her power to make such a thing happen.

"I do not know what to say," Matthias said.

"You can start by promising me that you will not do anything stupid and that you will heal quickly," Aleksandra said, then turned back to Rain. "I will need you and my new ward to join a contingent of the wounded back to Arachovia tomorrow. He needs to heal, and you need to begin the process of rebuilding the fourth battalion. You will have my full support when I return, but you should get started as soon as possible. Matthias, you can receive your armor once you recover from your wounds and I have returned. For now, you will have to make do with just the two Signata."

"Yes, Heptarch," Rain said, "Where will the rest of the legion go in the meantime?"

"We will stay here for a few days and then follow you north," Aleksandra explained. "The Queen of Raephina, their version of a Solarch, is to journey here to sign a treaty with the Kyriaki, and General Zsolt has requested my presence for the summit. If all goes as planned, we will finally have peace in the south. Now I must get back to command; it seems like no one can move a stone in this camp without my signature. Get some rest, and I will see you again in Arachovia."

Aleksandra nodded with a satisfied smile and promptly left the tent, leaving the three with their heads spinning and mouths agape.

"Well, that was quite an audience," Kadri said, "I was half expecting us to get court-martialed, the way she walked in like that."

"I can't say that I disagree with you, Kadri," Rain said, "though I would have been less surprised by that outcome."

"Two promotions and an adoption within a few minutes," Matthias said. "Technically three promotions, for what she promised Kadri about those strategy meetings."

"Priestesses transcend outdated notions like rank," Kadri said, voice filled with fake grandeur. "But Aleksandra told the lot of you to rest, and I'll not let the two of you squander her good graces by staying up all night. Now go back to your quarters, Commander Rain."

The priestess shooed the sulking Rain out of the tent and forced another glass of water into Matthias' hand, compelling him to drain its contents. He obeyed and soon he was drifting off into a dreamless sleep.

The following day was a flurry of motion among the healing tents. A long caravan was assembling on the outskirts of the camp. Nurses and furies rushed between a couple of dozen wagons, loading them with scores of wounded soldiers, and even more poor souls with maimed arms or missing fingers stood alongside the wagons. Since there were no plans for more battles, anyone who was not in fighting condition was ordered to march northward. Matthias was roughly transferred to his own small wagon, pulled by two study mountain elk. He was surprised at first by the accommodation and then realized that he was now an officer and had access to such privileges.

His wagon jolted, and he noticed Veiko clambering over the wooden edge. The wiry man smiled brightly as he tumbled into the wagon and embraced Matthias enthusiastically. He smiled back, ignoring the stabbing pain in his gut as the petite man hugged him.

"Careful with him, my love. The man had a hole in his stomach less than three days ago," Darius leaned over the wagon, towering over Matthias. "It is good to see you, lad."

"It is good to see you both," Matthias said, "How has the Devoted Company been? I have heard all of the stories."

"Oh, it's amazing, Matthias," Veiko said, grinning, "I have never felt more part of a family in my entire life. Oh, we have so many stories for you."

"Which can wait until we are all safely home in Arachovia," Darius said.

Matthias smiled; seeing his friends again brought tears to his eyes. "You have no idea how much I missed you. You should have seen the pups they had to replace you..." He trailed off, realizing the young men and women he was gossiping about were all dead.

"Those poor souls," Veiko said. "Curse that Commander Vallin, may he rot in hell. We heard how the bastard ran with his tails between his legs. Good riddance, if you ask me."

"We also heard about you, lad," Darius glanced down at the new Signata on Matthias' left arm. "Seems like the stories are true. You were always losing your shield in battle, just as well you have a sword instead. Will the officers allow you to keep your new sword?"

"Aye, Aleksandra visited me last night," Matthias said, "Promoted Rain to the position of commander and adopted me as her ward and promoted me. You can refer to me as Captain Matthias Passiflor from now on."

"Now that is a juicy piece of gossip that I am ashamed I haven't heard yet," Veiko said. "Though I could hardly imagine a novice like you leading his own squad. I still remember seeing you vomit at your first battle."

"Easy on him, my love. He will make an excellent officer, and Rain will make an excellent commander," Darius said, beaming. "We heard all of the tales of him from the battle, as well."

"Oh yes," Veiko said. "I heard that the man killed two dozen Raephinans while protecting your body, thinking you were dead. The two of you must have...bonded a lot in the last few months."

"What do you mean?" Matthias asked, not quite sure what his friend was suggesting.

"The way the capt...er...Commander Rain fought to protect you with such ferocity. The entire legion is talking about it. I would fight for my Darius the same way if he were mortally wounded in battle," Veiko said. "Only a great love would cause a man to fight like that."

"Love?" Matthias said, laughing at the statement's absurdity. "We are good friends, yes. And I respect him more than anyone I've met, but the man was rejected by the love of his life less than four months ago. He is still healing. We are friends and confidants, but lovers? I think not."

"Whatever you say, lad," Darius chuckled as he shared a knowing look with Veiko. Matthias' face flushed and he cursed at the pair, forgetting how much they enjoyed torturing him. "We must get going, Matthias. Have a safe journey and take this soup Leonas made for you. He and Bruno send their regards."

"Goodbye, my friends," Matthias said, hugging the pair, immensely grateful for their friendship.

Within the hour, Rain joined his wagon, sitting on the driver's seat and the pair chatted aimlessly as the caravan heaved forward towards the north. Matthias looked up at his aloof friend and for some strange reason, he could not shake Veiko's ludicrous suggestion that Rain loved him. They were shield-brothers; Matthias would do the same for the man if the need arose. Yet, the more he convinced himself of it, the less he seemed to believe it. As the journey continued northward, Matthias could not help but wonder if there was an inkling of truth to Veiko's joke.

12

Recovery

The caravan moved slowly across the plains, frequently stopping for rests and setting up well before the sun began to set. The back of a wooden wagon that jolted and bounced over every rock and rut was not ideal for convalescing, but each passing day took Matthias closer to a real bed and a warm bath. A thin canvas was draped over the wagon's wooden frame, doing a less than stellar job protecting his skin from the harsh sun. Rain had proven to be quite the excellent caretaker by driving the wagon at a leisurely pace to accommodate a smoother ride, often taking breaks to make sure Matthias was watered and fed and redressing his wound every few days. The new commander would tell stories during their daily travels to help Matthias keep his mind off the pain and play soothing melodies on his flute each night to make it easier for him to slumber.

His friend made the arduous trip much easier, but Matthias could not shake what Veiko said the day they left on the journey. Were Rain's actions on the battlefield a product of a great friendship like Matthias had believed them to have been? Or were they rooted in more profound feelings of a different nature?

During their journey, the pair discovered how much fame they had garnered from the siege of Phalanaea. The rest of the soldiers of the caravan kept a great distance during the marches and at night. At first, Matthias believed it was a sign of respect for their new titles but soon realized that many of the wounded in the other tents and wagons were officers mixed in with the enlisted. The tales of what Matthias and Rain had done during the siege of Phalanaea had twisted and grown throughout the army until it made the pair seem like heroic legends from the days of old. Those they interacted with would stare at them with admiration, excitement, and fear. It was strange, but Matthias did not mind having space from the others. Rain's companionship was more than enough. His slow driving allowed the pair to keep an excellent distance between their wagon and the rest of the caravan.

Despite the constant motion and poor conditions on the road, Matthias felt his body gradually healing each day. The pain dwindled from a continual throbbing to a dull pang, and by the time the caravan traversed the Gap of Tanaegra, he could sit up without crying out in pain or getting lightheaded. After hours of incessant pleading, Rain finally allowed him to sit up with him on the driver's bench for an hour or so a day.

They were a few days south of Arachovia when Rain began to grow silent. There would be long gaps of silence, and when the man did speak, it was only to talk about the logistics of their journey. The man's behavior reminded Matthias of how Rain acted in his first days in the army.

"You have been fairly quiet today, Rain," Matthias said

teasingly. "Do you have no more stories to entertain me and distract me from my wound?"

Rain returned his jest with a deadpan glare. "If you were still in so much pain, you wouldn't demand sitting with me, and you would return to the cot where you might heal," Rain said dryly.

"Maybe it's because your sunny disposition is the best medicine for an invalid like me," Matthias said, ignoring his friend's scowl.

"If you must know, I hate this part of the country," Rain said.

"What did this land ever do to you?" Matthias chuckled, "What makes it so different from every other place we've passed? All I see are plains, mesas, shrubs, and rivers."

"My parents own it," Rain said softly. Matthias' grin immediately fell off his face, and he bit his lip, embarrassed.

The only subject the pair avoided like a disease was Rain's family. Matthias would even talk about his own father, who disowned him, before his friend would discuss the lavish wealth into which he was born. Matthias looked out across the plains to the half dozen farms in the distance; it was hard to believe that Rain's family owned everything in sight. Matthias wracked his brain, thinking it best to change the subject to something that would boost his friend's mood. Perhaps the logistics would do; the odd man seemed to love administration and organization, something Matthias would never fully understand.

"What are your plans for the fourth?" Matthias asked. "What will you do first once we return?"

"I suppose I will start at the Officer's Academy," Rain said, the gears in his brain immediately going to work, and Matthias knew he had succeeded in distracting the brooding man. It was too easy. "There are only eight captains that survived the siege besides myself, and I am assuming some of them will request a transfer to a more established battalion, and some will not want to be commanded by someone my age. So I will recruit as many brilliant minds as possible; age has nothing to do with intelligence and worth. The wisdom that builds over time is a fallacy told by old codgers like Vallin to keep themselves in power. An old man can be a fool just as easily as a child."

"Hopefully, you have room for at least one fool captain among your ranks," Matthias said, "It would be a fun challenge to rebuild the Sand Ferrets into a better unit than before. I heard its last captain was a lazy lout."

"I suppose I can allow one fool captain in the fourth; it will give the rest an example of what an officer should not be," Rain said. The sarcastic grin faded, and his eyes shifted past Matthias to the plains beyond. "It looks like a storm is coming."

Matthias turned around and saw a massive cloud on the horizon. It was odd-looking, much darker and almost brown instead of the dark gray of a regular rain cloud. It was a dust storm. He had heard of such a thing, but he had never actually witnessed the rare event in all his years.

A few moments later, a warning horn sounded from the caravan ahead. The canvas-covered wagons were specks in the distance, opposite the storm, and were probably a league away. Rain urged the mountain elk into a gallop, and Matthias gritted his teeth as the jostling sent pain shooting from his abdomen. The wind began picking up, carrying an odd musty smell. Matthias looked back to see the brown clouds much closer. They were hundreds of paces high and began blocking the afternoon sun.

"We will never make it to the caravan in time," he shouted over the howling wind.

Most urban Arachovians had never experienced a dust storm, but it was common knowledge how the rapidly flying sand and dirt could tear the flesh off the bone. The best way to survive was to find shelter and avoid it altogether. He could see the caravan heading to the nearest farm where they would be safe. Matthias and Rain did not have that luxury; they would be overcome by the storm well before they reached the nearest farm.

"Hold on and do not fall off," Rain said, turning the wagon violently to the left. Matthias screamed as he almost flew off the driver's bench, clinging precariously to the small wooden railing.

"What are you thinking?" Matthias yelled. Now the pair were racing in the direction of the violent storm.

Rain pointed to an obscure, dark shape almost a few hundred paces in front of them. "I told you these are my parents' lands," Rain yelled, barely audible over the gale.

The mountain elk bayed in terror but obediently galloped forward, nearing the rough shape in the distance. The turbulent wind picked up dirt and sand, creating a dense fog around them, though the storm-front was still a league behind. Matthias pulled his shirt over his nose to avoid breathing in the dirt. The wagon hurtled at the object, and Matthias realized it was a butte, a stony spire jutting out from the plains. It could provide excellent cover from the deadly winds. Rain steered the wagon directly at the rocky wall, elk running at full speed. He showed no signs of stopping and urged the elk forward, desperate to reach the cliffs; they would collide at any second. Matthias closed his eyes and braced for impact, but none came. The temperature suddenly dropped and had a slight scent of mildew. The wagon stopped after a few more moments, and Matthias opened his eyes, and his mouth opened at his new surroundings.

The wagon sat in the center of a large cavern, near the entrance of a narrow tunnel; a beam of sunlight illuminated the cave from a thin crack above. A sea of bright green moss covered the whole cavern floor, save for the back section, which held a large pool of water.

"I used to play here as a child," Rain explained, helping Matthias off the wagon and onto the soft moss, "My mother and father made a habit of touring their lands often and would always take me along so that I could learn about our family's duties. I would sneak off and explore when my parents were busy with the tenants and farmers. We were lucky that this was so close by; it will be a perfect place to wait out the storm."

"Maybe the rach don't want us to die, after all," Matthias said, looking around the cavern in amazement. It was large enough to hold the entire caravan and still had room to spare.

The elk began to graze on the subterranean vegetation as Rain half-carried Matthias closer to the pool of water and laid him down on the soft bed of moss. Matthias let out a contented sigh; after months of sleeping on the ground and in old cots, it was the most comfortable he had been since enlisting.

While Matthias luxuriated and regained his composure after the mad dash to safety, Rain quickly set up camp next to the pool of water. He tied the elk to the wagon and built a simple fire near Matthias. The smoke floated upwards into the unseen crack, seeking the sky beyond. The sounds of the storm echoed through the rocky walls and were almost soothing.

"You saved my life, yet again," Matthias said as the other man was cooking a quick dinner by the fire. "Thank you."

"No need, Matthias," Rain said absentmindedly. "I swore to protect you as a shield-brother, and that does not change now that I am a commander, and you are a captain."

The pair ate in silence, enjoying the haunting beauty of the cave; Matthias glanced over at Rain, distracted by a flurry of disjointed thoughts. Rain was considerate, immensely intelligent, with a unique sense of justice for the disenfranchised, and a disdain for the nobility that Matthias thought he would never share with another. On top of that, he kept his word and fiercely protected those he cared for, and Matthias felt lucky to be counted among that number. The firelight danced off Rain's face, handsome features, and dark, curly hair. He was a bit smaller than Matthias, but years of combat toned his muscles. Not big and bulky like Bruno, but athletic and strong.

Matthias felt his face flush and pulse raced as he quietly observed the man. Had Rain always been so attractive? Or had Veiko's words twisted Matthias' feelings?

No. Matthias could not speak for his friend's actions on the battlefield, but he could not deny the feelings that began to stir in that cavern by the pool. After Anton's betrayal, he had been afraid to trust anyone, but Rain had given him reason a dozen times over that he would always be there.

His thoughts helped him drift into a lovely sleep, in which he dreamed of Rain holding him in the cavern, both naked. At first, he had thought it was real but soon realized he was no longer wounded. Once he comprehended that he was dreaming, Matthias gave in to the dream and allowed himself to be swept up by the lust of his inner desires.

He woke with a start the following day, feeling Rain's hand on his shoulder. The pair were both clothed, and the healing wound on his stomach had returned; Matthias' face flushed as his mind wandered back to the dream. Rain pursed his lips, confused, then helped him to his feet.

"It is time to go," Rain said, "We are only a two-day ride to the city, and the rest of the caravan no doubt assumes we perished in the storm."

"Rain…" Matthias said. He held his breath when the man met his gaze. He desperately wanted to share his newfound feelings for the man. His brain began to form the words, but fear crept in. Rain was still dealing with a broken heart, and he no doubt just saw Matthias as a shield-brother and nothing more. "Never mind, we should get going."

Soon the pair were on their way northward, across the plains that held no signs of the previous storm. After two exhausting days of travel, Matthias and Rain finally arrived home. They discovered, upon their arrival, that the rest of the caravan had returned a few hours before and had indeed taken refuge at a nearby farm during the storm. Luckily, they suffered no additional casualties and could transfer all the wounded to the large hospital building at the edge of the army encampment. Matthias was given a small, cozy room on the third floor with a small window that overlooked the training field.

The priestesses and nurses in the army hospital may have been better equipped to aid in his recovery than the new commander, but Matthias after the first few days, began to miss his time with Rain. The busy officer spent his days interviewing prospective candidates from the Academy and reorganizing the remaining soldiers into a few squads. Rain would visit Matthias after the sun set and discuss everything that transpired that day. Time did nothing to dispel Matthias' feelings for Rain, which had blossomed from their deep friendship. Each day, he waited in boredom, alone in his room, eagerly awaiting Rain's visit, yearning to confess his feelings, but his fear would get the better of him each time.

Matthias had never been one to be shy or coy about his thoughts and emotions. He had professed his love to Anton the day he found out himself. The impetuous ex-noble was never reluctant to share his mind and was often considered too blunt and rash, so what made this any different? As the days turned into weeks and Matthias' wound healed, he slowly understood it was trepidation. After everything the two men experienced together in the last few months, Rain had undoubtedly become his closest and dearest friend. He did not want to risk their friendship, which he cherished so deeply.

Then one day, a few weeks after he arrived in the hospital, a priestess told him that he was ready to return to the barracks the next morning, though he should still be mindful of his injury for the next few days. Rain arrived with a bottle of wine at dusk, and the pair feasted and celebrated the end of Matthias' hospitalization. The sun had long since set, their meal devoured, the wine bottle emptied, and the conversation depleted when Rain bid farewell and turned to leave.

He did not know if it was the late hour, the changing circumstances, or the wine, but something possessed Matthias and he decided it was finally time. Matthias leaped from his bed and grabbed Rain's hand; it was surprisingly soft but firm.

He stared the man directly in the eyes, stomach fluttering as the other man returned his gaze.

"Wait," Matthias said, taking a deep breath in preparation. "You need to know how much this all has meant to me. Saving my life, helping me recover, and being my friend. I care for you deeply, Rain."

"I care for you, too," Rain said awkwardly. The man was not as forthright with emotions as Matthias was. "I am glad you have recovered and have been proud to be your shield-brother. It will be an honor to serve as your commander."

"I think you are missing the point," Matthias said, sighing deeply, "I have cared for you as a shield-brother since the beginning of our first campaign. But that has grown into something else…something stronger."

Rain raised his brows when the meaning behind Matthias' statement finally dawned on him. The man was quiet for what seemed an eternity, his brain processing the new information and calculating a suitable response. Matthias swallowed hard. If the man felt the same way as he did, it wouldn't have taken so long to respond. Rain's brilliant mind was trying to plan a way to let him down gently. He was a fool to have been so bold.

"Matthias," he said slowly. "I am not sure if I'm fully over Hendrick yet. I have loved that man for most of my life. I don't know if I am ready to open it to someone else. I do not think I will ever be. I am sorry."

His words seemed final, but Rain's pained expression betrayed that he was genuinely conflicted by his own response. Matthias' heart jumped with revitalized hope. His feelings were not entirely unrequited.

"But I am not Hendrick," Matthias said firmly. "I do not

care about promotions or glory or victory. I will not put my pride before you as he did. And you are not like Anton. You have shown me that you will always keep your word. I was afraid to reveal my desires for fear of losing your friendship. Honestly, I have never been afraid of anything more in my entire life, including my first day in battle. But I see the way you're looking at me now, and I know that you feel the same way I do. Rain, I believe that I love you. Do you have feelings for me as well?"

"I…" Rain said, "I think I do…but…"

Matthias could not wait for the man to finish. He put a hand gently on his neck and stepped forward, so the two men were inches from each other. Eyes locked, Matthias hovered his lips a hairbreadth from Rain's, stopping his sentence in its tracks. The pair breathed heavily, and Matthias could feel the man's pulse begin to race. Veiko had been right all along. Rain felt something special for Matthias.

"You do not have to say it," Matthias whispered. "I would rather you show me instead."

Rain threw his arms around Matthias and leaned in, pressing their lips together. The wiry man was surprisingly strong and held Matthias tightly as the pair kissed passionately. His whole body was on fire, threatening to explode as he felt Rain's lips and tongue work their way skillfully around his.

There was a sudden knock on the door, and Rain pulled back quickly and stepped across the room. A plucky captain slowly opened the door and entered the room, one of the fourth's recruits. He stood awkwardly in the doorway silently, studying his feet with a strange intensity, until Rain nodded for him to speak. Matthias hoped against hope that the officer hadn't heard anything from the other side of the door.

"Your presence is requested at the front gates. Heptarchs Aleksandra and Hendrick have returned from the south and are holding council this evening," The man, who was more a boy, spoke shakily, "General Zsolt has joined them with a small force of Kyriaki; they are camped outside."

"Very well, I will be there shortly," Rain said brusquely. "You are dismissed."

The officer saluted and sped out of the room nervously, leaving the pair alone.

"Interesting," Matthias said, "I wonder if the Kyriaki seek to add our city to the treaty they drew up with Raephina. You have a fascinating meeting in front of you."

Matthias, heart still pounding from their first kiss, leaned in close, hoping for another before Rain left him. But, to his dismay, the other man pulled away and stared at the floor, unwilling to look Matthias in the eyes.

"I am sorry, Matthias," Rain said. "I do not think I can do this."

He slipped out before Matthias could object, leaving him alone in his chamber.

* * *

Hendrick sauntered through the dimly lit streets of the upper city, freshly bathed after weeks of hard campaigning. The only thing that felt better than a warm bath after a journey was the acclaim his Devoted Company had garnered since he left Arachovia all those months ago. Achieving his dream of winning the title of Heptarch was only the beginning.

He would have preferred to be in his bed at this late hour, but General Zsolt's letter seemed urgent, and he did not want to be rude to his guest. The Kyriaki leader had proven to be an unequivocal ally on the field, and Hendrick admitted that the two men had slowly become friends. It was refreshing to meet a man with similar ambitions and skills. It seemed as if the two were kindred spirits. Inviting the Kyriaki northward into the city had been Hendrick's idea, seeing how well the pair worked together during their war against Raephina. He couldn't even imagine the fantastic feats they could accomplish by signing a treaty binding the two influential cities together. The histories would sing Hendrick's name for years to come.

Finally, Hendrick arrived at the peculiar meeting place established in Zsolt's letter. The Cassian villa. It had been years since he had visited, before he became commander, back when he was still Rain's tutor. Hendrick had heard what happened to the young man during the battle of Phalanaea and was glad that he had garnered some notoriety for his achievements. As long as Rain's glory did not eclipse his own, he was fine.

Hendrick strode past the Cassian guard and down the gilded path to the giant villa. It was an unexpected place to meet the general. Not only was it strange that the foreign leader was admitted into the upper city unguarded at such an hour, but Hendrick had no idea that the man had any connection to the Cassian family. Regardless, he entered the gorgeous building and found himself staring at a small group of people surrounding his Kyriaki friend. Hendrick recognized each of the dozen men and women mingling in the grand foyer; each was the head of some of the oldest and most powerful houses in Arachovia, including Lord and Lady Cassian. It was an odd assortment, since half of the room had ancient and public feuds with the other half.

Hendrick scowled when he noticed Heptarch Paulius among them; there was no love lost between the two leaders. The silver-haired man had gained his crown by the depths of his pockets and his personal connections, not his courage or love for the city. Paulius' presence did, however, explain how Zsolt was able to enter the city with such ease, as the older man controlled the very city guard that patrolled the gates.

When the Kyriaki general noticed Hendrick, his face broke into a broad smile, and he tore himself away from a discussion with Lady Cassian. The man still wore his red armor, as was customary in his homeland. Zsolt strode towards Hendrick and shook his hand with vigor.

"It is good to see you, my friend," Zsolt said in his heavily accented voice. "I am glad you could join us tonight; we will need your help in the days to come."

"I'm not sure if I follow, Zsolt," Hendrick said slowly, "What is the meaning of this meeting?"

"Let us retire to the library," Lady Cassian said abruptly, peering around at the servants standing near the doorways. "We have much to discuss."

Zsolt nodded and turned to follow the other nobles. Hendrick followed the others into the library. What had he gotten himself into?

13

Celebration

After a restless night of sleep, Matthias woke up in his soft bed well before sunrise. Instead of falling asleep, the young man analyzed every second and every word he said the night before in futility. He had always acted too rashly and recklessly; it was why Matthias enlisted in the first place. Now it would be why he ended the closest friendship he had ever known.

He mentally kicked himself, staring up at the ceiling in the dim early morning light. It had taken Matthias months to get over his feelings for Anton, and Rain had loved Hendrick for half his life. Of course, he hadn't resolved his feelings for the charismatic Heptarch who taught him everything. How could he possibly love Matthias, whom he had known for less than a year? If anything, it was Matthias who took advantage of Rain's confusion and broken heart, a fact that made him sick to his stomach. But all that considered, he could not stop thinking about the kiss he and Rain had shared. He could not deny the feelings he held for Rain, no matter how the man reacted the night before.

The sun rose, but Matthias could not find the strength to get up and face the day. If he left the bed, he would have to pack his things and move back into the barracks, risking a run-in with Rain. Matthias could not face the man yet; he needed time to process the kiss and Rain's rejection. Old wounds in Matthias' heart threatened to reopen when he compared his rejection the day before to the night with Anton at the Shrine of Isemelith.

An hour after sunrise, a nurse visited his room to discharge him from the hospital, but he refused to speak to her. A second nurse came and met a similar reaction. A flying wine glass chased out the third. The small hospital room was his respite from the rest of the world, and he would not allow anyone to tear him from it until he was ready to face Rain, which would never be.

A few hours after midday, the door opened yet again, and Matthias grasped the remaining wine glass from the bedside table, ready to hurl it at the blasted nurse. The glass dropped from his hand as the woman entered. She was not a nurse but Heptarch Aleksandra herself. She stormed into the room, her golden crown on her head and Insignis armor summoned, regarding Matthias with her hawk-like eyes as she would a petulant child.

"When I adopted you as my ward, I did not think you would need any parenting, being a grown man. But apparently, I was mistaken." She tossed a large parcel at him, which he fumbled and dropped into his lap. "I had these sent to your room in the barracks, but I was told you refuse to leave the hospital."

"The nurses said I was well enough to leave, but I think I need a few more days to rest," Matthias said, trying his best to sound hoarse.

Aleksandra raised an eyebrow at Matthias. He could not help but look down sheepishly. "If the priestesses and the medical professionals tell you that you are well enough to leave, then make way for the poor souls who need the bed you are lazing about more than you do. Judging by your lack of bandages, you are in good enough shape to leave today. And to dance."

She motioned to the package in Matthias's hands. He opened it obediently and discovered a freshly pressed dress uniform.

"The Solarch is hosting a gala in the upper city tonight to celebrate our victories against the Raephinans and formally greet General Zsolt and his Kyriaki delegation," Aleksandra said. "And since you are both the ward of a Heptarch and the apparent hero of our most recent battle, you will be expected at the ball. In that uniform. Within the hour."

Matthias took the uniform in his hands, waiting for Aleksandra to turn or leave the room. Instead, she stared expectantly, losing patience.

"What are you waiting for?" Aleksandra said, gesturing towards the uniform in his hands. "Get dressed. We must be off immediately."

"Can I have some privacy, please?" Matthias asked. She glared at him for a few moments, but he did not back down. The newly appointed captain was not about to let her see him naked. He would respect her, but he had his limits.

"Very well. I will shut that door and count to thirty," Aleksandra said sternly, "If you are not fully dressed by then, you will sorely regret being adopted by me. Now move."

Before the door shut, Matthias was scrambling out of bed, frantically throwing the uniform over his head and jumping into the freshly pressed pants. The shirt was only half-buttoned when he threw himself out into the hallway, nearly crashing into the Heptarch.

"Seems like you can listen to direction, after all," Aleksandra said, smirking. "Come along now, Matthias, and straighten out that uniform while you're at it. We have an entire city of self-interested fools and charlatans to impress."

Aleksandra led him out of the hospital and through the encampment. Officers, soldiers, and furies alike took great care to avoid her path. She strode past them, ignoring their stares and whispers. As the pair entered the maze-like streets of the lower city, Aleksandra's demeanor slowly changed. Her shoulders relaxed, and her stern expression melted away.

"It is good to know that you respond well to vinegar," Aleksandra said, smiling devilishly. "I will remember that when you need motivation in the future."

"I would rather you didn't, Aleksandra," Matthias replied, not trying to look too incredulous.

She had been almost too convincing in the hospital, though her strategy had been effective. He probably would have still been in bed if she hadn't been so persuasive. The pair reached the grand steps that led to the upper city and began their long ascent. A few groups of officers and Kyriaki officials were not far ahead on the broad stone staircase.

"Have the Kyriaki come for any particular reason?" Matthias asked. "It is unheard of for any foreign forces to enter the city under any circumstances, even our allies."

"That is true," Aleksandra said. "However, it seems we live in unprecedented times. The summit with the Raephinan Queen was so successful that the two southern cities decided to sign an official treaty of peace. General Zsolt wanted to bring the document himself for our Solarch to sign as a gesture of good faith and acknowledgment of our assistance in the war."

"So it is true?" Matthias asked, "There will finally be peace?"

"In the south, at least, spirits willing. Though treaties have never been ironclad," Aleksandra said. "We still have bandits and tribes to the north to contend with, so our bloody work continues. But enough talk of work. Matthias, try to enjoy yourself tonight. You truly have earned it."

The broad road cut through the upper city from the stairs directly to the Solarch's Palace. Ornate bouquets, golden lanterns, and silken banners lined every wall and door frame. It was Matthias' first time back on the top of the mesa since the night Anton had broken his heart. He gaped at the elegant buildings as they passed by. Had he completely forgotten the city of his youth? It had barely been more than a year, but after spending the entirety of that time in military camps and battlefields, it seemed as if Matthias had jumped into a fairy tale. He felt guilty about how much he relished returning to the upper city after so many discussions with Rain criticizing the lavish lifestyle of the nobles. They had agreed it was unnecessary and needed to be changed.

The sun was nearing the horizon when Aleksandra and Matthias reached the great plaza before the Solarch's Palace. Dozens of pavilions had been constructed around its edge, filled with tables and an array of delicious foods and desserts. The plaza's center was free of structures, instead filled with hundreds of dancers in fine outfits and jewels. An orchestra sat on the giant steps playing a complex and beautiful melody to which the nobles danced.

As Aleksandra led him around the dance floor and into a tent nearest the orchestra, Matthias looked around nervously to see if anyone from his past life was in attendance. The only person he caught a glimpse of was Kadri. She was busy dancing with Vilja. The two furies swayed together rather sensually, their arms wrapping around each other. The sour-faced Silja danced awkwardly off to the side, looking sluggish with boredom. Most priestesses did not attend such functions, and the poor woman was stuck as a tag-along. Matthias smiled. He would have to find Kadri later and interrogate her for the juicy details. He hadn't noticed how close she had become to Vilja, but he had his own drama to preoccupy his time.

Matthias kept close to Aleksandra as the pair entered the tent, filled with the city's highest nobles. Three men stood off to the side, speaking in hushed tones, two in golden crowns and one in intricate red armor. Their conversation halted as they noticed Aleksandra approach.

"I would like you all to meet my new ward," Aleksandra announced, with an oddly dignified tone. "This is Captain Matthias Passiflor, or as the soldiers call him, Matthias Two Blades. Matthias, please meet Heptarch Hendrick Ixora, Heptarch Paulius Serriphine, and General Zsolt of Kyriak."

Matthias bowed to each man, frantically trying to remember the intricate etiquette lessons his mother and father had taught him. Paulius nodded back curtly, pursed his thin lips, and turned to Aleksandra, immediately forgetting Matthias existed. The gray-haired man was like most nobles Matthias had known from his past life. People beneath Paulius did not matter unless he had use for them. General Zsolt, however, kept staring at Matthias, his dangerous eyes drawn to his forearms. The foreign general had blunt features and a severe expression that regarded the newly appointed captain like he was some dangerous wild animal. Hendrick, however, greeted Matthias warmly and energetically.

"Matthias Two Blades, it is good to meet you finally!" Hendrick said, slapping Matthias on the back. "I have heard so much of your feats during the siege of Phalanaea. You must tell me all about it."

The large man pulled Matthias to the side and began rapidly asking him questions about the battle. He reluctantly answered Hendricks's long line of questioning; he hated how kind the man was, fully expecting him to be a monster after Rain's stories. It was irritating that the man was so funny, intelligent, and mild-mannered.

"And what about the enemy…oh hold on, the other hero of Phalanaea is here, one moment, Captain Matthias." Hendrick paused. "Commander Rain! Do you have a moment?"

Matthias' heart stopped, and he whirled around to see Rain sulking quietly in the corner. He had ducked into the least populated tent to avoid the crowds he so disdained. Rain was equally horrified to see the group whose attention he had just garnered as Matthias was to see the man who dismissed him the night before. Rain slowly made his way toward the group, and Hendrick threw his arms around his shoulders, congratulating him with deep sincerity. The annoyingly charming Heptarch introduced the man to the three other generals, who regarded Rain similarly to their reaction to Matthias.

The pair stood awkwardly next to one another, trying to avoid eye contact. It was torture. Matthias hated the way Hendrick possessively regarded Rain so casually and began to detest the man once more. Thankfully, Paulius whispered harshly into Aleksandra's ear, and she saved Matthias from further awkward agony.

"Commander Rain, Captain Matthias, will you please excuse us?" Aleksandra asked, "We have some confidential matters to discuss."

The pair bowed and departed briskly, eager to leave the tent; they continued in silence but stuck as closely together as if the party were a battlefield.

"Matthias, I wanted to apologize," Rain began, but the words froze in his mouth, "My parents!"

Looking around his shoulder conspicuously, Matthias saw an older couple in gold-fringed clothing, and there was no mistaking them for Lord and Lady Cassian.

Without thinking, Matthias quickly grabbed Rain by the waist and spun him around, pulling them both out of the pavilion and onto the dance floor. Rain initially resisted but soon understood Matthias' intent and placed his hand on the other man's waist, dancing further into the moving crowd. The grand anthem that the orchestra was playing swelled towards its climax, stirring emotions in Matthias as the pair spun in circles. Their faces close together, he admired Rain and his beautiful, dark features and resisted kissing him once again. The world fell away until there was only Matthias, Rain, and the music. Rain returned his gaze, and his ever-calculating expression was relaxed for once, also enraptured by the thrill of the party.

"Matthias," Rain said softly in his ear. "As I said before, I wanted to apologize for last night. I—"

"You have nothing to apologize for, Rain," Matthias interjected. "I should not have been so forward, knowing your feelings for Hendrick. It was selfish and should not have happened."

"No," Rain said. "I…I am happy that it happened. I wanted to apologize for reacting the way I did. Having slept on it, I was able to think upon your words. You were right. You are not Hendrick and what he did to me has nothing to do with how I feel about you. When I thought you had died in Phalanaea, I couldn't bear it. I believe…that I love you, too, Matthias. I love you."

His self-control depleted, Matthias leaned in and kissed Rain, holding his body tightly against his. Rain returned the kiss with an equal amount of passion and desire; Matthias closed his eyes and allowed himself to be swept up by pure, unbridled joy. His love was not unrequited, and he hadn't misjudged the aloof man's feelings for him.

His hands caressed Rain's firm body, moving southward, his excitement growing as the other man's strong hands did the same. He wanted the man more than anything, wanted him there on that very dance floor. He pulled back abruptly realizing where they were.

"Perhaps we—" Matthias peered around at the dancing nobles around them; their display was beginning to attract unwanted attention.

"Yes," Rain said instantly. "Follow me."

Rain took Matthias by the hand and led him off the dance floor. They picked their way through the crowds, and soon they were almost jogging down a nearby street. Matthias breathed heavily, eyes focused on the tight muscles beneath Rain's uniform, fighting the urge to tear it off of him. If they did not find a private spot soon, there was no telling what Matthias would do. Luckily, Rain stopped at the first gate they passed. The two men standing guard recognized him and allowed the pair to enter with a salute. Matthias was so focused on Rain's athletic frame that they were halfway through the gardens when he realized where they were. The ancient villa of the Cassian family.

"Not to worry," Rain said, "They will be at the gala for quite some time; they will have no idea that we were even here."

Rain led him down a path gilded in roses to a small patio on the side of the great house; the Helianth estate could have fit ten times over in the gigantic structure. Rain pulled him into the door, kissing him as they shuffled inside. Voraciously, the pair ripped the dress uniforms from one another as they made their way across the luxuriously soft rug. They were in a giant bedroom that seemed as if it hadn't been touched in years, which he assumed must be Rain's. By the time they reached the massive bed, both men were completely naked, feeling each other's warm bodies with trembling hands. Matthias kissed Rain's lips and neck, chest, and tight stomach. He bent his knees to continue lower, but suddenly Rain grabbed him by the shoulders firmly, pulled him up for a long, fiery kiss, and then threw him onto the bed behind him.

Breathing heavily, hands shaking, Rain looked down on Matthias, cheeks flushed with longing. Matthias found himself examining the man's naked body, a heavily toned frame covered in the dark tattoos of his Signata, yearning to touch the man again. Rain stood there for a long moment, allowing the tension to build, for their desire to grow. He jumped on top of Matthias. His naked body pressed up against him. Taking the lead, Rain pinned Matthias' hands firmly on the soft bed, kissing his neck and biting it gently.

Matthias let out a loud moan of pleasure as his lover's mouth worked its way down his chest, lingering at his nipples, gently down his tender abdomen, and resting between his legs. Eyes rolling back into his head, Matthias allowed Rain to take control, wave after wave of ecstasy crashing into him. Suddenly it stopped. Rain sprung to his knees and threw Matthias' legs up in the air. Teasing, Rain leisurely eased back onto him, leaning in for a passionate kiss. Matthias allowed Rain to take him, grunting at every gyration and thrust, focused completely on one another, bearing each other's souls.

Matthias twisted his hips and forced Rain onto his back; now on top, he ground against him eagerly. His thighs burned, and he began to sweat, but he continued, seeing the look of pure pleasure on his lover's face. Rain smiled devilishly and the pair tumbled yet again until he was once more on top.

Rain built up speed as the pair continued. The moment his body threatened to climax, Matthias pulled away from Rain. Nimbly, he rolled out from under Rain and positioned himself behind him, both men standing on their knees. He kissed Rain's neck and teased the rest of his body with his hands. As much as he enjoyed the man taking control, Matthias wanted to have his own fun with Rain before they finished.

He leaned forward until he was laying on top of Rain, bare chest touching bare back, lover on top of lover on the soft, luxurious bed. Matthias took control of the other man, chest heaving, and thrust into him aggressively. Where Rain had gradually built up speed, Matthias bombarded his lover with an aggressive torrent of pleasure. Rain moaned loudly, taken in entirely by the fast rhythm. Matthias smiled and kissed the man's neck and continued to make love to him.

Without warning, Rain pushed himself on his hands and knees, forcing Matthias back on his knees, taking control of the rhythm. He grabbed Rain's hips and resumed control of the smaller man. Faster and faster, the two men became one, their moans growing into a loud crescendo of passion. The climax engulfed them simultaneously, so intensely that Matthias felt his head spin. It lasted for seemingly a lifetime, aftershocks pulsing through him one after the other until finally, he collapsed onto the bed next to Rain.

The two men lay naked among the ruined sheets, limbs intertwined, foreheads touching, chests heaving, and eyes interlocked. They lay there in silence for quite some time, breathing in one another and slowly allowing their bodies to recover from their joint activities. Matthias never wanted to leave that bed. He desired to hold onto the man next to him for as long as possible. Rain smiled, and the pair simply lay in silence.

"I love you, Rain," Matthias said after a long while.

"And I love you, Matthias," Rain replied, looking up at the darkened windows, "But we should be getting back to the gala soon. I do not want to run into my parents, and Aleksandra is probably looking for both of us."

"Very well," Matthias said, sighing dramatically. "I suppose the heroes of Phalanaea must make another appearance at the gala thrown in their honor."

Reluctantly, the pair got dressed and picked their way through the moonlit gardens, hand in hand. Rain spoke of stories from his childhood every once in a while, pointing at the spot of its occurrence. A fountain where he had his first kiss, a topiary where he played his first tune from a flute, and a secluded patch of grass where he read frequently. Matthias silently followed and listened, soaking up each memory and piece of knowledge from the man.

Regrettably, their meandering stroll finally ended at the

front gates. As they approached, Matthias realized one of the two guards remained. Only then did he hear the distant screams. A torrent of nobles sped around the corner and down the cobblestone street, many had their clothes torn and others covered in blood. City guards, swords drawn and shields raised, pushed through the stream of fleeing people to the plaza beyond the corner. Matthias could hear familiar and horrifying sounds of metal clashing against metal more clearly. As they reached the gate, the second guard had returned, panting and holding a bloody forehead.

"What is the meaning of this?" Rain asked quickly.

"The plaza is under attack, sir," the second guard said breathlessly. "It is the Kyriaki. The Solarch is dead."

Matthias and Rain bolted down the road, their Insignis steel fully summoned and drawn by the time they took a dozen paces.

14

Flee

By the time Matthias and Rain reached the source of the commotion, the central plaza of Arachovia had fallen into pandemonium. Lifeless bodies, broken and maimed, littered the ornate mosaic. Splintered wood and torn canvas from the ruined pavilions lay haphazardly about the city square. Scores of soldiers in red Insignis armor overwhelmed the crowd, cutting down the dwindling number of defenders.

To Matthias' shock, most of the members of the civil guard were not protecting the civilians from the attacking Kyriaki but instead aided the enemy in their assault. The civil guard captured and arrested Arachovian officers and nobility alike. Matthias' attention was immediately drawn to the grand steps leading to the Solarch's Palace. General Zsolt stood at their apex, looking down at the chaotic scene with a smug smile. At his feet lay the crumbled body of the Solarch, white robe stained red with blood. Matthias noticed Heptarch Paulius to the Kyriaki general's immediate right; the arrogant man watched the grizzly scene with a blank expression. Matthias' blood boiled at the sight of it. Paulius had betrayed the city, using his power over the city guard as a weapon rather than a shield. It was a disgusting display of corruption and toxic ambition. Matthias cut down a soldier in red absentmindedly as he and Rain pressed into the plaza, focused on the palace.

Suddenly, Matthias thought back to the odd conversation between the three Heptarchs and General Zsolt, wondering in horror if Hendrick and Aleksandra were also responsible for this disaster. He frantically searched the crowd and eventually found Hendrick, Insignis steel summoned and fighting off a dozen Kyriaki invaders. Hendrick had formed his sword in the fashion of a heavy war ax, two crescent moons covered in blood. Rain slashed at the nearest soldier, making his way through the chaotic throng to reach the besieged Heptarch, it was a small consolation that the man had nothing to do with the betrayal, but it still irked Matthias to see his lover rush to the man's aid so eagerly.

Before they reached Hendrick, a ball of fire hurtled through the air above them, crashing into a nearby group of Kyriaki soldiers. Matthias whirled and saw a trio of women standing a few dozen paces away, surrounded by a score of red-armored warriors. Vilja and Kadri flanked Aleksandra, tentacles of flames sprouting from their hands. Aleksandra had summoned her Insignis armor and engaged the enemy with a torrent of slashes and jabs. Her giant blade decapitated four soldiers in one arching attack.

For each Kyriaki slain, two more would spring up in their place. The three women were drenched in sweat and blood, most likely a combination of their enemies' and their own. Matthias feared that the enemy would soon overtake the women without reinforcements. The battle priestesses were famous for their ferocity and resolve, each would die before surrendering to the enemy.

"Rain!" Matthias shouted over the din, pointing at the women. "We must help them! We cannot lose Aleksandra."

Rain studied the scene before them, adopting a grave expression when he came to the same conclusion as Matthias. Rain glanced back at the stairs, at Hendrick with a pained expression, but turned to aid Aleksandra and the priestesses, charging across the plaza. Matthias followed, hacking through soldiers with his pair of blades, trying his best to forget the conflicted expression on Rain's face.

Within seconds, the pair crashed through the knot of Kyriaki and joined the trio in the small clearing. Rain impaled a soldier who had snuck up behind Vilja, and Matthias kicked one of the three attacking Aleksandra. Her blade flashed through the night, slaying the remaining two, and a gale of powerful wind blossoming from Kadri's hands sent the remaining soldiers flying. The armored soldiers picked themselves up slowly and charged with a chorus of screams, but the first few crumpled to the ground as if they had run into an invisible wall; they slashed at the shimmering barricade, swords bouncing off with a strange sound. Matthias turned to see Silja, who had abruptly appeared to his left, face blooded and hands extended towards the rushing soldiers, chanting under her breath.

"Hold!" A voice bellowed through the square, stopping the red soldiers and the treacherous city guards in their tracks.

The source of the call drew every eye in the plaza to the top of the palace steps.

General Zsolt was still at the zenith of the stairs, and Paulius remained at his right shoulder, standing over three crowned men, bloodied and bound, their heads hanging in defeat. One of the three was Hendrick.

"Surrender, please!" General Zsolt cried, "I have no interest in razing this magnificent city! I mean to help it realize its full potential! Lay down your weapons, and my troops will not harm you. Heptarch Aleksandra, please see reason and surrender. Your fellow rulers are either dead, captured, or already aligned with the glorious city of Kyriak. Let us help you bring glory to this city!"

The Kyriaki troops and civil guard cheered, and the remaining defenders dropped or retracted their weapons, kneeling on the ground in defeat.

"I will not be so easily swayed by the words of a man as treacherous as you!" Aleksandra spat. She lowered her voice and whispered something unintelligible to Kadri, then raised her voice once more. "You have broken a sacred covenant to your allies that will anger the spirits and send their wrath upon you and your city. I swear that your head will be cleaved from your body before this night is over!"

Aleksandra continued to criticize the general loudly as Kadri had begun to chant in unison with Vilja and Silja. The hairs on Matthias' neck stood up, and the wind began to blow wildly around them. A few soldiers shifted restlessly, muttering to each other under their breaths, but Aleksandra continued to pontificate. She was buying the priestesses' time.

Suddenly the wind gathered in front of Kadri, tearing and whipping violently, then pushed out into the crowd, sending soldiers flying. The mighty gale shot across the plaza and dissipated at its edge, creating a clear path between the group and the nearest street.

When the priestesses launched the wind stream, Aleksandra

abruptly cut her speech and sprinted down the newly cleared path as fast as possible. The Kyriaki soldiers lunged forward, stopped by Rain and Matthias' swords before the pair turned and dashed after Aleksandra and the priestesses. The group ran closely together across the plaza as the general bellowed orders and the dozens of soldiers charged at them from all sides. Silja lifted her arms, and a shimmering barrier appeared on either side of Aleksandra's group, stopping the enemy soldiers who lunged at them from either side. Matthias and Rain repelled soldiers that ran from behind while Kadri and Vilja threw the Kyriaki in their path into the air with a gust of wind.

"To the stairs!" Aleksandra shouted as they reached the plaza's edge and bolted down the wide city street. "We must reach the barracks and rally the troops before the rest of the Kyriaki forces breach the city."

The small group frantically dashed down the cobblestone streets, past screaming nobles, corpses, and enemy soldiers. Kadri and Vilja rained fire upon the wave of Kyriaki who pursued them as Aleksandra, Matthias, and Rain cut down any red-armored warrior in their way with their swords.

When they arrived at the small courtyard built on the top of the stairs, the six men and women were panting heavily, near exhaustion. Matthias' heart leaped to his throat when he saw what awaited them. Forty Kyriaki soldiers blocked the top of the stairs in a tight defensive formation. Dozens of corpses lay before them of poor souls who had attempted to flee to the lower city. Four neat rows, each with ten soldiers, their round shields raised high, and swords shaped like pointed spears; all of them were Insignis bearers. The front two rows held their swords out level to the ground, while the back rows angled theirs upwards. The formation was wedged neatly between two pillars that marked the top of the grand stairs; they could not avoid fighting these dangerous and well-trained warriors. The group waited warily in the center of the square for a brief moment, caught between their pursuers and the wall of shields and swords.

Matthias and Rain nodded at each other and rushed the enemy formation, swords drawn, Matthias in front and Rain directly behind him. Matthias waited until the spear points were two paces in front of him before falling to the ground. He reshaped his swords into long, deadly scythes and sliced at the ankles of the front row. A sickening sound, accompanied by screaming sent the middle four soldiers crumpling to the ground, their feet separated from their legs.

Rain leaped into the air as their spear-like swords clattered against the cobblestone, launching himself up from their falling bodies and stabbing viciously at the second row. With four swift motions, four rear soldiers toppled to the ground dead. By the time Rain had eviscerated the second row, Matthias was on his feet, cutting down the nearest survivors of the first row from the side. He reached Rain and side by side, they crashed into the third row, which had no time to lower their spears. Within seconds, the pair had slain ten of the Kyriaki and punched a hole into their formation. A few unlucky souls from the back row screamed as they tumbled down the stairs, accidentally pushed by their compatriots who were driven back by Matthias and Rain's onslaught. The survivors dropped their shields and broke formation, slashing at the pair violently.

A fierce gust of wind tore through the left flanks, throwing a dozen Kyriaki into the abyss. Their screams echoed as they plummeted off the cliff's face. The trio of priestesses chanted louder and another violent blast of wind tore through the stone columns, sending the remaining soldiers careening over the edge, along with Matthias and Rain.

Desperately, Matthias plunged his left-hand sword into the stones below and hung on tight as the wind threatened to throw him into oblivion. Rain was not so lucky and blew past him, screaming into the night. Withdrawing his free sword into his forearm, Matthias lashed out at Rain, frantically reaching for his hand. Their hands connected, and Matthias screamed in pain as the wind threatened to tear him apart, but he endured. He clutched the hilt of his sword with one hand while holding onto his lover with the other. The wind died down, and the pair collapsed in a heap together on the top steps.

"Sorry about that last one," Kadri said as the four women reached the top of the stairs, "I—"

The words froze in her mouth as she saw the lower city below. Fire tore through the rooftops as Kyriaki tore through the streets, corralling terrified citizens into homes and slaying those who resisted. The barracks were dark, but a few flashes of steel against the moonlight and familiar clangs echoing off the cliff walls told Rain that there was a ferocious battle below.

"We are too late," Aleksandra breathed, "Paulius' guards must have let the Kyriaki in before they attacked the palace."

"Our brothers and sisters below will still need your help, Aleksandra," Rain said, beginning his descent into the chaos below.

Aleksandra nodded resolutely and tailed the commander and Matthias, with the three priestesses in tow. The grand stairs were empty, the soldiers below were too engaged with the enemy to attempt a climb, and the formation Matthias, Rain, and the priestesses had just destroyed had prevented anyone from descending. The screams from the lower city grew in volume and ferocity the further they traveled, and smoke began to fill their lungs. A similar Kyriaki formation sat at the base of the steps from the one above, obviously placed to prevent soldiers from ascending. Kadri and Vilja hurled lightning down upon them, quickly dispatching the knot of soldiers and sending the survivors retreating into the maze of streets.

Matthias jogged behind Aleksandra into the lower city with the rest of the group, but at one narrow junction, Silja stopped near a burning home. The shrieks of those trapped inside could be heard over the chaotic din. They weren't the only pained cries within earshot, the lower city was filled with the wails of the dying.

"Wait," the short-haired priestess announced, "I must stay."

"You cannot," Vilja said. "It is not safe here."

"That is precisely why I should!" Silja said fiercely, gesturing to the flames tearing through the rooftops. "The city will burn to the ground if I do nothing. Go! Get the Heptarch and the others to safety. I will find you when I can, sister."

The twin sisters embraced, tears falling down their cheeks. Silja hugged Kadri fiercely, nodded to the others, and ran into the city, chanting loudly. The rest of the group reluctantly left the fury and made their way through the twisting streets in the direction of the barracks and the sounds of battle. They had only made it a few hundred paces before water began to pour from the sky, dousing the rooftops and quelling the fires that raged all around.

"Your sister is commendable," Aleksandra told Vilja as they ran side by side, "The lives she has just saved are countless. Her actions tonight will prove to be the most important of all."

Vilja smiled in admiration as the group continued their race through the winding dirt streets, past fleeing citizens, overturned carts, and corpses. Soon they made their way to the empty barracks save for the clanging noises ringing from beyond. They followed the sound and found themselves on the edge of the practice ground.

A small group of Arachovians engaged with a much larger force of Kyriaki. The defenders had been pushed back against a large building; the red-clad soldiers filled the space around them, pressing in on them. Matthias realized that members of the Devoted Company comprised the majority of the defending formation. His heart sank, imagining his friends amid the carnage.

Rain drew his sword and bent his knees, ready to charge forward. "We must save them. Kadri and Vilja, can you summon more lightning to disperse the Kyriaki? Matthias and I can—"

"No," Aleksandra said, holding a hand up. "A wise officer must know when to embrace defeat to save the lives of as many of her soldiers as possible. Their lives are more important to waste on a pointless battle."

"But—" Matthias protested.

"This is not a discussion," Aleksandra said, turning to the priestesses. "Kadri, can you hold a barrier as well as Silja?"

"No," Kadri admitted, "But it will be strong enough for a few moments."

"Good, that is all I will need," Aleksandra said. "Vilja, can you tear a hole in the outer city wall on the far side of the practice field if I give the signal?"

"Yes, I can bring that entire section down," Vilja said, pointing to the nearest portion of the wall.

"Perfect. Kadri, lift the barrier," Aleksandra said, then called out for the whole field to hear as the space between the two forces began to shimmer. "This is Heptarch Aleksandra! The city has fallen. The enemy killed Solarch Eirenan and captured Heptarch Hendrick. Flee or surrender! Live to fight again! I order you to flee or surrender!"

She gestured to Vilja and the priestess screamed, lashing out towards the high wall across the field, the stone shook and collapsed in a cascading display of destruction. The stone and mortar crushed the unsuspecting Kyriaki below, creating a massive opening between the practice fields and the dark plains beyond the city.

The shimmering subsided when the Arachovian formation dissolved and the field erupted into pandemonium. Hundreds of soldiers poured across the rubble into the plains and many ran in the opposite direction, to the safety of the lower city. Hundreds of Kyriaki tried in vain to stop them but managed to kill and capture dozens of fleeing soldiers. Aleksandra led her group through the battle, toward the large gap in the wall. Suddenly, Veiko and Darius appeared from behind a group of retreating soldiers. Matthias threw his arms around his friends, delighted to see they survived the attack.

"What is happening?" Veiko asked, "Is what the Heptarch said true? What do we do now?"

Aleksandra put a calming hand on the wiry soldier and pointed to the gap in the wall. "We flee tonight and regroup in the wilds, then plan how to—"

The words caught in Aleksandra's throat as an enemy spear impaled her on the shoulder. She grunted and dropped to the ground.

Before anyone else could react, Darius knelt, broke the handle off the spear, scooped Aleksandra in his arms, and carried her gingerly. "We must get her to safety and be quick about it."

They started for the breach in the wall, but Matthias shot his hand up, "Wait! We cannot get very far with her on foot. They will run us down within the hour. We need another way out."

"The stables!" Rain said suddenly, pointing to the small grouping of buildings nearby. "We can find a wagon and flee through the nearest gate."

Veiko, Rain, and Matthias formed a wedge and cut through the enemy, while Vilja and Kadri flanked them, catapulting the enemy with a gust of wind. Darius ran in the formation's center, carrying Aleksandra.

After minutes of fierce battle, the group finally arrived at the stables, a low, sprawling building on the edge of the complex. They found a small wagon, and Veiko and Rain hastily prepared it for the journey. Darius placed Aleksandra in the wagon, and Kadri climbed in and immediately began to chant over the Heptarch. Within a few minutes, the group harnessed the two mountain elk to the wagon, Veiko and Darius at the helm and the priestesses sat in the wagon with Aleksandra. Rain opened the far door for their escape. A nearby group of Kyriaki noticed them when the wooden doors swung ajar, and rushed at the opening, flooding the stables. Vilja stretched out her arm and punched a hole through the wooden wall in front of the elk. The terrified beasts reared and

Veiko struggled to control them. Rain and Matthias swung their swords, keeping the rushing enemy at bay. The cart lurched forward through the ragged wooden hole.

"Hop on first," Rain said, gesturing at the wagon. "I will be right behind. Be quick about it."

Matthias nodded, leaped into the cart, and turned with his hand outstretched. Rain kicked a soldier back and leaped at Matthias. Suddenly, another soldier lunged from the shadows and tackled Rain from the side, pinning him to the ground.

"Leave me!" Rain shouted. He withdrew his metal and held his hands up in surrender. Matthias screamed and lurched forward to save Rain, but the bear-like embrace of the burly man behind him prevented him from moving.

"No point in getting killed, lad," Darius said gently. "They won't kill an officer like him, they will want to keep him alive. Settle down, he will be fine. I promise."

Tears streamed down his face as Matthias struggled against Darius' tight embrace. The wagon turned the corner, and the last thing he saw was a Kyriaki soldier kicking Rain in the stomach and others towering over him with thick ropes. The wagon raced through the barracks, careening towards a large wooden gate in the outer wall. Vilja cut a hole through it with a blast of fire, and the elks raced into the plains beyond. Matthias did not stop screaming or fighting Darius until the city wall was obscured from view by shadow.

Aleksandra groaned quietly but was alive, her pain soothed by Kadri's soft chants. Darius held Matthias in his large arms as the young man cried in despair. He should have let Rain board the cart first. Or they should have gone together. He should have fought Darius harder. It was his fault Rain was not with him. Now he was in danger.

His chest felt hollow. He had just connected with Rain, and now that had been torn from him. For all Matthias knew, Zsolt would execute his lover before the night was over.

"Where do we go from here?" Veiko called from the driver's seat.

"Head south," Matthias said grimly. "I know of a place we can go. Then we will return for Rain. And I will have General Zsolt's head."

15

Exiles

The wagon rolled slowly across the desolate plains as the wind tore at its thin canvas cover and the sun beat down unforgivingly. The passengers were quiet, sullenly staring southward as the elk plodded along with deep grunts of effort. Matthias, however, was staring in the opposite direction, northward towards Arachovia. Towards Rain. The farther south Matthias was, the more his heart hurt. Images of Rain being kicked and captured flashed constantly through his mind. He would never forgive himself for leaving, allowing Darius to hold him back; if something happened to Rain…Matthias shoved that thought out of his head. It was unthinkable.

The cart jolted, and someone's knee jabbed him in the side; it had become crowded after two long days of travel. They came across six soldiers hiding among the plains and the farms they visited throughout their journey. They all decided to join Matthias' group when they recognized Aleksandra resting in the front of the wagon.

She was pale, the spear tip still lodged in her shoulder. Kadri continued her prayers for healing, but she did not have Silja's propensity for restorative arts. She simply kept Aleksandra stabilized and nourished her with the food and water they collected from the farms along the way. Word traveled quickly across the plains, and news of the coup reached each farm they passed. The charitable country folk were eager to help wounded soldiers and promised to keep their lips tight about their encounter. Veiko aimlessly drove the cart in random directions despite the farmer's promises, sometimes even double tracking to ensure the Kyriaki would never uncover their true destination. Even the kind-hearted farmer would loosen their tongue if they faced a Kyriaki interrogation.

On the third day of their journey, the wagon came across a young couple from the Devoted Company, Jonas and Taimo. Matthias had served with the men during his first campaign with the Sand Ferret Squad. The pair were kind, amiable, and excellent trackers, as they had been following the wagon since the night of the invasion.

The eclectic group numbered fourteen in total, too many to ride, so they were forced to take turns walking alongside the wagon, all except for Aleksandra and Kadri. By the end of the fifth day, Matthias was glad to see the lone butte jutting out from the plains in front of them. He was surprised he remembered the location of Rain's secret cavern, he felt almost drawn to it.

The wagon entered the vast cavern, and many in the group looked up at its high walls in awe. For the first time since the attack, Aleksandra lifted her head, her hawk-like eyes scanning her surroundings intently. Veiko parked the wagon next to the large pool at the cavern's edge, and Darius yelled at the two soldiers who tried to jump in it. A few of the more sensible soldiers began to unload the supplies they had gathered from the farms and lit the abandoned fire Matthias and Rain had previously built on the shore of the underground lake. Matthias helped Kadri and Darius remove Aleksandra from the wagon and laid her down gently on the mossy bed.

"This was a nice selection, Matthias," Aleksandra said, gesturing to the cavern around her. "Highly defensible, replenishable source of drinking water, decent airflow, and large enough to hold an entire battalion or two. Are you positive that no one knows about this place besides you and Commander Rain?"

Matthias felt a pang in his heart at the mention of his beloved's name. "I am certain, Aleksandra. Not even his family knows about this place. We should be safe here for a time."

"Excellent, though we will gather for a moment to discuss our next steps," Aleksandra said. "Matthias, can you gather our forces? We must take care of a few things before the day is out."

"You can wait on the council for another few hours, Aleksandra," Kadri said firmly, and the Heptarch did not argue. "We need to remove that spearhead from your shoulder, or you will not last the week. I may not be Silja, but I can at least keep you alive until we find her or another priestess with the right talents; Darius, could you assist me?"

"Yes, priestess," Darius said, "I have dealt with many similar wounds in my day. We will need water, fresh towels, and fire."

The odd pair quickly went to work. Matthias' stomach turned just thinking about the procedure, so he sat by the water and became lost in his thoughts. He looked out onto the nearby lake's calm surface, and his mind went directly to Rain. In this very cavern, he had realized his true feelings for the aloof man. He wondered what would have transpired if he confessed his love for the man on the spot, next to the underground pool. They would have at least had more than one night together. Matthias couldn't bear the thought that he would never see Rain again; that possibility was out of the question.

Given the circumstances, Kadri and Darius made reasonably quick work of Aleksandra's wound. She barely made a sound when the priestess ripped the metal spearhead from her flesh, and Darius' blade cauterized the wound. She only needed a few hours to recuperate before calling the cavern's inhabitants together near the fire. If it wasn't for the large bandage that covered her upper torso, Matthias wouldn't have known that Aleksandra was gravely injured.

"Before we start our council," Aleksandra began, "I wanted to thank all of you for your part in our journey here and saving my life. What has happened to our city is tragic and unforgivable. But you have all shown me that Arachovia's strength does not lay within her walls or her defenses or her armories but in the hearts of her people. If we remain unbroken and unified, even the smallest group of us, our city will not fall. An enemy force may occupy it today, but it is only a matter of time before those who took our city from us will see our passion. Who will fight with me, to reclaim our city?"

A roar tore through the cavern as the small group cheered for Aleksandra's speech.

Matthias understood what made a leader genuinely great for the first time. It was not the number of battles won or the power and notoriety one garnered. It was the ability to inspire others, lift people out of the darkest of times and shepherd them to their true potential. That was why Aleksandra was the most powerful leader in the city. She may have been a brilliant tactician and a ferocious warrior, but the way she inspired those she commanded was an unparalleled talent.

"The first major obstacle we must overcome is our numbers," Aleksandra said. "We will need more than fourteen to retake the city. Jonas and Taimo, you have proven to be swift, agile, and excellent trackers. The two of you will leave here tonight and travel to every farm, mesa, and hiding place in the valley. By now, those who fled the city will have found their respective places of refuge. Find who you can and direct them back here. Make sure you do not speak too specifically; we would like this location to remain a mystery. Start with the farms and villages closest to the city and work your way outward. The Kyriaki will undoubtedly begin to scour the land for dissidents once they have full control over the city. Can you handle this mission?"

"Yes, Heptarch," the couple said, in unison, beaming with pride from the words of their superior.

"Good," Aleksandra said. "Now, our defenses are the second obstacle we must address. As Taimo and Jonas spread the word, the information they divulge will undoubtedly reach enemy ears. Matthias has found us an excellent hiding place, but these rock walls will do nothing if the enemy finds us and we remain unprotected. We must station two guards outside the cave at all times to act as lookouts, watching for enemy activity and for allies who are searching for our location. We will also need to dig two trenches, one surrounding the perimeter of the butte and the other inside, at the tunnel entrance. We can construct a drawbridge from surrounding trees. Kadri and Vilja can create the exterior trench while the rest can dig the interior."

"How will we dig, Heptarch?" one of the soldiers asked.

"Your sword can make a fine shovel, lad," Darius said, "Have you never dug a latrine before?"

"Excellent point, Darius," Aleksandra said. "I will entrust you and Matthias to coordinate and build our camp here. I believe we have enough tents for the fourteen of us, but that brings us to our next obstacle. Supplies. Veiko, how many days of provisions did we gather on our journey here?"

"Enough for roughly two weeks if we do not include Jonas and Taimo, possibly more if we hunt and forage for ourselves," Veiko said. "But that will change once our numbers grow."

"Very well," Aleksandra said. "In that case, you and Darius will continue to help construct the camp and set out a week from today to the nearby farms. Use the same strategy and random pattern you used on our journey here, but try to collect as many supplies as possible. Fill the wagon. We will want to establish relationships with the farmers and offer them protection, if necessary. If our food runs out, so will our hope for victory. Any questions?"

The Heptarch patiently answered a flurry of minor and petty questions, mainly from the less experienced soldiers, though she answered each one like it was the most important thing she had ever heard, regardless of how stupid it was. After a lengthy discourse, and a bevy of senseless questions, in Matthias' opinion, Aleksandra dismissed the council. The small group set about to complete the tasks she had set forth.

"Kadri and Matthias, could you both stay back for a moment?" Aleksandra said. "There are a few things I would like to discuss with you."

"Yes, Heptarch," Kadri said.

"Of course," Matthias said, waiting for the others to walk out of earshot before continuing, "That speech was moving. I am glad to see you feeling better."

"On the contrary, Matthias, I am in so much pain at this very moment that I could pass out. But I refuse to faint, for I would be useless in an unconscious state, so here we are. We all must do what we must in times like these," Aleksandra said, sighing, her fatigue finally showing. "Which brings me to the matter I wanted to discuss with you two. I am not mentally or physically capable of leading now, and I will need to rely on you both to help us through this."

"You can rely on me, Aleksandra," Kadri said, beaming. The priestess had been waiting her entire life to be in this exact position.

"What can I do?" Matthias said, "Kadri is a genius and master tactician, but I have almost no leadership experience, and it seems that you've already established an excellent plan."

"That 'council' was to boost morale and take the necessary actions for our survival, not victory," Aleksandra said dismissively. "We will need soldiers, defenses, and supplies to continue living in exile, but we will need a strategy to reclaim our city. Soon the Kyriaki forces will make outposts throughout the land and threaten farmers who do not submit or who are known to support us actively. They will call for reinforcements and rebuild our city's defenses, and it will all be under the direction of a military genius. General Zsolt may be a pompous ass, but we should not take his prowess in these matters lightly. To defeat and outwit him, we will need to devise a strategy that he will not expect, something to take him off his guard. I will need your help to plan and command in my absence. I cannot lead soldiers in the field in this state, and I need you to."

Matthias nodded slowly, trying to comprehend what Aleksandra was asking. He was decent in a battle, regrettably so, for he took no joy in killing and found it all to be senseless. But things were different now. His battle was not for some southern fortress or a disputed piece of land. It was for the lives of every person in the valley. For the farmers whose crops and lands would soon be seized by the occupying army. For the citizens of the lower city whose homes had burned in the fire and who would be terrorized by the enemy soldiers every day. For the citizens of the upper city whose villas were being raided and sacked. For the men and women who would be forced to fight against their own, conscripted into a foreign army. For Rain. Matthias had never taken any pleasure in battle since enlisting, but now was the time to act to save lives and save the Arachovian way of life.

Matthias and Kadri sat with Aleksandra for a long while, discussing the future and laying out plans and contingencies for every possible outcome and surprise, no matter how likely. It was grueling work, but they needed to do it. By the time the trio finished their talks, the sunlight through the cracks above had diminished, and the others had set up a neat camp along the water's edge. Half a dozen tents surrounded a small fire, with one of the soldiers already tending to dinner. Darius and Veiko came by and set up a small tent for Aleksandra by the original fire, off to the side of the others. Kadri slipped into the Heptarch's tent, staying there for a while. Exhausted, Matthias found a free spot of moss and gazed up at the cave's intricate ceiling, desperately wishing that Rain had been lying beside him.

After a while, Matthias heard footsteps on the moss nearby and looked up to see Veiko and Darius making their way over, the latter holding a bowl of stew. The pair sat down gently on either side of Matthias, and Darius held the bowl out.

"You should eat before you waste away, lad," Darius said. "We have plenty of work to be doing, so don't go dying on us just yet."

"I'll try my best to stay alive," Matthias said, accepting and devouring the food. His words felt a bit hollow. He hadn't talked to Darius since the night of the invasion, and he wasn't sure if he was ready to forgive him.

"Beautiful place," Veiko said, breaking the silence. "How did you ever find it?"

"Rain. He used to play here as a child. He showed it to me on our journey back from Phalanaea," Matthias said between bites. Veiko fell silent.

"I am sorry, lad," Darius said, finally. "For what I did the other night, holding you back and all. But if I hadn't done what I did, both you and Rain would be dead right now. I hope you can forgive me."

"What would you have done if the Kyriaki captured Veiko and I held you back?" Matthias said, surprised by the bitterness in his voice.

"I would have broken your neck," Darius admitted, "and rushed to my death. Sometimes the heart fogs the brain and makes us do reckless things. That's why you have Veiko and me to steer you clear when that happens."

"You were only trying to protect me. And you succeeded," Matthias said. "I understand that. And I forgive you. But that doesn't change reality. Rain is in danger, and I will not rest until he is free. I cannot rest."

Tears started to fall down Matthias' cheeks. He hadn't cried since the night the universe tore Rain from him. Darius threw a massive arm around him and held him tight, allowing him to cry until his emotions receded and a new calm washed over him.

"Aye, we will free him, Matthias," Darius said resolutely. "I can promise you that. But you need to take care of yourself in the meantime. You can't help Rain if you're dead. Do you promise us that?"

"I can," Matthias said, finally.

"So," Veiko said, beaming. "Does all of this mean that you have finally admitted the love you share with Rain? Did you finally realize what we knew to be true?"

Matthias blushed and looked down at the moss bashfully, "Yes...we have."

"When was this? Did you profess your love in this cave?" Veiko asked, leaning in. "How romantic!"

"No," Matthias said. "It was the night of the gala...of the attack. I told him the night before and he ran off. Rain found me at the plaza, and we danced...and he told me he loved me too. He kissed me, and we snuck off to his—" He cut himself short, realizing how much he had already revealed so freely. His face burned as the mere thought transported him to that magical moment in the Cassian villa.

"Go on," Veiko said playfully, "I always wondered what the captain...er...commander was like in bed. How long did the two of you last?"

"Quit it, you," Darius said seriously, swatting at Veiko, who dodged the playful blow. Then his face broke into a garish smile. "But I was curious about that. Who was on top?"

Matthias nearly choked and let out a hoarse cackle causing his friends to join in. The three friends laughed and bantered as the beams of sunlight faded from the cavern and darkness fell upon the plains. They chatted about minor things, keeping the topic light to forget their current situation for just one evening. The weeks ahead would be arduous, so Matthias relished the small moments like this. As the fires faded, Darius and Veiko invited Matthias back to their blankets to hold him as they did the night after his first battle. Though he was grateful for the pair and their unwavering friendship, he politely declined.

As his loving friends retired for the evening, Matthias stayed on the bed of cool moss and drifted to sleep. His head swarmed with the plans he had discussed earlier with Aleksandra, but he had only one goal he obsessed over. Saving Rain, even if it cost him his life.

16

Governor

The cell was cold, dank, and musty, but Rain did not mind the peace and quiet it allowed him. The small room had housed four others after the invasion secured the city almost two weeks ago, but after daily interrogations, each one disappeared until only Rain remained. The other prisoners had all been captains and commanders, just like the dozens who had crowded the small prison wedged under the cliffs next to the River Palanthia. There was never much reason for long-term incarceration in Arachovia; petty misdemeanors always resulted in fines or service, and violent crimes were practically nonexistent. Most of the cells had been vacant before the enemy gruffly escorted Rain and the other captives through the prison the night the Kyriaki overtook the city.

The night in which he had utterly failed.

The enemy had not executed the other prisoners; the interrogators had simply asked them the same question they had asked Rain a hundred times before: "Will you pledge allegiance to General Zsolt?"

It was a proposition to which every Arachovian agreed, eventually. The question would always come with pain, bribery, or a threat. Rain did not condemn the others for breaking and swearing allegiance to the enemy. He did not know how he had resisted himself. Slowly, the crowded building grew quiet, and by the time two weeks had passed, Rain believed he was the only soul left in the cells.

It had been precisely fifteen days since his incarceration; he paid close attention to the sliver of sunlight trickling in from the tiny, barred window high on the wall. Rain always had an excellent memory and an impressive internal clock; he always knew where and when it was.

Between the daily visits from the guards, the only thing Rain had to keep himself company was his dark thoughts. He had always been introspective and had a bad habit of dwelling on emotions and memories, but he could only focus on that night during his quiet contemplation. Dancing with Matthias, being held in his arms, professing his love, leading the handsome man home and making love with him.

Rain had been surprised when Matthias first kissed him. Part of him knew that his feelings for the sarcastic and bombastic man had been stirring for some time, especially during the siege at Phalanaea, but he dismissed them for misplaced feelings he hadn't yet resolved with Hendrick. But after the kiss in the hospital, Rain could not stop thinking about Matthias.

Rain had never met a man who would fight for him as fiercely as Matthias had. The audacious man was exactly what Rain had always wanted. A true partner. But he failed him, made a foolish mistake, and allowed the enemy to capture him. Matthias probably thought he was dead. If the man wasn't dead himself. Rain shook the thought away. The image that haunted Rain's dreams was the look on Matthias' face as the wagon pulled away into the night. The fool would have leaped into the soldiers and gotten them both killed if Darius hadn't been there to restrain him.

But that was enough for Rain. Matthias was willing to lay down his life for him, which was more than anyone else would have done. Hendrick would not even give up his ambitions for him. Rain was beginning to believe that Hendrick did not want to bring him into battle because he knew he would be unable to put his lover's life before his own. Rain had finally found someone who understood the Vows, but he would most likely never see him again. Rain would probably never see the outside of these cells.

The heavy door opened, yanking Rain from his melancholy thoughts. It seemed too early in the day for his appointment with the interrogator, but the monotony of his captivity must have been playing tricks with his mind. A Kyriaki soldier strode in, and Rain raised his wrists to be restrained, which was customary every time the guards brought him to a special chamber for questioning.

"No need for those," the guard said gruffly, pulling Rain roughly to his feet and dragging him into the narrow hallway beyond.

Rain followed the man hesitantly down the dark hall, passing empty cells as they went. He was indeed the last officer left in the tiny prison. Instead of taking Rain to the interrogation room, the soldier blew past it without a second thought and continued up a nearby staircase. Puzzled, Rain climbed after the sullen man, unsure where they were going. He had assumed that all the others had been set free after pledging loyalty to Zsolt and Kyriaki regime. It seemed as if the general had no use for prisoners and the only other option was execution.

The winding steps led up to a small landing with a heavy door. Beyond the door lay a large courtyard. Rain remembered the place from the night of the invasion; it must be where the more stubborn Arachovians who refused to pledge loyalty would be hanged for treason and displayed as a warning to others. Rain squinted as he stepped outside into the mid-morning sun; after days of darkness, it took a while to recover from the shock of sunlight. The guard was neither patient nor sympathetic to Rain's reaction, shoving him across the courtyard. As his vision adjusted, he noticed that the yard was empty. Only a pair of guards on the other side protected the large gate that led out of the compound. His keeper sped toward the entry gate, and Rain found his legs struggling to keep up, weak after days of misuse.

"Where are you taking me?" Rain said, ignoring the glares from the other guards as they passed through the front gate.

"I am to escort you to the upper city," the man said, tersely. "General Zsolt has requested an audience."

The guard spoke in a tone that told Rain he was in no mood to divulge even if he knew more details. So he let his dozens of questions loose, giving birth to countless more. General Zsolt had never struck Rain as one to negotiate or to extend mercy. He simply took what he wanted and killed those who got in his way, as he had done with Arachovia. With the other officers and nobles who hadn't bent to his will, the most common outcome had been a public execution.

Rain and his reluctant companion plodded through the lower city; many buildings were blackened, burned, and without roofs. There had been no effort to repair or rebuild anything, and commoners walked sullenly around the winding streets with their eyes downcast to not attract unwanted attention. There seemed to be as many Kyriaki soldiers as civilians in the lower city. Rain passed dozens of squads of red-clad soldiers patrolling the streets, more often than not with prisoners in tow or bursting open the door to a nearby building.

Rain's stomach turned as they reached the first city square. Hanging in the center by their necks were a few dozen corpses of men, women, and children. Children. They all wore tattered clothes and looked like peasants, no one important or threatening, no one with real power or influence. But there they hung as a gruesome example, just the same.

A quiet rage began to roil over Rain, and he suppressed the thought of summoning his steel and decapitating his guard. The Kyriaki had been fools to allow him to keep his Signata, but a sudden outburst would attract the nearest patrol, and then Rain would be as good as dead. On top of that, it was not the soldier's doing, though it may have been his hand. Only one person was to blame for the cruelty and horror Rain witnessed. General Zsolt.

The rest of the lower city was just the same, filled with burned buildings, scared and starving civilians, troops of enemy soldiers, and scores of bodies hanging, limply swaying in the wind. He was relieved as they climbed the wide steps, nearing the upper city, though Rain was terrified of what he would find above. He gritted his teeth nervously, his weary legs pushing him up from the final steps and over the zenith of the grand stairs.

What lay beyond in the upper city was much worse than

he could imagine. The chaos and fire had touched not one building during the night of the invasion. Children ran in the streets, laughing and playing. Nobles strolled leisurely down the cobblestone boulevard and into neat shops and stalls. The civil guard still lightly patrolled the gardens and plazas, as they always had done, but not once did Rain see a single soldier in red armor. It was just as the upper city had been before the attack. As if nothing had happened.

Rain had never considered himself mercurial like Matthias. He never acted rashly and always chose his words and actions with careful precision. But it took every ounce of strength he possessed not to summon his steel and begin wreaking havoc on the nearby nobles and guards. The Kyriaki had only been invited to Arachovia because of their agreement with its ruling class, to sign a treaty that would only benefit the wealthiest in the city.

Now, the lower city lay in shambles, and the nobles continued their daily lives as if nothing had happened. His anger quickly morphed into shock as his escort led him to his destination. Right before they arrived at the Solarch's Palace, the soldier took an abrupt turn and walked to the nearest villa gate and the lavish gardens beyond.

The Cassian estate. Rain's childhood home.

The two of them strode briskly through the grounds, and Rain could not help but notice the increased defenses. Six soldiers had guarded the gate, and many more lined the path to the main entrance, each heavily armored, face obscured by elaborate helmets. The guards wore the emblem of Kyriak on their chests, but Rain deduced they were not Kyriaki themselves, but Arachovians conscripted into the enemy's ranks. The symbols betrayed an unsettling truth that not only had Rain's family pledged fealty to Zsolt but that the new regime had their full, unyielding support. Rain wondered if they had known anything about the coup beforehand, or worse, if they had helped orchestrate it.

A few minutes later, Rain sulked cautiously in the corner of the massive Cassian dining room, alone after his escort had stiffly bowed and exited the way they had entered. Three people sat before him at a large oaken table. In the center was General Zsolt, wearing his red Insignis armor from the neck down, but instead of his helmet, he wore the tall and thin crown of the Solarch. The severe man was busy flipping through dozens of papers, signing a few, and tossing others into the bin near his feet. To his left was Paulius, who barely seemed to notice Rain as he entered. The silver-haired Heptarch seemed intent on sloshing wine in his goblet as he swirled it around gently in his hand. To the general's right was the only person in the room who seemed to notice him, and she glared at him with disdain and utter contempt—his mother.

"Governor Zsolt," Lady Cassian said. The new title that the noblewoman used to address the Kyriaki leader was not lost on Rain. It was a title the Kyriaki used to distinguish the leaders of their nation's vassal states. Arachovia was now fully under Kyriak's control. "The...commander has arrived, as you requested."

Zsolt's eyes left his work and fell upon Rain with the intensity of a raging fire. The intimidating man assessed him with an acute curiosity until, finally, the sour-faced Kyriaki pursed his lips.

"So this is the boy who helped Aleksandra escape," Zsolt said. "The only officer left in the city who has refused to swear loyalty to me. How come I find that so hard to believe?"

Rain opened his mouth to respond, but his mother quickly cut in. "If I may explain, your eminence, the reports from the night of your victory must have been misconstrued. True, my son was seen with the treacherous Heptarch Aleksandra; he has always been drawn to people more powerful than him to hide his own failings. But he could not have possibly achieved the feats reported from that night. It must have been that treasonous Two Blades fellow. Rain has always been as stubborn as a mule, which is why he hasn't accepted your most gracious offer. He probably did not fully comprehend it. My son has also always been a little slow."

Rain clenched his jaw, hands shaking and desperately trying to keep his steel retracted in his forearms. His parents had consistently underestimated him and always assumed the worst of him. Rain had always been a quiet and reserved child; he never spoke unless he was sure of his words. Lord and Lady Cassian mistook his gentle demeanor as stupidity and often lamented at the disappointment that was their youngest child. When he joined the Officer's Academy, they were almost glad to be rid of Rain. His parents had always assumed that Rain only achieved his successes because of his connection to Hendrick, a man they had wished to be their son instead.

His mother was not lying to Zsolt; she fully believed her words. But his mother's disapproval would work in Rain's favor today. He kept his shoulders hunched and his eyes downcast. If they wanted to think he was meek and benign, he would not give them a reason to think otherwise.

"And what say you, Commander Rain?" Zsolt asked. "Am I to believe Lady Cassian's account?"

"I...I..." Rain stammered and fell silent, studying the ground.

Zsolt was too smart to see through his ruse if Rain spoke too much. The less Rain said in front of the city's new leader, the better. He would play the role his mother had assigned him since he was a child and act the meek and incapable idiot she thought he was.

"Enough," Zsolt said, turning to his mother. "You were right, Lady Cassian. It seems that your son indeed achieved his reputation by simply his proximity to a greater man. I see no threat standing before us. I grant you the wish you requested of me. You may have custody of your son, but he must have a constant escort. Arachovia is now under my protection and governance, and I will see it protected. Your family has been instrumental in my efforts, but there will be grave consequences if your son steps out of line. Do I make myself clear?"

"Yes, your eminence," Lady Cassian said quickly. "We will keep him under strict guard at all times. You have my word, governor."

"Excellent," Zsolt said, returning to his papers. He waved his hand casually at Rain. "You are dismissed."

Rain bowed, faltering a bit to maintain his charade, and sulked out of the dining room. One of his parent's guards, a hulking man, strode forward from the wall and lumbered after him, following him to his room. Thankfully, the brute stayed outside in the hall when Rain entered his apartments. He glanced out onto his private patio and saw two other guards stationed outside to prevent his escape. But their efforts would be in vain, for he would not attempt to flee.

Why would he leave when he was in the best position he could hope to be? He had already ensured his parents and the other leaders would pay him no attention, and he could move about the city unhindered, save for his guard, who was probably too stupid to know what direction the sun rose in the sky. Aleksandra and Matthias were out there on the plains, being hunted by Zsolt, and they could only reclaim the city if they had help from inside. They would need sensitive information about its new defenses that he was now in the perfect place to gather. He would watch, he would wait, and he would plan.

A few days later, Rain was strolling along the southern edge of the upper city, gazing down at the streets below and the vast plains beyond. His massive, armored guard walked directly behind him, casting a shadow over him wherever he went. The pair ignored the screams of a noblewoman outside the nearest house as her son was carried away by a dozen civil guards.

Rain soon discovered that even though the upper city seemed to be untouched by the coup, that was hardly the case. Nobles of lower houses were disappearing every day. The new governor had decreed that each youth would be legally required to be conscripted into his new army regardless of birth. Gone were the days of voluntary service. Zsolt was forcing Arachovia into the archaic ways of the southern cities. The Kyriaki usurper had also introduced new and strict laws, including a curfew. Breaking any of the new edicts would result in public beatings in the central plaza. It may have been less cruel than what was happening in the lower city, but the pained cries of children who had broken curfew were too much for Rain to bear.

Unfortunately for Rain, it seemed as if Zsolt's presence in the Cassian household was an anomaly and the man barely left the palace, putting a damper on Rain's plan to spy on him. Nevertheless, he could still walk the upper city freely and had soon memorized the pattern of the city guard's patrols. Any information would be crucial, and Rain would gather as much as he could discover.

The group of civil guards carried the poor young noble across their paths. Rain's heart broke as he ignored the man's desperate cries for help. He shuddered as the guards spirited him off, undoubtedly to forcibly enlist him in the new, growing army.

"Disgusting," the colossal guard behind Rain said. "They have no honor."

Rain whirled around to the giant man, who hadn't spoken a word since he had become Rain's shadow. Other guards were assigned to him, but the huge one who had first escorted him to his room was his most common companion. Rain had never given the man much heed since he always walked behind or off to the side. But there was something about the man's voice. He studied the man intently now; only his thick brows and bearded jaw were visible underneath the helmet. Rain's eyes narrowed.

"Take off your helmet," he commanded.

The hulking man obliged and removed his helm for a brief moment with a smile, then rapidly put it back on before anyone noticed. Rain gasped.

"I wondered when you would notice me, Commander Rain," Bruno said.

"How is this possible?" Rain said, clasping the giant man on the back. He had served alongside Bruno for his entire military career, and he was shocked he hadn't recognized him, even when heavily armored.

"Was captured that night, after the outer wall fell. It took six of them to knock me out," Bruno said, in a deep voice filled with regret. "Woke up in chains, then brought to your family's villa. They forced me to serve as their guard. Lots of good folk were forced to do the same for the great houses, many of them from the Devoted Company."

"I see," Rain said, "They do not trust the veterans enough to allow you in their new army, but they still have a use for you to protect the high families. I assume the other noble houses have just as large a force as my parents. You spoke of other members of the Devoted. Do you know where they all are?"

"Aye," Bruno said, "Arvo serves Heptarch Paulius' estate, and his Devoted, Gvidas, serves with me at the Cassian estate. There are a few dozen more I can think of."

"Excellent," Rain said, starting to formulate plans and countermeasures. "You all must be able to connect without much notice, seeing as even I did not recognize you for days. Can you tell me the exact location of every veteran and member of the Devoted Company that you know?"

Bruno nodded, and the pair walked along the edge of the city, Rain listening to the hulking behemoth list each man, taking note of their locations. His heart panged when the massive man mentioned Hendrick. He had been one of the last to break in the prison, but eventually, Hendrick pledged his allegiance to Zsolt and was living comfortably yet isolated in his small villa. Hendrick barely left his estate and made no effort to contact or lead the Devoted. Bruno was disgusted by his former commanding officer, but Rain felt pity for him. In the end, his resolve wasn't as strong as he'd believed.

"And what of Leonas?" After Bruno had exhausted his list, Rain said, "Who is he serving? He must be close by."

"No," Bruno grew dark and scowled, pointing towards the plains. "My Leonas is not here. We were separated when the walls fell. He's either dead or out there somewhere. Every day I look for a way to break out and find him."

"I know the feeling, Bruno, trust me," Rain said softly, putting a comforting hand on the large man's armored shoulder. "We will do what we must here, and soon we will be reunited with those we love. I promise you."

Bruno smiled, the pair continued their stroll, and Rain began developing an elaborate plan. He looked out across the plains. In his head, he promised Matthias that he would see him again one day.

17

Rebellion

Matthias lay with his stomach on the cold ground, peering over the short hillock and studying the farm below in the early morning light. Darius' large frame lay to his right while Kadri and Vilja were on his left. A large field boasted bountiful, green crops that separated their hiding place from the cluster of farm buildings. On the far side of the farm, cattle grazed on the sun-dried grass. It was a moderately sized ranch located near the road that connected Arachovia and Tanaegra, almost a day's journey south from the secret cavern. But once one examined the farm properly, it was anything but ordinary.

A deep trench surrounded the farmhouse and its outlying buildings, where the Kyriaki had erected a makeshift wall of neatly constructed logs inside the circular rut. The occupying troops had set up dozens of tents in neat lines near the barn, and soldiers in red armor walked casually between them. Next to the central gate, a crude lookout tower soared above the outer wall, where a pair of soldiers stood alert at its apex.

An aggravating Kyriaki tactic during the month since

Arachovia fell was to occupy as many farms and villages in the outlying countryside as possible and convert them into military outposts. Matthias was almost impressed by how diligent the enemy had been and how quickly these makeshift strongholds had sprung up in the last few weeks. The soldiers allowed the farmers to continue working the land as long as they pledged allegiance to Kyriak. This strategy allowed the new regime to have tighter control over their precious food production, but moreover, it limited the places rebels could gather themselves and supplies. It also resulted in the capture of countless rebel Arachovian soldiers who used these farms as hiding places from the invaders.

The crops below rustled, and Matthias summoned both of his swords. He held his breath and tensed his body, prepared to fight. He exhaled when the green stalks parted to reveal Veiko, sweaty and out of breath. The wiry soldier clambered up the hill with graceful speed and dropped to the ground between Matthias and Darius.

"Any news?" Matthias asked calmly, speaking in a whisper even at this distance from the enemy camp.

"It is just like the last three farms we visited," Veiko said, slowly catching his breath. "The outer wall was clumsily built and easy to slip inside, but the Kyriaki troops kept the compound heavily patrolled. I would estimate the farm is now home to over a hundred troops. There are also a dozen or so officers, each being Insignis wielders. About thirty troops from the prisoner escort are in a smaller camp along the northern wall."

"Are the captives being held in that camp with them?" Matthias asked.

"No," Veiko said, "They are using the barn to hold them for

now. I overheard a pair of officers near the wall; they plan to leave before midday."

"Can you tell how many prisoners there might be?" Kadri asked.

"No," Veiko said, "But judging by the security, there could be a hundred poor souls locked in that barn."

Matthias gritted his teeth; they had chased the caravan southward for a few days now. It was transporting every captured dissident in the region to Tanaegra, which had fallen into Kyriaki control shortly after Arachovia. If they escaped now, the enemy would send all of those soldiers to the southern plains, destined to live out the rest of their lives as conscripts in a Kyriaki legion. Matthias could not allow that to happen. The caravan guards believed they enjoyed total protection within the walls of the newly constructed camp, but they were mistaken. Matthias had waited to strike until now, when he could solve two problems with one blow.

"Let's waste no time, then," Matthias said, turning to Kadri. "Please be careful."

The priestess nodded gravely, hastily rose, and sped down the hill. Matthias watched her stealthily make her way around the crops, skirting their edges and running eastward, in the opposite direction of the farm. She ran until she was almost out of sight, making her way to a rocky outcrop next to the road that connected the farm to the surrounding countryside.

She hid behind the rock formation for a few moments and then promptly re-emerged, leading a force of forty soldiers. Shields held high and Insignis swords drawn out like spears, the heavily armored troops accompanied Kadri down the path toward the farm's front gate. Within seconds of the force's appearance, a Kyriaki horn blew from the lookout tower and the camp jolted alive like an anthill. The large gate opened, and scores of armed soldiers poured out into the road beyond into a tight, well-organized formation. Matthias counted over a hundred Kyriaki soldiers as the heavy gates closed once more, most of them conscripted and armed with ordinary weapons and armor. Half a dozen Insignis wielders stood behind them in a neat line, wedged safely between the wall and the knot of their subordinates. Kadri continued to march her small force towards the gate until they were in the range of the defenders' arrows. A few volleys hurtled through the hair, but a wall of shimmering air materialized before them and caught them mid-flight; Kadri had been practicing her barriers. The rebel soldiers let out a yell in defiance that echoed across the fields and continued their relentless march at the Kyriaki.

"Now," Matthias said as he sprung up and dashed into the crops below.

Veiko dashed forward and led the small column, blade summoned and shield raised, Darius and Vilja fell in directly behind Matthias. The three men had their weapons drawn when they reached the small hole in the wall Veiko had mentioned earlier. Vilja extended her hands and began to chant as they traversed the shallow ditch and lashed out at the logs. The nearest ones to them began to turn color and rot. Vilja continued to chant, and the logs decayed more rapidly until they disintegrated into sawdust, leaving a wide gap in the fence.

The four clambered up quickly and helped each other through the breach and into the camp. The compound was mostly deserted; Kadri's advance had lured out most of the forces. But Matthias knew they would still have to deal with the archers on the lookout tower, the highest-ranking officers, and the few soldiers left to guard the camp. They crouched and snuck through the base like a pack of predators, sneaking to the front gate where the high officers gathered. Hiding behind a wagon next to the clearing by the gate, Matthias surveyed the area. Eight of the warriors wore red Insignis armor, and about a dozen were merely foot soldiers. There were no sounds of battle on the other side of the gate, which meant Kadri had not engaged with the defenders yet.

"Vilja, take care of the archers. Darius and Veiko, follow me. Target the officers and kill them swiftly," Matthias whispered to the others. "Incapacitate or wound the conscripted soldiers, but do not kill them unless you have no other choice."

"Aye," Darius said, shaping his sword into a heavy cleaver, "as you've said before. But I still think it's a dangerous strategy. A man can't kill me if he is dead."

"Focus on the officers," Matthias said sternly. "Avoid the soldiers. I do not want a repeat of last time."

Darius grunted but nodded, nevertheless. Matthias smiled, leaped from behind the small wagon, and dashed at the enemy, his two friends in tow. He shaped his left-hand sword into a spear and hurled it at the nearest officer. It spiraled forward and impaled the unsuspecting man through the neck. The others turned and drew their weapons as the first soldier fell to the ground dead, but their reaction was too slow. Darius barreled into the formation, bashing a soldier in the head with his shield and cleaving the officer in half with his heavy sword. Veiko was right behind his lover, his blade thin and sharp, weaving through the soldiers gracefully and stabbing at the officers. After his friends, Matthias collided with the Kyriaki, cutting down an officer with his remaining sword. He extended his left hand out, and the discharged sword flew back into his grasp just in time for him to slash at the nearest officer.

A pair of screams followed a strong gust of wind that shot from Vilja's hands into the tower. The two unfortunate souls were picked up and tossed like rag-dolls, colliding against the ground with a sickening crack. Another blast crashed into the four soldiers trying to flank Veiko, sending them careening into the gate. By the time Vilja's victims hit the ground, every officer in the clearing was dead, and the soldiers lay on the ground unconscious or clutching wounds. Two soldiers lay at Darius' feet with sightless eyes; Matthias furiously clenched his jaw and glared at his friend.

"I am sorry, lad, it was either them or Veiko," Darius said. "There's no way I'm choosing them over my love."

"No, Darius, you had a choice. But those people you just slaughtered had their choice stolen from them by the Kyriaki," Matthias said. "Use your rage against those who benefit from the bloodshed, not the ones forced into it. I have had it with senseless killings."

Darius growled and lumbered off, mumbling under his breath. Matthias' clenched jaw. He regretted yelling at his friend, but things would be different now that he was in charge.

Vilja wasted no time after firing her tempests and quickly picked her way up to the top of the tower. She looked down at Matthias expectantly, and he nodded gravely. Turning to the field beyond the gate, Vilja raised her hands, and six ethereal golden arrows materialized in the sky above her. They hovered in place before flying over the wall like half a dozen lightning bolts. Matthias heard six unique screams as the arrows fell home, killing every officer outside the gate.

Matthias grimaced and grabbed the red helmets of the nearest fallen officers, climbing up the stairs to join Vilja and the top of the rickety tower. He could see the hundred Kyriaki conscripted fighters standing insecurely between the locked gate and Kadri's forces, which stood a few hundred paces from him. Holding up the bloody helms in either hand, Matthias yelled loud enough for the entire compound to hear.

"Your officers have been slain!" Matthias yelled. "We have taken your fortress! Surrender now, and we will spare your lives. Lay down your arms and leave this place. Attack, and we will destroy you!"

A murmur tore through the enemy soldiers, and a few dropped their shields and spears. A few others in the front broke ranks and charged at Kadri, lances extended. Vilja chanted, and lightning rained from the heavens, colliding with the shrieking soldiers. Matthias closed his eyes as the debris of their smoking remains littered the ground. If only the poor fools would listen.

"Surrender now!" Matthias yelled. He signaled Kadri, and her forces immediately walked in perfect unison off the road and reformed on the edge of the crop fields.

In a crescendo of metal clanging against the earth, the remaining soldiers dropped their arms and hesitantly retreated down the road, out of sight. Matthias smiled as they disappeared along the horizon, regretful for the death of the few but glad that the majority acted as he had expected.

Today's raid was Kadri and Matthias' fourth attack in the last week. Each one ended in a similar fashion; he had killed the officers and the weary Kyriaki soldiers withdrew. They did not fight for the honor of Kyriak; most of the conscripted were prisoners of war or residents of lands invaded by the powerful city-state. If they had no one to answer to, they would surrender, preventing mass bloodshed. It was exactly what Aleksandra, Kadri, and Matthias had designed.

Matthias and Vilja descended the steps and opened the large gate in time to see the last of the Kyriaki soldiers disappear around the rock outcropping. There was another Kyriaki outpost less than a day's walk in that direction; the raid survivors would be able to reach it by nightfall.

"I must agree with Darius," Vilja said as Kadri and her soldiers approached. "It seems odd to allow such a force just to slip our grasp. We will never win by letting so many escape; we must crush them when we have the chance."

"Our fight is not with the conscripted," Matthias said, sighing. It would take a while for the others to see his point of view, but he must remain steadfast. "They are victims in all of this as much as you and I. The Kyriaki lead their conscripted with fear and the unearned power of their nobility. We will chip at their strength until nothing is holding their forces to these lands."

"I hope you are right," Vilja said, turning back towards the wall.

As Kadri drew near the gate, the formidable host behind her began to shimmer and fade into nothing. The priestess had discovered her power with illusions during their first raid, which proved to be an invaluable skill. Using soldiers as pawns during battle was commonplace, and now, with Kadri's talent for conjuring fake armies, Matthias could wage war without risking lives.

"That was larger than last time," Matthias said, smiling at his friend. "Are you able to touch them, or are they like mist?"

"Touch them?" Kadri chuckled, "Sounds like we need to

rescue your lover sooner rather than later, or who knows what you will try to stick your dick in."

Matthias playfully pushed Kadri but blushed. He had missed Rain and the romantic advantages of their relationship. His heart panged again, as he still did not know whether the man was alive. Pushing the thought out of his head, he turned and joined Darius and Veiko, who were on their way to the barn.

Kadri and Vilja began to walk around the farm's perimeter; the former strode outside the defenses and the latter on the interior. Vilja dissolved the gate while Kadri raised the earth to fill the trench. Their force was not large enough to protect the farm from another invasion, but they could make it harder on the Kyriaki if they tried to reclaim the area. There were few trees among the plains, and the force had probably cut down every tree for leagues to build the wall; it would take a much greater effort to rebuild.

By the time Matthias caught up to Darius and Veiko, they had already crossed the farmyard and opened up the great doors of the barn. Dozens of haggard and thin men and women stumbled out, eyes squinting in the sunlight. The Kyriaki locked up the poor farmer and her family with the others during the battle. Matthias hastily established a rapport with the family elder to ensure a smooth transition. He informed her of what happened; Kyriaki forces had vacated, and Matthias' squad destroyed the defenses. They could not provide further help but would send a patrol to check on things weekly. If the enemy returned, so would Matthias.

Veiko's assumptions had been correct; the convoy was trafficking almost a hundred prisoners, and he was happy to find a handful of furies and even a dozen members of the Devoted Company among their number. Even better, it seemed as though each Devoted couple had remained intact. Matthias knew only too well the pain of such a separation. A few of the furies specialized in healing, and he promptly dispatched them to tend to the wounded Kyriaki soldiers. They hesitated but obeyed when Matthias repeated his command more firmly. The surviving enemy soldiers silently left the restored farmland within the hour, wounds freshly healed, confused by Matthias' generosity. Mercy was not something they were accustomed to, and it would be Matthias' most important weapon.

By midday, Matthias and his friends led the column of released prisoners across the plains. The grateful farmer insisted on the rebels taking provisions and a wagon to transport them. Matthias gladly accepted her offer, knowing that most of the supplies would have gone to support the Kyriaki forces.

The small column of rebels carefully made their way northward, avoiding roads, villages, and other farms. Luckily, they did not run into enemy patrols on their way to the secret cavern. On the contrary, the only people they encountered were a handful of Arachovian soldiers wandering the plains searching for their destination, attracted by Jonas and Taimo's message. Three soldiers they met on the journey home were from the Devoted Company, a veteran couple, Derra and Lucia, and the grizzly Leonas. Matthias was surprised to see the man without the equally massive Bruno but thought it best to avoid the subject. If the pair had been separated during the attack, it was by force or, even worse, by death. Besides that, he was happy to see his old Sand Ferret companion and to have an excellent fighter—and an even more excellent cook— for the camp. The growing number of rebels meant that good meals were in short supply.

They walked through the night and arrived at the lone butte during the small hours of the morning. Matthias was happy to see six people guarding the entrance rather than two. When the large host entered the cavern, he was surprised by how many others had successfully discovered their hiding place. The rebel camp was now home to around three hundred people, including the prisoners Matthias and Kadri had just freed. Almost a hundred elite fighters from the Devoted Company, a handful of furies, and nearly two hundred soldiers, the forces under Matthias, Kadri, and Aleksandra had grown to almost a battalion within just a month.

Upon their arrival, Kadri immediately sent the furies with talents in restorative arts to the Heptarch's tent. Aleksandra did not outwardly show it, but Matthias knew she was barely hanging on. The healers had been the most important discovery in the past week as they were the first healers they had come across, and the rebels desperately needed their aid. They had still heard no word from Silja, and Matthias hoped the priestess had found a safe place to hide.

The newcomers were assigned their own tents and camp duties by one of the more senior rebels, and Matthias' friends retired to their tents, weary after a long journey and a handful of battles. Matthias trudged through the camp without having that luxury, solving dozens of minor issues and disputes. A soldier wanted a new tent after discovering holes in his current one. A few newcomers wanted to relay intel they gathered on their way to the cavern. A couple of drunken soldiers were still trying to bathe in the underground pool and needed discipline. It was all part of the daily duties of command that Matthias hadn't anticipated and the part that was slowly wearing him down.

His inspection of the camp ended with a joyous tone when he learned Jonas and Taimo had finally returned from their long journey spreading the word of the rebel hideout.

"It is good to see you both," Matthias said, gesturing to the camp around them. "We owe you a large part of this. More than half of these soldiers credited you by name as the pair who directed them here, and we haven't seen a single Kyriaki patrol within ten leagues of this location. A commendable effort."

"Thank you, Captain Matthias. Taimo's idea was to use old folk tales to describe the location. Stories like that are just gibberish to the Kyriaki," Jonas said, "Though I've heard you freed over half of the men and women here."

"Well, I don't know about that," Matthias said, "but please sit and tell me of your travels. I need some food and could use some company." He gestured towards the nearest fire.

"There is something important we wanted to tell you," Taimo said as the three men sat down, "On our return journey, we decided to scout Arachovia before returning."

"You managed to infiltrate Zsolt's defenses?" Matthias breathed, "What did you discover?"

"It is mostly bad news, I'm afraid," Jonas said, his blank look telling Matthias everything he needed to know. Death. Lots of death. "But we did come across one of the Devoted hiding in the lower city. He told us that Commander Rain is alive and living in the upper city."

"Alive?" Matthias said, leaning forward intently, "Are you sure?"

"As good as proof as we could find." Taimo said, "Apparently, he is under constant guard and living at his family's estate. Rumors say that Rain was the only one to refuse to surrender and was only released due to his parents' connection to Zsolt. The other officers pledged their loyalties to the new governor, Zsolt, even Hendrick himself. Rain held steadfastly."

"Sounds like him," Matthias whispered. "Though I am sure he isn't too happy with his parents' connection to the coup. What else can you tell me?"

Jonas and Taimo answered every question regarding the occupied city and Rain for the better part of the day. He sent the pair to Aleksandra's tent to relay the same information. While they were gone, he composed a lengthy note and found the young lovers later that evening.

"Do you think you will be able to sneak into the upper city?" Matthias asked.

"It will be difficult, but we can manage," Jonas said.

"Excellent," Matthias said, "In that case, I would like you to locate Commander Rain and deliver him this letter. He will undoubtedly have crucial information about the upper city's defenses and the ability to rally our allies within the city. I would like you to leave at first light."

Jonas and Taimo left the next day, and Matthias watched them fade into the horizon. His entire body screamed at him to follow, to join them on their mission to the upper city itself. But he was needed here, with his troops and his plans with Aleksandra. The note would be sufficient for now.

But none of that mattered save for one fact. Rain was alive.

18

Correspondence

The city square was brimming with activity; children chased each other across the cobblestones, merchants called out to attract the business of wealthy citizens, and groups of nobles clustered by the fountain or at the stalls gossiping in not-so-quiet volumes. None noticed Rain, who walked among them silently, listening intently to their private conversations. They did not even heed the massive Bruno, who lumbered menacingly in his wake. Lady Cassian's story of Rain's incompetence quickly affected the upper city. The nobles had already seen him as an odd bird and had always been baffled by the stories of his successes in the field. Now his reputation had fully cemented as a lazy youth who had risen on the coattails of others, hardly the favored topic of gossip.

It was a perfect disguise for Rain, who used his anonymity coupled with his peers' disdain to walk around unnoticed and absorb as much information as he could grasp. He already knew the exact size of every major house's private guard, the exact patterns of the civil guard, even which families were faithful Kyriaki sympathizers and which were just paying lip service. The nobles' favorite topic of discussion seemed to be the city below; it was always juicy to talk about less fortunate people for the pride-focused nobles. Rain knew most happenings in the lower city, the arrests, the hangings, and the number of newly conscripted Arachovian citizens.

Gossip was a powerful tool, and it would allow him to gather beneficial intel in the days to come. However, he regretted his lapse of knowledge when it came to the Kyriaki high command. Zsolt had not visited his family's villa once since Rain's mother freed him, and he did not dare go close to the Solarch's Palace, now named the Palace of the Governor. Rain had seen Hendrick once as the man passed the Cassian estate on his way to the palace. The pair made eye contact, but Rain sped off into his mother's garden before the older man could react. Rain could not bring himself to face Hendrick, though he contemplated reaching out to his former lover after each passing day with no word from Zsolt's inner circle.

The most thrilling news Rain overheard had come from outside the city walls; there was much talk about a force of soldiers led by the rogue Heptarch Aleksandra. Most days, the upper city buzzed with gossip and reports of either Kyriaki outpost destroyed or a farm freed from the grasp of Governor Zsolt. What surprised most of the nobility in Arachovia were not the raids themselves but the number of casualties. Oddly enough, only the conscripted soldiers survived the attacks, but the rebels never spared a single officer of Kyriak nobility. Rumors said that the higher ranks of Kyriaki officers were becoming sheepish about being deployed in the valley, for their chances of survival had plummeted in recent weeks. There was even talk of Governor Zsolt replacing his officers in the field with Arachovian nobles. This thought terrified the families of the hundreds of officers now under the rule of the Kyriaki. By the sound of it, the rebels had grown to the size of a legion, destabilized Zsolt's control of the southern valley, and essentially cut off Arachovia from Tanaegra to the south. What Rain was most interested in, however, was the captain, who was said to have led most of the raids. A fierce fighter and brilliant strategist, Matthias Two Blades. It was enough for Rain to know Matthias was still alive, but his heart burst with pride, knowing he had been thriving in exile.

Rain left the square and began his daily stroll along the cliffs at the city's perimeter, Bruno in tow. The man was a lousy companion, but Rain was not bothered by silence. Moreover, the Devoted veteran proved to be a crucial asset in his endeavors. Bruno was much sharper than his gruff demeanor suggested and could easily see patterns in patrols and hear gossip that Rain had missed.

As Rain reached the southern cliffs, he looked down at the lower city below. The Kyriaki had been busy rebuilding, not the burnt homes of the commoners but reconstructing the section of the city wall that Vilja had brought down. They had also constructed a large gatehouse of stone and mortar at the base of Arachovia's grand steps. The Kyriaki heavily guarded the garish building, and even merchants who made the journey every day to sell their wares were searched extensively on each trip. Governor Zsolt was accustomed to the fortress-like architecture of the southern cities. The Kyriaki ruler's goal was to make Arachovia even more impregnable. He had stationed dozens of guards around the half dozen lifts on the cliffs used to transfer supplies to and from the upper city.

They continued their journey around the city, moving

counterclockwise until they reached the section of the city near the Temple. Rain tried not to notice the path that led to the Shrine of Isemelith, for it brought back too many bitter memories. However, that was a common emotion experienced by every man who wished to be Devoted and could not secure the Vows from his lover. Bruno tensed suddenly, and Rain followed his gaze, resisting the urge to summon his steel. Two guards appeared from the nearest alleyway and marched right towards them; they wore the armor of the House of Serriphine, Paulius' private guard. Rain knew the man had no love for him and even viewed his family as a political threat, but he did not think the man would try to assassinate him. Rain tensed up and called upon his sword, ready to dispatch the assassins.

"It is safe, commander," Bruno said, putting a reassuring hand on Rain's shoulder, relaxing as the two men approached, "It's Taimo and Jonas."

Rain's Signata roiled on his forearm as he hurriedly retracted his blade. Luckily the street was empty, and no unwanted eyes saw the display. Rain gave the couple a brief nod as they approached. Jonas and Taimo had been the newest additions to the Sand Ferret Squad before Matthias; he had fought alongside them in many battles and respected each as an excellent soldier. The men paid Rain no mind and passed by them with as little as a nod, making their way down the path toward the Shrine of Isemelith. Understanding their desire for discretion, Rain waited a moment, ensuring the street was utterly vacant, before following Jonas and Taimo to the shrine. The pair had picked an excellent meeting place. Unless a pair of lovers entered the shrine to say their Vows, which was an uncommon occurrence as of late, they would be able to talk uninterrupted for hours.

"I did not know the Kyriaki had captured either of you. I was under the impression we knew the location of each of the Devoted," Rain said, raising an eyebrow at Bruno. "I'm surprised you are working for someone as high profile as Paulius, and Bruno was unaware."

"Because the enemy did not capture us, Commander Rain," Jonas said, "We just arrived today."

"A veteran hiding in the lower city gave us these as disguises," Taimo explained, "He said that there were so many private armies in the upper city that no one would pay attention to us. That proved to be right."

"Very sensible," Rain said, silently commending the couple's genius. No one would look twice at the personal guards of a Heptarch, and even those under Paulius' employ would think anything odd of two men they did not recognize in the constantly growing private force. "But that does not explain why you are here. Why would you risk so much to come?"

"For this," Jonas said, pulling a crumpled envelope from his pocket and extending it outward. "It is from Captain Matthias."

Rain was slightly embarrassed by how quickly he snatched the letter from Jonas' hands, but he was too busy tearing the letter out to care.

"Thank you, both of you," Rain said, "Will you give me a moment?"

The men nodded and chatted softly with Bruno while Rain found a bench on the far side of the shrine. He eagerly opened the letter, and his eyes poured onto the page. The letter was not very long. Matthias had always been a man of many words, but the art of writing was not one of his strong suits.

The letter revealed that Matthias and the others had fled to the secret cavern Rain had shown him on their way home from Phalanaea. Rain was shocked but impressed that Matthias chose such an excellent hiding place of which only two people in the world were aware. The letter detailed a rough estimate of the forces Matthias was able to muster, around the size of a battalion. Aleksandra was alive but gravely injured, but there were a few furies who had just arrived who might be able to save her. Kadri had discovered a talent from the rach that was proving essential in their battle tactics. Then the letter shifted, and Matthias asked Rain to respond with any crucial information and a request to locate as many Devoted, soldiers, or influential nobles as he could rally within the city and prepare them for a future attack. The letter ended with a brief remark. *I am glad you are alive. I love you, my Rain.*

Rain chuckled, and his heart began to fill. Any other man would have been offended by such a brief sentiment from an estranged lover, but instead, Rain chuckled. "What an idiot," he said, then corrected himself. "My idiot."

Rain read the letter once more to make sure he did not miss anything essential and then tore it into small pieces and shoved them into his pocket. His life would be forfeit if anyone else read the letter's contents. Luckily, the unassuming noble had always possessed an excellent memory and had already memorized the letter word for word. Then he walked across the shrine to join the three soldiers, whose quietly excited conversation ended abruptly upon his arrival.

"When will you return to Matthias?" Rain asked.

"After nightfall," Jonas replied. "It will be the safest time to sneak out."

"Excellent. Meet me here at sunset, and I will have a letter for Matthias with all the information he requested. Stay safe, and thank you both," Rain said.

The pair nodded and quickly exited the shrine. Rain and Bruno waited a while before leaving in the other direction. Bruno was in an uncharacteristically good mood. According to Jonas and Taimo, Leonas was alive and safely hidden in the cavern with the other rebels. Rain spent the entire walk home convincing the large man not to immediately run off across the plains to be with Leonas. He reminded Bruno that he was not the only one who was separated from his lover and that the two had a duty to the city to remain. Bruno accepted reluctantly, especially when Rain mentioned honor and commitment, and instantly reverted to his grumpy disposition.

Rain wasted no time writing a lengthy letter in his Cassian villa chamber. He used a few pages; it just so happened that writing was his favorite form of communication, and he had much to say. That night he snuck back to the shrine of Isemelith and gave Jonas and Taimo the letter. He trusted the men to safeguard the envelope, so he did not deem it necessary to write in code or leave anything out.

The following day, Rain took longer than usual to rise. His dreams were a blend of pleasant ones involving Matthias and nightmares that depicted the city crumbling to the ground around him. He was in a foul mood because of his tumultuous sleep and what he was about to do. After getting dressed and having a light lunch, Rain and Bruno made their way across the city to a small villa near the cliffs. The estate was devoid of life and in disrepair, and the gate remained unguarded, a notable anomaly during these days. He left the hulking soldier by the entrance, walked up to the large doors, and knocked.

After a few minutes and some cursing from within, Hendrick opened the door and peered out at Rain. The man's skin was pale, eyes bloodshot, clothes wrinkled, and his breath smelled strongly of stale wine. The once bright and confident man was now a sulking husk standing amidst a crumbling house. Rain had wondered how his old lover could have possibly sworn allegiance to Zsolt. Whatever their personal grievances had been, Hendrick was a somewhat honorable man. Now Rain saw the toll that such a decision had taken on the once proud man. It had utterly broken him.

"What do you want?" Hendrick asked, voice hollow and head tilted downward in shame.

"To talk," Matthias said simply. "Can we go inside?"

"No," Hendrick said, a bit too forcefully. He looked beyond Rain to see Bruno lurking by the gate and gave a start. "I…I do not want you to see me like this. Can we please stay out here?"

Rain agreed, though he was taken aback by the man's behavior, he had always been assertive and sure of himself. Hendrick had never acted so meek before.

"Very well," Rain said, keeping his voice low. There was no telling who could be nearby. "I would like to ask you a favor and a chance to reclaim your honor in return."

"I am not interested, sorry," Hendrick said, turning and closing the door behind him. Rain grabbed the door forcefully and pulled the man back.

"The very least you could do," Rain seethed, "is to hear me out. For the first time in your entire life, you can listen to what I have to say and not dismiss it like you always have done."

Hendrick's mouth opened; Rain had never spoken to the older man like that before. He had never shown anger or resentment, just blind, foolish loyalty.

"I had to submit," Hendrick said. "If I didn't—"

Rain held his hand up, cutting the man off mid-sentence. He surprised himself with his own assertiveness. Anger could do strange things. "I do not care for your reasons, though I guess it has something to do with keeping that crown you fought so hard to gain. Not a soul in this city can say they resisted the Kyriaki's will. Except for me. But whatever oath you pledged can easily be broken and forgiven by the spirits."

"You mean to attempt a coup," Hendrick said, his eyes narrowed.

"Yes, there is a group that I believe to be strong enough, but they will need help from those closest to the palace. You and I." Rain chose his words carefully. He still did not trust the man enough to disclose precious information about his allies.

"Matthias Two Blades and Aleksandra, you mean," Hendrick said, nearly spitting venom when he said their names. "The heroes of the south. Of course, I have heard of their battles on the plains. I haven't completely shut myself out of society."

"Then you know there is a chance, but we need—" Rain began, but Hendrick cut him off.

"I took Oaths, Rain!" Hendrick said, "I cannot simply forsake them. What kind of man would I be if I did?"

"You already betrayed the Oaths you spoke when you received your Signata," Rain said, ignoring the stung expression on Hendrick's face, "But you still have your tattoos, don't you? You can manage to break another set but save more lives in the process."

"What can I possibly do?" Hendrick said, finally.

"You will show me the man I thought you to be for all those years. Honorable, steadfast, and loyal. If you ever actually loved me, you will help with this. To reclaim this city and save her people," Rain said. "Will you?"

"I…I think I can." Hendrick said, his voice softening but still filled with doubt. "But there are too many spies in the upper city, and Zsolt is suspicious by nature. I may wear a crown and have access to some meetings, but I am truly powerless."

"There are quite a few things to help our efforts," Rain said, "As you said, you have access to meetings and Zsolt."

"But he does not tell me much, nothing of importance," Hendrick said dismissively. "And nothing he doesn't disclose to at least two dozen noble families. Your parents aligned with Zsolt before the coup. They would know far more than me."

"I have tried to discover his plans in my family's villa, but it hasn't resulted in anything," Rain said. "Zsolt may not disclose everything to you, but you still have access to crucial information that will be essential if we wish to succeed."

"You have a point," Hendrick said slowly, "but intel is not much if we do not have a force to act upon it."

"I already know the locations of at least sixty Devoted in the upper city, and you can help us add to that number," Rain said. "We will need as many Devoted or loyal soldiers as possible in the upper city, and people are talking about how it is odd that you are the only Heptarch without a private guard. No one would think twice if you finally started filling your estate with soldiers like the others. There are many Devoted hiding in the lower city, risking their lives daily, avoiding capture, torture or conscription."

"That is actually a brilliant plan," Hendrick said. A familiar determination began to return to his drunken face. "I could host at least forty in my household without anyone batting an eye at it. That, along with the others already in the employ of other houses, would make a considerable fighting force when the time comes. I should have thought of it myself."

"But you didn't," Rain said firmly. "I did."

"You are right, Rain," Hendrick said, "This is *your* brilliant plan. Thank you for giving this tired man some hope."

Something didn't sit right with Rain; his mind was pouring over the last few minutes, and one thing did not quite add up.

"You said that my parents were plotting with Zsolt before the invasion. How could you possibly know that?" Rain asked. Hendrick wrinkled his forehead briefly, and suddenly, all was clear. "You were close with Zsolt during your campaigns in the south. Did you know about the coup beforehand?"

"Yes," Hendrick said, shifting his weight nervously. "There was a meeting at your parents'—"

"Enough," Rain said, backing away from the man, realizing his folly. He just divulged his entire plan to a conspirator of the very incursion that destroyed the city. Rain summoned his blade, putting it between him and Hendrick.

"You saw me in the square, Rain," Hendrick said desperately. "I did not go along with it. You must understand."

"Even so," Rain said, "you knew of the plot and did nothing to stop it. You are as culpable as my parents and Paulius."

"I know," Hendrick said. The disheveled man grabbed Rain's sword and pressed it against his neck. "I deserve death, I know. Kill me. Please. Release me from this torment."

Rain stared into the bloodshot eyes of his former lover and suddenly realized why the man had been reclusive since the city's fall. Guilt. Hendrick knew precisely what he had done, and it was slowly eating away at his soul.

"No," Rain said, retracting his blade, "I will not execute you for your crimes. Your penance will be to help me reclaim this city. If you do anything shady, my blade will seek retribution. Do you understand?"

Hendrick regarded Rain with an expression he had never seen from the man before. Respect. Then, without warning, Hendrick grabbed him by the shoulders, pulled him in, and kissed him. Rain initially accepted the kiss, a small part of him longed to be in his former lover's grasp once more, but the smell of rancid wine quickly pulled him out of the moment, and he roughly shoved the man away. Hendrick had never been the man Rain had wanted him to be. The sterling image was created by a foolish boy blinded by love. He was a weak-minded, self-centered lout and would never be the man Matthias was.

"I made a mistake," Rain said, turning to leave. "I should have never trusted you. Good day, Hendrick."

"Wait!" Hendrick grabbed Rain by the wrist, preventing him from leaving. "I am sorry, Rain. I truly am. Not for the kiss. I enjoyed that immensely. But for betraying your trust. For taking your love for granted and never seeing you for who you truly are. I should have brought you to the Devoted Company with me. I should have professed my love for you and spoken the Vows with you. But I was a coward and wanted glory for myself. I was a fool, Rain. I was only a great man because I had a greater one supporting me. I will help you in your efforts to retake the city if only to show my true love for you."

Rain stopped and thought for a moment. His chest ached with regret, for he had just kissed a man after pouring his heart and soul into a letter for another. Hendrick said everything

Rain had been waiting to hear for years, and his words did seem to soften the contempt he used to feel for the disgraced Heptarch. There was no chance he would ever truly forgive Hendrick and love him again, but he did not need to know that. If they were to save Arachovia, they would need his help. There was no other way.

"Very well," Rain said, ignoring his conscience, which screamed at him loudly. "I will allow your help, but I do not promise anything in return, Hendrick. You have broken my heart, though I may learn to love you again. You may not kiss or touch me. But I do thank you for your words, and I will allow you to prove them to me." He avoided the topic that was Matthias. If the man knew that Rain loved another and, of all people, the leader of the rebels they were helping, there would be no telling what the man would do.

"Deal," Hendrick said. "I will start preparations this evening."

Rain nodded and turned to go, not looking back. He was taking a risk in trusting Hendrick, but he believed that the man still loved him in his own twisted way. Rejoining Bruno, the pair walked through the city. Rain ignored the massive man's judgmental looks; they were nothing to match the guilt that tore through his soul. What he did today might save the city in the coming days, but it could not help him from thinking he had just betrayed Matthias, the man he truly loved.

19

Reunions

Matthias woke to the bustling sounds of soldiers packing, which echoed across the cavern walls. Sitting up lazily, the dark canvas of his tent slowly came into focus. He stretched his long limbs and begrudgingly left his cot. His hands went directly to the stack of letters lying in the corner, picking up the nearest one and reading it thoroughly. It had been months since Rain sent his first letter, and Matthias made it his morning routine to read the most recent one to pull him into the day. Rain may have been soft-spoken, but the way he wrote simply transported Matthias into another world; Rain's letters were filled with colorful imagery and passion and always ended with the declaration of his love. Over the past few months, the pair shared dozens of letters, and Rain's words were the primary fuel to Matthias' fire. They sent Jonas and Taimo each time as their personal couriers. However, Matthias practically restrained Leonas from joining them when the muscular behemoth discovered that Bruno was alive and living with Rain. Matthias hated keeping him from his lover, intimately understanding the pain of being separated from the one he loved.

Besides words of encouragement and romantic words, the pair discussed strategies and tactics in their war against Zsolt and the Arachovians. Rain disclosed the city's defenses, the location, and numbers of both soldiers and civil guard, and even was able to intercept sensitive intel from the Governor's Palace. Matthias, in turn, was able to share placements of Kyriaki troops in the surrounding plains, alerting Rain when his scouts spotted convoys between Tanaegra and Arachovia. Together the pair devised strategies that kept the Kyriaki forces reeling and unable to take hold of the valley. It was wonderful having a true partner who understood his way of thinking and helped him hone his ideas.

Aleksandra fully recovered from her wounds thanks to the efforts of the furies. The Heptarch was a veteran strategist and more often than not, her sage counsel saved the rebel forces from being obliterated. Kadri proved to be an excellent tactician; her talents in the divine arts were evolving every day and were crucial for battle strategies. Though he could not help but miss Rain, who understood him the most.

In a few short months, the rebels pushed the Kyriaki army back into Tanaegra and Arachovia and killed hundreds of officers. Matthias' insistence on sparing soldiers' lives resulted in the rebels being outnumbered by one to twenty. Still, his resolve remained unwavering, and he promised the others his scheme would soon pay off. Governor Zsolt eventually sent battalions composed mainly of Arachovian officers and soldiers, just as Rain had warned. The enemy's hope to foil the rebel's strategy by sending Arachovians into the field was quickly dashed when their soldiers simply turned on the few Kyriaki officers and joined the rebels, significantly strengthening their numbers.

That blunder enraged Zsolt and prompted the severe man to heighten his savagery and ruthlessness by demolishing farms and villages and increasing executions in the lower city. His cruelty forced the rebel leaders to accelerate their plans. If everything went their way in the coming days, there would be no more needless death in the valley. Matthias set the letter back on the top of the pile, which would be the last Rain would ever send. Their time to strike had come, and soon the pair would be reunited.

He left his small tent and headed out into the camp for breakfast. He was surprised to find Kadri eating alone by the fire outside his quarters, for the priestess was almost always accompanied by Vilja. It was apparent the women were much more than colleagues or friends, but their body language and hushed tones when they were together suggested the couple valued their discretion. Matthias had never found the time to bring up what he witnessed at the dance; so much had transpired. He instead waited for his friend to tell him when the time was right for her.

Kadri smiled when he sat down to join her.

"You never were a morning person," Kadri said slyly, "though I thought that might have changed once you became a leader of an entire army."

The priestess gestured to the camp around them; tents filled the cavern, and soldiers flitted in between them like hundreds of metal ants. Aleksandra and Matthias had nearly six battalions crammed together in the cavern, which seemed much smaller now than when he had first ventured there with Rain. The camp had become almost unmanageable, and

Matthias spent most of his days simply ensuring soldiers did not end up in brawls after living in such close quarters for so long. Yet another reason Matthias, Rain, and Aleksandra decided to move up their schedule.

"Some things will never change," Matthias said, grinning. "Like how putrid your breath is."

He dodged a rock aimed for his head, thrown by an invisible hand.

"I know the rach listen to you more than most priestesses," Matthias pouted, "but that does not mean you can abuse their power."

"Crushing pests is not an abuse of power, in my opinion," Kadri said.

Matthias chuckled, and the pair continued their meal. "When do you leave?" he asked seriously. The nearby soldiers were busy packing their belongings and breaking down their tents.

"After I finish breakfast," Kadri said. "I'm afraid I may extend myself too far this time."

"Nonsense," Matthias said, "You have done more wonders than any other fury in a thousand years. They will be singing songs about you for another thousand. No one else can complete this task other than you."

"You're a terrible liar, you know," Kadri said, "and an even worse friend."

"The worst," Matthias said. He launched himself across the fire and threw his arms around the priestess. "Please be safe."

"You will be in more danger than I," Kadri said. "You are going into the wolf's den; I'm merely drawing them away."

Matthias held his oldest friend for a few more moments until she sat up and left him alone next to the fire. He could not lose her, at any cost.

Matthias stood by the mouth of the cavern as Kadri and a handful of furies led two battalions marching southward. The air shimmered, and four more battalions materialized on either side of the original host. It was a larger force than the rebels possessed altogether, but luckily the Kyriaki high command had no way of knowing their actual numbers.

"She can handle herself, you know," Aleksandra said, causing Matthias to jump. He hadn't noticed her sneak up next to him. "Watch out for that one; she will change the world. Though I believe that she already has."

"I know," Matthias breathed, looking out toward the fake army with pride. "How long do you think it will take Zsolt to notice?"

"He will dispatch his forces within the day," Aleksandra said. "A force that size marching on the main road to Tanaegra will attract attention. Six battalions are more than enough to take the small city. If we control the gap, Zsolt loses the access he sorely needs to Kyriak after all of the farms he has destroyed."

"Are the scouts already in location?" Matthias asked.

"Yes, we will know the moment Zsolt's forces pass our location," Aleksandra said, "Then all we have to do is wait until his forces are too far south to be of any help, then we make our move."

"Wait," Matthias said, testing the word in his mouth. He was not very fond of the concept of patience.

And wait they did. An entire day passed, and Matthias could do nothing but pace by the mouth of the cavern, anxiously scanning the horizon. He barely slept that night, plagued by terrible dreams of Kadri and Rain falling from the cliffs of the upper city. There was nothing he could do for his priestess friend now, but as each day passed, being apart from Rain was torture.

Two days passed before the scouts finally returned. Matthias was napping near the pond when he heard the call. He scrambled to his feet and dashed through the camp, eager for the latest report. Aleksandra was already waiting at the cave mouth when he arrived, looking eastward diligently. Two small shapes along the horizon, the scouts were less than a league away. Of course, Jonas and Taimo had been selected for the task, proving themselves to be the quickest and most effective scouts in the rebel army.

"Something is wrong," Aleksandra said as more shapes came into view behind the Devoted couple. "Vilja and her priestesses are returning with them."

Matthias' heart sank as he noticed the robed woman strolling behind the two scouts. Jonas and Taimo ran through the camp's outer defenses within a few moments, panting heavily.

"What news do you bring? Have the Kyriaki forces passed?" Aleksandra asked immediately. She apparently deemed the pair's intel more important than allowing the couple to catch their breath.

"Aye," Jonas said. "They are marching south, two legions, one Arachovian and one Kyriaki. Only soldiers. No cavalry."

"So we gathered," Aleksandra said, gesturing to the women who had almost nearly reached the cave.

The furies had been waiting along the main road to ambush the cavalry that Matthias presumed would be sent south to Tanaegra to prevent them from reaching Kadri. She did not have enough troops to defend against a party that size, let alone take Tanaegra. That had never been her goal. She was merely meant to draw the Kyriaki forces out of the city.

"Zsolt knows it's a trap," Matthias said, kicking himself. "According to Rain's estimates, he has at least that many soldiers left in Arachovia, not to mention his cavalry. He is not concerned about reaching Kadri in time because he has enough soldiers to reclaim Tanaegra while still having enough to effectively guard Arachovia."

Governor Zsolt was an intelligent man and played his hand to maintain his tactical advantage. The severe general divided his Kyriaki officers equally, so Kadri could not simply assassinate a few enemies to regain the forces following her. And there were still too many soldiers guarding the city for their plan to succeed.

"We have contingencies, Matthias," Aleksandra said reassuringly. "There are still three battalions at our disposal. We will still be able to draw enough of the Kyriaki out beyond the city."

"Ah," Matthias said, "are you sure about that? I think it is too risky."

They had discussed this strategy before. Aleksandra was to take the remaining soldiers along the main road to draw more of Zsolt's forces from the heavily guarded barracks in the lower city. They would only be drawn out a day's ride away and could easily wipe out Aleksandra's forces. The plan was near suicide.

"It is our best option in the current circumstances," Aleksandra said, "Zsolt will dispatch the remainder of his forces if I am seen at the front of ours. Otherwise, he will suspect that we have divided ourselves yet again. Which we have. And do not worry about my safety. You should know by now how hard I am to kill."

"Only too well, Aleksandra. But please take the furies," Matthias said, "According to Rain, there are enough furies gathered in Arachovia to help me accomplish my mission. Your chances are better with the might of the spirits behind you."

"I am going with you, captain," Vilja said firmly. "Silja must be in Arachovia, and I must be there to protect her."

"Very well."

The priestess seemed surprised by Matthias' quick acceptance, but Vilja had become a close friend, and he couldn't keep her from finding her sister.

"Then it is settled," Aleksandra said, "You will immediately lead our Devoted Company troops to Arachovia. I will simultaneously take my battalions slowly to the road, which should draw the remaining troops out far enough. Fate has prevented me from being by your side at the end, Matthias, but may the spirits have favor upon you."

"You as well, Aleksandra," Matthias said. "May the spirits protect you."

Matthias saluted her and prepared his troops; there were about sixty couples from the Devoted Company, over a third of its original force, but enough for Matthias to defeat Zsolt. He tried not to worry about the Heptarch, who had become his mentor and friend, but he could not help but think she was about to sacrifice herself. Even if Matthias and Rain's plan succeeded and the rebels took the city, they would never be able to send out reinforcements in time to save Aleksandra.

Time. It was all about timing. That is all Matthias could think as he ran north across the plains with Vilja and the Devoted at his back. Aleksandra was already heading east towards the main road with her battalions marching behind. The Devoted Company left the cave around midday and needed to reach its destination before sunset. They would have to run hard through the night, but they had rested enough the past few days.

This plan was messier than he intended; unforeseen circumstances caused them to split their forces three ways, sandwiched between two enemy strongholds and two deployed forces. There would be complications to deal with later even if Matthias and Rain succeeded in their mission, but he had to focus on what he could control, and that was to reach Arachovia as soon as possible. But most importantly, to reach Rain.

The sun was beginning to descend on the second day when Arachovia's mesa came into view. Matthias' company gave the city a wide berth, looping around its northern cliffs until they reached the banks of the River Palanthia in the east. By the time they arrived, Jonas and Taimo had joined their ranks. The couple had already scouted the main road to Tanaegra. Almost two legions had left the city walls around midday, marching to meet Aleksandra's forces. Matthias couldn't believe their good luck. Zsolt meant to crush the attacking force, sending out enough soldiers for the rebel's plan to prevail. The man must not have believed there were enough soldiers for a third attacking force. Hopefully, the cruel tyrant would be dead before the night was over.

Matthias led his troops to a bend in the river. The banks here were steep and tall enough to hide their numbers from the watchful eyes of the city above. Their hiding place was only a few hundred paces away from the cliff base. A walled compound was built against the rock, protecting one of the dozen lifts that led up to the upper city. The Kyriaki lightly guarded the fort, which would be an easy target for the Devoted Company's elite soldiers. Once the Devoted took the fort, the rickety wooden lift would be enough to carry their entire unit in one trip. But Matthias would not be leading them. There was only one way to signal Rain above, and that was in person. He bid farewell to Darius and Veiko, whom he had faith in to lead the others with honor and began to sneak south along the river with Vilja, Jonas, and Taimo. Before they took ten steps, Leonas stepped out of the ranks and blocked their way.

"I will not fight another battle without Bruno," Leonas said. "You must take me with you, captain."

Sneaking five people into the city would be risky, but Matthias did not want his arm torn off, so he reluctantly allowed the large fellow to join. Leonas moved surprisingly fast and silent for a man of his size; Matthias barely noticed him as they crept southward along the River Palanthia.

The sun had set by the time the small squad had reached the walls of the lower city. The tall battlements had been constructed centuries earlier along the riverbank. A large gate and protected harbor sat halfway down its width; Matthias could see red helmets along the wall. The port was one of the weakest points in the city's defenses, but that was not their destination.

Jonas and Taimo secretly entered the city dozens of times in the last few months, and Matthias had always wondered how they successfully snuck past the defenses without being seen. The young couple led the way and guided the group to where the city wall met the cliff's face. A few paces up, Matthias saw a shadow in the moonlight and quickly discovered a small crack.

Jonas promptly clambered up the rock wall and slipped into the dark slit, disappearing in seconds. Matthias drew near and sighed when he saw how thin it was; Leonas scowled at the tiny crevice.

"Allow me," Vilja said, placing her hands on the cliff wall.

The fury chanted quietly, and the wall hummed slightly. Suddenly the rock gave way and disintegrated into sand, dropping like a waterfall onto the riverbank below. Leonas smiled and climbed into the hole. Matthias clambered into the dark opening after him, glad that he was crawling through a narrow tunnel rather than shimmying through a tight crevice. The other end of the tunnel deposited him on the backside of an ancient and decrepit building. Matthias had never seen the place before, but from Rain's letters, he recognized the prison in which his lover had spent a few rotten weeks. It had been completely abandoned since Rain's stay, and they did not encounter any guards as the five made their way into the city.

Rain had described the horrors of the lower city to Matthias in his letters, but seeing was a much different thing than merely reading. Tears of anger welled in his eyes while Taimo and Jonas led them through the decrepit streets to the safe house. The civil guard had not repaired one burnt roof since the night of the Kyriaki invasion, dozens of poor souls hung by their necks in the squares, and starving beggars littered each corner.

The safe house was tiny, sparse, and empty. Jonas explained that the old veteran couple hiding there had already joined the others in the upper city. Taimo opened a trunk and revealed three sets of guard outfits with the house of Serriphine crest; he peered up at Leonas sheepishly.

"We did not know there would be more than three of us, captain," Taimo said, "Vilja will be able to pass fine by herself, they never stop priestesses, but Leonas will be an issue."

"Wait a moment. I'll take care of that," Leonas grunted and left the safe house quietly, leaving the others confused.

Not sure what to do, Matthias began equipping his armor and helm in silence, as did Jonas and Taimo. By the time the three had fully dressed, the door opened again, and Leonas walked in wearing the armor of a civil guard. Matthias thought he saw a dark stain on the sleeve and realized it was blood. Deciding not to ask questions, he cleared his throat.

"Now that we have a disguise for everyone, we should head out," Matthias said.

The group agreed and crept out of the safe house into the twisting streets; Jonas and Taimo led the way, walking with newfound swagger in the center of the road. Matthias followed suit, trying to imitate the gaits of the men in front of him.

"Vilja, go first and wait for us at the top," Taimo said quietly. "They won't look twice at you if you are alone, but it will raise an eyebrow if you are in the company of four guards."

Vilja nodded and walked forward, past the guards, through the guardhouse, and onto the stairs above. Like Taimo said earlier, not a single guard seemed to notice her. The group waited a few minutes, and then Jonas and Taimo strode forward directly at the guardhouse, Leonas and Matthias in tow.

"Ah, Godfrey, Julius, spent another night at the brothels, have we? Kind of early to be heading home," the old officer at the gate said in a raspy voice, greeting the couple like old friends. "But I don't recognize your companions."

"Met them in the brothel," Jonas said, his voice lowered to a deep baritone.

"Ah, I see," the grizzled guard said. "Well, have a good night."

Without missing a beat, the four passed the guard and began to ascend the steps after Vilja. Matthias arched an eyebrow at Jonas as they climbed. The man blushed and stared away abashedly. Matthias chuckled but soon grew quiet, his palms sweaty with anticipation as they climbed. He was so distracted by their journey that he had forgotten what was at its end.

Rain. Every step took him closer and closer to his love. It had been so long since he touched him that he could not wait any longer.

The upper city was quiet, but in much better condition than the section Matthias had just walked through. This angered him even more. He was too distracted to dwell on the inequality and eagerly marched after Jonas and Taimo toward the Shrine of Isemelith. It was a fitting place to reunite with his love, even though Matthias hadn't been since Anton rejected him. None of that mattered now; he simply needed to find Rain.

Finally, they reached the high hedge that surrounded the shrine, and Matthias gave a start when he saw a hulking shape lurking in the shadows under it. The wind whipped by him as Leonas sprinted forward at the dark figure. Matthias nearly drew his swords before Leonas threw his arms excitedly around the stranger and tackled it to the ground. The pale light soon revealed the man to be Bruno, who didn't care about being bowled over and was too busy kissing Leonas enthusiastically. The pair rolled around in the dirt before composing themselves.

Matthias could see the others blushing, but his chest swelled with joy. He was about to experience the same thing as these two men, and he could not wait a moment longer. Matthias ignored Bruno's greeting and tore off through the archway and down the hedged path. He could feel Rain's lips and arms around his body, his feet beating against the cobblestones as hard as his heartbeat in his chest.

The shrine was showered in ethereal moonlight and possessed an otherworldly beauty that Matthias hadn't noticed on his last visit. Rain stood in the middle, next to the central statue, pale skin glowing in the moonlight. Matthias made his way to his lover but stopped in his tracks. Rain was not alone.

Facing the curly-haired man was Hendrick. The two men were standing close together; Matthias leaned in close and had his hand on the small of Rain's back. The shorter man craned his neck upwards, meeting Hendrick's smoldering stare. And slowly, he brought his lips closer to Rain's face.

Matthias stopped in his tracks. The words "My love!" had already escaped his lips, causing the two men to turn towards him. Hendrick furrowed his brow in confusion, but Rain practically jumped in horrified, face pale with shock and guilt.

For the second time in his life, Matthias' heart broke in the Shrine of Isemelith.

20

Convergence

After Rain received Matthias' final letter, he began his preparations at once, sending word to every Devoted in the upper city and smuggling anyone he could from the lower city. When Zsolt only deployed half of his forces in response to Kadri's ploy, Rain became anxious, despite knowing there were contingencies for this particular outcome. Still, they were rapidly approaching the worst-case scenario. Then, only a few days later, a second force was dispatched from Arachovia, and Rain knew that it was finally time; the strike would happen that night. And soon, he would finally be reunited with the love of his life.

He alerted his troops expeditiously and commanded them to gather at their secret rendezvous by nightfall, a location in the city where no one would notice a large force of soldiers. A place citizens avoided more than the Shrine of Isemelith. Instead of joining the gathering forces, Rain took Bruno and headed to the shrine itself. He and Matthias decided they would meet there the night of the attack. He was filled with joy at the thought, though the familiar sense of guilt that had consumed him over the past few months followed in its wake.

There was nothing more he wanted in the world than to see Matthias; the letters they had exchanged had strengthened the pair's bond and sustained Rain through dark and difficult times. His guilt was rooted in the fact that he had entirely left out Hendrick in all of his letters; Matthias did not even know he had joined their cause. Rain did not have the courage to tell the man about his former lover in his first letters, feeling guilty about Hendrick's surprise kiss. Soon too much time had passed to reveal it, even though he knew his omission would only complicate things further.

Rain knew he would always care for the disgraced Heptarch, but his feelings for Matthias were stronger than anything he had felt before. Merely looking at Hendrick reminded Rain of the heartache and betrayal of their relationship. His reservations, however, did not prevent Hendrick from trying his hardest to win back the affections of the commander. Flowers sent to his room, daily professions of love, attempts at more non-consensual kisses. Rain began to avoid Hendrick as much as possible and used Bruno as an emissary. As a result, he hadn't seen the former Heptarch in weeks. Rain would never see him again if he could have things his way, but they needed him if they hoped to reclaim the city. In fact, Hendrick's villa had rapidly become home to dozens of Devoted soldiers.

When he and Bruno arrived at the shrine, he stationed the giant man at the entry and entered alone. Rain stopped in his tracks when he saw Hendrick waiting for him.

"You are supposed to be with the others in the Temple," Rain said, "What are you doing here?"

"What I should have done a long time ago," Hendrick said, looking over at Rain longingly, "Something you have asked of me, and I was too foolish to grant you, my love. I want to say the Vows with you. Tonight."

Rain was stunned. The guilt that had lurked on the edges of his mind now washed over him. He had tried his best to keep Hendrick at a distance, but he also hadn't told the man about his love for Matthias. There was no telling what the temperamental man would have done if he had known.

"Hendrick, this is hardly the time," Rain said in hushed tones, closing the space between them.

"On the contrary," Hendrick said, "There is no telling what will happen in the battle to come, and I want to be Devoted to you if this is our last night on earth."

Rain scoffed. "So after years of me begging and pleading for you to bond yourself to me after I bared my heart and gave my life to you, you denied me your loyalty because you were obsessed with your future. Now, on the brink of our deaths, you may not have a future, and that is the time you are willing to Devote yourself to me."

"It is not like that," Hendrick pleaded. He grabbed Rain on the small of his back and pulled him close.

Rain was taken aback by the move and stared up at the man he once loved, there was no denying the heated look on his face, and he couldn't help the dormant feelings that crept to the surface. Hendrick no longer smelled of stale wine and had cleaned himself up since their first meeting after the invasion. It felt nice to be in his strong arms once more, and for a moment, Rain forgot himself, forgot everything the man put him through. Hendrick leaned in for a kiss.

"My love!" a voice called from the other side of the shrine.

Rain jumped in horror and saw Matthias standing at the entrance. His joy quickly fell off his face and was replaced with deep agony.

"Matthias," Rain said, pushing Hendrick away, desperate to create distance, "please—"

Hendrick interrupted him by grabbing him by the wrist, and lips pursed in agitation. "What is the meaning of this? Why did he call you that?"

Rain faced Hendrick, unsure of what to say, "Matthias and I—"

"The night of the gala…I saw the two of you dance," Hendrick said, his grip growing tighter, "You were in love with him this entire time, weren't you? Then why did you let me kiss you?" His face darkened. "You used me!"

"I needed you, yes." Rain said, "But I did not say or do anything to suggest I loved you. And you kissed me without my consent or desire."

"But you kept it from me," Matthias said, his voice trembling. "If it did not mean anything, you wouldn't have hidden it from me."

Across the small courtyard, tears streamed down Matthias' face. The damage of Rain's lies had already been done. Hendrick leered down at him, brimming with anger and malice. He was caught between the two men who glared at him, unsure what to say. Rain's analytical mind reeled as he tried to find the right words. He had lost them both in a single second. After an eternity of silence, Bruno entered the shrine arm-in-arm with Leonas and Jonas, Taimo and Vilja directly behind.

"We must be off to the Temple of Sorilea before—" Jonas said, cutting off when he saw the state of the three men.

"Yes, we must go," Hendrick said, his voice hollow. "We have little time to waste."

"You will still come?" Rain said, "After all of that, you will still help?"

"Of course," Hendrick said flatly, "I am not the monster you believe I am, Rain. Arachovia is my home, and I will fight for her. It was never about you, anyway."

The sullen man shoved Rain aside and strode across the shrine, glowering at Matthias and gesturing for the group to follow him. Tears still falling down his blank face, Matthias stared past Rain and gazed at the statue in the center. Rain rushed to the man's side, but Matthias ignored him, concentrating on the shrine.

"Matthias…what I said was true, I no longer have—" Rain began.

"I always thought our first time at the Shrine would be different," Matthias interrupted, his voice cracking. "But it seems the spirits have decided to make this place a reminder of my place in this world. To be alone. You will never be over your feelings for Hendrick. I know that now. We shared one night together, and that is all it was to you."

"But I am over my feelings for him! Matthias, you must—" Rain said, but the distraught man raised a hand to cut him off.

"Hendrick is right. We have no time to waste," he said, turning and following the others into the city beyond.

Rain hurried after him, begging him to respond, but the man ignored his pleas and walked briskly until they reached the others. They continued in silence, with Jonas leading the way. Both Hendrick and Matthias ignored Rain as they made their way through the city. He decided it was best to keep quiet for the time being. His love problems did not take precedence over the freedom of Arachovia, though Rain would gladly give it all up just to see Matthias smile once more.

The neighborhood surrounding the Temple of Sorilea mainly consisted of lavish gardens, various shrines, and a few villas owned by the more pious noble families. The temple itself was a low and sprawling building with dozens of annexes, wings, and courtyards surrounding a towering dome in the middle of the complex. It was home to scores of chapels and shrines dedicated to the thousands of rach that priestesses communed with and relied on, some were tiny and dedicated to a single spirit, while others were large sanctuaries that celebrated a group of spirits. Most spaces in the gilded labyrinth were rarely used and, in those cases, only by priestesses. It was a perfect place to hide an army.

Once they drew near, Rain quickened his pace and led the pack through the nearest courtyard and into the maze of long halls. He had chosen a rather large chapel dedicated to the spirits of death to gather his forces that evening. It was a dusty and massive chamber with dozens of statues for each of the deities, and due to their morbid nature, worshipers rarely visited.

When they reached the heavy iron doors of the chapel, Rain knocked on it and a priestess greeted him. The woman had short-cropped hair and a permanent scowl on her face.

After saving the lower city from destruction by fire, Silja had snuck back to the temple's safety. Rain had found her a few days after his discussion with Hendrick, and Silja went to work gathering the furies hiding in the temple or throughout the city. The door had barely opened before Vilja rushed forward and threw her arms around her sister. The pair held their embrace for a few moments, and Rain could not help but be jealous of their reunion. It seemed as if everyone in their small group would have a sweet reunion that evening but him, though his own actions were to blame for the fiasco at the shrine. He shook the thought out of his head and tried to focus on the task at hand.

Over a hundred Devoted pairs sat throughout the large chamber, intermingled with a few dozen furies. When Rain walked through the doorway, the men and women leaped to their feet and gathered close, soldiers scooping up their shields, ready for battle. All of their careful planning and organizing had led up to this night.

Rain opened his mouth to speak but was pushed aside by Hendrick, who swiftly made his way to the center of the room and began to address the Devoted gathered there. It had taken Hendrick a while to regain their trust after he swore fealty to Zsolt and abandoned them. However, Hendrick reverted to his charismatic and passionate self, allowing his subordinates to remember why they loved and followed him in the first place.

"Here we are, my friends," Hendrick began, "on the eve of battle. Our city has been ravaged and terrorized by a foreign power for too long. A malevolent dictator seeks to exploit our people and leech off the bounty. The prosperity that the strength of your shields and the might of your blades secured. Tonight, we show them the glory Arachovia has garnered over the centuries was not created by its buildings or its lands but by the hearts of its defenders. By you. Now join me tonight to take it back!"

The warriors knocked on their shields deftly, in unison, they could not cry out or chant since stealth was still paramount to their mission, but their drumbeats showed their passion just the same. Rain grimaced at the cheesy speech. How could he have loved a man that pompous and full of himself? He made brief eye contact with Matthias, who was reacting similarly. The lanky man smiled for a moment, but soon the pained expression returned to his face, and he turned away. For that fleeting moment, Rain had forgotten what occurred in the shrine and hoped that one day he could reclaim the bond of the man who was not only his lover but his closest friend.

Time was still of the essence, and Hendrick wasted none of it as he led the small force out of the chapel and into the maze of halls. As they reached the exit, Vilja chanted softly and sent a small ball of fire up into the night sky. It flashed through the air in seconds, so fast that no one would have seen it unless they were looking in that exact spot. But, of course, Matthias' forces lying in wait at the mesa's base were scouting that same patch of sky, waiting for that signal to overtake the small fort below.

The Devoted padded softly out of the Temple and onto the cobblestone streets, one pair at a time. It was slow-moving but proved to be the best way to avoid detection. Rain marched at the end of the train next to the furies. He hadn't tried to partner with Matthias, though he was horrified to find him paired with Hendrick. The two led the front, stopping at each corner to ensure the path forward was clear. He dismissed the petty behavior, which was somewhat justified, but he could not imagine the two men fighting together.

They encountered a few civil guards on patrol; Hendrick and Matthias dispatched them with relative ease before they could sound an alarm. They wound through the city until they finally reached the small square on the city's edge that held the lift station. A short wall separated the sturdy wooden frame of the lift that jutted out into the inky abyss. According to Rain's scouting efforts, about twenty civil guards stood in a loose formation next to the wall. They would be easy to overcome, and soon the Devoted Company would be complete for the first time since the invasion.

"Form up!" Hendrick said, not caring to conceal his voice. It did not matter if the civil guards heard, there was nothing they could do against the mighty Devoted Company.

Shield-brothers linked up into four neat lines, Hendrick and Matthias front and center, and Rain brought up the rear among the furies. He had imagined this night very differently, but there was nothing he could do now.

At Hendrick's call, the formation of Devoted lurched forward, shield high and swords summoned and extended like spears. They marched swiftly into the small square, but Rain's hair stood on end before they made it to the center. Something was amiss.

"Halt!" Rain cried, but it was too late.

Another score of guards sprung up from behind the short wall. Suddenly, the streets on the left and right filled with civil guards and Kyriaki soldiers. The road behind them rumbled at the force of hundreds of armored boots that blocked their exit. Within seconds, the Devoted Company was surrounded by enemy soldiers.

It was a trap. And they had walked directly into it.

"Circle!" Hendrick bellowed, and the formation shifted instantaneously, shields pointed outward defensively. Rain remained outside of the circle, along with the furies. They chanted and the air around them shimmered into a protective barrier as strong as any shield.

"Hold!" a thin voice called from the left-hand road. A man walked out from the line, slender and silver-haired. Heptarch Paulius. His face was smug and contorted into a nasty sneer, body covered in elaborate Insignis armor.

"Bastard," Hendrick seethed.

"You never were an intelligent man, Hendrick," Paulius called out from the safety of his troops. "Anyone with a brain knew that you relied on the strategies of others, but you were a fool not to think we were watching you. We raided your villa a few hours ago and I will give you some friendly advice. If you are planning a coup, do not leave evidence of your plans lying around for anyone to find. I am shocked you have survived this long with a skull that thick."

Rain flinched. The idiot. He had been careful to destroy every letter and plan he had drawn up. On the other hand, Hendrick did not have the sense to do the same. He cursed the day he asked that man for help.

"You will not leave here alive, you sniveling weasel," Hendrick said, shaking in anger. He and Matthias were on the other side of the formation, and Rain had trouble seeing either.

The two Heptarchs continued to exchange vitriol, but Rain was busy analyzing his current circumstances. Despite the protective barrier conjured by the furies, he felt vulnerable outside the formation. It could not hold forever, and eventually, the collision between the two forces would crush them when the fighting began. The weakest spot in the enemy defenses was the formation nearest the lift, which was also precisely where Rain needed to go. He slowly motioned to Vilja and Silja, and the group of furies around him slowly inched their way around the Devoted, in the direction of the lift. He knew enemies constantly underestimated the robed women in battle. They were always seen as less of a threat, even though everything Rain had witnessed proved otherwise. He hoped their underestimation would be their saving grace.

"I have had enough of this gloating," Paulius said, turning to his troops. "Destroy them."

The small square erupted into chaos as the Kyriaki and civil guard rushed forward from all sides. Rain had already drawn his armor, sword, and shield; he rushed at the thin line in the formation near the lift. Vilja, on his right, lashed her hands out and sent a dozen enemies flying into the darkness with her signature gust of wind, their cries echoed through the night. Dozens of fireballs slammed into others when Rain crashed into the first guard. He hacked his way through their ranks, desperately trying to reach the lift.

"Vilja, with me!" he cried as he leaped over the wall, slicing through another guard.

The other half of the Devoted Company were waiting at the bottom of the lift, and they were his only hope out of this mess. The long-haired woman followed him over the wall, gracefully pushing the remaining three soldiers over the cliff's edge. When they neared the lift, Rain's heart stopped. The platform wasn't there. He inspected the frame above and realized there were no ropes. Someone had cut them long before the ambush. The lift was useless.

He peered over the side and could see the glint of a hundred Insignis blades in the moonlight far below. They were ready and waiting, but now there was no way of them ascending. Frantic, Rain surveyed the square, which was filled shoulder to shoulder with the enemy, pressing in. Silja and the other furies were straining to keep the enemy at bay along the short wall but had already suffered a few casualties. The Devoted held their formation, though it was only a matter of time until the hundreds of soldiers would push in. Rain scanned the battle and noticed that more red-armored fighters marching toward the courtyard. Every soldier Zsolt had left in the city was about to descend upon them.

He turned his attention back to the Devoted, straining to find Matthias. He had to save Matthias.

"Can you lift them?" Rain cried over the din of the battle. "Can you lift the others from above?"

Vilja furrowed her brow and began to chant. The wind howled around them and then ceased entirely. "The winds could propel them upwards, but I cannot promise any of them could survive the journey so close to the cliffs."

Rain's mind raced for another solution, anything that could get them out of this situation. Then it came to him. If he could not bring the reinforcements to the fight, he could try to bring the fight to them. It had been a joke he and Matthias used to make when they talked about making a better Arachovia. A united Arachovia.

"Then bring it down." Rain said firmly, "Bring it all down."

"Bring what down?" Vilja said.

A priestess near them screamed, chest impaled with a sword.

"The mesa!" Rain cried frantically, "Make the earth swallow it whole so we are level with the plains."

"You won't risk the lives of the Devoted, but you will risk the lives of everyone in the city?" Vilja said wryly.

"If we lose the Devoted, the city is as good as lost," Rain explained, "Besides, Matthias said he has seen you do similar things with trenches, and the rach won't allow the city to be destroyed."

"That is different!" Vilja said, "And I wouldn't be able to do it alone."

"Then chant loudly so the others can join you!" Rain said, gesturing to the few dozen robed women next to them.

"Fine," Vilja said, "but this might destroy us all."

"Good," Rain said. "Now try it."

Vilja nodded and began to chant loudly, her voice echoing off the cliff-side, the shocked priestesses near her began to turn, eyes wide with shock and fear. At Rain's behest, they began to join her, forty voices booming through the night. The ground started to shake, and Rain grabbed hold of the short wall. Men screamed and toppled to the ground as the mesa shifted. The stones beneath his feet cracked slightly and shingles flew off the nearby roofs.

Rain looked off the cliffs as the mesa sank into the ground. For centuries the great city of Arachovia sat in its place near the clouds, keeping it safe from enemies. Rain and a handful of priestesses would change that forever.

21

Reclamation

Matthias lifted his buckler high, locking it in place with Hendrick's metal shield as the Kyriaki pressed in from all sides. The disgraced Heptarch was not who he had imagined fighting alongside this night, but things had changed in the Shrine of Isemelith. Surprisingly, he decided to join Hendrick's side and was more surprised when the man did not refuse.

Throughout the evening, up until now, Matthias had remained in a fugue state. After seeing Hendrick almost kiss Rain, his initial shock and sorrow quickly faded into numbness. Only now did the adrenaline of battle make the pain and anger surge back like a tidal wave. Despite his feelings, he could not stop thinking about Rain, trying to see the glint of his steel armor through the chaos of the square. Matthias couldn't help feeling guilty that Rain stood outside the circular formation, unprotected, but there was nothing he could do about it now.

The enemy crashed in, throwing Matthias against the buckler of the Devoted behind him. A poor civil guard ran directly into his sword, impaling himself. He retracted the metal and lashed out again, finding another unfortunate soul. Hendrick bellowed, slashing and cutting enemies down as they charged forth. Despite the overwhelming number of Kyriaki, the Devoted Company maintained its formation. Not one man allowed his lover to fall to an enemy blade. Matthias hoped that the man next to him would do the same, but Hendrick had every reason to resent him and let him fall. Matthias missed feeling the safety of Rain by his side in battle. The enemy soldiers kept coming, pressing in until Matthias felt like the sea of metal and humans would crush him.

The air filled with shrill chanting, and the world shifted. Matthias tumbled over onto his back as the earth buckled beneath his feet, avoiding the flailing swords and shields crashing down around him on all sides. The stones beneath his feet cracked, and he could barely hear the screams of horror around him over the rumbling din of moving earth. Hendrick dropped next to him with a grunt, shoving an enemy soldier as he went. The ground continued to shake, and Hendrick and Matthias helped each other up onto their knees. Matthias retracted his swords and discarded his heavy wooden buckler. He would try to finish a battle with a shield someday. The rest of the battlefield was in a similar state, but most of the survivors remained prone on the violently shaking ground; it took all of Matthias' strength to stay upright. Leaning against the massive Hendrick certainly seemed to help. The men scanned their surroundings calmly, unphased by the quaking earth below.

"What are the furies thinking?" Hendrick shouted, looking towards the mesa's edge. "What sort of magic is this?"

Matthias followed his gaze, forty furies were still standing and chanting despite the tremors. Beyond them was the lift frame, sans any rope. Rain hung on tightly next to the women, bracing himself against the low wall that separated the square and the lift. Matthias found himself smiling. Unlike the others, he knew exactly what was happening. Rain and Matthias flippantly joked about such an occurrence months ago, hoping it would somehow destroy the inequality that plagued the city. Now Rain was doing it through the raw power of the furies. He was eliminating the mesa entirely.

"Paulius sabotaged the lift," Matthias explained, "Cutting us off from our reinforcements. Rain decided to bring the fight to them."

Hendrick's mouth hung open as he realized what Matthias meant. Then he pursed his lips and stood up, pulling Matthias with him. Bending his knees and keeping his feet wide, he managed to stay upright without Hendricks's help.

"Devoted! Stand up and fight before our enemy recovers!" Hendrick called, urging his troops. The shell-shocked soldiers scrambled to their feet clumsily as the earth was still shaking uncontrollably. Hendrick turned to Matthias and gestured outward towards the sea of writhing soldiers. "Matthias, with me."

Hendrick drew his sword and stepped through the masses, most of whom were still struggling on the ground. Stepping over the fallen enemy, the man savagely stabbed each soldier he passed. Matthias followed but could not bring himself to be as cruel as Hendrick. He only slashed at a few enemies who had managed to stand and merely kicked at the prostrate soldiers who had avoided Hendrick's sword. Behind him, many of the Devoted had climbed to their feet and mimicked Hendrick, mercilessly cutting through the defenseless Kyriaki forces. Matthias' stomach turned. There was no honor in this. This was not how he would have led his forces, but unfortunately, Hendrick outranked him. No matter how badly he wanted to change that fact.

As Hendrick and Matthias continued through the crowd, leaving a trail of blood in their wake, he could see where the large man was leading him. A man adorned in Insignis armor was only a few paces away, struggling to his feet. Heptarch Paulius sported a gash on his forehead, blood trickling out from behind his helm. Once his eyes reached theirs, he let out a roar of anger. Only a few more paces, and they would catch him off guard. The others around him were trying to stand up in vain. They were almost upon him.

Then the earth grew still. Paulius was obscured from view by a line of shields, and suddenly, enemies who had finally regained their footing surrounded the two Arachovian officers. Matthias held out his blades. There were too many to overcome, and they had traveled too far from the rest of the company for reinforcements to send aid. He looked over at Hendrick with a somber face of resignation.

A battle cry tore through the night. Matthias whirled around, and over dozens of heads, he saw what used to be the lift station. Instead of an empty night sky, three tall walls were beyond the knot of priestesses and broken wooden frame. A hundred armed soldiers waited, weapons drawn, beyond the fractured lift, Veiko and Darius at the forefront. Matthias noticed a figure amid the furies, who signaled the force forward with a hand cased in gray metal. Rain.

With a defiant yell, the other half of the Devoted Company lurched forward, shields up and swords extended, charging behind Rain. The furies quickly parted and allowed the soldiers to leap over the wall and crash into the unsuspecting Kyriaki. In moments, the reinforcements tore through the smallest part of the enemy and joined their allies near the center. Finally, Rain had unified the Devoted Company once more.

Matthias had no time to celebrate, dodging an arching sword and parrying another slash simultaneously. Rain's charge had pulled the focus of many of the soldiers surrounding Matthias and Hendrick, but they were still in immediate danger. Hendrick bellowed and swung his sword, shaped like a heavy battle-ax, cutting through men. He was focused only on Paulius. Matthias hurried behind him; fighting alongside Hendrick was nothing like his experience with Rain. He could not get close to the large man, who swung his weapon wildly and chaotically. The ferocious man barely noticed his companion, giving Matthias no aid. So he had to protect Hendrick's rear and his own at once. It was exhausting. Fire fell from the sky, exploding on unsuspecting Kyriaki forces, burning them alive. The furies were standing on the short wall where the cliffs used to be, protected by the entire host of the Devoted.

A long, thin sword lashed out from behind, and Matthias barely caught it between his two blades before it sunk into his flesh. The needle-like sword retracted and shot out once again towards Matthias' midsection. Bending his body, he threw himself to one side, but the pin-sized blade grazed his side, and he screamed in pain. Matthias followed the weapon to its bearer and realized it was Paulius himself. Somehow the man had snuck through the ranks unnoticed and decided to strike at them from behind. Hendrick heard Matthias yelp, noticing him seemingly for the first time. The crescent moons of Hendrick's blade flew through the air, cutting the stones where Paulius had been only seconds before. But the aging Heptarch was surprisingly agile and light on his feet. Paulius sidestepped and thrust his needle-like blade at Matthias' throat. Hendrick threw his massive shoulder at Matthias, knocking the wind out of him and pushing him out of the path of Paulius' blade. The hair-thin sword glanced off Hendrick's shield as he barreled forward. The smug noble pulled his blade back into a thicker shape to parry the second swing of the ax head expertly.

The instant Matthias fell to the ground, he shaped both of his swords like scythes and sliced at the man's ankles. Paulius vaulted forward without missing a beat and easily avoided both swipes, landing spryly on his feet as the blades cut through the Kyriaki next to him. Matthias had always believed the conniving Heptarch had gained his military position due to his political prowess and fortune, but the man proved to be an unparalleled swordsman.

As soon as his feet touched the ground, Paulius launched a flurry of swipes at Hendrick, who grunted and desperately swatted them away with his sword and shield, taking a step back. Paulius shaped his blade into its preferred state, long and thin, and left dozens of minor cuts on Hendrick's exposed skin. The two Heptarchs exchanged blows in intense combat while Matthias climbed to his feet, fighting off a couple of Kyriaki who had decided to take advantage of his prone state. Then Matthias rotated and whipped his blades at Paulius.

Instinctively, the silver-haired man whirled around and blocked both blows with ease and, as quick as lightning, twirled again to block Hendrick's strike. Even with three blades vying for his neck, the pompous man avoided them without breaking a sweat. A few Devoted had pushed through the fray and engaged with the enemy, allowing Hendrick and Matthias to focus their combined energies on Paulius. The three of them danced around each other in a flurry of dark gray metal.

While the battle raged around them, the enemy and allied soldiers alike kept out of their way, careful to avoid being the collateral damage of the storm of steel. As partners, Matthias and Hendrick were clumsy and could not seem to time their blows correctly. Paulius' blade and reflexes were too quick, and he had the two of them on the ropes. But he was weaker and had kept his shield retracted, relying on his blade. A thought suddenly sprouted in Matthias' mind. He formed a hook with his right blade and swung it at Paulius.

The man blocked it, but as he swept upward, the needle hit the end of the hook. Matthias swung his hook-shaped left blade from the other direction, locking Paulius' sword between the two, and pulled them down with all his might. Matthias pulled down his sword arm, and his opponent's eyes grew wide. He was too weak to resist. The second Matthias trapped the Heptarch's weapon between his, Hendrick swung his sword at Paulius. The pompous man screamed and began to summon his shield to protect him, but it was too late. The great sword of Hendrick fell on him and decapitated the man in one grisly motion. His helmet clattered to the ground, quickly following his limp body.

"Civil guard, hear me!" Hendrick screamed, picking Paulius' head up from the ground and brandishing it in the air. "Heptarch Paulius is dead! You are Arachovians, not Kyriaki! As your Heptarch, I order you to fight the Kyriaki!"

The civil guard around them grew still, shifting on their

feet, unsure of themselves. A few dropped their swords in surrender, while others decided to heed Hendrick's request to fight off the Kyriaki. Soon there were more allies than enemies in the square. However, many civil guards chose to run down the main road, away from battle. Suddenly, arrows sprung forth in the night sky, colliding with the retreating guard. A line of red officers came into view, each armed with a bow, flanking an office in particularly intricate red armor.

"Zsolt!" Hendrick screamed. "Your ally is dead, and your forces are losing. Come face me and end this!"

The Kyriaki leader summoned his great-sword made of red metal; it gleamed evilly in the moonlight. The red-clad man stepped forward, and the battle seemed to dissolve before him, opening up a path between him and Hendrick. Matthias stood shoulder to shoulder with Hendrick, blades drawn. Then, Zsolt stopped walking and raised his free arm in the sky. Matthias furrowed his brow, confused.

Then the arm dropped. The world slowed as dozens of arrows flew through the air directly at them from the archers behind Zsolt. They cut through Kyriaki and Arachovians alike, slicing through air, flesh, metal, and bone.

In a flurry of motion, Hendrick whirled around and threw himself in front of Matthias, protecting him from the deadly volley. There was a sickening sound of arrows tearing through the Heptarch's body, and the pair tumbled to the ground.

Matthias struggled on the cobblestone, turning the man over to his side. At least a dozen arrows protruded from his back. His chest was heaving, his breath rasping, as a pool of blood began to form beneath him. The clicking boots of Zsolt and his soldiers clacked against the ground as they advanced.

"We must get you to the furies," Matthias said. "Hold on just a little longer."

"No, it is too late for me," Hendrick said, "but not for you. You must leave me."

Zsolt was only a few dozen paces away; the general hacked through a civil guard, jaw clenched and focused on Matthias.

"Why?" Matthias said, "Why would you die for me?"

"For him," Hendrick said, "You must survive for his sake."

"Rain?" Matthias said, "But he—"

"He loves you," Hendrick insisted.

A great cry tore through the night, and a column of Devoted crashed into their area of the square. Matthias could see Rain leading the charge as they crashed into the Kyriaki archers. Zsolt spun around and lunged at the men, forgetting Hendrick and Matthias. The lanky captain propped the larger man up, desperately searching to see if a fury was close, but it was too late. The man was dying.

"Promise me you will keep him safe. Protect him with your heart, mind, and body," Hendrick said, coughing profusely.

"I...I will, Hendrick," Matthias said. "I promise you."

"Then I can leave this world happy. Knowing my love will finally have the Vows he deserved," Hendrick said, voice wavering. "Good luck to you, Matthias."

Matthias cradled the man, his breath grew laborious, and his body grew limp. The once-great leader lay in his arms in a pool of blood. Matthias had envied and hated the man for quite some time, but the moment the light left Hendrick's eyes, he couldn't help but weep. Matthias bore no love for the man, but his final words did more to ease his pain than anything he could have imagined. The man's last act saved his life, and he would never forget it.

Suddenly he felt a presence above him; realizing he was

still in the middle of a battle, he wearily began to lift his sword in defense. The sword clattered to the ground when he saw it wasn't a Kyriaki soldier but Rain standing above him. The small town square was almost empty, save for the dead and wounded. Matthias gingerly set Hendrick's head on the ground and stood up slowly. Rain looked down with a blank look of shock at the body.

"Rain," Matthias said, "I am so sorry, I could not prote—"

Rain pulled him close and threw his arms around him in a tight embrace, cutting Matthias' words short. Rain's strong hands held him close, and his soft lips were on his own before Matthias realized it.

"All that matters is that you are alive," Rain whispered, kissing him once more. "I could not bear it if something happened to you."

Matthias gave in to the kiss, despite his mixed feelings. Regardless of Hendrick's confession, Rain still had a lot to answer for, but it felt good to be in his arms. They had both survived the fight thus far.

"This place cleared out quickly," Matthias said, gesturing to the empty square. "Where is the battle now?"

"Over," Rain said, gesturing to the plains beyond. Dark shapes ran along the horizon in the pale light of early morning. "Zsolt and his forces fled the moment the tide of battle turned. The man is too wise to continue a hopeless battle."

"So the city is saved?" Matthias said, smiling. Rain did not reciprocate one in return.

"For now," Rain said. "No doubt Zsolt will try to rally his previously deployed forces at the garrison at Tanaegra and attempt to retake the city, which has considerably fewer defenses now, thanks to me."

"And I always thought I was the dramatic one," Matthias said, looking around at the plains around them. The only thing that marked where the mesa had been was the low-lying wall that surrounded what once was the upper city. "When I said we should do our best to bring equality to the upper and lower city, this wasn't what I had in mind."

"It was your idea," Rain said, pretending to be offended. "I specifically remember you suggesting this exact scenario."

"You really need to understand what a joke is, my love," Matthias said. His voice stuttered when the last words dropped out of his mouth. He had forgotten himself and his conflicted feelings.

"I…I am sorry, you must know that," Rain said sincerely. "What happened between me and Hend—"

Matthias put a hand up to Rain's lips. "I know. But you truly hurt me, Rain, and it will take some time to heal. Please allow me that."

Rain nodded. His face grew serious as he pushed his emotions aside, scanning the carnage around them. "Very well. For now, let us assess the damage and see what we can do with the survivors."

"And do our best to avoid the nobles," Matthias said, gesturing to the buildings around them. They were mostly intact, but many had bowing walls or caved roofs. "They will flay you alive once they realize you were behind this."

"They will forgive me one day," Rain said, "and things will be better this way."

The pale sun began to rise above the dusty plains, shedding light on the chaotic city. Furies carefully stepped through the casualties, healing the wounded as they went. Citizens in dusty clothes carefully peeked their heads out of doorways, mouths agape when they saw the plains around them.

As Rain and Matthias strode through the streets, pair by pair, the Devoted Company joined them, most having survived the brutal night. Grizzled Arvo and Gvidas. Burly Bruno and Leonas. Spry Jonas and Taimo. And finally, beaming Darius and Veiko. The final pair hugged Matthias tightly before falling in line behind them. The triumphant Devoted walked into the city they had destroyed and saved in one night.

22

Coronations

Smoke from the hundreds of funeral pyres lingered in the air and slowly dissipated into the morning sky. Dozens of priestesses danced around the fires, their robes flowing in the gentle breeze, which carried their anguished voices across the plains. Hundreds of mourners had poured out of the city to pay their respects, clumping between the pyres and the ancient city's fortifications. Matthias hung off to the side, watching the flames climb high and carry the souls of the men and women who had lost their lives five nights earlier.

Aleksandra stoically stared at the somber display from her place at the front of the crowd. She returned to the city with half her troops the day after Matthias and Rain reclaimed Arachovia. According to her, the entire valley felt and heard the mesa fall to the earth. Many thought the world was about to open and swallow them whole. Luckily, the tremors scattered the Kyriaki forces sent to destroy her. However, she still had to fight her way to the city, losing many good men and women in the process. Not one Kyriaki officer in her path survived.

Naturally, Aleksandra oversaw the city's recovery since she was only one of three Arachovian Heptarchs left alive. The other two survivors were weak-minded men who previously pledged loyalty to Zsolt. Matthias was thankful for her arrival, for he had been too mentally and emotionally exhausted to assume leadership. Matthias slept most of the hours before her arrival. Aleksandra promptly set about reclaiming order, clearing the streets of corpses, and chasing out lingering Kyriaki troops. Rain had compiled a list of high nobles, including his parents, who had aided Zsolt in his coup; Aleksandra expeditiously rounded up each of them. They were currently sitting in the dilapidated prison in what once was the lower city, awaiting judgment.

Aleksandra was more than displeased by how their mission had unfolded. Zsolt was still alive, his forces rapidly reforming in the south, the Arachovians wounded, and their city less fortified than it had been in centuries. Dozens of Arachovian soldiers who had deserted the Kyriaki armies flooded into the city each day, but it wouldn't be enough to defend the city against an attack.

On her first day back, Aleksandra commanded the furies to walk around the city's northern perimeter, tracing the path that used to be the mesa cliffs, raising the short wall into similarly high fortifications as the ones on the southern side. The nobles were less thrilled when Aleksandra commanded the robed women to destroy the short wall that used to lie on the southern cliffs rather than raising them to separate what used to be the upper and lower city. Much like Rain and Matthias, she was also hopeful for a better Arachovia.

His eyes drawn southward, Matthias scanned the plains for

any sign of movement, just as he had done every morning since the fall. Kadri and her two battalions still hadn't returned to the city, even though five days would have been plenty of time for her to make the journey. So many different scenarios flowed through his head, and most of them resulted in Kadri's death. Thousands of Kyriaki soldiers lay between her position and Arachovia, and her force was considerably smaller than Aleksandra's. Kadri's survival chances were slim, and Matthias was powerless to change that. All he could do was wait.

Rain stood on the other side of the mourners, gazing into the flames with a blankly serene expression. Matthias had not spoken to him since the night the mesa fell, but it was finally time to discuss what had happened at the shrine. Mustering up the courage, Matthias willed himself through the crowd to speak. He carried too many thoughts and emotions over the past few days for his liking and desperately needed the man to hear them. Rain was only a few paces away when Matthias felt a hand on his shoulder. Turning, he met Aleksandra's intense gaze, her jaw firmly clenched resolutely.

"Please follow me," Aleksandra said quietly, not to disturb the surrounding mourners. "We must have a discussion."

Silently, Matthias followed her through the crowd, looking back at Rain with regret. Aleksandra's tone left no room for negotiation, and his discussion with the handsome comman- der would have to wait a bit longer. The pair strode through the front gates of Arachovia and into the city.

The streets were abuzz with people scurrying between buildings. Merchants were hawking their wares, and soldiers were helping citizens rebuild walls and re-thatch roofs. Alek- sandra and Matthias garnered a lot of attention as they passed.

He could hear his new moniker, Two Blades, whispered as they went. It was an odd feeling, being so well known by so many. Of course, every noble gossiped about him when he enlisted, but they did that secretly, behind his back. Now every Arachovian knew Matthias' name, not for his misfortunes but for his courage and contributions to saving Arachovia. The city was still in mortal peril, with thousands of Kyriaki forces scattered in the surrounding plains. Matthias was reminded of that daily when he saw farming families streaming into the city by the droves, abandoning their farms and land from the chaotic soldiers who burned their homes and stole their crops.

"What is this about, Aleksandra?" As they made their way northward through the winding streets, Matthias said, "We have barely spoken since you arrived."

"We must prepare you for the elections," Aleksandra said simply. "They will take place midday."

"Elections?" Matthias said, stunned. "The Kyriaki could be at our gates any minute. I don't think this is the right time for something like that."

"That is why they should take place this instant," Aleksandra said. "Only three Heptarchs remain, and the other two are hair-brained fools. We will need leadership in the battles to come, leaders that the whole of Arachovia will respect and follow. I should have held them the day I returned. I have every power to do so, given we are without a Solarch."

"But what officer would be able to gain favor from the entire city at a time like this?" Matthias said. "Many have died, scattered, or remained conscripted with the Kyriaki army."

Aleksandra turned and considered him with a sharp expression, "Well, I am looking at one of them right now."

"You can't possibly think I could be Heptarch," Matthias said. "I am too young. Too inexperienced. Not a single person would vote for me if I tried."

"Nonsense," Aleksandra said. "You have excellent instincts, a good heart, and you cannot tell me that you do not hear people whispering your name. You are one of the most famous people in the city now."

"A nickname does not mean the people think of me as a leader worthy of a crown," Matthias said, "I cannot possibly think of becoming a Heptarch, Aleksandra."

"Interesting. Rain's response was similar," Aleksandra said. "You two fools are perfect for one another, aren't you? Both of you are too blind to see your full potential."

"You asked Rain as well?" Matthias said.

"Of course," Aleksandra said, "Despite…our current set-backs, the two of you have proven yourselves as the city's saviors. We still need both of you to save it. Please think about my words. You are more capable than most I have seen take the crown. You and Rain both."

Matthias could not find the words to respond, so he walked with her in silence for the rest of their journey. The pair eventually arrived at Aleksandra's villa, a handsome building that reminded Matthias of his family home. She bid him farewell, and he made his way to his large quarters, similar to his childhood bedroom in the Helianth estate. Thankfully, his family had survived the last few months and had nothing to do with Zsolt's coup. Lord and Lady Helianth remained in their villa just a few houses down from the Passiflor estate.

His father still refused to see Matthias and even ignored him the few times they crossed paths in the streets. Lord Helianth ordered the rest of the family to do the same, for Markas and

Lady Helianth also ignored Matthias just that morning, before the funeral. It hurt deeply, but Matthias had learned to live without his family's love and no longer needed the approval of his close-minded father.

He stared at the ceiling of his room, slightly cracked from the night the mesa fell, pondering Aleksandra's words. She had spent a lot of time with him during their days in exile, and he had led successful missions, but he was technically not an officer in the Arachovian army. Matthias was only a captain in name. The Kyriaki invaded before he was officially sworn in, he hadn't even received his Insignis armor. But Aleksandra had years of military experience, if she saw something in him, she must be right.

Matthias still hadn't made up his mind when there was a knock at the door, and a servant in livery made him go to the Solarch's Palace. It was already midday.

Matthias made his way to the palace; part of its dome had collapsed during the fall, so he was not surprised to see the masses who had gathered for the elections standing outside the plaza. Aleksandra and the other two remaining Heptarchs already stood at the top of the steps to preside over the proceedings. What shocked Matthias was how many had gathered for the ceremony. He was sure that the city's citizens would sparsely attend the occasion with so many nobles incarcerated, officers scattered, and the remnants of the military focused on preparing for another attack. Matthias was wrong, it seemed that the entire city had gathered, even commoners.

Aleksandra raised a hand above her crowned head and stepped forward next to a small pedestal where four crowns lay, representing each of the four dead Heptarchs. Matthias pushed through the crowd until he was near the palace stairs.

"People of Arachovia," Aleksandra said, her voice booming across the plaza, "The other Heptarchs and I welcome you to a special election ceremony. The unprecedented events we endured have led us to an unusual dilemma to fill four empty crowns. Important battles still lay ahead, and we urge our citizens to do their duty and select the chosen few to lead us to victory. We ask each citizen to do this, regardless of birth."

A murmur tore through the crowd. The nobles nearest Matthias spit in anger, the commoners near the rear yelled in joy, and most people gasped in surprise. What Aleksandra had just suggested was unprecedented. Matthias smiled. Aleksandra had listened to his ideas after all.

"Silence!" Aleksandra spoke. "As there is no Solarch, the three surviving Heptarchs have deliberated and come to this conclusion, using the sacred authority given to us by the spirits. The Heptarchs you elect today will be able to dictate what happens in the future. But today, the power rests with the people of Arachovia. Now, let us begin."

The old, stodgy Heptarch on Aleksandra's left stepped forward and addressed the crowd. "We shall start with the First District. If the incumbent Heptarch would like to maintain their position, please step forward."

"I, Heptarch Aleksandra Passiflor, hereby declare my intent on retaining my seat," she proclaimed. She handed her crown to the older man and stood patiently next to him.

"Does anyone elect themselves to challenge Heptarch Aleksandra's claim?" the elderly Heptarch asked. He waited a moment for someone to speak, but no one dared challenge her "Very well, who in this assembly accepts Aleksandra Passiflor as the Heptarch of the First District?"

Hands in the crowd shot up. Many nobles refused, but most commoners raised their hand. For the first time, all the people of Arachovia had a voice, not just the wealthy and fortunate.

"So the people proclaim! Heptarch Aleksandra Passiflor!" The proud woman bowed low as the older man placed the golden crown back on her head. The audience erupted in praise as the old ruler stepped back next to the other Heptarch.

"Very well," Aleksandra said, taking control of the function. "Now, onto the Second District. Does anyone elect themselves to take the empty crown?"

Silence fell over the crowd. Not a soul drew breath. Apparently, the mantle of Heptarch gave people pause, and for a good reason. Aleksandra's words were still buzzing in Matthias' ears, he could not possibly say his own name. However, he knew one man worthy of the crown —someone the city needed to lead them out of danger. There was only one choice.

"Commander Rain!" Matthias shouted, the name blurting out, his voice echoing across the silent plaza.

There was a gasp, and through the crowd, he could see Rain turn to him, his cunning eyes wide in shock.

"Commander Rain!" Matthias repeated. A few other voices had joined him this time, "Commander Rain!"

Matthias persisted until the plaza filled with the chant. Hundreds of voices called out for his lover to step forward. He knew the man well. Rain would only put himself forward if he knew he had the city's support beyond a shadow of a doubt. Matthias let him know that not only did he have the citizens' support, but he also had his lover's. After a few moments, Rain stepped out of the crowd and ascended the steps to a roar of applause. Aleksandra was right, and the people loved him. Though the screams and boos from the nobility showed a different side of the story; they thought the man to be the one who destroyed their way of life and doomed them all.

"Does anyone elect themselves to challenge Commander Rain's claim?" Aleksandra asked as Rain reached her. The crowd grew silent once more, Matthias was shocked that none of the nobles put their name forward, but obviously, none wanted to squander their only opportunity for power after a display of support like that.

"Very well," Aleksandra said, "Who in this assembly accepts Rain Cassian as the Heptarch of the Second District?"

Matthias' hand shot up, along with every commoner and a few minor nobles, an overwhelming majority.

"So the people proclaim! Heptarch Rain Cassian!" Aleksandra proclaimed, putting one of the free golden crowns on Rain's head. The plaza erupted once more, and Matthias' heart burst with pride. The city would undoubtedly be safer under the man's rule.

Rain descended the steps, and Aleksandra picked up the second empty crown. "Now, onto the Third District. Does anyone elect themselves to take the empty crown?"

Immediately a hand shot in the air, just in front of Matthias. "I, Lord Helianth, hereby elect myself as Heptarch."

Matthias was stunned as his father quickly ascended the steps. The man had never shown love for the military; he wanted to keep representation for the nobility and undermine Aleksandra and Rain.

"Does anyone elect themselves to challenge Lord Helianth's claim?" Aleksandra asked as Matthias' father reached her.

The crowd grew silent. Matthias' mind was a raging storm of conflicting thoughts. He could not allow a man like his father access to so much power. Lord Helianth would do everything he could to keep the commoners under his foot. It was unacceptable.

"I do!" Matthias yelled, "I, Matthias Hel…Passiflor challenge him!"

Ignoring the nobles' gasps and jeers, Matthias walked through the crowd that melted away before him. A hand suddenly reached out and clasped his tightly. He glanced over and saw Rain beaming. Matthias returned the man's smile and reluctantly let go of his hand. Rain's mere touch had given him strength despite everything that transpired between them.

A few chanted "Two Blades" as he ascended, and he thought he recognized Veiko and Darius' voices among them.

As he reached the top of the stairs, he first saw his father, face red in a fury, spitting curses at him under his breath. Matthias smiled back at the foolish man, which infuriated him even more. Instead, he focused on the loving and proud gaze of Aleksandra. She may not have given birth to him, but she had been more of a parent to him in the last few months than Lord Helianth had been in a lifetime.

"Very well, who in this assembly accepts Lord Helianth as the Heptarch of the Third District?" Aleksandra asked. Most of the nobles' hands went up and some of the commoners. Matthias swallowed hard. He would need every other hand in the plaza to defeat his father.

"And who accepts his challenger?" Aleksandra asked. Matthias saw Rain, his hand held high with pride. The Devoted Company near the middle had their hands raised, along with every priestess, and most commoners. Over half of the crowd had their hands in the air.

Matthias' heart stopped. He had done it.

"So the people proclaim! Heptarch Matthias Passiflor!" Aleksandra said, emphasizing his new surname. The crowd erupted as Matthias knelt and accepted his crown, which felt heavy and cold on his forehead.

"False!" Lord Helianth spit, throwing his arms up, and the crowd gasped. "I claim folly! There were clearly more hands for me. You are biased because my challenger is your ward!"

"I have spoken," Aleksandra said, stepping forward and towering over the man, "And the spirits bind my word. The only way to overturn my ruling is to challenge the victor to combat. Do you accept?"

The pompous man shook with fury, eyes filled with hatred, but Matthias simply smiled at the man and lifted his forearms, brandishing his dual Signata. The man growled, whirled away, and strutted down the stairs.

"Well done, Heptarch Matthias," Aleksandra said quietly. "What a satisfying display."

"I have you to thank for everything," Matthias said, turning to go. "A man could not hope for a better mentor."

Beaming as he descended the steps, he joined the crowd. Suddenly Rain materialized next to him and threw his arms around him. Matthias hesitated at first but returned the hug and held the man's hand as the ceremony continued.

Four more elections followed, and neither of the remaining Heptarchs regained their crowns. The first lost to a noblewoman from a lower house, and the second lost his crown to a charismatic merchant, the first-ever Heptarch not of noble blood. The citizens of Arachovia gave the remaining crowns to an older commoner who proved to be extremely popular and an austere officer whom the people seemed to trust.

However, Matthias and Rain barely paid attention and

focused on one another. When the day started, neither man wanted the crowns they had just won, but the adrenaline of the elections caused both to relish their victory. Aleksandra was right, neither one believed in themselves, but they always had faith in one another. It was their mutual respect that made their victories possible. Matthias' win over his father was particularly sweet but not as good as sharing a crown with the man he loved.

The ceremony concluded, and the crowd began to disperse. Dozens of people swarmed the two new Heptarchs, congratulating them with enthusiasm. After they survived the onslaught, Matthias led his companion near the plaza's edge.

"We must talk, Rain," Matthias said, dropping his hand from Rain's and clenching his jaw, "Can we go somewhere quiet? There are many things I wish to discuss with you."

Rain seemed nervous, unsure what the conversation would entail, but he nodded. "Of course. We can use my family's villa."

Horns abruptly sounded throughout the city, blaring and ominous. People began to scream and run in every direction. Officers summoned their armor and ran south to the front gates; Matthias and Rain followed. They had reached the gate in a few minutes, dashed up the stairs, and stared out along the southern plains.

"They have arrived," Matthias said under his breath. "To reclaim the city once more."

Thousands of soldiers marched along the horizon, stretching as far as the eye could see. Every Kyriaki soldier and conscript in the valley gathered together, outnumbering the surviving Arachovians by at least forty to one.

The time was upon them. Zsolt had come to destroy the

city.

23

The Battle of Arachovia

Within the hour of the first alarm, Matthias found himself standing in front of Arachovia's main gate, watching the sea of enemy soldiers slowly approach. He could not help but feel vulnerable. There had been no time for him to acquire Insignis armor in all of the confusion, so he simply wore a foot-soldier's leather armor and a wooden shield lifted high. The Arachovians assembled every able-bodied soldier in the city in a tight formation outside the gate. It was a pitiful amount compared to the veritable force marching their way.

Aleksandra demanded that she command the defenses from the front lines, forgoing the usual battle etiquette for Heptarchs to stay protected in the rear. Instead, she positioned herself in front and center of the Arachovian soldier formation. To their right lay the remnants of the Arachovian cavalry. They had been lucky that Zsolt had never deployed the mounted force, and the Kyriaki had taken less than half of the mountain elk during their chaotic retreat the night of the fall. The cavalry would be able to prevent the enemy from spreading too far and attacking the city from the west.

Scores of archers perched along the battlements, intermingled with robed priestesses, who were already chanting in preparation for the battle. Vilja and Silja, two of the most formidable furies in the city, positioned themselves directly above the gate. Matthias had just wished Kadri was with them; their chances for success would have increased tenfold if his friend had survived. But if she hadn't returned by now, she had most definitely been overtaken by the massive force currently bearing down on Arachovia.

The final piece of the city defenses was the Devoted Company, situated on the left-hand side of the formation, between Aleksandra's host and the swift waters of the River Palanthia. Matthias and Rain were situated at the forefront of the company, shoulder to shoulder, with a wooden buckler locked in place with the glinting metal shield. Their piece of the formation would be the most critical if they hoped to survive the impending assault. Despite their distance as of late, Matthias knew Rain would do anything to protect him, and he would do the same in return. It was the first time since the invasion that Matthias felt some sort of security before combat

However, today was different. He had never faced an enemy this size with so few behind him. Matthias did not allow his fear to show, but it raged inside him like a wildfire that threatened to burn him alive. Veiko and Darius were next to Matthias, while the lumbering Bruno and his lover Leonas towered over them on Rain's far side. The rest of the Devoted Company filled in the column, longer than it was wide.

The company had regained its full strength of three hundred.

Dozens of couples had clamored to join their ranks the night after the fall, and Rain promptly accepted the best applicants to replenish their forces. Not a single one shook or trembled in fear, for they felt the same security that Matthias felt standing next to Rain. The Devoted Company was arguably the safest place within the entire formation, for the lovers would protect one another until the last.

Matthias carefully studied the approaching forces, which spread from the River Palanthia out farther than the city wall. They sought to engulf the city from the south and the west, rolling over it like a tide. Peering through the troops, Matthias hoped to find any sign of Zsolt. He and Rain had positioned their company near the river, predicting that the Kyriaki leader would use its natural defenses to post his command center. He desperately hoped that their instinct would be proven correct. If they were to be victorious today, Zsolt would have to die.

Matthias' heart sank, however, when he realized that not one soldier within view was wearing red armor. Turning to the right, he saw that the rest of the enemy front lines were the same. The front line of the Kyriaki host consisted solely of conscripted Arachovian soldiers. The Arachovians fighting for the enemy outnumbered those defending the gates. They were to be used as fodder, pitting brother against brother in hopes that Zsolt would not spend a single Kyriaki life to reclaim the city. Matthias thought about shouting to the enemy front lines in hopes of inspiring the conscripted Arachovians to turn and fight the Kyriaki in defense of the city. But they would be slaughtered before they could be of any use. Zsolt was ruthless and a genius in battle.

The enemy abruptly stopped, just out of range of the archers and furies on the battlements, and Matthias could finally see a sea of red armor behind the conscripted soldiers. A horn sounded near Aleksandra, and dust flew as the defending cavalry fanned out past the wall to match the width of Zsolt's army. The mounted force would have to hold their thin line. Otherwise, the enemy would easily swallow the city whole.

A Kyriaki horn blasted its terrible, reedy sound. The battle had begun. Matthias bent his knees and braced for the flood of steel and muscle. Nothing happened. Not a single enemy soldier moved. The horn sounded once more, this time more forcefully, and again, the conscripted at the front lines did not charge. Matthias smiled. The Arachovians would never attack their own.

However, his smile fell when the front lines before him began to waver as if Matthias were looking through a layer of water. Suddenly, the conscripted soldiers shimmered and disappeared, followed by the others beside them and behind. One by one, the soldiers faded into oblivion and revealed an empty field in their stead. A gasp tore through the defending ranks. Only soldiers in red armor remained in front of them. Matthias furrowed his brow, confused, and scanned the empty field to realize it was not as vacant as he thought. One figure stood alone between the Kyriaki and the Arachovian armies, robes flowing in the wind. Kadri.

Matthias yelled in pure joy seeing his friend. He still did not fully understand what he saw, only confused further when Kadri sent a fireball into the air, aiming westward. Matthias' jaw dropped, eyes following the flare when Arachovian soldiers began pouring over a small hillock in the west. The force was equal in size to the defenders and lined up in a tight formation in preparation for an attack. His head was still swimming; the fake host had looked incredibly real and must have been to fool an entire army. Maybe Kadri had finally found out how to make her illusions corporeal. How the priestess snuck so many soldiers out of the clutches of Zsolt, he would never know. Regardless, she may have saved them all with her genius.

The Kyriaki horn bellowed again, and the red-gilded soldiers on the western flanks pivoted and rushed out to meet the ambushing force. Meanwhile, the newly formed front line rushed the wall with a chorus of cries. Kadri ran for the gate as fast as she could, hurling fire back at the enemy on her heels. Matthias turned his attention to the enemies running at him and the Devoted along the river bank.

"Brace!" Rain bellowed.

The company tightened its ranks. Matthias extended his right-hand sword like a spear, his left still dormant in his arm. The Kyriaki soldiers sprinted across the dusty field in a messy line. They had not anticipated being on the front lines, and their unpreparedness showed. At twenty paces, Matthias could see the fear in their eyes.

Suddenly Rain yelled, "Now! Push!"

Seconds before the impact, Matthias felt the weight and strength of hundreds behind him, catapulting him forward into the charging mass ahead. The two forces collided, but the Devoted Company's sudden charge took the Kyriaki by surprise. Their red shields and bodies broke against the human battering ram that was the company. The screams of Kyriaki followed as they fell against the swords and bucklers of the front line, the force of their charge used against them. The Devoted did not stop, charging over the fallen bodies of their first victims and into the next wave. The enemy began to brace back, but the deft thrusts of the Insignis swords cut them down one by one. Spear-like steel shafts matted in blood shot out from the soldiers behind him, grazing his head. Even against the new resistance, the Devoted Company did not slow its advance. Matthias felt the force of their power behind him as he was pushed forward through the unfortunate enemy in their way. They kept close to the river, and soon the enemy was forced away from the Palanthia to avoid the deadly column of elite soldiers.

"Push! Push!" Rain continued to chant, urging the Devoted Company forward in their deadly advance. Rain's eyes narrowed in fierce determination, and his jaw set tight; Matthias found it difficult not to find the man attractive and forced his thoughts back to the battle.

Matthias was relieved to see their efforts positively affect the rest of the battle. The defending soldiers nearest them advanced through the chaos and protected the company's right flank, driving the enemy further from the river. Across the vast sea of chaos, Kadri's forces reached the battle. Together with the cavalry, they pushed the Kyriaki in from the west. Aleksandra's steady force held the gate, and Zsolt's army was now hemmed in at three sides. Arrows and fire alike flew from the battlements into the heart of the enemy horde, but for every slain Kyriaki, four more took their place. There were too many to be overwhelmed, and their sheer numbers would soon push the tide of battle back into their favor. They must find Zsolt.

As the rear guard of the enemy forces came into view, both Matthias and Rain scanned the fray as they continued their push. Only a dozen lines of the enemy remained, but there was no sign of any officers taking refuge behind them. They had been wrong; Zsolt was not along the river.

"There!" Rain shouted.

Matthias turned and saw a brief glimpse of an ornate red helm a hundred paces from the river, not in the back but close to the center of the horde. He kept scouring the area around and soon saw dozens of ornate helms of enemy officers and the familiar frame of the general. They had found the Kyriaki high command, but rows upon rows of soldiers protected it.

Matthias glanced at Rain for a brief moment. They were always able to communicate with one another without words during a battle; it was one of the things that bonded them the most. Both knew what they had to do with just a glance, though the risk was high and could cost them the entire battle.

"Forward and out!" Rain called.

They meant to break free of the battle, leaving the left flank of Aleksandra's unit defenseless and easily flanked. Matthias' heart was heavy. He would never be free of the guilt for the Arachovian soldiers who were about to die, but Matthias and Rain would save many more if they could reach Zsolt.

The Devoted Company complied and intensified their charge, bowling their foes down in a frenzy until the Kyriaki's last line had either been slain or pushed entirely away from the river. Once they were past the battle, Matthias and Rain dropped their shields to their sides and sprinted forward, beyond the struggle. The rest followed as Rain guided them behind the enemy forces and marched them back until their deadly column pointed directly at Zsolt's location.

"Charge now!" Rain yelled.

The company raised their shields once more and ran full speed at the back lines of the Kyriaki. The poor soldiers in red had little to no time to respond; many were cut down from behind as Matthias and Rain led the Devoted Company like a deadly arrow deep into the center of the invading force.

The invaders were all but defenseless from an attack from behind. Within a few bloody seconds, Matthias could already see the ornate helms of the Kyriaki high command. The officers only noticed the attack from the rear when the company was a few dozen paces away. In moments, deadly arrows rained from above, launched from the very bows responsible for Hendrick's death. They had found Zsolt and his elite guard.

The arrows fell and peppered the Devoted from above, slaying a few and injuring many more. Leonas grunted as a shaft sunk deep into his shoulder. Matthias urged the company on after another deadly volley, and finally, they reached the high command. The world exploded as the Devoted Company broke against Zsolt's elite troops. Their formation dissolved and split into pairs as they hacked into the enemy.

Jonas and Taimo weaved and dodged through the fray with ease until they reached the closest line of archers and began to cut through them. Veiko and Darius led a group of three other couples and pushed the front line of guards back, leaving the Kyriaki command vulnerable. Matthias and Rain took advantage of the breach and rushed in, with Bruno and Leonas on their heels, who slashed through the enemy as if there weren't arrows protruding from their massive frames. Matthias immediately dropped his shield and summoned his second blade, staying close to Rain as the four men cut nearer to Zsolt.

The Kyriaki leader waited warily in the center of a dozen swordsmen, their eyes glistening with bloodlust. Zsolt stepped forward slightly and brandished his sword as a challenge. Then Zsolt raised his arm in the sky, and Matthias' stomach lurched, thinking he was about to die like Hendrick. However, when the red gauntlet descended, no arrows came. Zsolt cocked his head in confusion and yelled in fury when he realized a group of Devoted had slaughtered his precious archers. Matthias recognized Jonas, Taimo, and a few other couples who had joined the sneak attack.

"Focus on Zsolt" Bruno bellowed. "We will keep his guard occupied."

"No," Rain said, looking around and seeing no other Devoted close by. "There are too many. It is suicide!"

"Then we will die with honor. Together." Bruno said. "It was a pleasure to see you flourish, Heptarch Rain. These men and women are lucky to have you as one of their leaders."

With a final nod, Bruno and Leonas barreled into the heavily armored guard, killing two immediately and scattering the rest, but the enemy soon regrouped and surrounded them. Even for two veterans like Bruno and Leonas, the chances of surviving against that many master swordsmen were slim at best.

"Hurry, Zsolt is vulnerable," Rain said, a tear falling down his cheek. "Let us not squander the opportunity they gave us."

Matthias nodded and extended his swords into scythes. Bruno and Leonas' rampage created a small clearing in the melee where only he, Rain, and Zsolt remained. Insignis shield held high and sword-shaped like a spear, Rain stalked towards Zsolt warily.

Stabbing once, twice, three times, Rain fired a volley of jabs, testing the enemy's reflexes. The Kyriaki leader made the late Paulius seem like a novice, batting away the attacks with precision and ease. His large, two-handed sword flowed like thick, red water, changing shape instantly over and over again. The man did not stay on the defensive for long and swung his sword savagely at Rain, who blocked with his shield. Matthias stalked around from the side and aimed his scythes at Zsolt's neck. The red-clad man pivoted expertly, kicking Rain back and batting away Matthias' blows with the same ease as deflecting a child's arm. Rain recovered first and slashed at Zsolt's midsection, but the red sword flowed through the air and reshaped at an odd angle to block Rain's blow.

The fight continued in such a manner, the two Heptarchs slashing desperately at Zsolt, foiled at every moment regardless of their combined efforts. Instead, the Kyriaki warrior held the upper hand, despite being outnumbered. After a short while, Matthias and Rain were each bleeding from numerous cuts and scrapes. Since Rain had his highly protective armor summoned, he was in much better shape. Matthias' body screamed with pain and fatigue from dozens of wounds.

Zsolt had separated the two Heptarchs and kept them on the defensive. The man was an unrivaled swordsman, the best Matthias had ever seen. Rain glanced at Matthias and the pair locked eyes for the briefest moments. An odd glint in the man's calculating gaze told Matthias that his love was about to do something stupid.

He was not wrong. Before Matthias could shout, Zsolt brought his colossal sword high above his head and swung it down in a mighty blow. Rain quickly raised his shield to block it, and the two metal objects hummed when they connected. However, instead of pushing the strike aside, the shield began to pulse. Matthias and Zsolt gasped.

No one had ever seen an officer manipulate their shield like one did with a sword; it was deemed impossible.

Nevertheless, the dark gray surface of the Insignis shield pulsed and wrapped itself around the red broadsword. Zsolt violently pulled the sword back, but it wouldn't budge. He flashed a cruel smile and Matthias realized that half of the enemy's sword was between Rain's shield and his body. The red metal flowed and sprung out, slicing Rain in the shoulder where he was unprotected. Rain cried out in pain as the colossal blade skewered him, and the red metal sprouted from his back.

"Now! Do it now, Matthias!" Rain screamed.

Almost forgetting the horror before him, Matthias turned towards the red-clad man, whose sword was deep in Matthias' lover and unable to protect him. Zsolt had caused so much death and pain in such a short time. For what? His pride? For power? None of that meant anything. It was all meaningless. The world needed to be free of Zsolt.

With a scream of defiance, Matthias willed his swords into a pair of spear-like rods and stabbed ferociously at Zsolt's face. The man threw his free hand up to protect himself and withdrew his sword from Rain's shoulder to attack, but it was futile. Rain's shield deflected the attack, and Matthias' blades cut through the gauntlet and impaled Zsolt through the head with a sickening crunch.

Matthias pulled the swords out; blood flowed like a waterfall from the dead man's skull, the limp body crumpled, and the sword fell from his hand, still trapped in Rain's shield. Rain dropped to his knees next to the dead general. Matthias retracted his blades, rushed to the man's side, and held him close. Blood flowed freely from his deep wound and his pale face was contorted in pain as he gasped for breath. It reminded him of Hendrick in his final moments.

"Breathe slowly," Matthias said, voice shaking. "Hold on, and I'll get you to safety."

"Matthias…" Rain said, "I am sorry, but this is the end…I love you."

Not accepting reality, Matthias groaned, lifted Rain into his arms as gently as possible, and climbed to his feet. Kyriaki soldiers, having witnessed Zsolt's death, retreated around the Heptarchs and scattered into the plains. Every other enemy officer was already dead by the Devoted Company's hand.

Next to Matthias, beyond Zsolt's body lay his dozen guards—all dead. In the center of the carnage lay the bodies of Bruno and Leonas. The two massive soldiers grasped their hands tightly together, foreheads touching. They had left this world together, taking a dozen enemies with them. Nothing would separate them ever again. Matthias saw the spectacle and refused to lose Rain.

Holding Rain carefully in his arms, Matthias ran towards the gate as fast as he could, screaming for a priestess. A few moments later, he saw Veiko and Darius running next to him out of the corner of his eye. Jonas and Taimo were close behind, followed by the survivors of the company. Unable to rejoice in the survival of so many friends and compatriots, Matthias ran through the battlefield, checking every few seconds to ensure his lover was still alive.

After Matthias and Rain slew Zsolt, the Kyriaki army slowly broke and fled, realizing the Devoted Company had executed their entire leadership. Darius and Veiko cleared any resisting soldiers from their path as they quickly made their way closer to the gate. There. He saw a woman bloodied in a tattered robe but alive and upright. Kadri. When he reached her, his lungs were on fire and his muscles were about to give out, covered in Rain's blood. She turned and smiled as she saw him.

"Matthias, it's so good to see—" Kadri began, stopping when she saw Rain's mangled body.

"Save him," Matthias said, tears streaming down his face, falling to his knees in exhaustion. "He needs healing. Now."

Kadri knelt next to the two men and softly put a hand on Rain's shoulder, his breaths were hoarse and shallow, and his skin pale.

"This wound is beyond me," Kadri said. "If Silja was here, she might be able to do something, but I am sorry, Matthias, she is up on the battlements. He is too far gone."

"No," Matthias said. "Do not say that. I have seen you do impossible things, Kadri. You are the most powerful priestess in this city. Probably in the world. You conjured an entire army from nothing. What is a small wound compared to that? Now. Heal. Him."

Kadri pursed her lips but nodded, laying a hand on the wound, and she began to chant. There, before the great gate of Arachovia, Matthias sat in horror as he saw the life fade from Rain's face.

Around him, the screams of the injured and dying on the abandoned battlefield joined the howling wind. But all Matthias focused on was Kadri's desperate chants and Rain's lifeless face.

24

Devoted

Matthias woke from an odd dream. He had been standing on the front lines of his first battle, back when he first joined the army. The enemy charged at him, and he suddenly realized he was standing all alone. Before the soldiers descended upon him, he was jarred awake with a start.

Shaking the disturbing images from his head, he crawled out of the large bed and quietly padded to the large window overlooking the city below. The Passiflor villa had an excellent view of the southern city, which had once gone by the moniker of "lower city." Hundreds of new buildings and freshly thatched roofs dotted the flourishing neighborhood. Its citizens had built markets, shops, and schools to sustain the rapidly growing population of the southern half of the city.

It had been almost three months since the Arachovians defeated Zsolt. Remnants of the Kyriaki army retreated back through the Gap of Tanaegra to their homeland beyond, leaving the valley in peace once more. However, many of the conscripted soldiers within their ranks decided to stay in Arachovia to start a new life for themselves, determining that the opportunities would be substantially greater under Aleksandra's benevolent rule. Matthias smiled at the thriving city, basking in the late morning glow. He knew the city's newfound peace would always be Rain's legacy.

Looking at his reflection in the glass, Matthias saw his own naked body covered in the tattoos of an officer. He received them shortly after the battle of Arachovia, which served as a constant reminder of his duties.

Matthias returned to his bed, where Rain lay naked among the blankets, and smiled. The two spent every night in that bed since the Battle of Arachovia while Rain healed from his wounds. Rain had given his family's villa to Silja and the other furies to convert it into the city's first hospital. The unassuming Heptarch had no use for it and had always despised it, referring to it as a garish monstrosity. Aleksandra had barely used the Passiflor villa since the Heptarchs unanimously voted her as the Solarch of the city, giving the couple their much-needed privacy in the sensible but lavish home. She was more than capable of handling her new regime, which gave Matthias and Rain many months to spend with each other uninterrupted before their duties as Heptarchs called them out of their sabbatical. They were the city's heroes, but that did not excuse them from shirking their responsibilities to make love all day.

Matthias smiled at the last thought, crawling back into bed with his love, and ran a hand along his tattooed body. It lingered over the scar on his shoulder, which matched the one on Matthias' stomach. Now he knew precisely how Rain had felt during the battle of Phalanaea, where Matthias had received that mark. After holding Rain's limp body on the battlefield, Matthias knew that he could never be separated from Rain again. And he wouldn't. Matthias had planned to forgive Rain for what happened with Hendrick, even before the battle of Arachovia, but watching him almost die made him entirely forget the episode at the shrine.

Matthias' hand caressed the man's chest softly, grazing across the tight muscles of his abdomen, and kept moving southward. With a quiet groan, Rain began to stir and opened his eyes with a broad smile.

"So it will be another good morning, I see?" Rain said, looking down to where Matthias' hand had gone.

"I promised you that day on the battlefield that we would begin every morning like this," Matthias said, working his hands deftly as he spoke. "You may have been unconscious at the time, but seeing as you came back to life after I said that, I want to keep my word."

"Always a man of honor," Rain said. "One of the thousands of reasons I love you so."

Rain suddenly jumped into action, grabbing Matthias firmly on the back of the neck and kissing him deeply, turning him until he was on his back and Rain was on top. Matthias moaned softly as their tongues danced together. His lover was always more aggressive in the mornings, and he would never let that energy go to waste.

Rain grabbed his wrists, pinning Matthias to the soft bed, and teased his neck with a deft tongue. Wrapping his legs around Rain's body, Matthias ground against him, teasing his lover and urging him on. Within seconds Rain was inside and in control. Matthias' face was flush and hot with passion, his entire body burning as Rain began to thrust hard and fast. His eyes rolled back into his head, and Matthias uttered a passionate scream. The man on top did not relent; the desperate moans just encouraged him to continue his onslaught. Matthias ran his hands along Rain's back, feeling each thrust that matched his heartbeat. Their heartbeats. Whenever they were in bed together, Matthias felt one with Rain. They were one body, one heart, and one soul.

Rain began to grunt loudly, and Matthias took it as a cue to twist his hips and roll the man to his back so he was on top. He could always overpower his lover at will, being a bit larger and stronger. The lanky man pinned one of Rain's hands and left the other free to caress his chest. Then the Matthias moved his hips rapidly, forcing himself down on Rain. He knelt and kissed him deeply, increasing the pace. Feeling Rain tense up, he continued faster. The moment's heat swept them up into a frenzy, and they climaxed together, their moans stifled by their kiss.

When the rush eventually subsided, and both men were heaving their sweaty chests in exhaustion, Matthias climbed off Rain and fell onto the bed beside him, wrapping the man in his long arms. They would have kept going, but they had spent the better part of the night prior making love. The two were more than exhausted and were content with lying in each other's arms, basking in the bliss of the late morning.

"You can never allow me total control, can you?" Rain said, chuckling.

"That wouldn't be fun now, would it?" Matthias said, "But if you were a bit stronger, maybe you could keep control when you wanted."

"I could always find some rope to tie you up," Rain said. "Maybe I could finally have my way."

Rain wrestled his lover playfully, the pair grappled for a

moment before falling back onto the mattress. Matthias scoffed, but his heart leaped at the notion, surprisingly it excited him.

"Perhaps we could try that," Matthias said mischievously. Then he looked towards the window and the rising sun. "Though we may have to wait for now, I'm afraid the day is getting away from us, and we have more important things to focus on."

"Spoilsport," Rain said. "But you are right. We shouldn't dawdle any more than we have."

Reluctantly yet excitedly, the pair crawled out of bed and readied themselves for the day. The couple were dressed, bathed, fed, and they walked hand in hand through the city streets within the hour.

Neither of them preferred to wear their crowns unless it was for a formal occasion where they were required, but everyone they passed in the street still bowed in reverence as they passed. Matthias and Rain were the saviors of the city, after all. Not only did they drive the usurpers out of Arachovia and beat them back when they attacked the gates, but they unified the city once and for all. The new Heptarchs confiscated the hoarded wealth of the corrupt nobles and redistributed it to the commoners, granting every citizen the opportunity to prosper and thrive. A few nobles still held ill will against them, especially Matthias' family, but change was never easy and did not happen overnight.

The pair passed the Solarch's Palace, complete with a freshly rebuilt dome, its plaza lined with a few new statues to commemorate the heroes of Arachovia. The first depicted a man with a buckler and sword, dedicated to the brave soldiers who fought and died for the city. The second statue was a trio of robed women, finally giving the furies of Arachovia their due. Without the power of the women who harnessed the mystic power of the rach, the city would have been destroyed. The third and final statue commemorated none other than the Devoted Company, two men carved from stone intertwined in a loving embrace. One held a mighty sword while the other held a shield.

It looked remarkably similar to the statue in the center of the Shrine of Isemelith, but Rain had done his best to persuade the statue's artisan to sculpt the men based on the likeness of Bruno and Leonas. Without their sacrifice, Zsolt would still be alive, and Matthias and Rain would certainly not be. Dozens of names, along with Hendrick's, were carved on a plaque on the statue's pedestal, so all would know who sacrificed their lives for Arachovia.

Despite the company's losses during the battle of Arachovia, there were plenty of couples who served in the army. Now that the name Devoted was renowned worldwide, Matthias and Rain had plenty of soldiers to choose from when they rebuilt their ranks. They conducted extensive assessments with the help of their friends, Darius, Veiko, Jonas, and Taimo, and soon their elite squad numbered three hundred once more. It was unusual for two Heptarchs to lead one legion, but Matthias and Rain insisted on working together, building an elite troop that would act as the sword and shield of the realm. They would work towards ending the needless violence of soldiers in Arachovia and throughout the world. The other city-states feared the new world power, and Matthias would ensure they used every advantage to keep the peace in the valley and the plains around it.

Darius and Veiko, in particular, had been crucial in their

rebuilding efforts. They always had a special place in Matthias' heart, but the pair proved to be unparalleled leaders and wise counselors. They had built a house in the southern city, not too far from the Passiflor villa. Matthias and Rain often joined the couple for dinner, though none were as skilled in the kitchen as Leonas had been. The wine Darius kept in the cellar made up for the lack of flavor in Veiko's food. Matthias seldom left their home sober, but he was always content and at peace.

Matthias and Rain passed the great plaza and continued past the old Cassian estate. Kadri, in her flowing robes and a golden crown, walked out of the new hospital grounds as they passed by. She smiled broadly when she noticed them and jogged over to meet them.

"I see the two of you have had a late morning," Kadri said, "And here I thought you would have finished before dawn. This has been a long time coming."

Kadri smiled and adjusted her crown. Unlike Matthias and Rain, she loved showing off her symbol of rule; she was the first-ever priestess elected to Heptarch, after all. She had taken Aleksandra's spot when the older woman ascended to Solarch, and there had barely been any dissent in Kadri's special election. The citizens of Arachovia regarded her as the third savior of the city. The conscripted soldiers would have never been rescued without her cunning and skill. After the mesa fell, Kadri hid her troops near Tanaegra and discovered Zsolt reforming his army nearby. Each night she would sneak into the camp and steal away Arachovian soldiers forced into service and replace them with copies that fooled Zsolt himself. It was such an unprecedented feat that the entire city regarded her as the most powerful priestess that had ever lived, and now she reigned as one of its Heptarchs.

"We are on our way right now," Matthias explained. "We had a few things to sort out first."

"Right," Kadri said, smirking, "I presume these important 'things' you speak of hang between your legs."

"Such a mouth on you, Kadri," Matthias said. "Do you kiss Vilja every night with that? She must find it quite foul."

Kadri pouted, but her face was flush. After the battle of Arachovia, it was no longer a secret that the two furies were lovers. Matthias was delighted his dear friend had found someone as equally ferocious and passionate as she. The two priestesses, in his opinion, made a lovely couple.

"She hasn't given me any complaints, Matthias, but you will be the first to know if she does," Kadri said. "Anyways, I am off with an audience with Solarch Aleksandra. I suggest you both come when you're finished. Congratulations to both of you."

Matthias and Rain bid Kadri farewell and continued westward, hands held together tightly. His heart began to beat faster as they continued further, filled with excitement and nervousness. Soon the great dome of the Temple of Sorilea came into view, and it took all of Matthias' strength to refrain from running forward.

Finally, after seemingly an eternity, the familiar arch in the center of elegant hedges came into view. Matthias' mind returned to the two previous times he had visited the Shrine of Isemelith, which had ended in heartbreak.

The first time he discovered the man he had loved since childhood had chosen his family and his "duty" to procreate over his love for him. He had long forgiven Anton, who had attempted in vain to rekindle their romance soon after the battle of Arachovia. Matthias turned him down rather gently and asked his first love to return to his wife and the miserable life he had chosen.

The second time Matthias entered the shrine, the hopeless romantic found his lover in the arms of another, but he forgave Rain the moment Kadri healed him on the battlefield. Matthias trusted the man with his life and knew he would never break his trust ever again.

The third and hopefully final visit to the shrine would prove entirely different.

The sun was high in the sky, not a shadow to be seen in the secluded place as Matthias and Rain slowly walked towards the statue at its center.

"Are you ready?" Rain said quietly as the pair turned to one another under the statue.

"I think I could use a few more years to decide," Matthias said wryly. "Perhaps when I finally know I love you."

Rain scowled and Matthias laughed playfully.

"Of course, I love you, you dreamy fool," Matthias said. "Start the ceremony already."

Rain smiled and looked deep into Matthias' eyes, holding his hands in his with a tight grip. Neither man had to look at the words etched on the stone plinth, for both had known them by heart for years. They were about to do something that they had wanted their entire lives.

"Matthias Passiflor," Rain said, "I Vow to respect your mind and consider you my partner in all things."

"Rain Cassian," Matthias began, staring deep into Rain's eyes, "I Vow to respect your mind and consider you my partner in all things. You are the best partner I could have ever hoped for, and I cannot imagine another day without you by my side."

"Are we allowed to embellish the script?" Rain said in a whisper.

"Probably not," Matthias said, "But given that we both can make laws now, I don't see why the spirits would have an issue if we take a few liberties."

"Very well," Rain said, "I Vow to protect your body, Matthias Passiflor, as it is more precious to me than my own. And it is an adorable body. I particularly like this bit."

Matthias punched Rain playfully. The man had adopted too much of his own sarcasm in the last few months for his liking. He did not like competition and desired to remain the funniest one in the couple.

"I Vow to protect your gorgeous, gorgeous body, Rain Cassian, as it is more precious to me than my own," Matthias said, gripping his lover's hands tightly.

"I Vow to cherish your heart fully and share mine completely in return." Rain said, his eyes began to well as they approached the end of the ceremony.

"I Vow to cherish your heart fully and share mine completely in return, Rain Cassian." Matthias simply repeated, not being able to quip at this moment.

Matthias' voice wavered, overcome with the sheer emotion of love and respect for the man before him. Without Rain, he would have been dead a dozen times over—and not only in the literal sense—and his life would have no meaning. Together, they were changing the world, making it a better place, and making each other better men.

They spoke the final line in unison, and Matthias could not prevent the tears from cascading down his face. "Until my own heart, mind, and body give way, until the end of my days."

The moment the final word left their lips, Matthias pulled Rain close, grabbed him by the face, and kissed him passionately. Rain wrapped his arms around him tightly and returned his kiss in fervor. They stood there in silence for a long while, taking in the words they had just spoken to one another.

Matthias had felt alone and listless for most of his life. He had never believed he had a true purpose. Now he was Rain's, and Rain was his.

Eventually, the men left the shrine, walking with their hands intertwined. Matthias looked out at Arachovia before him. It had changed as much as he had in the last few years, and there would be more if he had anything to say about it. There was so much to accomplish in the short life he was given, to leave the world in a better place than he had found it. And now, with Rain by his side, anything was possible.

Together they would see to the coming of a new and better world, free of suffering and needless death. A world in which the powerful would protect the helpless, not exploit them. They would do all of this in love. Together. Devoted.

Acknowledgments

While Matthias, Rain, and the Devoted Company are relatively recent creations, the book in your hands (or on your screen) has been over ten years in the making. Dozens of failed drafts, a few archived novels, countless sleepless nights, and a metric ton of anxiety later, this story has finally come to life. This would never have happened if it weren't for the people around me, and they have my undying gratitude. To Asher, Alec, and Jake, for being the first visitors to Arachovia and letting me know that this wasn't a heap of trash. To Mallory for taking my jumbled thoughts and making them coherent. To Chris for refining and propelling the material to greater heights than I could have imagined. To Emir, for bringing the images in my head to life and creating the most beautiful cover art. To Derek for encouraging me and guiding me through the scary process of turning one's dream into a reality. To Drew, Brendan, and Nancy, for keeping me balanced, acting as my emotional support, and being the best friends a mess like me could ever ask for. And finally to Dan, for putting up with my chaos every day and having faith in me when I didn't have any in myself. You have been my anchor, my sounding board, and this author's greatest champion. To everyone who worked on this dream with me, for everything mentioned and unmentioned, thank you.